Fifty Writers on Fifty Shades of Grey

EDITED BY
LORI PERKINS

An Imprint of BenBella Books, Inc.

Fifty Writers on Fifty Shades of Grey © 2012 by Lori Perkins

BenBella Books, Inc.
10300 N. Central Expressway, Suite 400
Dallas, TX 75231
www.benbellabooks.com
Send feedback to feedback@benbellabooks.com

Printed in the United States of America
10 9 8 7 6 5 4 3 2 1

Library of Congress Cataloging-in-Publication Data is available for this title.
978-1-937856-42-7

Copyediting by Don Weise
Proofreading by James Fraleigh and Michael Fedison
Cover design by Jarrod Taylor
Cover illustration by Ralph Voltz
Text design and composition by John Reinhardt Book Design
Printed by Berryville Graphics, Inc.

Distributed by Perseus Distribution
(www.perseusdistribution.com)
To place orders through Perseus Distribution:
Tel: 800-343-4499
Fax: 800-351-5073
Email: orderentry@perseusbooks.com

Significant discounts for bulk sales are available. Please contact Glenn Yeffeth at glenn@benbellabooks.com or 214-750-3628.

COPYRIGHT ACKNOWLEDGMENTS

CONTENTS

Fifty Shades of Sex

Fifty Shades of BDSM

Fifty Shades of Writing

Intermission

ACKNOWLEDGMENTS

BEHIND EVERY AUTHOR, there is a team. In addition to the Ab Fab writers in this book who wrote under extreme deadline and turned around corrections at lightning speed, I want to thank Louise Fury, my agent, who came up with the idea for the book and brought it to me; Debra Hyde, who kept me on track and pitched in on a moment's notice; and Leah Wilson, who was everything an author could dream of in an editor.

Fifty Ways to Look
at Fifty Shades

EVERYWHERE YOU GO people are talking about *Fifty Shades of Grey*, from the supermarket (where it is on sale!) to the airport to PTA meetings and even church socials. It is the book of the year, if not the decade.

You all know the stats. It has sold more copies than the Harry Potter series in a mere six months. It has dominated the *New York Times* bestseller list since April 2012. As of this writing, 32 million copies have sold this year in the US alone.

So the real question is: Why did this book, and its sequels, capture our attention now?

· • ● • ·

I WANT TO MAKE IT CLEAR THAT, as a literary agent who has toiled in the erotica fields for decades, I love the Fifty Shades trilogy. Its success has shown the world that a strong market exists for erotic fiction written, edited, and purchased by women.

To me, Fifty Shades is smut for women. I consider myself a "feminist pornographer," which always raises a few eyebrows. But I believe this movement of women claiming their own smut is part of the evolution of feminism—proudly owning your sexuality is a big part of equality.

When I was a young feminist, I was given *Story of O* by a lover, and I was offended by it—not because of its overt subject matter but because I knew that I was not a submissive woman (I didn't know the terminology back then; now every young woman will!). I've wrestled with this my entire life in my personal relationships, and I assumed that the submissive woman fantasy was a male one and part of the patriarchy.

Until I became an editor of erotic literature. I quickly learned that the fantasy of complete surrender to an alpha male is the leading daydream of the majority of American women.

As a young feminist, I equated all romance with submission, and I looked down on them both. I didn't think it was possible to be submissive and a feminist, just as old-school feminists were appalled that their well-educated daughters wanted to stay home and be mothers or learn to knit and bake. In a recent review of *The Hunger Games* movie, a feminist reviewer complained about the apparent need for "romance" in what is otherwise an action-based dystopian story. I used to decry this kind of "unnecessary" addition of romance, too, but I secretly went to romantic comedies alone so no one would see me cry. I was ashamed of my romantic side.

Until I came to see that you can be a feminist and a romantic. It's okay. And it's really okay to want, and believe in, a happy ending—even when you know that in reality 50 percent of all marriages fail. These movies and books are an escape, and a hope.

We've been saying for the past several decades that feminism is about having choices, and one of those is the freedom to indulge in our erotic fantasies. Everyone wants to fall in love and be swept away by its power, even men. But they don't have the emotional freedom women have. They don't have the emotional *choices* we have. In Western culture, you will never see a story about a man being swept away by love, unless it's a comedy or a cautionary tale.

Fifty Shades brings all these issues and more to the surface. But more than that, it has proven, once and for all, that women love to read smut with a happy ending.

Looking through my erotica reader and writer lens, I foresee that this phenomenon means that a whole new marketplace awaits these stories. *Story of O* is fifty years old and the current edition is a dated translation (I'd love to see it in contemporary language). We need new fantasies, which E. L. James has given us. I am awed to see the birth of a new erotica classic. (I had the same feeling when I watched Harry Potter become a children's literature classic in my time.)

Some have wondered how a "classic" can be so "poorly written." But I contend that it is not poorly written, but rather written in an everywoman's voice, a necessary part of its success. I once worked with an author who used plebian language (bringing me my first experience with the phrase "Holy crap!"). When she returned my edits, she told me that she did indeed know the word "simultaneously," but when she was fantasizing, she always used the phrase "at the same time as," and she knew that her readers did as well. When she saw the word "simultaneously" in fiction, she knew it had been edited up to *New York Times* standards, which was all well and good, but not the way she spoke in her head. These books are about being drawn into the fantasy—and E. L. James expertly takes her readers on that journey.

I hope Fifty Shades will be the tip of a rather large iceberg of erotic empowerment. And I hope that these books will usher in a publishing tidal wave of female-centered commercially successful erotica, giving women a new voice for sexual, political, and financial choices. It's what we should've had all along.

•   •   •   •   ○

THIS IS THE WAY I look at Fifty Shades. But there are many, many others, from what its story says about us as a society to the role of women in and out of relationships to our hidden fantasy lives. This book offers fifty of those ways, from readers who love it and a few readers who don't, because their voices are important, too.

Is Fifty Shades literature? Postfeminism? Or just the end of civilization as we know it?

I hope you will find all of those answers in here.

And then continue discussing amongst yourselves.

Lori Perkins
August 2012

Fifty Shades of *Erotic Fiction*

M.J. ROSE

Between the Covers

THE SHEETS WERE SMOOTH. Cool. And that smell! Fresh linens scented with jasmine and orange blossom. She breathed in deeply as she settled down. For a few moments, she concentrated on just being there. On relaxing. On trying to let go of the minutiae... of all the ordinary and unimportant million things that had happened. Or barely happened.

She knew he wouldn't mind if it took her a little while. He was patient. He would wait for her. Yes, he would wait for her.

The day had seemed like it would never end. There were arguments at work that had been exhausting. Her family was always demanding but today they had been relentless in their needs. She'd thought this would never come.

Her fingertips made circles on the bedding. She listened to the jazz she'd put on. The slow, hot music was perfect. Just loud enough to drown out the sounds beyond this room...beyond this house...beyond this world. Drown it all out so she didn't have to be aware of anything but what was going on inside of this cocoon she was spinning around herself. Where no one else was invited.

No one but him.

She'd dressed for him, putting on a thin nightgown that clung to her and skimmed her skin. A pressure so light it was like butterfly kisses. For now, the silk was pulled down demurely, covering her to her ankles. Only the soles of her feet and her toes were exposed to the cool air.

Even with his first words her breasts began to push against the fabric. More of his words. More push. Even gossamer would have been too constricting now. Her breasts were ready to be released. To be touched. To be squeezed and pinched and...

No, not yet...all in time...because there was time...with him there was always time, and what a luxury that was.

As she relaxed into the act, he told her more about what he wanted and her imagination soared.

How would her skin feel when he slapped her?

How would her mouth be able to take so much of him inside her?

How would she react to being bound?

Scared? Excited?

Would it be frightening to do only what he allowed?

How could she accept being controlled?

She could accept it because this was control by invitation. This time she wanted to be told. Yes. Wanted him to demand she perform for him and do these things to him, and she wanted him to do those things to her.

It was all new. It was heady. She'd never imagined any of this before him. She would have been ashamed if anyone else had asked all this of her.

But not him.

The sensation between her legs intensified and teased. Hovering deliciously. The twinges and very first throb of an orgasm beckoned. Maybe there would even be more than one. Hard to come by more than one in most situations.

But this wasn't most situations.

This was a sexual heaven. This was being taking by the hand and led gently into a different world where nothing was wrong...nothing was obscene...nothing was forbidden.

Orange moved to red. Red moved to scarlet. Scarlet pulsed to purple. Lightning jolted inside her. She flared.

Yes, he had been patient...but now he was demanding. He was a frightening lover. Yet, because he made sure she understood the word *love* was encapsulated in the word *lover*, she was safe. Everything he was suggesting, was insisting on, was all for one reason...to take her further into the colors...into the music...into the smells and the touches...all to make her feel more...and feel more deeply.

She didn't understand how such a simple act made excitement like this build in her. How it aroused and hardened her nipples. How it made it so she could barely keep her hands away from the warm, wet space between her legs.

But she had to keep her hands away. Because he was telling her to. Because he was demanding she wait until he allowed her to have it. Because if she did, he told her, it was going to be better than she could conceive of. And she believed him. These promises he was making, here in the dark, in her private velvet and jasmine-scented secret garden were like no other promises she'd ever heard.

If she obeyed...if she followed where he led...he pledged she would find that deepest purple answer she craved.

There was sex and then there was ecstasy. There were orgasms and then there were orgiastic mind-numbing experiences. The kind that she disappeared into and got lost inside of. The kind that only he gave her. And only in this place and only in this way.

Passion could obliterate reality. She'd learned that from him. She'd found out that whatever you thought you knew about yourself, you could learn more. That every pleasure could be heightened. And turned to pain that turned back into more intense pleasure. She'd discovered that just thinking about this man, about his desires, his yearnings, and his demands created waves inside of her. She'd learned she could think about what he wanted and the waves would build. He'd taught her to block out the world and ride those waves and travel to other worlds she'd never been to before.

And no one could take any of it away from her. No one could interfere. No one could say she was wrong for giving into the fantasies he offered. No one could tell her she was dirty or pagan or that she was breaking her vows or hurting her children or abandoning her responsibilities or negating the teachings of her church or her temple. No one could stop her from the delight and joy and bliss that she now knew was her right—and such a simple right to claim at that.

Now he was asking for more. Demanding it.

As she gave him what he wanted, her own moans—throaty and raw—drowned out the music. Her own scent—the musky rich incense of her own heated cunt—overwhelmed the jasmine and orange blossom perfume. She was floating on the waves...waves he shaped by blowing gently on her ocean. Giving her the ride of her life. Again. And then, yes, again.

This wasn't about power or pain...not about risk or reward...not about fidelity...this was what she took for herself. She gave herself up to him and his fiery, arousing words. And in giving, she got. He gave her burning, roiling seas that grew and grew inside of her.

Fingers moved on her lips. Teasing. Tickling. Rubbing in exactly the right way, in exactly the right rhythm. Slowing. Then hurrying. Slowing. Then hurrying. Inside, her seas burned hotter. His words were waves rising higher. Receding...bringing her to the brink. Receding. And then to the brink again. And then to the brink for the last time.

Her gift to herself was him. His gift to her was freedom. And fantasy. The ability to be a wild and abandoned sexual adventurer in this safe place under the covers...between the covers...because this is what erotica is...this is what it does. This is the gift of it.

Is there a secret? Yes. Anaïs Nin and Pauline Réage and Anne Rampling and Erica Jong all knew it. E. L. James knows it.

It is the secret behind all of our writing. And our reading. Arousal starts in the mind. And grows in the mind. The brain is the most erogenous zone in a woman's body. That is our secret. And it is what we share.

M.J. ROSE has been reading erotica since she was eleven and found *The Story of O* on her mother's bookshelves. Rose's first novel, *Lip Service*, was chosen by Susie Bright for the Best American Erotica series. International best-selling author of a dozen novels, Rose continues to mix genres and include both the erotic and the suspenseful in her work. In addition to her fiction she has written three books on marketing for authors and is one of the founding board members of International Thriller Writers. Rose is also the founder and president of the first marketing company for authors, AuthorBuzz.com. Visit her online at www.MJRose.com.

manner of a bedtime story told to children. *The girl meets a wolf on her walk through the forest and she is very afraid*...Or in the style of words whispered in the dark between lovers in the act. *It feels so good...I need this...I'm begging*...The prose has the aura of a dream to it, as if the writer is dictating something she's seeing from a distance and yet experiencing at the same time.

Once sent, the letter proves her point—a woman can write an erotic book. But she miscalculated, wrote it far too well: her married lover thinks it should be published. She finishes it, though it is difficult for her. The plot meanders and the tortures of O increase. She finishes what she can and the book comes to a dark, abrupt ending as dreams often do—especially dreams of falling to one's death and jerking awake.

The book is published under the pen name Pauline Réage. A furor erupts. Many women hate it and say a man who loathes women must have written it. Other women adore it as it speaks to a part of them no one has ever before addressed. Some women burn the book. Other women read the book and burn. And the author stays silent and admits nothing. The book is brave but the author reticent. Is it the content of the story that makes her hide her identify? Or is it that the recipient of the first letter is married and her lover? Although this is Paris, it is still 1954.

An erotic love letter never meant to be published for the masses—it is a story not unfamiliar to modern readers. Other women will follow in Réage's footsteps. Often these women will be plain and unremarkable just as Réage was. Older, long past their sexual prime. Their beauty faded, if ever they were beauties at all, they will still have the longings of their youth. The world will see them merely as wives or mothers and not objects of sexual attention. They write, as Réage did, to prove someone wrong. A woman can write erotic fiction. A woman who is not beautiful can write something beautiful. A woman who is not the object of sexual desires is still shockingly sexual. A woman who is a wife or a mother or a nobody is, on paper, a goddess, a slut, a slave, a body to be taken and used for the pleasure of a man. Réage writes her letter to her lover for the same reason the mistress of any married man attires herself like a prostitute or a princess. It is her way of saying, "I am not your wife. I am not an ordinary woman. I am so much more."

•   •   •   •   •

I SCOWL WITH FRUSTRATION at myself in the mirror...
This is the story. Another version of the story, true perhaps or perhaps not, perhaps merely another fever dream...another woman, not young or physically remarkable, a woman with two children, a husband, nothing to distinguish her in a crowd, finds herself unable to stop dreaming about a man twenty years her junior. A beautiful man who is adored by women the world over, he is utterly unattainable. They have nothing in common. They will never cross paths. If they do by accident or whim of fate, he will not notice her. At most he'll sign his name on a scrap of paper for her, and she will already be forgotten by him before he's taken two steps from her. She will never have him. But in her mind, she is twenty-one years old, not forty-seven. In her mind she has no children and no husband. She is, in fact, an untouched virgin, untouched even by her own hands. And the man is someone else. He has the same face, the same eyes, the same body she dreams of, but he is a darker version of himself. The real man leads a tame life and is devoted to one woman. The man she desires is damaged and distant. He has desires that inflame and terrify her. She wants him to be broken so she can heal him. She wants him to be lost so she can save him.

And so she begins to write. Unlike Réage, who wrote in pencil in school exercise books in the dark, this woman writes on a BlackBerry during her commute. She has children and must steal the time from her everyday life to lose herself in this fantasy that will never come true. It is a child's fantasy—a girl with nothing special about her except her incredible ordinariness captures the heart of a beautiful man flush with wealth and power. Like Réage's, her story isn't written to be published for profit. It's put online, given away to others who, like her, love the same Unattainable. An editor finds the book, changes it, publishes it. The ordinary wife and mother has, without trying, become an author, garnered an audience, fame, millions of dollars, and the adoration of legions. Some women burn the book. Other women read it and burn.

•   •   •   •   •

THIS IS THE STORY.

TIFFANY REISZ's books inhabit a sexy shadowy world where romance, erotica, and literature meet and do immoral and possibly illegal things to each other. A seminary dropout and semi-devout Catholic, Tiffany describes her genre as "literary friction," a term she stole from her main character, who gets in trouble almost as often as the author herself. Reisz's debut novel, *The Siren*, was published by Mira on July 24, 2012. Reisz describes it as "not your momma's *Thorn Birds*," and she means it. Reisz lives in Lexington, Kentucky.

M.CHRISTIAN

The Game Changer

XCUSE THE HYPERBOLE, but there really are moments when everything just...changes: the wheel, the internal combustion engine, antibiotics, the personal computer. It would just be nice that the paradigm shift in literature and publishing would have been better written.

To be polite—at best—*Fifty Shades of Grey* has been called...well, let's let Margot Sage-EL, co-owner of the Watchung Booksellers in Montclair, New Jersey, say it: "Our customers are very smart and they say it's badly written, but they are in the middle of book three."

As with anything hugely popular, the trilogy has received just about an equal amount of scorn to match its sales. Even Susan Donaldson James called it "a cheese-ball narrative whose heroine is incapable of using adult language. She refers to her genitals euphemistically as *my sex*." But popular *Fifty Shades* is—to a staggering degree: in March it reached the number-one spot on the national e-book fiction bestseller list. Naturally there's going to be a film.

Putting aside the mumbles and grumbles from the legions of hardworking, and unarguably more talented, erotica writers out there (*ahem*...M.Christian...*ahem*), *Fifty Shades* will, no doubt, be remembered as when *everything changed.*

Okay, it may not be as big as the wheel, the internal combustion engine, antibiotics, or the personal computer, but it's still a total and complete game changer. For one thing, it's pretty much the final nail in the old-school world of print publishing. Sure, that model has been gasping and wheezing for a few years now but for a teeny-tiny—and badly written—little book to do what New York dreamt of doing shows once and for all that they need to burn down their old ways and finally begin to embrace the lean, mean, and cutting-edge world of e-books.

It's also the final shovel of dirt on another corpse: the concept of old-school marketing. *Fifty Shades of Grey* didn't succeed because of its brilliant prose, its immense advertising budget, or inspired publicity: it scored that coveted number-one spot because "mom" E. L. James jumped right in, feetfirst, to social networking and viral marketing with a dogged persistence that's, frankly, a bit scary. The only bad side of this is—sigh— that for the next five to ten years we're gonna be bombarded not just with *Fifty Shades* knock-offs but all those authors trying the same tricks James did.

Still, while a lot of them won't succeed, *Fifty Shades* has proven that it's time to bury what doesn't work—like dead tree book printing—and try to really, completely rethink marketing and publicity.

The bottom line is that the Fifty Shades trilogy is pure, unadulterated smut.

Porn? PORN?! The mind boggles! Sure, anyone with two brain cells to rub together could see that the world of advertising and marketing was due for a major overhaul, and only people with some serious stock holdings in paper were holding onto the fantasy that print books weren't dead, but no one could have seen that the book that would prove both would also haul

our beloved pornography out of the shadows and into the mainstream—and on to the *New York Times* bestseller list as well.

So while *Fifty Shades* may have shaken things up a bit, take
heart in that, while a lot of old traditions are tumbling down,
its success means that authors—especially erotica writers—may
finally get to remind the world that there's no gray area when it
comes to popularity... and money.

M.CHRISTIAN is an acknowledged master of erotica with
more than four hundred stories in anthologies such as
Best American Erotica, *Best Gay Erotica*, and *Best Lesbian
Erotica*, as well as many other anthologies, magazines, and
sites.

He is the editor of twenty-five anthologies, including
the Best S/M Erotica series, *The Mammoth Book of Future
Cops*, and *The Mammoth Book of Tales of the Road* (with
Maxim Jakubowksi) as well as many others.

He is the author of the collections *Dirty Words*, *The
Bachelor Machine*, *Filthy Boys*, *Love Without Gun Control*,
Rude Mechanicals, and *How To Write And Sell Erotica*, and
of the novels *The Very Bloody Marys*, *Me2*, *Brushes*, *Finger's
Breadth*, and *Painted Doll*.

Fifty Shades of Change

I STARTED WORKING as a literary agent two years ago, and one of the first books I signed was a self-published erotic steampunk novel. I discovered it on Twitter, seduced by its gorgeous cover. I emailed the author and read the book in a single sitting. The writing drew me in with seductive phrases and beautiful storytelling. I was hooked. Addicted. I took it into our office and everyone read it. Everyone loved it.

"This is a six-figure book," said one agent.

"This will go to auction," said another.

Both agents had been in the industry for many years. One of them didn't even read erotica, but like me, in reading this book, had been drawn into a world she couldn't forget.

Determined to break the stereotype of self-published books, I sent it out on submission. A good book is a good book, I figured. This one just happened to be erotic. The editors offered praise. One at a Big Six house emailed me halfway through and said she loved it. Some editors took it to their boards. But in the end the content was too scandalous, too controversial for their publishers. The main character was a man who liked to have sex—lots of sex—and the story was told in first-person from the male point of view. Because of that, we knew exactly how much he liked sex. A little rough sex even appeared. It was delicious. One editor emailed me several times to let me know it was fantastic and that she thought it would be perfect for her list.

Then her publisher canceled her erotic line, killing the potential deal.

For two years I shopped this amazing book, determined to find it a home. I felt frustrated by the market's limitations. Was the book too erotic? Was self-publishing its downfall? Those issues played a role. But an even bigger factor? The book was simply too kinky. Most publishers believed readers weren't ready for that.

But readers were ready for some kink, and they didn't care if the book was traditionally published. They just needed to be able to find it. They just needed to be able to buy it. And then they just wanted to read it and enjoy it—in the car, on the train, on the couch, or in the bedroom.

My struggle to find a publisher for that self-published book—which, months after *Fifty Shades of Grey* burst onto the scene, started receiving offers, both foreign and domestic—wasn't the last time our agency battled to break through the prejudices about erotica and BDSM writing. At the 2011 Romance Writers of America Conference, I sat down with a traditional, female-owned publisher and pitched them an exclusive erotica line. They said they didn't do erotica. However, after we revealed book sales and royalty statements for writers who were publishing in the digital marketplace they got excited. They thought it could work, especially because at that time a large book retailer was looking to fill a void left after the closing of an erotic publishing imprint.

Then they wanted the dirty details.

Exactly what kind of books were these, they wondered. Well, BDSM, male-male, and ménage. For starters. Those are the digital bestsellers, the genres readers crave. But when we sent one of their romance editors some erotic manuscripts, she passed on the entire line and said it didn't fit into their list. We knew it didn't fit into their list; that's why we approached them. It was something new and different. In the end, it was simply *too* different—too erotic.

Now? Just one year later, it's all changed, and it's all because of one English author, E. L. James, and her three naughty books. Foreign agents call wanting more erotica. Scouts approach us wanting to talk about erotic publishing. I have an exclusive erotic imprint now at Coliloquy, a digital publisher that delivers customized erotic adventures to their readers, and created an erotic audio imprint with Audio Realms just for my clients at royalty rates that beat all competitors. (Customers don't just want to read about spankings and bondage and dominance and submission—they want to listen to it, the better, I think, to free their hands.) A famous book packager approached me, searching for erotic authors.

The changes are obvious throughout the industry, marked by headline-grabbing sales. Berkley snapped up veteran romance writer Sylvia Day's self-published erotic romance in a major deal and later bought author Sylvain Renard's *Gabriel's Inferno* and *Gabriel's Rapture* from a small digital publisher for seven figures.

E. L. James helped BDSM and erotica burst onto the scene, but for a decade, a select few people—almost all of them women—have been working outside of traditional publishing, using their knowledge that women love to read sexy, scandalous books to create erotic digital publishing houses. This is not self-publishing; they support their authors in all the ways that count. These women built websites and published erotic writers, then provided gorgeous covers, amazing online and in-store distribution, wonderful editing, promotion, and high royalties. Today some of these companies are multimillion-dollar businesses. They were ahead of the trend, and now that the rest of the publishing world has caught on, they are leading the way.

Older publishing houses are trying to catch up, and one of the ways they are doing that is by buying out books from the digital-first publishers who have already figured out this new market.

Fifty Shades of Grey forced the world to accept that women have always enjoyed erotic romance. The reading public has spoken, even as the media, bloggers, and book world attempt to figure out what it all means. The traditional publishing industry has had to acknowledge that there is a strong market for erotic fiction written, edited, and purchased by women. These aren't the bodice rippers of old. These aren't the books you hide in your bedside table or inside a copy of *Ulysses*. Romance is a multibillion-dollar business and erotic content is a huge part of that market.

My colleague Lori Perkins likes to consider herself (as she mentions in the introduction to this book) a "feminist pornographer," a phrase that offends some people. Honestly? It makes me cringe, too, but I cringe not because I think the term degrades women, the romance genre, or the industry, but because I actually like the way it sounds and I know that as a publishing professional I'm not supposed to use words like "pornography," "smut," "bodice ripper," or "mommy porn." I cringe the same way when I add an extra scoop of ice cream to my sundae or sneak chocolate while on a diet—because what I'm doing feels so good, it must mean trouble. Secretly, I want to embrace those terms, wear them on a T-shirt, tattoo them to my body, and whisper them to those who take offense. What *The Vagina Monologues* did for women and their vaginas, *Fifty Shades* has done for women and smut. No matter what anyone says or thinks, no matter how they feel about the book or the author, E. L. James has revolutionized publishing. For fans of romance books, and especially for fans who enjoy erotica and a bit—or a lot—of BDSM in their stories, this is the best time ever to be a reader.

It's an even better time to be an author of erotic romance. E. L. James helped pave the way for these writers, but I can't wait for new voices to emerge and follow in her formidable, trailblazing footsteps. They might be longtime erotica writers finally being discovered by the public. Or maybe they'll be writers who have written traditional romances but have always cultivated naughtier ideas in their heart and can now sell those stories to mainstream readers. Maybe they'll be conservative writers who simply realize this is a viable market for their careers. Perhaps the new face of erotica will be an author who has only written thrillers or horror or nonfiction and was too embarrassed to write the story she's thought about for years, or a writer who had fantasies of telling the tale about that night her husband put her over his knee for a sexy spanking followed by a night of passionate lovemaking. Inspired by E. L. James' success—and by the response of readers—she'll finally be ready to write that book...but only after she makes her husband give her some more firsthand experience. These books sell. Not only can authors make money, they can make a living off books like these. Readers want them.

I want them, too. I want writers to send me their erotica. To paraphrase the poem associated with Lady Liberty—who may have been reading something a tad naughtier than the Declaration of Independence on that tablet of hers all along—give me your spanking tales, your bondage love stories, your fetish fanfiction, your sexy, forbidden fantasies yearning to breathe free.

Fifty Shades of Grey isn't the first popular BDSM romance, but it's certainly been the most successful at bringing erotic literature into the mainstream. I can't wait to sell similar books. And I can't wait to read what authors in this genre will produce next.

LOUISE FURY is an award-winning literary agent at the L. Perkins Agency and specializes in all forms of romance, children's books, and young adult material, as well as pop culture nonfiction. She has sold books to both traditional and electronic publishers and encourages authors to have one foot in traditional publishing and the other in the digital-first arena. She believes in staying ahead of the pack by embracing change, not just adapting to it, and is a huge advocate for exploring secondary rights. She's sold audio and foreign rights for her clients and was awarded the 2012 RWA NYC Golden Apple Award for Agent of the Year. For more information, visit www.louisefury.com or follow her on Twitter @louisefury.

SYLVIA DAY

The Brown Paper Bag

'VE BEEN TOLD I write "those" books.

The first time someone said that to me I was startled, then slightly offended as I realized she was referencing the erotic content in my stories. *Hell,* I thought, *didn't anyone tell you the days of brown paper bagging your naughty books are over?*

In a way I was right, but I was wrong, too.

I was a new author and an arguably lucky one. I sold my first story to Kensington's erotic Brava imprint less than a year after I began writing. A few weeks after that sale, the submissions I had out with Black Lace and Ellora's Cave—both erotic imprints/publishers—were acquired. Writing erotic romance is what I do, and I was very happy to be placing my stories with publishers who knew how to publish it well.

Within the next year, other publishers created erotic imprints, spurred by the stunning success of Ellora's Cave. Berkley and New American Library had Heat, Harlequin had Spice, HarperCollins had Avon Red, and Kensington added Aphrodisia, which was marketed as leaning more toward erotica than its sensual sister imprint Brava. By 2005, so many members of Romance Writers of America were writing erotic fiction, or wanted to learn how to write it, that I cofounded the Passionate Ink chapter with friend and fellow author Shayla Black. When we applied for affiliation, over four hundred writers' names were on the application paperwork.

But there was controversy surrounding the subgenre. It was said that erotic romance wasn't actually romance. Many disdained it. Others swore there was no market for it, despite the proliferation of new erotic writers and imprints. They were certain erotic romance would never sell in large enough quantities to hit national bestseller lists. And still others didn't believe that writers of erotic stories were "real" authors. After all, we didn't write "real" books; we wrote "those" books.

In the meantime, many of us writing erotic romance were making very good money. We had avid and dedicated readers. Some of us were selling an impressive quantity of digital copies before the invention of the Kindle or Nook.

But the writing community wasn't the only place that didn't embrace erotic romance in the mainstream. Some of the retail outlets that carry books didn't welcome them either.

Being a published author of erotic romance meant that your books were published as trade paperbacks at a higher price point. The titles were often suggestive (such as *Sex Drive* and *Pure Sex*) and the cover art left little to the imagination. As a result, distribution was limited and writers often heard from readers who had difficulty finding the books.

Some publishers, however, chose to publish erotic romance in mass-market paperback format with traditional romance titles and cover art—the new brown paper bag. Long before *Fifty Shades* disguised the sexual nature of the story through packaging, authors such as Lora Leigh and Cheyenne McCray were being published incognito. And with the expanded distribution the format and packaging enabled, the books were easier to find and therefore easier to buy, and they hit the national bestseller lists—the very ones the naysayers had insisted were beyond reach. Lora Leigh swiftly hit the number-one spot on the *New York Times* bestseller list.

Is that the happily-ever-after to this tale? Not quite...

Distribution was still problematic if the erotic content wasn't subtly conveyed. The mass-market format remained key, but it was a format in decline in the industry as a whole. Trade paperbacks still held a steady market share, but it was rare to find a trade paperback romance outside of traditional bookstores. It's very difficult, if not impossible, to reach a large audience if your books aren't conveniently available. Many books are acquired at grocery stores, membership warehouses such as Costco and Sam's Club, and at general stores such as WalMart and Target. Readers want to one-stop shop, not make an extra trip to a specialized store, where most romance trades are sold at full cover price sans the hefty discounts general retailers and e-tailers often apply.

The media spotlight on *Fifty Shades of Grey* changed that. In a tragic economy, retailers couldn't afford not to stock an in-demand item. They made room on their shelves, and once that room was made and the demand remained, they continued to fill it. My novel *Bared to You*, which was a *New York Times* and *USA Today* bestseller as an e-book but had nonexistent print distribution, was suddenly eagerly welcomed in brick-and-mortar venues where erotic trades had previously never been stocked.

Yes, the covers being used on erotic trades are now uniformly subtle, with flowers, scarves, feathers, pearls, belts, and stilettos, but the latest brown paper bag is an immediately recognizable one, which means it's not really there at all. We know something sexy is going to be found between those innocent-looking covers and we don't care who sees us with them. Better yet, we can buy them pretty much everywhere.

Erotic fiction is finally out, proud, and widely available.

SYLVIA DAY is the *New York Times*, *USA Today*, and in-ternationally bestselling author of seventeen novels. Her stories have been translated into over thirty languages. She's been honored with many awards, including multiple nominations for Romance Writers of America's prestigious RITA® Award of Excellence. Find out more at www.SylviaDay.com.

Labels, *Schmabels*, I'll Take the Publicity!

FIFTY SHADES OF GREY. It's been called porn, erotica for women, and, more recently, mommy porn (or mummy porn, as we British would say). It's also been called a lot worse, but I won't get into that.

My opinion is that labels don't matter. The media can give *Fifty Shades of Grey* whatever nickname they like. What does matter is the huge popularity of the book, and the fallout that is affecting the publishing industry, particularly in the romance and erotica sectors. As a UK writer, I'm going to give my perspective on the Fifty Shades trilogy and how it's affected things here in author E. L. James' home country.

Whether you love or hate the book, there's no doubting that it's been a game changer. Nielsen BookScan, a company that compiles official UK chart figures, released the information that the book is the fastest selling paperback since records began, outstripping J.K. Rowling and Dan Brown of *Harry Potter* and *The Da*

Vinci Code fame respectively. That's a huge feat for any book, let alone one belonging to a genre that, up until recently, was pretty much confined to bedrooms and talked about only amongst the most open-minded of friends.

In the UK, certainly, very few bookstores stocked erotic fiction. Now they have tables full of stock of *Fifty Shades of Grey, Fifty Shades Darker,* and *Fifty Shades Freed.* Even the supermarkets are stocking the trilogy, often as part of special promotions. If you want a copy of the books, then you don't have to go very far—they're everywhere. I'm half expecting to spot a copy in my local post office.

Even the UK media, previously so aloof toward erotic fiction, has gone crazy for it. E. L. James has appeared in countless newspapers and magazines and on national television, talking about the books, how they've taken off, and where her inspiration to write them came from. She comes across as quite surprised by the flare-up of interest and the resulting worldwide boom, but I'm sure that, despite her surprise, she's happily counting her money. And I don't blame her.

So, how has all this affected the other erotic writers out there? In a hugely positive light, in my opinion. E. L. James' books have taken the erotica and erotic romance genres and thrust them into the limelight, making them more socially acceptable. The power of word of mouth has been colossal, and women are rushing out to buy the Fifty Shades books on the recommendation of their friends, or borrowing them from one another. You can scarcely have an hour pass by where the books aren't mentioned on the various social media networks. This free publicity is backed up by a huge marketing campaign. For example, there are advertisements in the London Underground and on the sides of buses, which are seen by millions of people. I dread to think how much *that* has eaten into the publisher's advertising budget. But I'm sure they'll make it back many times over.

Of course, once readers have finished all three books, they'll be looking for something else to read. And this is where writers belonging to a genre largely ignored by the mainstream up until now come in. These writers and their books have always been there; it's just that many people hadn't noticed them before. Now, however, e-readers have really come into their own, and more and more people are happy to load up their devices with erotica and erotic romance, and read them in public, as well as in private. For the braver contingent, going into a bookstore and browsing the erotica section—if the store has one, of course— has become a much more acceptable thing to do, as has reading an erotic paperback on the Tube, bus, or train. The genre is no longer confined only to the privacy of homes and bedrooms.

Now that E. L. James is well and truly out there, the UK media are seeking out the next news article to ride the same wave. As a result, other erotic writers are being spotlighted. *Channel 5 News* did a segment on erotic fiction and the rise of e-readers, bringing in a popular erotic writer to give her opinion—and to plug her own books. The *Guardian,* the *Daily Express,* the *Independent,* the *Mail Online,* the *Huffington Post* (UK), and several regional newspapers have all published pieces on erotic writers and erotic fiction. The writers included have all benefited greatly from the publicity, and although they may not yet be counting their millions, it is having a very positive effect on sales for them and for the genre as a whole.

These writers are also taking matters into their own hands. Realizing that the reading public is now hungry for erotic fiction, particularly in the BDSM subgenre, they're promoting their books with a vengeance. There are pages on Facebook, hashtags on Twitter, groups on Goodreads, and boards on Pinterest dedicated to recommending books to read after *Fifty Shades of Grey.* Articles and blog posts with the theme "If you liked *Fifty Shades of Grey,* you'll love this" are springing up all over the web. Whether they love or hate—or haven't read—the book that started it all, writers are taking advantage of the sudden popularity of the genre. And why shouldn't they? Like E. L. James, they've worked hard to write these books, so it's only fair that they should get some recognition for it, and hopefully gain lots more new readers.

Publishers have jumped on the bandwagon, too. Erotica had already been experiencing a rise in popularity due to the increasing sales of e-readers, but following the *Fifty Shades of Grey* media furor, publishers are seeing huge increases in sales of erotica, so naturally they want more of it. Companies that already published erotica are desperate for their writers to pen more of it—particularly if it's BDSM—and several publishers that didn't have an erotica list have now started one. Black Lace, one of the earliest—and arguably still the most popular—erotica imprints, stopped commissioning new content back in 2009, much to the dismay of readers and writers alike. However, the veteran erotica imprint is reopening its doors. June 2012 saw the rerelease of an older title with a redesigned cover bearing no imagery and few colors, aimed at the *Fifty Shades of Grey* readership. A bright pink flash on the cover proclaims, "If you like *Fifty Shades of Grey* you'll LOVE this!" Many popular titles are being given new covers, and a peek at Amazon reveals that brand-new erotica and erotic romance titles from Black Lace can be expected starting September 2012.

So, in my opinion, particularly as an erotic writer, this is good news all round. It doesn't matter what labels are being given to *Fifty Shades of Grey* and other books in the erotica and erotic romance genres. What matters is the amount of publicity and increased sales and readership that have come from the media uproar. Personally, if I were selling millions of copies of my books, the media could label it anything they wanted, and I wouldn't care. I would simply laugh all the way to the bank, and I know many writers that feel exactly the same way.

LUCY FELTHOUSE is a graduate of the University of Derby, where she studied creative writing. During her first year, she was dared to write an erotic story—so she did. It went down like a storm and she's never looked back. Lucy has had stories published by Cleis Press, Constable and Robinson, Decadent Publishing, Ellora's Cave, Evernight Publishing, House of Erotica, Ravenous Romance, Resplendence Publishing, Sweetmeats Press, and Xcite Books. She is also the editor of *Uniform Behaviour*, *Seducing the Myth*, *Smut by the Sea*, and *Smut in the City*. Find out more at http://www.lucyfelthouse.co.uk.

RACHEL KENLEY

Porn Writer on the PTA

*H*AVE YOU READ..."

And then there's a pause. There's always a pause and once I hear it, I know what they are going to say.

"*Fifty Shades of Grey?*" I finish for them.

There's a sigh of relief, followed by, "Yes, how did you know?"

The pause told me. Even though women are reading it, they still aren't completely sure about admitting to anyone they are reading it. With me, however, they know they are safe. In fact, the next sentence is frequently, "But of course *you've* read it."

It's been over five years since my first published fiction was released. Not just fiction—an erotic romance e-book. I don't know which confused people more back in 2007: the fact that the book was only available for download or that I wrote something erotic.

For some reason, most people weren't able to bring themselves to ask me much about my books. "Erotic romance? So that means it's..." More unfinished sentences.

Yes, it's a romance where the number of sex scenes is higher than the average book and the descriptions of what happens in those scenes are hotter and more graphically described.

If there's another question, it's usually, "What made you decide to write *that* kind of book?" There's an emphasis placed on the word "that." If I were writing about murder or horror, no one would ask, but for most of my peers they seemed to have trouble thinking about either reading or talking about sex in this way.

The truth is, most people who knew me weren't terribly surprised by the genre I chose, just somewhat uncomfortable with it. I love romance and relationships and the things someone can discover about herself within a relationship. Genre romance books focus on this. I've never hidden the fact that I've always found merit, strong writing, and great characters in these books. While at college, during long conversations about guys, friends would ask, "This isn't going to end up in one of your books one day, is it?" I would answer with a smile. No sense in lying.

In nearly each decade of my life I've discovered something new to read in the erotic/romantic genre—and I'm getting progressively spicier and more discriminating in my tastes. What pleases me most is when I look back I can see that I have also learned something lasting and important to my personal and sexual awareness from these books.

I read my first romance at fourteen when my mother gave me Kathleen Woodiwiss' *The Wolf and the Dove*. Woodiwiss was credited with "opening the bedroom door" in romance. Thanks to the book's historical setting, I knew more about 1066 and the Norman conquests than any of my friends. I also came to believe deeply in the existence of strong alpha males who knew how to cherish those they loved, something that came in handy after a series of horrible relationships.

In my midtwenties I found the Beauty books by A.N. Roquelaure. My copies are so old, Anne Rice's name isn't on the cover. This was the first time I'd read anything in the BDSM realm or a M/M sex scene. I loved the entire series, and, more importantly, discovered I wasn't alone regarding some of the sexual fantasies and fascinations I had (have!). It gave me the courage to go to clubs and meet others with similar interests in power exchange relationships. It is something that has informed my writing and my life. What relationship isn't an exchange of power?

When I reached thirty, I discovered the Black Lace book imprint—erotica written for women. I was—and still am—hooked on many of the books and authors from this publisher, several of whom now write for mainstream houses. Here I found nearly every relationship combination and setting imaginable, past, present, and fantasy all presented in a way that involved love, character development, and a powerful conclusion. This was when I first started to consider writing erotic romance rather than more traditional romance. It was also when I was truly able to embrace how important sexual power is for a woman who wants to be completely powerful. It's a lesson I practice frequently and is, I think, part of the reason women ask me the questions they do.

I am now in my forties and was published not long after my fortieth birthday. My tastes haven't really changed, but they are more refined. I want something new, more gripping, more imaginative. Something that pushes the envelope, broadens my thoughts and my fantasies. When I read the first book in Laura Antoniou's Marketplace series, I knew I'd found what I wanted to read next. These books are beautifully written with love, sex, passion, and intellect combined—it's magic. In the more traditional romance genre, I discovered Joey W. Hill, who brings a level of both sensuality and sexuality throughout her books that is breathtaking. In these two women, and a few others, I found writers who inspire me to create books that are more erotic and populated with vivid characters on deep emotional journeys. It's going to be a lifelong journey.

So what does this mean for the married suburban mom and erotic romance writer I've become? Because I am fortunate to have friends to whom I can tell what I write, I have become the go-to person on questions of romance and sex. "Talk to Rachel. She's comfortable with these things." "I know you won't be offended if I ask..." "Have you ever heard of..." "What do you think it means if he..."

And now, "Have you read..."

It doesn't matter to them what I answer or what I thought of *Fifty Shades of Grey*. They simply want to be able to talk about it. What it made them think, what it made them feel. And what should they read next. Suddenly I'm the local X-rated librarian.

So then I have a question for them. "What did you like most about the book?"

The pause returns.

I find it curious that even though they've read the book and, more often than not, liked it, they still can't tell me why. I am saddened to realize that even though they are thrilled—and titillated—to have read something in "my" genre, they haven't let it touch them. They still don't know what they like.

The good news is, I think thanks to *Fifty Shades of Grey* more of my acquaintances have respect for and an interest in what I write. There is less judgment all around. Not that they pause any less when they talk about it with me or others, but that is their sexual issue, not mine. They realize that the genre doesn't deserve to be stereotyped or automatically discounted. There is more to it than they thought, and it has become something they are willing to enjoy now that they've opened themselves up to the possibility. Perhaps soon they will even be proud to read the books that I, and other erotica and erotic romance authors, write.

Still, their continued shyness makes me wonder what they are like—and what they are missing—in their current sexual relationships. And once I start thinking about that...I end up having the beginning of a new manuscript.

RACHEL KENLEY writes from her garage office in New England. Her current erotic romance novels and stories are published with Ravenous Romance and Ellora's Cave. Rachel's days consist of an unending quest to balance her many roles while maintaining her sanity and sense of humor. She is currently working with Scott Goudsward on a two-volume anthology for Chaosium Press entitled *Once Upon an Apocalypse.*

me, and give me the eye—the eye that says, *surely you must be joking.*

My inclination is to say, "Don't call me Shirley," but I refrain and tell them that, yes, I really did enjoy the books. And then I ask the million-dollar question: "How far did you read?" There's always a bit of hemming and hawing and the answer comes out as "I read the first chapter" or "About fifty pages," which is closely followed by "I just couldn't do it; I couldn't read any more—it was just so awful" or something to that effect. I don't believe one writer of whom I've asked that question has actually read the books—or even just the first book—but somehow they feel compelled to render a critique of them anyway.

Sure, there are problems with the books. The BDSM isn't always accurately drawn. A virgin probably isn't going to experience multiple orgasms the first time she has sex. I don't like the pop psychology attitude regarding BDSM or Christian's adolescence. But, hey, it's fiction. Let me say that again: it's fiction, folks.

When all the hoopla started, I made a pact with myself. I decided that I would read the entire first book before making any decisions. Even if I hated it, I would finish it. I figured that was the only way to give it a fair chance. And my first thoughts were that *Fifty Shades of Grey* was not particularly well written, although it was not particularly badly written. Its two main problems, in my opinion, lay with a poorly drawn main character and poor editing. I'm an editor, as well as a writer, and a real stickler for the quality of editing in everything I read. I knew E. L. James was British (that's fine with me; I tend to be a bit of an Anglophile), but she was writing a book that took place in America, with American characters. That might be fine, except that you can *tell* she's British. Let me tell you, if you haven't already figured it out—there are differences in British and American English. We don't speak the same; we don't even think the same. No American can hope to fool a Brit and, I'm here to tell you, no Brit can fool an American—not without the right editor.

I think it was the idea that one could commute between Seattle and Portland—or even worse, Vancouver, Washington, and Portland—that made me want to throw the book against the wall. I had occasion to make that drive a few years ago, while doing a West Coast book tour. It's long. It took four, four-and-a-half hours. It's not any kind of commuting distance, and like I said, I almost threw the book against the wall then. But I didn't, because you see, I'd made a pact with myself. And when I decided to let go of geography and the occasional sentence structure that no American college student would utter, I got sucked in. After all, it's a good story, and I'm the kind of person who eagerly anticipates suspending her disbelief. If I'm having fun, I'm happy to be taken for a ride, kinda like the dog that hangs his head out the window of the car on the way to the vet. He has no idea where he's going, but he's having too much fun getting there to worry about it.

And I had fun with Fifty Shades. Ana's annoying; she's a little too naïve to be believable, but she was patterned after Bella in the Twilight books.[1]

But now we come to the main premise for my rant: Is it erotica? I say no. I say the three Fifty Shades books are erotic romance, and there is a definite difference.

Because there's sex on every page (actually, there isn't. There's sex on a vast majority of the pages), and because Christian and Anastasia fuck like bunnies, the books have been billed as erotica. But whether erotic romance authors, editors, and publishers wish to admit it or not, it isn't the amount of explicit sex that makes a book romance or erotica, it's the plotline and the *happily-ever-after* contrivance.

---

1 Yes, I did read the Twilight books, too, and no, I'm not a closeted romance fan. I suppose I'd gotten used to the movies' characterization of Bella and had forgotten just how wimpy and annoyingly naïve she was in the books. I reread the last book recently and realized I greatly preferred the screenwriter's version of Bella. But I digress: Ana is just as annoyingly naïve as Bella was, except it's worse, because she's graduating from college with a high school girl's experience and sensibilities—a very immature high school girl's experience and sensibilities.

What makes a book a romance? It's more than just a happily-ever-after or a love match; the book really has to be about the love story. It has to be boy meets girl, boy and girl experience seemingly insurmountable problems (such as they don't like each other, one of them is crazy, one of them is suspected of committing murder, one of them is actually an alien, they might be related, and so on), and boy loses girl. Boy and girl overcome their problems, get back together, and live happily ever after. Although I say *boy and girl*, these days I could just as easily use *boy and boy*, *girl and girl*, or *boy and boy and girl*, and so on. The point is, it's a love story with roadblocks thrown in.

Erotic romance means there's explicit sex in the story, but it's still essentially a romance, based upon the aforementioned plot points. What *explicit sex* in the story meant, up until fairly recently, is that there are a few sex scenes, maybe three or four, that escalate in intensity until the final scene, which is unbelievably (in erotic romance terms) sexy, hot, or erotic, because the couple is finally married, or they're committed to each other, or they're together forever, or at the very least, they're together for the foreseeable future. The sex scenes are explicit in that body parts are named and there is a description of what those body parts are doing as the action gets hot and heavy.

Based on a piece of erotic romance I heard read aloud recently, those body parts might consist of nothing more than lips and nipples and the action might not get much heavier than light petting, but, that particular piece notwithstanding, erotic romance has been heading in the direction of the explicitness of erotica for quite a while. And now, sex can happen in erotic romance before the couple makes a love commitment—just as long as they *do* make a love commitment before the final page.

Erotica, on the other hand, is more about the sex than the undying love. That doesn't mean that there can't be undying love in an erotic novel, it just means the undying love isn't the reason for the story's existence, as it is in a romance. No, in erotica the *sex* is the reason for the story's existence. I would argue that the main purpose of erotica is to arouse and titillate and, while that might be a by-product of erotic romance, it is not the main purpose. Is that an oversimplification? Yes, but just bear with me for a moment, I know a little something about this, you see; I'm an erotica writer, and along with short stories and novellas, I've also written two erotic novels.

As with Fifty Shades, my novels share a BDSM milieu, although they are intrinsically different, as my books are set in a world of female domination and male submission.[2] They are also different in another, very fundamental way: while my books also include a romantic love match and a happily-ever-after, or at least a happy-for-the-foreseeable-future, ending, the sex is what drives the plot, rather than the love relationship.

Here's a little secret about the difference between erotica and erotic romance: you can take the sex out of an erotic romance and the story will survive just fine (although it won't be nearly as much fun to read), but you can't take the sex out of erotica. If you do, you'll be left with nothing to hold the story together. Go ahead, think about it. I'll wait.

It took me a while to recognize the difference, a difference that is usually apparent to erotic romance writers, editors, publishers, and readers. I say "usually" because it doesn't seem to be as apparent to readers and critics of the Fifty Shades books, who continue to call them erotica. Granted, if you took the sex out of *Fifty Shades of Grey*, it would be a lot shorter, but if every time Christian got ready to do something really perverse to Ana, or every time they wound up in bed, the scene faded to black and ended with them cuddling together afterward, her crying on the floor or him playing the piano in the living room, the story would still be there. Yes, it would be pretty boring, but it would hold together just fine.

If you took the sex out of my Melinoe books, you'd have nothing. You wouldn't even have the love match, as the main

---

2 As you may imagine, Ana was not the character with whom I, personally, identified.

characters are together *because* of the sex, not regardless of the sex, as Christian and Ana are.

When I sent the manuscripts to erotic romance publishers, the books were resoundingly rejected. After they were published, as erotica, I tried sending them to reviewers of erotic romance. They didn't like them—at all. It turned out there was nothing but sex in them and the love match wasn't at all romantic.[3] But mostly, the complaint was that the books were just sex, sex, and more sex. And, of course, they are. Some people like that.

If, like I said, you can take the sex out of the book and still have a story, it's an erotic romance. On the other hand, if once all that sex has been extracted, you're left with a loose array of characters in search of a plot, you can be fairly certain you're reading erotica.

E. L. James' books are generally termed erotica, because a lot of people think that, based on the fact there's an overwhelming amount of explicit sex in the books, they can't be considered romances.[4] Those people, however, would be wrong. These books are unabashedly romantic. They follow the tried-and-true formula for romance and the series ends happily. And, as previously stated, this would hold true even if aliens came down and vacuumed all the sex out of all the copies in existence. With that in mind, there can be no denying that the Fifty Shades series is a romance.

In the past, the movers and shakers in the world of romance have eschewed sex in their novels. Sex was somehow base and didn't belong in the rarefied realms of romantic love. Of course, if sex weren't intrinsically bound to love, the human race would have died out long ago. We are sexual creatures.

---

3 For a lot of erotic romance folks, you need an alpha male to sweep the main character off her feet. A submissive man who craves the application of a woman's itchy palm applied to his needy backside, among other acts, is not as romantic as the reverse, it would seem.

4 A lot of romance purists don't think there should be *any* sex in romance, much less the amount ladled into the Fifty Shades books.

We not only enjoy but indeed live for sex, whether it's an imperative or not. Why then, as sexual beings, wouldn't we want to read about it, too?

Readers, worldwide, have answered that question. And they have answered it resoundingly, with their wallets, something that all publishers, whether of romance or anything else, use as the ultimate measure of acceptance. With the introduction of *Fifty Shades*, an awful lot of people have read books containing an awful lot of explicit sex for the very first time—and they've liked it. I think the floodgates have been opened. Now that they know what they've been missing, they're going to want more, and who can blame them? After *Fifty Shades of Grey*, *Fifty Shades Darker,* and *Fifty Shades Freed*, I don't think it will be possible to put the genie back in the bottle. Of course, being an erotica writer, I wouldn't want to.

D. L. KING's (http://dlkingerotica.blogspot.com) short stories have appeared in titles such as *Best Women's Erotica, One Night Only, Luscious, Please, Ma'am,* and many others. She is the editor of *Seductress, The Harder She Comes, Spankalicious,* IPPY Gold Medalist *Carnal Machines, Spank!, The Sweetest Kiss,* and the Lambda Literary Award finalist *Where the Girls Are.*

Fifty Shades of *Romance*

It's All in the Eyes

*N*EAR THE BEGINNING of *Fifty Shades of Grey,* our heroine, Ana, makes a profound and magnetic eye connection with Christian Grey. I understood that connection completely, because just about everything romantic in my life has started with my eyes. Ana knows how I feel, and *vice versa.* Christian's eyes haunted her dreams and burned into her "with some unfathomable emotion."

All my life I've been told I have unusual eyes. I guess they are rather large. They have green irises sprinkled with red and gold flecks and my pupils have dark purple rings.

Eyes have been on my mind since I read the novel, and I started thinking about something that happened when I was a teenager—the first time I was aroused by someone's eyes. At a New Year's Eve party I caught a cute boy looking at me from across the room. No matter where I was, when I looked up, there he was, watching me. It wasn't creepy, just very sensual, although I wouldn't have known to use that word back then. I eventually understood the feeling was a combination of curiosity, lust, and being teenagers. Eventually the boy spoke to me. I can't recall what he said, but I remember his sparkling green eyes.

At eighteen, a man entered my life. He was twenty-one, older, and he was definitely a ladies' man, with twinkling brown bedroom eyes that seduced me the moment I met him. He loved women and they loved him. At least, I sure did. We dated for five years and we had some amazing sexual experiences together.

I watched my first adult movies with him, the famous *Deep Throat* and *The Devil in Miss Jones*. These movies were very controversial—everyone was talking about them in hushed voices—and my reaction was total fascination. I understood why some people objected to them. I felt that anyone had the right to object to sexy movies but not the right to tell me I couldn't enjoy them. While watching these movies, I still remember watching the eyes of the actors and it always seemed to me the ones who were having the best sex were the ones making the most intense eye contact.

The sexual allure of eyes has also been a part of my reading experiences, too, especially books with sexual content. I had an active sexual imagination, knew that sex was a natural part of life, and I felt that reading about sex was part of the fun. As a young girl, I quickly graduated from Harold Robbins and moved on in my literary sex quest by reading erotic books by Anne Rampling and A.N. Roquelaure (both, I later learned, pseudonyms used by Anne Rice), who easily tapped my desire button.

Fast-forward to today. I've now read most of the best erotic literature, and as Vice President of Vivid Entertainment, helped design beautiful and erotic video and DVD covers and met many famous porn stars. Having been in the adult entertainment industry most of my adult life, I believe the fine line between porn and erotica has all but disappeared. One person's erotica is another's porn. Whatever you call it, it was created to stimulate and arouse.

And, with all these experiences, it is still the eyes that get me, just as they did that memorable New Year's Eve so many years ago.

It's been said that the eyes are the windows to the soul. Throughout *Fifty Shades of Grey*, Ana and Christian are blessed with the ability, whether conscious or not, to look deep inside each other's thoughts—including their sexual thoughts—through the intensity of their gaze.

What I have come to realize is that we don't wear our hearts on our sleeves, we wear them in our eyes. Some eyes are mischievous, some twinkle, others sizzle. They didn't coin the term "bedroom eyes" for nothing. I can tell immediately if there will be sexual compatibility with someone if our eyes lock. For me, everything romantic or just plain sexual starts with a look, and sometimes the response is a jolt so strong I can feel it with every sense of my being.

Sexy eyes are the biggest turn-on there is for me. They provide an immediate sexual connection. Whether what's there is romantic or animalistic, it's always hot. Conversely, if there's nothing going on with the eyes, I give up all sexual interest.

Attraction starts with a look and sometimes that is all it takes, because just one look into someone else's eyes can put us on the same wavelength. Once the connection is made, I find it hard to break. As E. L. James writes, "He [Christian] has beautiful eyes—captivating, intelligent, deep, and dark, dark with dominant secrets." Oh my!

For some people, it's the kisses. Not for me. The first kiss may be electric but only my partner's eyes can shake me to my core. Seeing the effect I have on my partner increases my pleasure and can take my breath away.

Come to think about it, I don't know why kisses are always portrayed with closed eyes. You miss so much when you can't see each other. During my best sexual encounters, I've looked into my partner's eyes during the entire experience.

An urgent, open-eyed kiss sets the tone for what's to come. Ana felt, "I'm hypnotized by his eyes staring fervently into mine." Combine eye penetration with great sex and it is guaranteed to be an experience that won't be forgotten...ever! A look can transport you to another place. A place where no one else exists but you and your partner.

In my day job I see women having sex and being photo-graphed in sexy poses all the time. I have watched the girls dur-ing photo shoots and often wondered what they were thinking about that gave them that smoldering look. The best pictures depict girls who look like they either just got laid or are about to. The eyes of a top model almost always express sexual arous-al. When she's looking deeply into the eyes of her lover, imagi-nary or real, suddenly the rest of the world no longer exists. Everything she needs to communicate is said through a look.

E. L. James vividly captures this reality in *Fifty Shades of Grey*. Christian's eyes show his desire and need for Ana, just as hers do for him. Christian uses Ana's looks as a barometer as to how far he can go with her. It's the same for me. From the first kiss through orgasm I like to know what my partner is feeling. If we are look-ing at one another, we can adjust our movements and make those tiny changes that can increase the intensity of the moment. If we're clamping our eyes closed, or looking somewhere else, we may never know when or how to do that one subtle thing that can make all the difference, and it is amazingly empowering.

Ana had power over Christian. It just took her a while to figure it out and make it work for her.

Just as Ana and Christian did, leave the lights on, keep your eyes open, focus on your partner, and let your mind and body fol-low the wave of arousal you feel. And, just as they did, you might find that new layer of sexual arousal you never dreamed of.

MARCI HIRSCH is Vice President of Vivid Entertainment, the world's leading adult film studio, where she heads up production, licensing, and international sales. The second generation of her family to work in the adult industry, Marci lives in Southern California with her two sons.

JENNIFER SANZO

The Byronic Hero Archetype and Christian Grey
Why America's Favorite Sadist
Is Nothing New

OU KNOW THE TYPE: powerful, mysterious, brooding, and unbelievably sexy. He is the reason you watch period dramas even though you have no interest in literature or history. He's the brilliant, cynical bad boy with a heart of gold—seemingly unobtainable, yet flawed just enough to make you think you stand a chance. In literature, he is referred to as the Byronic hero, and much to the dismay of feminists everywhere, women have been lusting over him for centuries. Now joining the ranks of literature's sexiest protagonists is Christian Grey, the beautiful, twitchy-palmed control freak who has captured our hearts and excited other parts of our anatomy.

If you have a pulse, you have heard about the Fifty Shades trilogy and America's favorite sadist, Christian Grey. I am a stay-at-home mom, and this series has become the topic of conversation at every playground, story time, and ice cream social from Rochester (where I live) to Timbuktu (assumption not based in fact). Last I checked there were over 1,000 people on the waiting list for *Fifty Shades of Grey* at my library alone. So, what is all the fuss about? Why have so many women fallen in love with Christian Grey? Why the overwhelming obsession?

Honestly, it is nothing new. Christian Grey joins the company of some of literature's most famous panty-droppers, including Mr. Rochester in *Jane Eyre*, *Gone with the Wind*'s Rhett Butler, Heathcliff in *Wuthering Heights*, and *The Count of Monte Cristo*'s Edmund Dantes. Christian Grey is Mr. Darcy with a darker past, a few more scars, and a more extensive sex toy collection. He's the Rhett Butler who gets the girl. He's a modern-day Heathcliff, sharing the crappy childhood but maintaining more self-control, less self-indulgence, and sparing us the ghost of his dead girlfriend. Think of Fifty Shades as your favorite epic romance with a touch of BDSM. With Christian Grey, E. L. James gives us the modern manifestation of the Byronic hero archetype—only this time the reader gets to know him more intimately than ever before. His allure is rooted in the qualities we have always been drawn to in our darkest romantic heroes, but now we get to go to bed with him (a lot), and women (myself included) just can't get enough.

So, what makes a hero "Byronic" and how does Christian Grey measure up?

Originating with Lord Byron's *Childe Harold's Pilgrimage*, the term "Byronic hero" is defined by the *Oxford Dictionary of Literary Terms* as a "boldly defiant but bitterly self-tormenting outcast, proudly contemptuous of social norms but suffering from some unnamed sin." In other words, he's a sexy badass who might have a chip on his shoulder, but is naughty in all the right ways.

Classically, this type of character possesses similar physical attributes. At first glance, the Byronic hero is utter perfection.

He is usually handsome and sexually attractive, seductive, mysterious, and charismatic. He is physically powerful and has a commanding presence. When we first meet Christian Grey, protagonist Anastasia Steele describes him as "tall, dressed in a fine gray suit, white shirt, and black tie with unruly dark copper-colored hair and intense, bright gray eyes." Much of Ana's inner monologue is devoted to obsessing over his beauty, how good he smells, and his overall physical perfection. In a nutshell: this guy is hot.

In addition to physical beauty, these characters tend to be worldly and cultured, arrogant yet charming. Think: Christian Bale in *American Psycho*, without the chainsaw and psychopathic tendencies. Christian Grey drinks the best wine and orders the most expensive champagne. He knows his gin; he has cucumber in his Hendricks and lime in his Bombay. He is a brilliant piano player who speaks fluent French and quotes Antoine de Saint-Exupery. A pilot, a sailor, an opera enthusiast, he is the epitome of sophistication.

The Byronic hero also fits a certain intellectual persona. Since he is perceptive, intelligent, and enlivened by a good challenge, he often partakes in witty banter, which is aptly demonstrated by Ana and Christian's email exchanges. Determined, capable, and bright, these men are typically wealthy and successful. In Christian's case, he's a twenty-seven-year-old CEO who makes about $100,000 an hour. Helicopter and a private jet? Homes in Aspen and New York? A fifty-foot sailboat named after his adoptive mother? He has all these things and more. He tells Ana that he wants to lavish money on her: "I could buy you your heart's desire, Anastasia, and I want to." Just in case I've lost you, let's recap. Drop-dead gorgeous sex god? Check. Ridiculously wealthy? Check. And he wants to take her on a shopping spree with his black Amex. Are you swooning yet?

Ah, but there is a catch: beneath his physical perfection, sophistication, and wealth lies a complicated emotional persona.

Christian, our self-proclaimed "dark knight," has perfected the art of brooding. Like his fictional counterparts, he can be solitary, moody, aloof, and distant. His self-critical and self-deprecating tendencies can escalate to self-loathing if not kept in check. He can be obsessive and controlling to the point of suffocation.

A few minutes into their first meeting Ana calls him a "control freak," to which he responds: "Oh, I exercise control in all things, Miss Steele." He likes to be in charge and his penchant for social and sexual dominance allows him to use sex as a weapon. Repeatedly described as "mercurial," Christian Grey is a "mass of contradictions." He is strong, yet fragile, presenting himself as the quintessential alpha male only in an effort to mask his vulnerability. At times he is uptight, selfish, and depressive; at others, carefree and playful. Christian's moods change so frequently that Ana actually Googles "multiple personality disorder"! It does not get much more confusing or frustrating than being in a relationship with a Byronic hero.

Sure, Christian Grey is conflicted, cynical, and at times quite unreasonable, but like many of the Byronic heroes who came before him, underneath his tough exterior are glimpses of his integrity and soul. Deep down he is a good man. He has a heart for philanthropy and dedicates much of his time and creative energy to feeding the world's poor and developing technologies to better life in the Third World. However, unlike many of his Byronic predecessors, Christian recognizes his shortcomings and is well aware of his baggage. In this respect, he is a more evolved version of the Byronic hero. He is drawn to goodness and even though he struggles with integrity, he wants to do the right thing. He warns Ana, "You should steer clear of me. I'm not the man for you." He marvels at her innocence and doesn't want to taint it, yet he finds himself "like a moth to a flame." The feeling is mutual. Ana expresses on numerous occasions that she fears she is "Icarus flying too close to the sun," but no matter how hard she tries, she cannot resist "poor, fucked-up, kinky, philanthropic Christian."

These emotional discrepancies result from yet another factor that Byronic heroes have in common: they are haunted, tortured souls who wrestle with demons from their past. In Christian's case those demons would include being raised by a "crack whore" mother, beaten by her pimp, and left alone with her dead body for four days, scared and hungry, at the age of four. Oh, and one of his adoptive mother's friends seduced him at fifteen and turned him into her BDSM boy toy. In turn he has learned to channel his anger by beating and having sex with girls who look like his birth mother. Super healthy, I know. "Paging Dr. Flynn!" So, in other words (Ana's inner goddess', to be exact) he "has a 747 cargo hold's worth of baggage," including a suicidal, gun-toting ex. (That being said, I would take Christian's mommy issues over Mr. Rochester's crazy, pyromaniac wife in the attic any day!)

Despite his beauty, intelligence, wealth, and power, the Byronic hero's emotional baggage would prove too much for most women to handle. Is it any wonder that Ana, our heroine and Christian's love interest, is a dewy-eyed literature major? Who better to fall for our Byronic friend than someone who has spent her entire life in love with his fictional counterparts? She even looks to her favorite romantic heroines for guidance: "Elizabeth Bennet would be outraged, Jane Eyre too frightened, and Tess would succumb, just as I have." Christian and Ana are a perfect illustration of opposites attracting. Fifty Shades tells a tale as old as time: beauty tames the (sexy) beast; only a true innocent can unlock the Byronic hero's heart.

What is it about the Byronic hero that certain women can't resist?

Even Ana, our Austen-loving, Brontë-reading, Hardy-quoting protagonist, has trouble putting her finger on it: "No man has ever affected me the way Christian Grey has, and I cannot fathom

why. Is it his looks? His civility? Wealth? Power? I don't understand my irrational reaction." Right now millions of housewives
are questioning their own reactions (irrational or otherwise) to
Christian Grey. Why do we love this guy so much? The answer is
simple: we love him for all the reasons we have always loved our
Byronic heroes.

Perhaps the most obvious trait we fall for is how ardently
they love and adore their women. Byronic heroes say romantic things like: "If he loved you with all the power of his soul
for a whole lifetime, he couldn't love you as much as I do in a
single day" (Heathcliff, *Wuthering Heights*). And this: "You have
bewitched me, body and soul" (Mr. Darcy, *Pride and Prejudice*).
And this: "You are exquisite, honest, warm, strong, witty, be-
guilingly innocent; the list is endless. I am in awe of you. I want
you, and the thought of anyone else having you is like a knife
twisting in my dark soul" (Christian Grey, *Fifty Shades Darker*).
I mean, come on! That's some good stuff! These men are passionate in their work, their causes, and their relationships. They
are not afraid to tell you that you are beautiful and make no
secret of how much they love you; they shout it from the roof-
tops. When Christian pays $100,000 for a dance with Ana at
the Coping Together benefit, I couldn't help but be reminded
of a similar scene in *Gone with the Wind* when Rhett exclaims,
"Mrs. Charles Hamilton—one hundred and fifty dollars...in
gold." How could you not fall for these rebels who will sweep
you off your feet at any cost regardless of who they shock in the
process?

In addition to being natural-born romantics, Byronic heroes
are great listeners and are attentive to their lady's needs. They
recognize that women want someone to take care of them. From
the beginning, despite his stalker-esque tendencies, Christian
makes Ana feel safe and protected. These guys pay attention.
After one coffee date, Christian knows how Ana takes her tea,
what size she wears, and that the key to her heart lies in a first
edition of *Tess of the d'Urbervilles*. When she is hung over, he

is there waiting with orange juice and two Advil. She's feeling naughty; he's got Ben Wa balls for her to wear to a black tie charity gala at his parents' home. Job security? He buys her a publishing company. Clothes? Personal shopper. Unsafe car? Have this Audi. Your Audi got trashed by my psycho ex? Here's a Saab. Like to read? How about the entire British Library on an iPad? Her wish is his command.

These characters give their women all they ever wanted and expose them to things they never even knew existed. Ana says, "It makes me feel powerful, strong, desired, and loved—loved by this captivating, complicated man whom I love in return with all my heart." Isn't that what we, as women, long for? To be pursued and desired? To find someone to love and cherish us? Women have always wanted honest, trusting, and committed relationships, and now we are thinking we would also like a playroom with a "soft-boudoir Elizabethan-torture setup." What better testament of trust than letting your boyfriend tie you up when you know his butt plug collection is vast enough to encompass an entire bureau? Implicit trust, giving yourself over—mind, body, and soul—to someone else... well, it doesn't get much hotter than that. We crave that level of ultimate intimacy; the mind-blowing, kinky sex is just an added bonus.

Romance, undivided attention, and being desired beyond our wildest dreams are all known to get our juices flowing, but there is one more thing that makes the Byronic hero irresistible: he resonates with the female fantasy of bad boy reformation. Ana's dilemma is age old: "He's not a hero; he's a man with serious, deep emotional flaws, and he's dragging me into the dark. Can I not guide him into the light?" Ah yes, the thoughts of every girl in love with every bad boy since the beginning of time. What makes Christian different from that tattooed guy with the motorcycle you dated senior year of high school just to piss off your parents is that this beautiful and broken man is flawed but willing to change. His admission that he is "fifty shades of fucked up" gives us hope that, with a little faith and some patience, any flawed man can be saved. By nature, it is his very brokenness that makes this otherwise "unobtainable" man attainable. The fact that this ridiculously handsome, powerful, wealthy, and kind man could fall for any one of us if we took the time to care, took the time to save him, is appealing on multiple levels. Christian Grey is perfect in his imperfections because we want to save him and be saved in the process. Ana says, "There's nothing I can teach him. I have no special skills," but ends up teaching him the most valuable lesson of all: how to love and be loved in return. She becomes his lifeline; in the end love saves the day.

It is a beautiful thought that love really can conquer all, and it is obvious that Fifty Shades is an erotic, modern fairy tale complete with happy ending (no pun intended). However, merely establishing that Christian Grey is a Byronic hero and discussing the overall appeal of these characters still does not explain the insane obsession with him. He is just one on a list of many dark, sexy, brooding literary hunks.

So why the astounding, inescapable popularity of the Fifty Shades series? The novels are not well written; in fact, many would argue they are poorly written. Grammatical and punctuation errors abound, Britishisms pop up all over Seattle, and redundancy runs rampant. Yet, much to the chagrin of many academics, literary critics, and general condemners of erotic fiction, this series is resonating with people unlike any book I've ever seen. When I taught Effective Reading to college freshman, I would always tell my students: "If you think you don't like to read, you just haven't found the right book." Whether we like it or not, *Fifty Shades of Grey* has become "the right book" for millions of people, the majority of whom are women. Am I advocating its addition to the literary canon? Do I think it should appear on every Brit Lit reading list? Of course not. Actually, I shudder at the thought. But just because it isn't on par with Shakespeare or Austen and Brontë doesn't mean it isn't valuable. *Fifty Shades* is clearly meeting a need in the literary market by giving its reader exactly what she wants: sex and lots of it.

This series is successful because James has given the reader her ultimate fantasy: experiencing the Byronic hero in the bedroom. What woman wouldn't want to read (in explicit detail) what happened after Rhett carried Scarlett up those stairs? Or what Darcy and Elizabeth's wedding night was like? Jane's sex life after Mr. Rochester regained his sight? Christian Grey epitomizes the sexy, brooding hero that women want and the love life that goes along with him. It is no longer left to our imagination. We get to hear the rip of every condom packet, every moan, every breath. We get to feel every touch and relish each caress. For the first time we get the hedonism along with the happily-ever-after. Cliché? Sure, but the cliché exists because of our common desires. Christian Grey is all of our fantasies wrapped into one.

As it turns out, deep down we're all a little "sex mad and insatiable." We want it all. We want the love and the lust. We want a man who will dance with us to Sinatra, take us soaring, and buy us our 12,000-square-foot dream home overlooking the Sound. We want the guy who can say, "I want you sore, baby" one minute and make love to the music of Roberta Flack the next. The guy who will whisk you around the world, drench you in diamonds, outfit you in designer duds from Louboutin to La Perla, reenact the piano scene from *Pretty Woman*, and make you come on demand. (Seriously, he says, "Come on, baby," and poof, magic orgasms!) A loving, committed relationship with a hottie billionaire who is good in bed? Who turns out to be a spectacular father and still thinks you're sexy when you're bloated and pregnant? Who only asks for the occasional spanking in return? Hello!! Where do I sign up? With Christian Grey, we get to fall in love with the reckless bad boy who wants us mind, body, and soul, and we get to experience him in the bedroom. Dreams really do come true, "kinky fuckery" included.

JENNIFER SANZO holds a BA in English from Seton Hall University and a Masters from William Paterson University. She is a recipient of the Elizabeth Ann Seton Women's Studies Writing Prize, a published poet, and former English professor. Jennifer lives in Rochester, New York, with her husband and two children.

Grey Is the New Black

FADE IN:
>Somewhere...
>In a fantasy far, far away...

We see Carrie Bradshaw's *Sex and the City* apartment (circa the TV show), New York City.

Next to a copy of *Fifty Shades of Grey*, we see Carrie Bradshaw's fingers whisk across the keyboard as sentences form on her backlit computer screen.

What is all the fuss about regarding this book?

Why is Grey the new black?

* * * * *

FADE IN:
>Somewhere...
>In *your* fantasy life—your place, present day...

Christian Grey's long, tapered fingers lace his silky silver tie tightly around you, the weave from his tie imprints your flawless skin. You inhale his freshly washed linen scent in a sharp intake of breath as his fictional persona imprints on popular culture and you anticipate the smart of his hand smacking your (roll fantasy sequence, it goes here).

* * * * *

DOES THIS AROUSE...your interest, Miss Reader?

Honey, take a number—these days we're all "in the kink."

Fifty Shades of Grey hit the 20 million mark the week I'm writing this and author E. L. James is signing them from Comic-Con to Costco.

Never before has one throbbing manhood held a nation in such sexual thrall.

What is his hold on our collective carnality, uh, I mean, our imaginations?

Looking at it as a literary agent—one of fifty takes on *Grey*—my thoughts center on why this is happening. This is the fastest-selling book of all time, yet it might not have been published on its merits alone had it been submitted to an agency slush pile. I decided to look deeper at why the bondage-themed novel is spanking the bestseller list and sparking a publishing phenomenon. What is it about this book that hits the sweet spot: the tipping point where culture really pops?

Here are a few thoughts on why *Fifty Shades* really hits the G-spot:

It is a very fresh and modern tale.

Fifty Shades tells an erotic story of desire and boundaries, love and dysfunction, trauma and trust issues. Anastasia Steele—who has never known a man's touch—or noticed she has a clitoris—meets Christian Grey. When Mr. Grey's steely gray gaze alights on Miss Steele, romance ensues. Guy meets girl. Girl is spirited to his millionaire man cave. Girl is deflowered, awakened, impassioned. Guy offers girl his hand in bondage.

We also get classic romantic tradition.

Girl with spirit and pluck meets man of property is ever a panty-peeling premise in the Victorian novel. Literature is riddled with submission/dominance themes. The very tales of literary heroines that *our* literary heroine, virginal Anastasia Steele, has been steeped in.

An expert on eighteenth- and nineteenth-century women's novels, Susan Greenfield, calls this hot title *recycled literature.* Indeed, *Fifty Shades* revels in the classic romanticism of Jane Austen and the Brontë sisters, and the plot specifically references Thomas Hardy. Echoes of each reverberate through *Fifty Shades* like the convulsions Christian expertly wrings from Ana with those long tapered fingers...um, where were we?

Oh, yes, so Ana's trio of literary heroines: Tess of the d'Urbervilles, Jane Eyre, and Elizabeth Bennet form a sort of *Sex and the City*–like posse for the virgin-turned-BDSM initiate. As she and Grey discuss their contract language and deal points to begin her new life as his submissive, Ana tells the reader, "[Austen's] Elizabeth Bennet would be outraged, [Brontë's] Jane Eyre too frightened, and [Hardy's] Tess would succumb, just as I have."

Anastasia Steele went out there an understudy...
and she came back a star.

Steele and Grey have joined the all-star cast of literary couples. The S&M-crossed lovers were first conceived as Bella Swan and Edward Cullen, the *Twilight* duo written as fanfiction for the Twilight fandom. For the literary zeitgeist, we could say that as the erotic trilogy draws on its precursors' influence, you start to see how *Fifty Shades* could be called Next Generation Jane Eyre or the literary lovechild of Lizzie and Darcy. We might call them the new Carrie and Mr. Big or something meets *Pretty Woman* (and that other rich corporate raider guy).

After all, these are the shades that launched a thousand 'ships.

Tess of the d'Urbervilles, referred to throughout the novel, put me in mind of the idea that perhaps the true origins of this trilogy were a term paper that James repurposed; the theme of a woman locked in soulful struggle over passion and power is a clear parallel between the tales. Ana has angel (her inner goddess) and devil (her subconscious) perched on each slender shoulder. While her inner goddess delights, her subconscious judges; when her inner goddess cheers at Ana's "OMG, he likes me, he really likes me!" attraction for a guy with "scary vices," her subconscious sneers. They haggle over his hard/soft terms, veering between sense and sensibility—so to speak. Tess, demeaned by a libertine (her cousin) and deified by an idealist (her husband)—true to Hardy's day, her story says "death before orgasm"—is now updated and re-created in Ana's conflict.

Love of *Pride and Prejudice* prompted Helen Fielding to modernize its plot for her novelization of her "Bridget Jones's Diary" column. With her mission statement being "simple human need for Darcy to get off with Elizabeth," with the couple as her "chosen representatives in the field of shagging, or rather courtship." The viral votes are in: Christian and Ana could now be said to be the new chosen representatives in the field of shagging, or rather courtship.

Christian Grey is a romantic hero.

Actually he is a very classic Romantic hero. And he is also a Byronic hero in the classic sense. This means Christian Grey is the quintessential hero of the Victorian literature that Anastasia is studying when the novel opens. He has every requisite for a Byronic hero: he is complex, he is a troubled soul, damaged from—and haunted by—a dark and mysterious past; he is extremely passionate, he exists outside the realm of the "norm."

Christian Grey seeks solace and control through micromanaging bondage-style sex. Christian Grey, CEO of Grey Enterprises, may be an all-powerful Pacific Northwest twentysomething magnate, but the vulnerable master of the universe has never known a genuine love connection and he is a virgin, too—to vanilla sex. Until he meets *her*—and then it is through Ana that Christian seeks sexual redemption.

In *Mad, Bad and Dangerous to Know*, Blogcritics' Barbara Barnett describes Byronic heroes as "charismatic characters with strong passions and ideals, but who are nonetheless deeply flawed individuals who may act in ways which are socially reprehensible, and whose internal conflicts are heavily romanticized. They are self-destructive and difficult at worst; courageous, intelligent, and noble at their best. Irresistible and magnetic."

So we can look to classic literature for the reason why the trilogy has us all by the nerve endings. This is also the answer to why this has become an internet sensation and why *Fifty Shades of Grey* is being read and embraced by girls coming of age in our era of economic anxiety and hot-mamas-turned-mommies are furtively downloading during the spin cycle.

Blame it on the Brontës. Charlotte's *Jane Eyre* and Emily's *Wuthering Heights*—Cathy and Heathcliff, Jane and Mr. Rochester—are in our romantic DNA. Christian Grey, literary heir to Mr. Rochester (Mr. Rochester hides his wife, the madwoman, in the mansion attic; Mr. Grey keeps his secret BDSM stuff in the man cave playroom), is the Byronic hero for our time.

Putting aside, of course, that Christian Grey's phantom-like menace is a portrait of the most literary stalker since Humbert Humbert's loins lit up for Lo-li-ta. But *Fifty Shades* is at heart a Cinderella story—perhaps we should think of it as the lost sex scenes of Cinderella.

E. L. James is redolent of the great doyennes of romance.

Author James likes to say in every interview that she knows she is not a great writer. But she sure knows how to rip a bodice, and she does it old school. Reading *Shades*, Georgette Heyer would have swooned from reading such explicit content; Barbara Cartland would have had the vapors from the fainting couch. But the cleavage-heaving greats would still have to agree E. L. has chops and craft, and holds her readers as the tension mounts...

• • • • •

So what if feminists decry the erotic lure of the powerful male over the vulnerable heroine thing? So what if you tend to nod off while waiting for the next sexually charged scene to get pulsing? So what if the book editors seem to have tossed aside their red felt pens and reached for their vibrators? *Fifty Shades* "gives new meaning to reading for pleasure," crows Vintage, an imprint of Random House, the publisher of E. L. James—as well as Flaubert.

Somewhere... in a bookstore, not far from you...

Madame Bovary just rolled her eyes.

KATHARINE SANDS is a literary agent with the Sarah Jane Freymann Literary Agency in New York City. Katharine represents a varied list of authors who publish a diverse array of books. She is "the agent provocateur" of *Making the Perfect Pitch: How to Catch a Literary Agent's Eye*, a collection of pitching wisdom from leading literary agents, and has written for *Writer's Digest*, *The Writer Magazine*, *Publishers Weekly*, and the *New York Times*.

For Katharine, watching ideas turn into books is magical—as if elves make them. Highlights include *XTC: Song-Stories*; *Mom's Choice*; *Hands off My Belly: The Pregnant Woman's Guide to Surviving Myths, Mothers and Moods*; *The Unofficial Guide to House, MD*; *Dating the Devil* by Lia Romeo; *The New Rules of Attraction* by Arden Leigh; *Make Up, Don't Break Up* with Oprah guest Dr. Bonnie Eaker Weil; *Writers on Directors*; *Taxpertise*; *Under the Hula Moon*; *The Complete Book on International Adoption: A Step-by-Step Guide to Finding Your Child*; Ford model Helen Lee's *The Tao of Beauty*; *Elvis and You: Your Guide to the Pleasures of Being an Elvis Fan*; *New York: Songs of the City*; and *SAT Word Slam*, to name a few.

Because Love Hurts

We are never so defenseless against suffering as when we love, never so forlornly unhappy as when we have lost our love object or its love.

—SIGMUND FREUD

ALL LOVE HURTS. At one point or another, it just does. How could an emotion so exquisite, so transporting, so complex and utterly consuming not be balanced by a shadow side?

The newly in-love are especially vulnerable, uniquely at risk. Be we sixteen or sixty, it is in forging the dark, unknown, and sometimes dangerous terrain of a new love that we are at our most blind and, yes, our most vulnerable. And yet arguably what makes new love so titillating, so entirely thrilling, so obsessively captivating is its very uncertainty, its implicit and, in the case of *Fifty Shades of Grey*, explicit danger. Will s/he hurt me? Is this going to work out? Can I possibly be...*enough*, whatever enough may mean?

Regardless of our sexual appetites, our kink, our desires in and out of the bedroom, when we're newly in love, we flog ourselves with feelings, excoriate ourselves with doubts. We may appear flawless and totally together on the outside but on the inside...we are raw, we are *bleeding*. What E. L. James accomplishes in *Fifty Shades of Grey* is to invite us inside a world where those inner hurts can be manifested in a very real, very tangible, very sexy way: BDSM.

In *Fifty Shades of Grey*, mega-mogul Christian Grey offers the young heroine, Ana Steele, an "indecent proposal" in the form of a three-month contract wherein she will be his submissive, his sex slave, and he her Dominant and tutor. Much later in the book (chapter 22), Ana eloquently expresses her internal conflict about their proposed arrangement to Christian.

"What you are offering is erotic and sexy, and I'm curious, but I'm also scared you'll hurt me—physically and emotionally. After three months you could say good-bye, and where will that leave me if you do? But then I suppose that risk is there in any relationship."

Yes, I suppose it is.

Love without some risk is like champagne without the fizz— flat, bland, and ultimately discardable. But how much risk is too much? And who in *Fifty Shades* really has the lion's share at stake?

The obvious answer is Ana and certainly on the surface that is so. It is Ana who starts and ends the first book as the vulnerable ingénue to Christian's jaded sophisticate. It is Ana, after all, who must cope with being whipped and trussed, blindfolded and belted. It is Ana who will require Advil and aloe and cuddling to recover from their encounters. It is Ana who is making all the concessions in their relationship. Or so it seems.

"I do it for you, Christian, because you need it. I don't," she says in the final chapter.

She may not need to be dominated, in fact she doesn't need it, and yet she likes it—and likes it fifty shades of a lot. Her true pain isn't found in the physical discomfort but in her emotional confusion, the cognitive dissonance she feels in being, on a very primal level, aroused by the punishment Christian inflicts. In the aftermath of her first light spanking, she bursts into tears, not because it hurts—of course it hurts!—but because she *liked* it. In contrast to Christian, who expects to enjoy their kinky encounters, Ana has no cognitive paradigm for interpreting her unanticipated sexual and emotional pleasure. Pain should be purely painful, and so it has always been, at least in her world. Pleasure-pain is a nuance she spends the entirety of the first book in the trilogy struggling to wrap her psyche around. Many of us struggle vicariously with her.

And yet if there is a true sadist in *Fifty Shades of Grey*, it isn't Christian Grey. It's Ana, or rather what she refers to as her "subconscious." Embodied as a pinched-faced, glasses-wearing librarian, Ana's "subconscious" acts much more as a flogger than a wake-up call to self-preservation.

"*Try to be cool, Ana,* my tortured subconscious begs on bended knee," Ana says to herself when Christian turns up in the hardware store where she works and coyly purchases cable ties.

Ana's is the most *conscious* subconscious of which one can possibly conceive. More properly, it's her masochistic *super-ego* that's doing double duty to sabotage her relationship with Christian, with any man, from their very first meeting when she nearly does a face plant inside his office doorway. The self-flagellation continues throughout the book with internal monologue such as:

"I still don't understand what he sees in me...mousey Ana Steele—it makes no sense," she silently laments, while continuing to covet her roommate Kate's attributes. "She is irresistible, beautiful, sexy, funny, forward...all the things that I'm not."

Ah, Ana...

Clearly it's not Christian's perennially "twitchy palm" that's the punisher here, let alone his sophisticated array of BDSM devices, but Ana's own insecurities and cognitive conflict, more properly the ongoing battle between her killjoy "subconscious" and her pleasure- and power-seeking "inner goddess."

Posed in direct contradiction to her "subconscious," Ana's "inner goddess" is a lush, Venus-like libertine who urges her on in furthering her sexual explorations with Christian, not only for the exquisite fifty shades of pleasure-pain to be had but, above all, for the power. Indeed, Ana's "inner goddess" grooves and gorges on the increasing servings of feminine sexual power she derives from each subsequent sexual encounter. As the book progresses, it is Christian who loses strength and Ana who gains it. Ana may strike the posture of a submissive within his "play-room" but at the end of each and every encounter, he is driven to his knees, not only sexually sated but emotionally helpless and in her thrall.

"You've completely beguiled me," he admits fairly early in the book, and while Ana still holds onto her doubts, we readers do not.

But then, as he rightly points out in one of their many email exchanges, in a BDSM relationship, the submissive holds the true power. This is news to Ana but not to us who have been watching Christian weaken progressively. Even the initially all-important contract governing their BDSM arrangement, which he sets out to impose but never quite does, isn't a protection for Ana so much as it is a protection for him, a presumed fail-safe in the face of the fear he feels in entering into a relationship, even a master-slave relationship, with a woman.

Christian may tie up Ana physically with an impressive array of cuffs, ropes, and chains, but he is the one who is bound emotionally and spiritually. He, not Ana, is the one in increasing danger of losing himself in their relationship, as evidenced by their ongoing negotiations over the contract, the terms of which weaken progressively in sync with Christian's weakening will.

The contract terms, such as the rule against her looking him in the eye and the insistence that she address him as "sir," are designed to enable him to objectify Ana both within and without his "playroom." Only Ana isn't the only one of them who rebels. Increasingly Christian, or rather his heart, rebels as well. By the end of the first novel, he relents on having Ana sign at all, too afraid of losing her to press for more than an informal understanding, a toothless tiger. Screw "hard and soft limits," not only are the "rules" all negotiable, they're no longer rules at all.

"Mercurial man" though he may be, as well as "fifty shades of fucked up," still he is willing to chart the scary, previously unexplored and unimagined path of "more" with her, where "more" presumably means a relationship that extends beyond playrooms and scripted BDSM scenarios and twitchy palms, a future that may as yet embrace darkness but also embraces light. Nor does Christian's willingness to try at having more come off as any kind of concession. Toward the book's end, he admits that the rigid power dynamic of their BDSM relationship isn't entirely satisfying his emotional needs, either. "I've never wanted more, until I met you," he tells Ana after their giddy day of gliding.

Christian Grey may be "fifty shades of fucked up," but he is also, perversely, something of a postmodern Prince Charming. Even the Red Room of Pain, as Ana calls his "playroom," is so lushly opulent and painstakingly well appointed that it seems more a backdrop for a Victoria's Secret catalog than an actual dungeon room.

Set aside Christian's proclivities toward dishing out punishment and what emerges is a portrait of a pretty princely boyfriend. Welts and whips and her own moribund insecurities notwithstanding, there were times when I found myself envying Ana. Scratch any "almost," I *did* envy her.

A man like Christian Grey is not trying to keep you off-balance or otherwise in suspense. He is not going to *not* call. Christian Grey will call, all right—as well as email and text message and even show up unannounced and uninvited in your very bedroom if he feels the situation warrants it.

Christian Grey is also not going to cheat on you. Once he chooses you, he is not going to take anyone into that Red Room of Pain but you. You need not doubt that those Ben Wa balls are shiny-new and bought just for you. He may insist on being the Dom to your sub, he *does* insist, but he is also unapologetically monogamous. And if in the past his monogamy has been of the serial sort, we're inclined to give the guy a break.

He *is* all of twenty-seven.

Obsessive and controlling as he is about your food intake and safety, traits rooted in the horrors of his early past, there is also something almost endearingly old-fashioned, even chivalrous, about such unwavering care and concern. When you drunk dial him, he'll not only come to your rescue but, unlike beta would-be boyfriend José, he'll also hold back your hair while you vomit. Post spanking, he'll voluntarily rub baby oil into your blistered bottom. Outside of bed, he'll shower you with first-class plane seats and first-edition books.

Christian is neither a hypocrite nor a liar. You *know* he's going to hurt you. The only issues in question are when, how, and where—all of which you ultimately get to decide.

Christian isn't afraid to commit. He won't blink about introducing you as his girlfriend. You will meet his mother on the Morning After, albeit by happenstance, and find yourself dining *en famille* with his parents, brother, and baby sister before the week is out. Sure, he'll try to finger you beneath the table linens and pitch a pouty fit later because you snapped closed your thighs, but then again, nothing in life is perfect.

Lastly but in no way least, he works for a living. He's not some trust fund brat with endless time on his hands to pursue his perverse passions. We're not precisely certain of the nature of his work but it involves overseeing a great many varied business interests and taking a great many 24/7 phone calls and employing a cadre of A-list lackeys, most of whom, like him, seem to have no need for sleep.

True, Christian may not be the most…emotionally available man, yet neither is he playing hard-to-get. Not only does he admit to being "beguiled," but later, in chapter 23, he goes much farther. "I don't want anyone but you. Haven't you worked that out yet?"

Only apparently Ana hasn't worked that out yet, certainly not by the end of the first book. Her final flight is not so much a response to the brutality of the belting, which she expressly demands, as it is a rejection of her "inner goddess" in favor of her safely familiar "subconscious." Above all, her decision to leave is a reaction to her own pervasive anxieties about not measuring up.

But then, whether we're newly minted college graduates or mega moguls, almost-virgins or sexual sophisticates, "love makes fools of us all," as Shakespeare pointed out centuries ago. Fortunately, E. L. James has given Ana and Christian—and us—not a single book but a trilogy in which to work out a better balance between dark and light, punishment and reward, vanilla and BDSM—and selfishness and selflessness.

Because while love will always hurt, for Christian and Ana and, indeed, for most of us, it will always be worth it.

HOPE TARR earned a master's degree in developmental psychology and a PhD in education, both from the Catholic University of America, only to come to terms with the truth: she wasn't interested in analyzing people or teaching them. What she wanted was to write about them! Today Hope is the author of nearly twenty historical and contemporary romances for multiple publishers, including Penguin, Harlequin, Medallion Press, and, most recently, her Suddenly Cinderella contemporary romance series with Entangled Publishing. Her nonfiction publishing credits span the spectrum from *Baltimore Magazine*, EuropeUpClose.com, and BootsnAll.com to academic journals such as *The Journal of Clinical Psychology*. Visit Hope online at www.HopeTarr.com, www.WriterNYC.com, and www.LadyJaneSalonNYC.com, as well as on Facebook and Twitter (@HopeTarr).

Every Breath You Take

"Please don't hit me," I whisper, pleading.
—E. L. JAMES, *Fifty Shades of Grey*

WHY CAN'T MY HUSBAND BE MORE LIKE
CHRISTIAN GREY?
—JENNY ISENMAN, *Huffington Post*

ON FEBRUARY 12, 2012, dangerously misguided young women took to their Twitter accounts to praise Chris Brown, the pop star best remembered for beating up his much more famous girlfriend, Rihanna, than for any talent of his own. They expressed such sentiments as "chris brown your sexy you can punch me in the face anyday" [sic] and "I know Rihanna didn't like it much, but Chris brown you can punch me in the face all you want" [sic]. These tweets were widely copied and reported and decried by internet media, because we're not living in a world where such talk is acceptable. We don't encourage women to sit idly by and let men abuse them, or fantasize about abuse.

Something happened between February 12, 2012, and March of 2012, when *Fifty Shades of Grey*'s stunning momentum dragged it from "that thing readers are talking about on the internet" into an honest-to-goodness media spotlight. Suddenly it was just fine for women to fantasize about an abusive, controlling man and to flood the internet with those fantasies, going so far as to lament the fact that their own husbands weren't just like the dangerously flawed hero of their dreams.

Surely we're not describing Christian Grey, the twenty-seven-year-old wunderkind who plays piano like a concert pianist, pilots a helicopter bought with his own vast fortune, and feeds starving children in Africa? Christian Grey is not an abusive boyfriend. He's gorgeous and kind; he lavishes gifts on the object of his affection, Anastasia Steele. Her Cinderella story culminates in the American dream of prosperity and two beautiful children. That's not abuse.

But he also stalks her. When Ana goes to a bar to get drunk for the first time, in celebration of completing her final college exam, she remembers his number on her phone and drunk-dials him. Within moments, Christian tracks her cell phone and arrives at the bar—despite her explicit request to the contrary—and spirits her away, unconscious. True, her friend José has gotten drunk and "handsy" in the parking lot, and Christian's arrival saves her from certain date rape, but still, she had asked him not to come. He admits, without any shame, that he used his considerable wealth and resources to track her cell phone. Christian showing up as the knight in shining armor—when he didn't know his intervention was needed or welcome in the first place—sends a very clear message to Ana and the reader: "Your personal wishes and boundaries are not important to me. I'm going to do what I want to do with you."

Later in the book, Christian tells Ana that no matter where she goes, he has the resources to find her. He proves this when she pleads with him for space and leaves Washington for Georgia to visit her mother and think about their relationship. Within two days, Christian shows up in his private jet, ready to be sexually serviced by Ana. Even though Ana's explicit wish was to be left alone for a few days, Christian cannot abide. If Ana is outside of his sphere of influence, he can't possibly control her, so he has to fly to Georgia to insinuate himself between Ana and her mother. He goes so far as to follow the two to a bar and watch them for an unspecified amount of time before contacting Ana. A reader can't help but wonder how many other times Christian Grey is lurking just out of Ana's sight, watching her every move. Some might call that romantic. Others call that stalking.

Crashing Ana's visit with her mother serves another purpose. By meeting and charming both of Ana's parents very early in their relationship, Christian can win them over to his "side," so that Ana has no neutral observer to whom she is emotionally close. The Georgia incident happens late in the book, but within days of meeting Ana, Christian forces her to introduce him to her father. When both of Ana's parents are impressed by Christian's wealth and charm, Ana has been cut off from two very important safe outlets in her life. They've met Ana's "boyfriend," they like him, and they both advise her, despite her uncertainties, to work out her relationship with him.

Ana has only one close friend, her roommate, Kate. From the beginning of Ana's association with Christian, Kate doesn't trust him or like him. She teases Ana at first about having a crush on Christian, but once she begins to see the toll their relationship takes on Ana, she encourages Ana to see Christian Grey for the control freak that he is. She also tries to get Ana to confide in her, but Ana can't. Christian Grey has already seen to that, with legal threats.

Paperwork is a huge object of manipulation in this series. Before Christian will even consider a romantic entanglement with Ana, he asks her to sign a nondisclosure agreement, prohibiting her from sharing details of their sex life with anyone. When Ana asks him for permission to talk to Kate and ask her questions, he refuses. While it is doubtful that this type of nondisclosure agreement would be legally binding (the BDSM contract he wants her to sign would not be legally enforceable, either), presenting these documents as though there will be severe consequences should Ana break their agreement is just another way Christian Grey manipulates Ana into behaving the way he wants her to behave. Later, in *Fifty Shades Freed*, Christian balks at the idea of a prenuptial agreement, while Ana is willing to sign one. Though Christian has more to lose from a failed marriage, Ana would also be protected by a well-executed prenup, and Christian's stern refusal robs her of the opportunity. He turns it into a question of love, rather than a question of fairness; if he deserved the protection of a nondisclosure agreement and a contract, in an equal partnership Ana should be given the same.

Though emotional manipulation and threats of physical punishment are the tools most often used by Christian Grey, he isn't above using alcohol to make Ana more malleable. In *Fifty Shades of Grey* he openly admits to purposely getting Ana drunk as they discuss her "hard limits" and other aspects of the contract. His motive is clear: if Ana's inhibitions are artificially lowered, she'll agree to more items on his list of desires, and when she does sober up, she'll be trapped into doing things she wouldn't normally want to do. That this behavior doesn't strike Christian as particularly unethical—and that he can rationalize that it's actually good for her—should be a concern for any woman wishing for a Christian Grey of her own.

In the middle of the *Fifty Shades of Grey* media furor, Dr. Drew Pinsky appeared on the *Today Show* and called the book "violence against women" due to the BDSM content. He suggested that men and women only become involved in a BDSM lifestyle as a consequence of a troubled upbringing, without addressing the emotional abuse in the story. Conflating consensual BDSM with domestic violence only served to muddy the waters of the very valid discussion of the relationship portrayed in the novel. Ana's consent is uninformed due to her sexual inexperience, and when you examine the words she uses to describe Christian's spankings, they're not sex-positive words. "Hit," "assault," and "beat" are all used by Ana to describe the way Christian treats her, and the first time he physically punishes her, she spends the night crying hysterically.

Christian doesn't appear to enjoy spanking Ana as part of a sexy game. He frequently threatens to spank her when he becomes frustrated with her, when her questions about his past become too personal, when she won't behave as he wants her to behave outside of the confines of the Red Room. And what does he want her to do? During a scene in which Ana is meeting Christian's parents for dinner—without any panties on under her dress—Christian tries to slide his hand between Ana's thighs, and she closes her legs. He feels provoked to physical violence because Ana won't let him finger bang her five feet from his mother.

Even if we remove the BDSM (and Ana's physical aversion to it, which Christian ignores), there is still the matter of his control. When Christian Grey buys Ana a gift, it is always for his own benefit. He buys her expensive books to warn her away from him because he's a dangerous man, thus building an aura of mystique around himself to draw her in further. He buys her a computer and a BlackBerry so that she can remain in contact with him at all times. He buys her a new car and a new wardrobe so that she fits in with his glamorous lifestyle, despite Ana's objections.

As the series progresses, the control Christian exerts over Ana's life becomes focused more on using his wealth as a weapon against her. When he feels threatened by Ana's male boss, Christian simply buys the company she works for. When she objects and threatens to leave her job, he tells her that he'll buy the next company as well. He learns her bank routing and account numbers and deposits large amounts of money into her account against her wishes, and reveals that he's done a background check on her.

Perhaps the most worrying of all the messages this series carries is that being completely dominated and controlled by a man is a natural part of a mature relationship. When Christian, finally confronted by Ana about her dislike of the BDSM aspect of their relationship, admits that she isn't a good submissive, he wants her to continue in the lifestyle, anyway: "And, as long as you follow the rules, which fulfill a deep need in me for control and to keep you safe, then perhaps we can find a way forward." He's unwilling to pursue the relationship outside of his parameters. When Ana protests that deciphering when he wants her to challenge him as a romantic equal and when he wants her submissive comes as too much "personal cost," saying, "I'm tied up in knots here," his response is to joke about bondage and coax her into another sexual encounter, thus ending the conversation. He never bothers to address her needs, because they don't fulfill his. Should she fail to meet his needs, however, he wants permission to physically punish her. Ana finds this unacceptable and breaks up with him at the conclusion of *Fifty Shades of Grey*, but at the beginning of *Fifty Shades Darker* she apologizes to Christian for not trying hard enough to fulfill his needs, going so far as to call herself "undeserving" of his affection. Though the physical punishments no longer involve whips and canes, they still persist, in the form of hickeys on her breasts when a wardrobe malfunction leaves her topless at the beach in *Fifty Shades Freed*.

It's not as though there aren't clues throughout the novels that total control of Ana is the ultimate end goal for Christian. Though the master/slave element is toned down in *Fifty Shades Darker* and *Fifty Shades Freed*, he continually tells Ana she belongs to him, that he knows what is best for her, going so far as to order her meal for her when they dine at a restaurant in the beginning of the second novel. After they marry, Christian is angered when she chooses to keep her last name for professional reasons, telling her, "I want your world to begin and end with me." Slowly, Ana begins to accept his total control, and this acceptance is portrayed as a positive progression in a normal and loving adult relationship.

But is *Fifty Shades of Grey* actually "violence against women" as Dr. Drew proposed? It's a fantasy—no one would want that relationship in reality, would they? The zeitgeist seems to believe otherwise. In her article for the *Huffington Post*, Jenny Isenman laments the ways in which her relationship with her husband pales in comparison to Ana and Christian's. In an article on CafeMom online, Andrew Kardon advised husbands to buy *Fifty Shades of Grey* so they could add little touches from the book into their marriages. The line between what women like to fantasize about and the way we want to be treated in reality is blurred in countless media discussions.

Fans of the books have reacted vehemently to criticism, going so far as to say the same troubling things about *Fifty Shades of Grey* as those young Twitter users said about Chris Brown. "I would let Christian Grey beat me!" is no less troubling a statement than the ones made about Brown, so where is a similar outcry?

The first step in correcting the misconception that the relationship portrayed in the novels is a romantic ideal is for fans to admit that the book is problematic. It would be enough to say simply, "While there are issues with the relationship portrayed in the books, I found them an enjoyable fantasy." Acknowledging that Christian Grey exhibits traits common to controlling, abusive men isn't admitting that the reader would like to be controlled and abused in real life. Many people can enjoy slasher flicks without actually wanting to be murdered or murder someone else, so the same considerations should apply to works of an intensely sexual nature.

Second, fans need to stop arguing that the relationship isn't flawed. Admitting that there is a problem truly is the first step to solving it, and it solves nothing for fans of the book to run around offering excuses. "He only wants to hit her because he had a bad childhood!" isn't a believable defense in real life, so it shouldn't be a valid reason to defend Christian Grey at book club. Attempting to explain away the troubling themes in *Fifty Shades of Grey* insults victims of domestic violence, many of whom have endured the same experiences of control and domination to which Ana is subjected. To revisit the slasher flick analogy, it's rare to find anyone who would defend the motives and actions of Freddy Krueger, and yet many people are capable of watching and enjoying *A Nightmare on Elm Street*.

Third, we must stop buying into the media obsession with equating female fantasy with female fulfillment. Discussions of *Fifty Shades of Grey* often include sly suggestions that reading the book will revitalize your sex life, that it will tell women what they really want from their men, and men what women want from them. It can be a satisfying fantasy without being anything else. *Fifty Shades of Grey* and its sequels are not, and shouldn't be touted as, nonfiction self-help books. Encouraging readers to emulate them is irresponsible in the extreme.

Finally, readers have to accept that if they're going to indulge in books with problematic themes, they will hear some criticism, and this criticism isn't personal. Many women reading the Fifty Shades novels are reading them as their first experience with erotica. The tie (no pun intended) between the sexual content of the book and the sexual fantasies of the readers builds a minefield critics have to navigate cautiously. In the company of other ardent fans, readers are safe to lavish praise on the books and the characters without any attention paid to the undertones of abuse and control in the story. Faced with criticism, many fans of the series interpret it as a direct attack on themselves and their sexual desires. Then the cycle of excuses starts all over again: "Christian bought her that computer because he loves her! He spanks her because he had a bad childhood!" When this happens, the reader isn't defending the series; they're defending their right to be turned on, which shouldn't be a part of the discussion. Or the fan resorts to ad hominem attacks on anyone who doesn't like the books, calling detractors "prudes" and suggesting they don't have satisfying sex lives. What was once a discussion about books is dragged into a quagmire of personal attacks.

Ideally, we would live in a culture where abuse and romance weren't so easy to confuse, where women could look at a man like Chris Brown or Christian Grey and see them for the predators they are. We would be able to draw a line between what women want in fiction and what they want in reality, and we would be able to draw a similar line between what we feel comfortable fantasizing about and our social consciences. To get there, we have to face some uncomfortable truths about ourselves and our culture.

So, imagine your daughter. She can be real, or hypothetical. If you're child-free, imagine your sister, or a friend. Imagine *Fifty Shades of Grey* never existed, and this woman you love has brought home her new boyfriend. He's rich, he's handsome, he's charming, although you suspect his charm is carefully tailored. He emails and texts her often, demanding to know her whereabouts. He has her cell phone traced, so he can follow her against her wishes. He reacts with jealousy to her friends. He physically hurts her when she's made him angry, but she assures you that she's okay with that, she's agreed to it and signed paperwork that makes it okay. Every time she talks about him, she's vague and moody. She cries often. She believes she can change him.

This is the deciding moment. Do you pick up the vibrator and fantasize about him, or do you pick up the phone and call the police?

JENNIFER ARMINTROUT is a *USA Today* bestselling author of urban fantasy and paranormal romance. She also writes award-winning erotic romance under the pseudonym Abigail Barnette. She lives in Michigan with her husband and two children.

Intermission

Fifty Shades of Play

A dame that knows the ropes isn't likely to get tied up.
—MAE WEST

HE WAS THE UGLIEST MAN I'd seen in a while. Bad teeth. Fat. Bald. Not at all the image of what my friends imagined I'd find desirable. At first glance he repulsed me. As did his atrocious grammar, stunning narcissism, and cocky demeanor, which were laughable.

But then something happened that turned my repulsion to attraction, my disgust to lust.

I was seated beside him at a dinner when he suddenly, boldly and unexpectedly, grabbed and squeezed my leg under the table.

His wife was seated across from us, which no doubt added to his thrill.

Here I was, a fiercely independent woman who'd loved and lost and loved again. I'd built a dazzling company, had beautiful, bright, loving children, an array of scintillating friends worldwide, and a bank account with enough fuck-you money to last a lifetime.

I had no time for romance, no interest in marriage, and a hot affair was the last thing on my mind.

He pursued me with a vengeance. He was powerful, too, and had his aides deliver a seemingly never-ending array of gifts: thousands of long-stemmed red roses, endless lingerie, and a life-sized stuffed lion with a motion detector that groaned and roared in his voice when I walked by. He even sent an Audi in my favorite color and a laptop fully loaded with erotic photos of a stunning twelve-inch cock attached to a hand masturbating it.

With each gesture I was repulsed and shocked and more and more titillated. It had been years since I felt so pursued. And despite all of his negatives, his allure was electric. He wanted to possess me, to own me, to make me his. For weeks he'd call at 1:00 A.M. and in his lowest, deepest voice he'd speak of the one thing every woman loves to hear: his desire for me.

I loved it. I wanted it. I fully imagined each and every cruel thing he said he wanted to do to me. He would make me beg for his cock, make me watch while other women prepped it for me. He would teach me to worship it, to run for it, to kill for it. He would handcuff me while he placed the large fat tip in my mouth and force me to sit still while he masturbated and poured his come down my throat, he would force me to put two fat dildos in my cunt while he pumped his throbbing meat into my ass. He would instruct me to lick the dicks of all of his friends under a table while they played cards, after which they would gangbang me.

I was his, and I would be his whore. When he called I would run. I would do as told. He would have me open my blouse while driving and expose my tits. I would have implants to make them huge for his pleasure. I would bring him women as toys, and I would hold their tits up for his sucking pleasure. I would lick them to prepare their juicy cunts for his hot cock. And if I pleased him, he would reward me with Take 3, his code word for one in each hole. In these late-night calls he reminded me again and again that I was his, that he would possess and control and own me, and that if I ever tried to leave him, he would kill me.

I started to believe him.

And as any forty-six-year-old woman with years of experience and a log full of memories of men would do, I agreed to meet him.

In a hotel room. Of his choosing. At his expense.

We set the time. One of his aides would arrive in advance and deliver the key to me after checking us in under an anonymous name. He was famous and didn't want to get caught.

The suite was huge. I was to arrive thirty minutes before him. He was military precise in his plans and maneuvers. Everything down to the second.

I was waxed and buffed and polished with new pearly white veneers, freshly covered grays, highlights, lowlights, brows shaped, seven pounds lighter, firmed up, semi-permanent lashes, stunning mouthwash, seven-inch Christian Louboutins, a black lace push-up bra peeking through my hot pink satin blouse and a desire that burned inside me in a way I'd never known.

After setting out my toys and gadgets (he'd had one of his aides hand-deliver the list) I sat on the plush, teal velvet couch in this massive suite, my leg bobbing nervously, freshly doused in Déclaration, his favorite Cartier perfume.

I was nervous, thrilled, excited, and ready. *Loaded, cocked, and ready.*

Thirty minutes passed. Then forty-five. Fifty. Sixty. For a man with a fierce dedication to detail, this was another surprise. I called his cell. No answer. I called his cell again. No answer. I called his cell a third time. It was off.

Was this to show me that he owned me? That my time was his? That I would wait? That he could keep me waiting? With each passing minute I grew more anxious. Should I leave? Had something happened to him?

He arrived eighty-two minutes late. He announced it as he came in, tore off his clothes, and jumped in the shower.

"I ran into Anna Kournikova at the airport. Her driver was late so I gave her a ride into the city. She invited me in. I didn't have time to call you," he said as he walked out of the bathroom soaking wet.

I was to wait. I was to submit. To accept. To take his crumbs. To honor his every move. Every word. I was to stroke his ego, to open myself up to any and all of his desires. I was to sit at his feet awaiting his next order, ready to serve, and be thrilled for the asking.

He pulled a whip and handcuffs out of his bag and threw me on the bed.

He placed the handcuffs beside me.

I told him I was nervous. I needed a drink to relax. I asked his permission. I begged him to join me in a toast to his cock.

I poured the champagne. We clicked. Sipped. Then gulped.

Within minutes he was drowsy and barely able to move. The drug worked quickly as promised. He collapsed on the bed and I quickly handcuffed him to the bedposts.

He was having a hard time comprehending what was happening but I lifted his knees to his chest, strapped a double dick strap-on to my waist, and told him to beg for more as I penetrated his eager ass.

He didn't know what he was saying, but I fed him line after line.

SAY IT!

I worship your dick.

Fuck my ass.

Rape my ass.

I am a cock lover.

I want to be fucked.

I am your cock slave.

Finally, I shoved a large, thick, black glass dildo into his mouth, two in his ass, and said, "TAKE 3, MOTHERFUCKER."

He passed out after that. I collected my things, including the hidden camera I'd installed in the room, turned on the iPod player on which I had downloaded our tape-recorded phone conversations, and pumped up the volume. I wanted him to hear it as his wake-up call.

Mae West said it best: "A dame that knows the ropes isn't likely to get tied up."

JUDITH REGAN is a publisher, talk-show host, and producer. She hosts *The Judith Regan Show* on the SiriusXM Stars Channel.

Fifty
Shades of
Sex

SUZAN COLÓN

Forbidden Fruit Is the Sweetest

*W*HEN I WAS ABOUT seven years old, I was at my very best friend Elizabeth's house when she took me aside and told me a secret: her mother had a stash of *Playgirl* magazines hidden somewhere in the house. "There are pictures of naked men in them!" she whispered.

When her mother said she was going to the supermarket and would be back in half an hour, we promised we'd be good. The moment the door closed behind her, the hunt was on: we ransacked that place like federal agents acting on a hot tip. And we found the magazines! Oh, the mysterious male anatomy, finally revealed...I think we even sneaked one of her mom's cigarettes to double the decadence.

We had only a limited time to fill our eyes and imaginations before Elizabeth's mother was due back, and almost as good as the discovery we'd made was covering it up. We ran around, giggling with nervous hysteria, as we tried to put the magazines back as we'd found them, then opened the window and fanned out the cigarette smoke. We might have gotten away with it all if we hadn't been standing stiffly in the living room, side by side, like two good little soldiers, when Elizabeth's mother returned.

That was my first sample of the unique and luscious flavor of a guilty pleasure, and understanding the ingredients—harmless naughtiness, mixed with a hint of secrecy—that went into one. I've been addicted to guilty pleasures ever since.

I'd read erotica before *Fifty Shades of Grey*, and each time I remembered the lessons I learned that day with Elizabeth: pleasure is fun, but a pleasure that gently tests the conscience and remains covert is even better. So I kept erotica, which sometimes overflows into mainstream popularity, as a hidden indulgence, one for me to enjoy in private. Especially when partaking of erotica that was rough.

Erotica has always been present in books and films, just out of view of the public eye. But every few decades, BDSM comes out of the dungeon (or, in this case, the Red Room of Pain) and has its moment in the mass market sun. Regular folks whose preference for whipping items usually extends only as far as a whisk for cream will line up to see Kim Basinger handcuffed in *9½ Weeks,* or to buy brutal and sexual versions of fairy tales by Anne Rice, writing as A.N. Roquelaure. And now everyone and my godmother have read *Fifty Shades of Grey.*

Why does BDSM have that mass moment? Maybe because we reach a saturation point with vanilla sex, as Christian Grey would call it, and we want a little...more (though not the "more" Anastasia asks Christian for, meaning a real relationship). If our society perceives sex as being naughty, and it does, then BDSM is the naughtiest of the naughty. BDSM is more than sex; it is potentially dangerous, not just physically, but emotionally. BDSM is sex with paddles and floggers, with handcuffs and clamps, and what truly makes traditional sex pale vanilla in comparison is the understanding that one person holds the flogger and the other is being flogged. In BDSM, sex is secondary to the true game of seduction: power and trust. The submissive must trust the Dominant to employ bondage, to administer corporal punishment, and, most important, to play by the rules: when the safeword is uttered, the submissive must have faith the play will stop.

But—and that is a big safeword in this scenario—BDSM is not generally considered completely unacceptable in the way that something truly harmful might be. Christian's own list of hard limits could have been taken directly from a romance publisher: no puppies or kitties, no kids, no fire, no unmentionable acts. Such high moral standards from a man who has a special drawer filled with whipping canes of varying lengths and widths.

Christian is also a man who knows the value of a guilty pleasure. Is he proud of the fact that he gets off on flogging the ladies? Not really, as Dr. Flynn's surely impressive therapy bill might suggest. But Christian isn't truly hurting anyone. Therefore, that guilt doesn't stop him from luxuriously kitting out an entire room for the discerning Dominant with taste and means, purely to indulge his, yes, guilty pleasure.

There's guilt, and then there's shame.

Shame can scare us off an action for life, or turn it into a hidden activity that can lead to obsession, which usually ends in remorse. Anyone who's been made to feel ashamed about the natural exploration of sex as a child has hopefully undone the damage with his or her own version of Dr. Flynn.

Guilt, though, is a lesser emotion, on just on the right side of that fine border between pleasure and pain that Christian tells Ana about. The difference becomes clear in the way Ana feels about her exploration of Christian's lifestyle. "Why does this feel so good?" she asks herself—usually right before asking for more.

In theory, being tied up and flogged by one's lover shouldn't feel good; in practice, however, it may. Even if it does, though, one generally doesn't admit it, for fear of being judged. The social stigma against such acts keeps them behind closed doors, safe in Red Rooms. (And think about it: if BDSM were acceptable enough to be spoken about over bagels at brunch, would it be as much fun?)

What keeps women who swap their bracelets for handcuffs quiet about it is the thick skin required to withstand not just a good spanking, but the withering stare that follows such admissions. Conventional society's judgment of anyone who likes painful games? They're weird, crazy, depraved, sick, and setting feminism back to the Stone Age. That nondisclosure agreement isn't the only thing that keeps Ana from telling her best friend, Kate, about what Ana and Christian do in private. Christian's binding (pun unavoidable) contract notwithstanding, Ana still can't bring herself to tell Kate, or anyone else, about what Christian wants to do to her . . . or why she wants him to do it.

Part of her silence may be due to embarrassment; Ana knows what people will think and is afraid of people talking her out of her own investigation. Another part may be the scandal that would ensue if word got out about what Christian, a well-known businessman and philanthropist, has going on in that Red Room of Pain.

Mostly, though, I like to think that Ana doesn't talk about what she does with Christian, or, more to the point, what Christian does to her, because she likes having a secret. *Yes, my boyfriend is a Dominant—and I think I like being his submissive.* Not exactly a line heard at most dinner parties. If it is, chances are good that the ante will soon need to be upped, because pleasures that come easily and become commonplace also get dull fast.

A few months before my wedding, I went on a diet. High fiber, low calorie, no fat, zero fun. Caning had nothing on this regime.

When the wedding day finally came, I had my first piece of cake in months. This was the best cake I'd ever eaten. This cake was like mind-blowing drugs in IMAX, it was so good. Deprivation had done more than get me thin; I'd developed a taste for forbidden fruit. To a mind trained to diet, the cake was still technically verboten. A cheat.

After the wedding, with a renewed hunger for sweets and no big event to diet for, I ate sugar with abandon. Chocolate craving in the afternoon? Have some. Want dessert? You bet. But when I gave myself permission to eat what I wanted without thought of consequence, that treat wasn't as good as when it was a cheat. The missing ingredient? The sweet taste of mild guilt, of doing something that I "wasn't supposed to do," and of having to hide my deed.

This is the problem with permissiveness; it's just not that much fun. In high school, the most messed-up kids I knew were the ones whose parents smoked pot and drank with them. How can a kid engage in rebellion—necessary for growth—against that?

My parents weren't terribly permissive, but there were some disappointingly easygoing moments. Every week I'd get together with my biological father, who my mother divorced when I was young. On one such visit, I remember finding *Story of O* in his bookshelf. (It wasn't even hidden.) He's an artist, so the version of *O* my father had was illustrated—what would now be called a graphic novel—by Guido Crepax. My father had a tendency to treat me, his teenage daughter, like an adult in matters of culture, so he didn't see why I shouldn't be allowed to look at a graphic novel about graphic sex. Graphic, sado-masochistic sex.

Well, I was thrilled. Not only was I being treated like an adult, I was being given free rein to look at penises and sex— very artistically rendered, of course. Fantastic! And yet...there was something missing from this transaction: everything that had been so fun the day Elizabeth and I found her mother's *Playgirls*. The sweetness of doing something naughty, the mild guilt of harboring this secret from authority figures, like my parents—hell, one of my parents had very nonchalantly given me permission to read it. Sure, I was going to look, but some of the thrill was gone before I even opened the book.

We love rules and boundaries. They keep order, but they also keep forbidden fruit sweet.

Women have a rich history of cheating on diets, starting with Eve. There was only one thing she couldn't have, and that was the only thing she wanted. I like to think of her in exile, wearing her fig leaf minidress, and saying to Adam, "Yeah, but it was *sooooo gooooood*. If I find more of that stuff, I'm making an entire pie out of it."

Pandora also had a craving. Only one thing she wasn't supposed to do. Only one thing she wanted to do. Cue the sound of a box being opened—consequences, *shmonsequences*. Which was more alluring for these women: the taste of the apple and the satisfaction of knowing what was inside that box, or doing these things despite the *thou shalt not*? There's something so bright and shiny about the thing you can't have or shouldn't do.

The recipe for a delicious guilty pleasure, then, is:

Naughtiness. For a guilty pleasure to work, it must have a piquant hint of being taboo. Remember, though, the guilty pleasure must be only slightly forbidden and not outright harmful. Anything that would harm you or another being is not a guilty pleasure, but something destined to bring on true pain. Conversely, if a relatively harmless action brings on too much internal agony, then an appointment with Dr. Flynn is in order.

Secrecy. Telling everyone about a guilty pleasure nullifies the guilt. The people who love you will say there's nothing to feel guilty about. Some people may admit that they do the same thing, in which case you're no longer the heroine of your own story; if everybody's doing it, what makes you special?

Yet what makes a guilty pleasure even better is telling someone what you've done. You need some sort of accomplice, even if it's only a diary. For Ana, that accomplice is Christian, who is deep inside his lifestyle, yet is brought outside of it by Ana's questions of how he became this way.

Long before *Fifty Shades of Grey* was discussed on the *Today Show*, my friend Donna said, "Have you heard about this book?

All the girls in my office are whispering about it." Whispering. Not discussing it openly, but speaking in hushed tones so the boss didn't hear them talking about how sexy a book about bondage could be. They knew how to keep a guilty pleasure good.

Recently, I was on the train and saw a woman who exuded an air of permissive entitlement. She was a person of size, possibly because she ate what she wanted, weight be damned. She defied societal norms by letting her hair go gray. Under her somber charcoal business jacket, she wore vibrant batik patterns. She was fierce.

The woman was reading *Fifty Shades of Grey*. I knew this because she had a paper copy instead of an e-reader in her hand, and she wasn't even attempting to hide the cover. A man was watching her read; he'd clearly heard the hype, knew what the book was about, and couldn't help a tiny *Tee-hee, you're reading lady porn* smirk from forming on his face.

The woman shot him a defiant look. She was going to read her erotica in broad fluorescent trainlight, and to hell with anyone who tried to imply that she couldn't.

Of course she could. But I felt like taking her aside as my friend Elizabeth had done with me many years ago and whispering an important bit of information: Madame, you're missing the point. I'm reading *Fifty* in public, too—but on my iPad, so no one can tell. Not because I'm ashamed, but because it's more fun this way. There's nothing more delicious than a guilty pleasure. The sauce, my dear, is in the naughty secret.

SUZAN COLÓN is the former senior editor for *O, The Oprah Magazine*. She is the author of the inspirational memoir *Cherries in Winter: My Family's Recipe for Hope*

in *Hard Times* (Random House); three young adult novels based on the hit TV series *Smallville*; *Catwoman: The Life and Times of a Feline Fatale*; and *What Would Wonder Woman Do? An Amazon's Guide to the Working World.* She has written for *O, Jane, Details, Harper's Bazaar*, and many other magazines. Her essays have been featured in three *O, the Oprah Magazine* anthologies: *O's Big Book of Happiness, Dream Big!*, and *Love Your Life!* Suzan's novel *Beach Glass* will be published by BelleBridge in spring 2014.

Visit her at www.suzancolon.net.

DR. HILDA HUTCHERSON

Fifty Ways of Looking at Sex in *Fifty Shades*

*F*IFTY SHADES OF GREY is an important book. It has single-handedly given millions of women permission to explore erotica, get in touch with their inner sexpot, and try new ways to heat up the bedroom with their partners. No longer is it embarrassing to read adult fiction on the plane, train, or in the checkout line of the local grocery store—where I recently saw a woman in her seventies eagerly devouring every word as she waited to pay. I can only imagine what the rest of her evening was like!

Women are reading it in book clubs. Friends are sharing stories about their sex lives. One woman told me that *Fifty Shades* saved her marriage. Women are using the book to learn new techniques and to begin a dialogue with their partners about sex.

Fifty Shades of Grey is a work of fiction based on fantasy and, as such, can take artistic license when describing almost anything. However, when it is read by millions of women—and men—around the world, from ages sixteen to ninety, one would hope that the fantasy is based somewhat on reality.

Fifty Shades also has a darker side that has led to my love-hate relationship with the book. Let's begin with Mr. Christian Grey. The man is a jerk. Pure and simple. As he himself said, "I am fifty shades of fucked up." He is not a jerk because he enjoys domination and submission or kinky sex. BDSM is an accepted way for consenting adults to express themselves sexually. Those that practice BDSM are not mentally ill, victims of child sexual or physical abuse, or just-plain-old-weirdo freaks. They don't need to be fixed. Many people enjoy the sensations that are created during this form of sex play. The motto in the BSDM community is "Safe, sane, and consensual," meaning that any activity must be safe and performed only between consenting adults who are fully aware of what they are doing. Trust and respect are key elements in BDSM play between consenting adults.

I can't imagine why any woman would want to be with this man. He is handsome, rich, and well endowed. But that's where it ends. He is selfish, a stalker, possessive, and controlling. He arranged her OB/GYN appointment, told her how to take her birth control pills, and didn't want her to masturbate, for example. He has a temper, mood swings, and doesn't want to be touched. He doesn't make love, withholds affection, and doesn't want to cuddle after sex or spend the night. He is simply emotionally abusive. Who would put up with that? Think of the young men reading this book who will get the wrong idea about sexual relationships.

All that said, the man knows his way around a woman's body! He tells Ana that she has a beautiful body, that she should not be ashamed or embarrassed, and that he derives pleasure from the sight of her naked body. How many of us have ever felt embarrassed while naked? Since most of us are having sex under the covers, in the dark, I would say that the number is large. Mr. Grey kisses her entire body, including her feet. He appreciates the scent of a woman. Running his nose up between her thighs, he murmurs, "You smell so good." Men of America, listen up! Many women fear that their natural scent is somehow offensive. Mr. Grey just helped millions of women exhale. He loves the taste of a woman: "'Oh, Anastasia, you taste mighty fine,' he breathes." After fingering Ana, not only does he enjoy the taste of her secretions, he offers his thumb for her to taste and appreciate her own flavor. Bravo, Mr. Grey!

Every woman should look at her vulva and vagina, appreciate her scent, and taste her secretions. Learning to love your body completely frees you and allows you to enjoy sex fully. Mr. Grey understands that the clitoris is powerful and needs lots of attention. He massages, circling slowly. He swirls his tongue around and around, taking his time. He massages her G-spot while he continues his gentle assault on her clitoris. He even appreciates her pubic hair. What a man!

Mr. Grey is responsible and practices safer sex, unwrapping a gold foil–wrapped condom—extra large Magnum, no doubt—every time they have intercourse. He has instant firm erections, is capable of having sex multiple times without rest, is never in a hurry, never boring, and never comes before his partner. Wow!

Anastasia Steele is just as problematic. She is a virgin who has never touched herself, yet she has easy orgasms, three her very first time having sex. Her first orgasm was through nipple stimulation alone. She comes easily with penetrative sex alone, even when he slams into her, and she has multiple orgasms every time. Her unrealistic responsiveness is annoying. Almost as annoying as her "inner goddess." She really got on my last nerve. Ana deep throats and swallows sperm her very first time providing oral pleasure. Whose fantasy is this anyway?

Anastasia comes on demand. Christian has only to command that she come for him—"Come for me"—and she explodes into a million pieces. Really? And the kicker: Anastasia Steele explodes into a massive orgasm when he flicks her clitoris over and over with a riding crop! I am expecting to see more than one bruised clitoris in my office in the coming months, as this is far from reality for almost every woman.

Since more than 75 percent of women do not experience orgasm through intercourse alone, many worry that something is wrong with them when they can't come within five minutes or have multiple glorious orgasms. And is this the message we want men to hear? They have already been telling women for years that they are defective when they don't come the moment their nipples are sucked or their vaginas assaulted by a stiff penis. It all makes me want to scream!

Anastasia allows Christian to abuse her emotionally and physically. She does not give consent to the spankings that she receives, so this is not BSDM play, but abuse. She allows herself to be treated poorly by this man simply because she doesn't want to lose him. What a poor message to send to young female readers.

I do applaud the book's instructional value when it comes to anal sex, woman-on-top positional sex, hand jobs, fellatio, cunnilingus, masturbation, Ben Wa balls, sex toys, ice play, erotic massage, safer sex discussion, and condom instructions. It encourages women to explore sexual pleasure without shame or guilt. And that is a good thing. I just don't think it makes up for the toxic relationship between Mr. Grey and Anastasia Steele.

DR. HILDA HUTCHERSON is a native of Tuskegee, Alabama. A graduate of Stanford University and Harvard Medical School, she is presently a Clinical Professor of Obstetrics and Gynecology and Director of the Center for Sexual Health at Columbia University Medical Center. Her commitment to women's health is evidenced by her monthly women's health column in Redbook, where she is also a contributing editor. She is a frequent contributor to *Essence,* where she had a monthly column for eight years. She is the former sexual health columnist for *Glamour* magazine and has been quoted in *Health, Allure, Seventeen, Self, Cosmopolitan, More,* and *O Magazine.* She is a frequent invited speaker on women's health and sexuality. Dr. Hutcherson is the author of three books: *Having Your Baby: A Guide for African American Women, What Your Mother Never Told You about Sex,* and *Pleasure: A Woman's Guide to Getting the Sex You Want, Need and Deserve.*

The McDonald's of Lust

E. L. JAMES' Fifty Shades trilogy is a by-product of feminism and women's equality. It's porn for women, and that's why it's so popular.

Porn and its softer cousin, erotic romance, are like the Dollar Menu at McDonald's. They're addictive, and what satisfies a craving one day just won't cut it the next. If you buy a hamburger today, then tomorrow you'll need a double bacon cheeseburger with large fries and a supersized Coke.

If male porn addiction arises from dopamine-oxycontin releases during orgasm, then the same is true for female porn addiction. In the best of times, repeated orgasms with the same person leads to bonding. Repeated orgasms based on porn or erotic romance means bonding with the fantasies. Male or female, the brain becomes neurologically hooked.

Today's women are overburdened. Single mothers struggle to earn a living while raising children alone, managing the home, paying the bills, and hoping they can cover college tuitions that cost more than houses. The workplace is infected by outsourcing, minimum wages, and no benefits. Despite so-called feminism and women's equality, single mothers are still in cages.

In the meantime, many stay-at-home mothers with college degrees don't know what they want or how to cope. They feel guilty if they leave their children at day care, feel guilty if they pursue careers or if they *don't* pursue careers. They worry that their husbands will leave them, because after all, the divorce rate just keeps skyrocketing, doesn't it?

Men also cope as best as they can. It's not that they're evil or hate women. Everyone's simply *coping*, and the focus has shifted from substance to whatever-gets-me-through-the-night. Jolts of Snooki and *Mob Wives*, dashes of Kardashians, a blip of fake-forever love on a dating show followed by two minutes of a sex tape. In 2012, life is an endless stream of 1980s MTV sleazed down to limp meaning and jacked-up excess.

As men turn to porn and away from reality, women become sexually frustrated. The women feel unappreciated, unloved, unattractive even in their youthful prime, and almost sexless. For a porn-addicted man, a real woman can't measure up, and increasingly, young girls and women find themselves with men who would rather have sex alone in the glow of a computer screen. For examples, just read any number of recent articles about the subject, such as, but certainly not limited to, Davy Rothbart and Alex Morris' 2011 *New York* magazine articles.[5]

Early feminists considered porn as something evil leading to rape. Gloria Steinem, who famously exposed *Playboy* in 1963 as a sexist empire when she became a bunny, labeled sadomasochism as pornography. One of feminism's earliest leaders, Steinem probably would have pegged *Fifty Shades of Grey* and the rest of the trilogy as porn. And she would have been right.

The difference is that Fifty Shades is *female* porn.

---

5 "He's Just Not That Into Anyone" and "They Know What Boys Want."

When men choose porn over their wives, why shouldn't women choose their own forms of erotica? This is exactly what women are doing with Fifty Shades and similar books, all of which are topping publishing charts.

Now, don't get me wrong. I was a fan of Steinem's back in the day. An elder stateswoman of feminism, she led the charge for equality. She came along in the '60s, a glamorous yet intelligent and strong female. But by the time I was a young woman in the late '70s and early '80s, many men equated feminism with "lesbians who hate men," or so they told me in the office. They made it clear that, if I was a feminist, I could lose my job. *I* didn't want to burn my bra. *I* didn't hate men. In fact, I rather *liked* men. Given that I worked for engineering companies where I was the only female professional in a sea of men, it was best for me to tell the truth, that I was working for the same reasons the men worked: I needed the money.

At first, I wanted a college education because I wanted to be a geneticist. I'd been a straight-A student in school. But my family had humble resources and told me that girls didn't need college. I should become a secretary, a teacher, or a nurse.

I didn't know anything about feminism or women's equality, but I did know that I was incredibly bored. Starting at seventeen and earning minimum wages, I wrote medical newsletters, technical manuals, and a book about poverty, and I also programmed in a variety of languages and studied engineering and circuitry. I somehow got lucky and had a couple of terrific bosses who promoted me into management. They only cared that I did a good job; my gender wasn't an issue. They liked the fact that I needed the money and had to support my family, that I had no choice. It meant that I worked all the time and did my very best for them. But being the *only woman*, I *knew* I was lucky.

In the late '70s and '80s, female professionals were supposed to dress like men. Shoulder pads in blazers hanging below our thighs, tentlike skirts hanging to our mid-calves, short spiky hair. Women's magazines told us to climb career ladders and break glass ceilings.

But I *liked* being a girl.

No shoulder pads for me. No drooping blazers and tent skirts. I didn't care about career ladders and glass ceilings. I was working to take care of my child, and I preferred intellectual stimulation to boredom. I remembered Gloria Steinem, who retained her femininity while projecting strength and intelligence, and I had no other role models. I forged my own path and made my own rules. I wore pants, simple button-down shirts, and loafers. I kept a casual blazer—short, without shoulder pads—on hand for meetings.

But after twelve to fifteen hours at work when I finally came home to my husband, I just wanted to be a girl. A physical entity, pure female, and with my brain switched off.

In those days, being a major breadwinner in pants could jeopardize a woman's relationship with her man. What if he stopped seeing her as a sexual object? What if he turned his back on her and fell in lust with *Playboy* centerfolds? My God, what if he became *addicted* to porn? Worse, what if she had to make do at a minimum-wage job with no benefits while raising three kids on her own?

Oh, wait. These are *today's* problems, only they're widespread and much worse.

Luckily, today's woman can do more than cry all night. If her man's grooving to porn in a dump somewhere, she can sit in her own dump and groove to Fifty Shades. She can stock up on all forms of erotica and download whatever-gets-her-through-the-night fantasies. If she wants, she can fantasize about a very rich bad boy who lusts after her, who finds her sexually attractive—one who has his hang-ups, all of which she's able to overcome, winning his heart. This is the potency of classic romance.

Anastasia Steele feels appreciated, desired, attractive. She has multiple orgasms. Her guy is consumed by angst. She must help him. It's *classic*.

And yet we live in the age of porn, and so modern romance novels come in all forms—cowboys, aliens, threesomes, para-normals, kinky, kinkier, and *kinkiest*. If yesterday, a woman got turned on by one subgenre—say, paranormals—today she might lust for other kinks. She might lust for a rich bad boy who's into BDSM and who ultimately finds himself and falls in love with her.

There's really nothing new here. It's traditional female sex fantasy, except hamburgers will no longer do. Today's woman demands a triple bacon cheeseburger with extra sauce.

LOIS GRESH is the *New York Times* bestselling author (six times), *Publishers Weekly* bestselling paperback author, and *Publishers Weekly* bestselling paperback children's author of twenty-seven books and fifty short stories. Her books have been published in approximately twenty languages. Current books are dark short story collection *Eldritch Evo-lutions*, *Dark Fusions*, and *The Hunger Games Companion*. Lois has received the Bram Stoker Award, Nebula Award, Theodore Sturgeon Memorial Award, and International Horror Guild Award nominations for her work.

Crass Is in Session

OR MOST TEENAGERS, high school is one long science class: the Petri dish, the litmus test, and the sludge test rolled all into one. It is a time of hypotheses tied to self-doubt and self-examination (and, if Christian Grey had his way, self-flagellation). High school students waver and hesitate and consider a whole plethora of possibilities before deciding—or, more often than not, *not* deciding—what their next steps will be.

This indecision was likely a primary impetus behind Stephenie Meyer's choice of teenaged Bella as the central figure in the Twilight Saga. She needed someone who could be both a clean slate and a messy blackboard, someone who was not yet realized as a sexual individual until presented with the most extreme of sexual partners and, later, equals. The teasing-out of her fledgling romantic impulses and the eventual fulfillment and satisfaction of them are what make her such an effective protagonist. We need our heroines to face conflict and be conflicted so that we can witness their evolution and realization. In the final tome of the series, *Breaking Dawn*, when Bella and Edward quite literally break the bed due to their passion, we see that Edward's influence on her has both introduced her to new physical worlds and brought to fruition her nascent, inherent longings.

Anastasia Steele, to be sure, is no pillar of confidence when *Fifty Shades of Grey* begins. She is the very definition of a wilting flower, with all of the connotations sexual and otherwise that such a term evokes. Most enthusiasts of the series know by now that the primary inspiration for Ana was the equally fraught Bella Swan. But Ana's main differentiating factor is that she is a college student; she has graduated beyond the lab test of high school and is ready for the sort of education that we do not readily attribute to those *au lycée*. It is a compelling decision on the part of E. L. James to choose this fulcrum on which to rest her story—compelling and fitting.

Whatever my other opinions about the trilogy may be, I find the *verboten* collegiate relationship that the author establishes in the first installment particularly sound. The student/teacher relationship is one that has appeared in art from time immemorial (paging Socrates!), but in pitting Ana as a finals-studying coed against the willful, dangerous, punitive power of business magnate Christian Grey, James makes explicit the steamy pedagogy that piques the fantasies of many a fledgling academic, while avoiding the creep factor that would define a similar relationship written about a high school student and educator.

After all, college is the real sexual awakening for many people.

I spent my undergrad years at Princeton, with its simultaneously gorgeous and lugubrious Gothic arches (networked in the famed ivy of yore), its atmosphere of reverence and academe, and, yes, its frequent bursts of bacchanalian delight. Here was at once a maddening intellectual paradise and a social playground, a gathering of similarly ambitious, often physically stellar, and sexually ravenous young men and women who fell into a frequent collegiate dichotomy: they either paired off and became entirely monogamous or trafficked in the kind of copious hooking-up that could be best compared to rabbit coitus. Naturally, as an awkward, dorky, if gregarious, student, I found all of this alternately thrilling and terrifying.

I shall emphasize the latter, for I was gay, though damn if I would confess it (lest I be damned). For however much I adored Princeton—and I still do to this day, in myriad ways—it was often a place that gave off the air of homoeroticism while still conveying a certain level of homophobia. Countless rituals played on the inherent sensuality of shirtless, athletic, lithe young men "roughhousing" and streaking, but when it came down to it, being actually queer mimicked that other dichotomy: you were either fully out and proud or you bore your identity quietly, moving as your other silent brothers and sisters did like so many dark satellites in the evening.

I remember when I applied to take a seminar on the history of human sexuality taught by a world-famous feminist scholar; I joked to my best friend that the fifteen of us who had actually gotten into the class after applying were the most sexually frustrated people on campus. And, indeed, even though many of us would eventually come out as queer later, only one or two of the students in the course publicly identified as such at the time. Meanwhile, I wore my L.L.Bean turtlenecks and drank vanilla lattes and thought insanely that I was a Sphinx of sexual discretion.

And even though, senior year, a few of us gay guys moved into a dorm called Foulke Hall and rechristened it "Queer as Foulke," we still kept a low profile in terms of our sexuality, opting for closed-door encounters that led to a rumor here, a possible confirmation there—a whole world of confusion and mussed sheets and hair. In college, we were playing at being gay the way people were playing at being adults: we were back in the Petri dish, just with more germs.

I lament the missed sexual opportunity that college presented to me. Too scared to come out fully, I slept through the kind of sexual examination that brings an entire universe of feeling to many people. Yes, it is a universe with as many perils as pearls, but I do envy those who had the chance to benefit from this romantic panorama and rejigger its contours to fit their own preferences. I felt a swell of pride when I recently visited Princeton for my tenth reunion and saw that the queer community was flourishing, with more students openly discussing their sexuality, a bona fide LGBT center founded on campus, and even a queer dance party scheduled the Saturday evening of the annual Reunions weekend. It felt like progress, like that naughty class that had eluded many of us was finally in session.

Perhaps this is why I find Ana and Christian's relationship enticing. Oh, to be the kind of college student who could find herself the unwitting, and then witting, accomplice of such sexual exploration. When Christian speaks at Ana's college graduation, he not only, as a literal motivational speaker, represents the culmination of Ana's awakening as a BDSM protégée, but also is an emotional lynchpin: he is the jolt that upends her otherwise staid romantic approach. Although I don't think a secret dungeon of toys would have been advisable during my Ivy League epoch, I do think that a similar guide might have jumpstarted my own exploration and quickened my sexual self-acceptance. Again and again, E. L. James reminds us that Ana is undergoing an academic transformation as well as a corporeal one, and the connection between the two becomes more and more pronounced—as well it should be. James seems to be telling us that the most important lessons in college are not found in leather-bound books but in leather-bound...well, I'll duly submit to whatever wording that you choose to finish that sentence.

I do think that this is why so many readers have connected with this story: it represents to them either their own sexual educations or, more likely, the kind of sexual education that they wish they'd had. Reading *Fifty Shades of Grey*, for them, maybe for me, maybe for you, is like hearing about someone's Rhodes Scholarship when you just passed an AP exam. Oh, how I'd like to study for *that* final.

RAKESH SATYAL is the author of the novel *Blue Boy*, winner of the Lambda Literary Award and the 2009 Award in Prose/Poetry from the Association of Asian American Studies. A former book editor at Random House and HarperCollins, he has edited such prominent queer voices as Armistead Maupin, Paul Rudnick, Terry Castle, and Vestal McIntyre. He also sings a popular cabaret show that has been featured widely in the press, from DailyCandy to *Page Six* to the *New York Observer*.

Sexual Empowerment
at the Water Cooler

FIFTY SHADES OF GREY is a book about a woman's sexual self-discovery. It dares to explore the forbidden territory of sexual pleasure and desire, and it does so in a way that allows the average woman entry.

Now, I would never pretend that my life is that of the average woman—whatever that is. In my private life I am surrounded by a very experienced, sex-positive cultural milieu in which orgies are common, BDSM isn't an acronym for evil, and people are polyamorous and polysexual. Nakedness is no shame: it's celebrated. All body types and sexualities are welcome, and people are respected and treated with kindness and grace. I choose to be partnered but nonmonogamous. I don't think it's fair to ask my partner to pledge sexual fidelity to me, nor do I wish that for myself.

To me, Christian Grey's proclivities for using rope, the flogger, or the riding crop simply express the desire to experience and provide intense sensation. The point of BDSM play is that you can experiment with sensations of pain and pleasure, and the roles of dominance and submission, without really hurting yourself or others. I've played with pain and pleasure. I've been flogged and spanked, and given such sensations to other consenting, requesting adults. I've done fire play, had my boots worshipped, and been rope suspended. I've done medical play. In short, I've even done things from Christian Grey's contract on his "no" list in Appendix 2.

My sexual self-expression is abundant, joyous, and adventurous. I believe that sexual pleasure is something wonderful, empowering, transformative. But conditions in America have not been such that I would feel comfortable talking about my sexual beliefs or practices around the water cooler at work. We are very comfortable with discussions of actual harmful violence. We freely talk about stories of dismemberment, the acts of psycho-killers, things blowing up, and hand-to-hand combat. I don't know why we are uncomfortable talking about bodies coming together in pleasure and joy instead of being torn apart in anger and hatred. Apparently, to the mainstream world, sex is unhealthy and dangerous on its face. Why else would Facebook ban the word "pleasure" from their list of acceptable page names? And if you try typing "sex" into Google you'll find no suggestions provided by their "auto-complete" function. It took me a long time to figure out one could change that by going into "Search settings" and resetting their automatic anti-sex filter.

In our daily lives, frank discussions or portrayals of pleasurable sex are virtually absent, unless you seek out illicit "adult" fare. The media is replete with stories of sexual abuse and misconduct, but there is virtually nothing about sexual pleasure, thus we rarely discuss it in polite conversation.

It wasn't always this way. In the '60s and '70s there was a cultural movement toward sexual exploration and openness. Yes, it was flawed, because it was often shaped by men, and certainly sexual behavior was frequently reckless and overindulgent, but its aim was self-exploration and liberation. The advent of AIDS, the general conservative political backlash, "abstinence only" education, and the bizarre coalition of the Christian right and anti-porn feminists caused the national dialogue about sexual pleasure and exploration to be shut down. Americans were left with warnings: don't explore, sex is dangerous, don't even think about the nuts and bolts of it—or should I say the sticky, sweaty, mind-blowing truth of it: that sexual pleasure is key to so much of our personal happiness.

Like most people, I live and work in places where I hardly ever give people even an inkling of my beliefs about sex and sexuality. In those rare moments when I drop little tidbits of information, people are generally shocked, and they think my championing of sexual pleasure is very outré.

This popular novel, *Fifty Shades of Grey*, exposes the general public, and especially women, to the deep and liberating exploration of sexual desire and experience. Through the experience of reading this book, women are given permission to have fantasies, get kinky, enjoy sex, experience pleasure, communicate equally, be strong, be adventurous, be fearless, be hungry and sensuous and celebratory and emotional and demanding, and—at the same time—be received, accepted, and seen as beautiful, loved, and appreciated.

Anastasia Steele is in essence an everywoman, "average." Through her, the book clearly exposes the truth that although our culture wishes to define women via the age-old patriarchal gaze, "average" women are not simply virgin, whore, nurturer, or seductress. Inside Anastasia Steele we find intellect, curiosity, fear, courage, anger, shame, love, passion, excitement, and joy. She is complex, intelligent, and sexy. She is not a cardboard cutout. She is not one-dimensional. She is a whole person. She is conflicted, pleasure seeking, and full of life. She is a fully sexual being who is being aroused and erotically awakened by this man, Christian Grey.

Throughout the book, we hear Ana's conflicting internal voices, and that gives her resonance. Inside of Ana there is "the subconscious," who "glar[es] at [her] over her wing-shaped spectacles." judging herself harshly and critically, and her "inner goddess" who wants to embrace life, dive into new experiences, and find where her passion and pleasure lies. The dialogue is familiar and authentic. These are the internal voices that articulate the struggle between what we think we ought to be and who we truly are.

Grey, too, is complex. The book is called *Fifty Shades of Grey* for a reason: Grey is a man of many facets. He's fifty shades of emotion and desire and conflict, as we all are. And like Ana and Grey, we are all goofy, imperfect, full of doubt, pain, fear, confusion. We are stumbling, funny, flawed, and full of laughter. We are all creative, active, passive, controlling, and surrendering.

Christian Grey—and the reader—recognizes Ana as a real woman in the full power of her intelligence, one who is questioning, reasoning, examining, and choosing, in her own time and in her own way, what does and does not give her pleasure. Grey gets his hands on a woman at the very beginning of her sexual self-discovery. He realizes this, and holds that precious, newly born sexual self with tender care. He helps her become orgasmic, initiates her exploration of her own body, and leads her to the discovery that there are things inside one's brain that can actually get best sorted out by fucking.

Fifty Shades of Grey allows people to think and have conversations about sexual pleasure and fulfillment. People reading this book experience the characters going through a journey of sexual awakening, and thus there is a possibility that they might come to think that they can explore their own sexual selves.

For me, it means that I might feel just a little more comfortable sharing who I am at the water cooler.

SELINA FIRE is a lifelong New Yorker, sex educator, pornographer, and hedonist. Corrupted by cult films and glam rock, she had her first threesome at age fourteen with her two best girlfriends while another friend watched. She had sex with a famously kinky rock star at age sixteen, and that set the tone for her life. She is most comfortable with the labels "bisexual," "kinky," and "nonmonogamous." She has been a columnist for *Penthouse Forum*, has written for Britain's *Swing* magazine, and was a regular contributor to the sex-ed website Carnal Nation. She is partnered and lives in Manhattan.

Fifty Shades of Women

*J*UST BEFORE I SAT DOWN to write this, I was speaking with a friend of mine. She's a beautiful woman, always together, very professional in her manner and appearance (no double entendre on the word "professional"). We're at a business con that deals with books and naturally the phenomenon of *Fifty Shades of Grey* came up. In a secluded corner with a few female authors, we joked and teased—and a few confessions came out: my very businesslike and together friend keeps her hair long because her husband enjoys schoolgirl braids, and yes, she has the schoolgirl uniform.

I was reminded of an occasion not that long ago when I was a guest at a Halloween event for a friend who has incredible sway in the "vampire" world, hosting parties across the globe. I attended with two friends, one whom I have often thought of as the contemporary equivalent to the moms in *The Partridge Family* and *The Brady Bunch*. She never wears provocative clothing; she's usually in jeans and a T-shirt, middle America clothing that might even be considered frumpy at times. She's a terrific soccer mom, keeps a warm and beautiful home for her young sons, and is a designer who works from home to be with her kids. How much more apple pie can you be?

So, we'd dressed up ourselves in something akin to vampire attire for the party; let's say we were in Victorian vampire mode. Around us, there was all manner of apparel being worn (and barely worn). As wickedly decadent costumes began to appear—and disappear—my apple pie friend was able to point out to my other friend and me exactly who was a submissive, what certain chains and binds meant, and something about the act going on at a long silver pole.

Go figure—still waters run deep! She went on to tell us about her life before marriage—the many S&M clubs she had joined and all the different roles she had played. She was still heavily into roleplaying; her husband not so much, but she'd been delighted when I'd asked her to this party because she still loved to observe.

In the past few decades the role of women in our culture has changed more drastically than in centuries before. Or let me say—the roles we show to the world have changed. Have our basic needs and desires changed on a purely carnal level? Probably not. Women with sexual prowess existed as far back as the days we lived in caves, but until relatively recently we didn't accept the idea of the wicked, wanton female as every man's wife.

Now, there's actually a bit of a biologic—not even dynastic, but biologic—reason for the way things used to be. Our fine early human males were on a mission and that mission was—spread your seed! But early females had to be far more selective, back in those cave days when life was hard. They didn't want just any old seed; they wanted the best seed out there, so that their offspring would survive the rigorous world. So—males run around everywhere; females seek out the best!

Then, of course, you get into the dynastic thing—property, who inherits what. The lord of the castle certainly didn't want his wife fooling around. I mean, really, should the groom's son inherit the great wealth of the lord's realm?

But we've now entered a world where our sexual roots aren't as important. Sex is an instinct, but our sexual mores are based on the world we live in now. Of course, in *Fifty Shades of Grey* we're going far beyond the simple concept of sex or promiscuity by either the male or the female of our species. *Fifty Shades of Grey* delves into areas of sexuality where many do not go—with any partner!

So, what is the huge draw? For some, it's curiosity. I believe we're voyeurs. "That's not something I would do—but how interesting!"

For some, it's because they find the book appalling. "I don't get it—what is fun or enjoyable about pain?"

For others, it's like a blessing. "Oh my God, I have always wanted to do that!"

Fifty Shades of Grey is far from the first book out there that falls into the category of erotica. It's just that, often, erotica is hidden deep in the cyberworld of the e-reader. In truth, authors have been writing erotica for as long as anyone can remember. And just as in any genre, there's excellently written erotica and erotica that isn't quite so well written. Why one story captures the popular imagination is often a mystery, but it's certainly evident that *Fifty Shades of Grey* struck the right chord somewhere. It might just have been the excitement of reading a book that "everyone is reading." I was watching a talk show last night that estimated there are 20 million copies of *Fifty Shades of Grey* being read worldwide. Other estimates have put that number even higher. To boot, the sales of merchandise in sex-toy shops has risen by well over 50 percent.

Maybe the reason the book is so popular is that it encourages freedom of expression. For some, like my friend who sometimes dresses up in a uniform and braids, it offers something of a blessing or a justification: our sexuality is something that we're free to explore and come to know. Most of my friends are not into being either dominant or submissive—but they are intrigued by the idea of climbing into costumes, roleplaying, and/or engaging in other little tricks to keep longtime marriages and/or relationships fun, new, sexy, and sensual.

Fifty Shades of Grey—with its amazing growth and viral popularity—has allowed us all to explore not just the "grey" shades of our sexuality, but all of the colors that lie between.

HEATHER GRAHAM is the *New York Times* and *USA Today* bestselling author of over a hundred novels, including suspense, paranormal, historical, and mainstream Christmas fare. She lives in Miami, Florida—her home, and an easy shot down to the Keys where she can indulge in her passion for diving. Travel, research, and ballroom dancing also help keep her sane; she is the mother of five, and also resides with two dogs, a cat, and an albino skunk. She is CEO of Slush Pile Productions, a recording company and production house for various charity events. Look her up at eheathergraham.com.

Fifty Shades of Snark

"CRAP!" we gasp. "I'm shocked! Truly appalled at the popularity of Christian and Anastasia's shenanigans," we scowl, appalled, clutching our collective pearls.

It's no surprise that the guardians of morality and arbiters of good taste scorn the books' popularity. It's not news that media loves a good titillation disguised as responsible cultural reporting. The most aghast, however, may be the practitioners of real-life kinky sex, followed closely by the writers of erotic romance and kinky fiction.

A central unspoken issue propelling the Fifty Shades controversy is about how women are using the books. It's not just escapist fantasy. Well-to-do women are turning to these books to advise one another on sexual information, better orgasms, and erotic agency. Women whisper to one another about how life changing this book was. With the money, education, and resources they posses, why turn to poorly written erotic romance as the source for advice? That the well-educated would be naturally better informed on the matters of sex and sexuality is a classist assumption; sadly, it isn't true. Privilege does not equal sexual fulfillment and relationship happiness. Frustration, sexual misinformation, and emotional discontent cross all socioeconomic strata. Enter *Fifty Shades of Grey*, sold in a pretty package or dressed in the anonymity of e-book, validated by the tacit media approval and thus accessible to this group of women.

This book has brought the notion of sex toys, whips, bondage, and erotic roleplay into mainstream discourse. Those who already practice toy-filled and kinky sex should be thrilled. But they're not. Far from it.

Many of my kinky pals just roll their eyes and rant about these books. And they assume that, as a sexual adventurer and educator who often travels among the realms of sexual subcultures, I hold the same disdain. So they tell me how they truly feel. They lament the onslaught of what they perceive as "kink-curious tourists" invading their realm. They snark bitterly about incorrect technique or criticize unrealistic play depictions. They belittle the questions and assumptions people bring from reading the book. They tell me proudly that they're above such drivel.

That's just snotty and condescending. It's particularly offensive coming from people who espouse sex positivity and promote self-actualization through the examination of arbitrary sexual taboos imposed on us by society.

Where did each of us find our first sparks of naughty adventuring? I doubt any of us had highbrow sources with cultural approval. Where do kinky people come from? They aren't brought up in some secret society of pervery. Ordinary people find inspiration in common places: stolen porn or dirty books, mischievous suggestions by a lover, something glimpsed on cable TV or late night in the back alleys of the internet. We all start wanting, curious, nervous, wrestling with unnamed desires.

I remember one night in Tokyo, many moons ago, when I was at the cusp of puberty. That night I was able to sneak some late-night TV viewing without my parents' knowledge. There

I came across a French movie with Japanese subtitles. It was about a French diplomat's wife in Bangkok. Shot in a dreamy and overly gauzy style, the wife looked steamy and exotic in every little gesture. Alone, she boarded a train car full of young football players. I remember how they all looked at her lustfully. The film cut to black. In the next scene all the men were strewn about the floor and seats, spent and sweaty. Some appeared to be passed out. At the time I didn't exactly know why they were all so exhausted, but I knew she had some amazing and mysterious power of womanhood. She sat glowing, victorious, and powerful. I didn't realize until I was an adult that the explicit sex scenes were edited out. That didn't matter, really. I was hooked on the story of desire, power, lust, and drama. I stared, aroused and shocked, at *Emmanuelle*. Perhaps that was my introduction.

Many years later at Berkeley, I was helping my college beau move. As I waited for him to return with the moving van I came across his stash of *Penthouse Variations*. I sat on the cardboard boxes devouring each dirty story from a magazine I would not have had the nerve to buy, much less actively shop for at an adult bookstore where such things were sold.

I was that nervous, hopeful "tourist" of my own awakening to power and desire. From there I began my exploration of adulthood and its sexual expression, tentatively at first, learning my own appetites and misadventures. Sometimes they were good, sometimes they were comically terrible, but all gave me insight into the complexity of my humanity.

If these books, or any other source, provoke people to examine their own desires and limits, to seek fulfillment, joy, and actualization, it's a good thing. Are the readers of *Fifty Shades of Grey* the new face of kink? Will this define a new generation like some sort of Summer of Love? Probably not—but maybe a little bit of unproductive sexual shame will fall away for some. What they devour and thrill to now may or may not be what they ultimately find sexual or personal pleasure in. We grow and evolve—this is the joy of a life well lived.

But I understand the kinksters' grief, their loss of the sense of uniqueness, or their woe at losing status as wild cultural rebels. It's okay to be sad or to feel misunderstood. It's not okay to be subcultural elitists and disparage others' erotic journey and discoveries.

As for my writer friends, they're groaning as well at the Fifty Shades hoopla. While they're thrilled at the attention the genre is getting, they also wish it had been them to hit the jackpot. That's entirely understandable. I feel the same way as I furtively tap away on my stories. The publishing industry is a fickle mistress. She is far more cruel and capricious than Christian Grey ever could be. Which among the many writers will earn her favors and the public's attention? So often that's a game of timing, perseverance, coincidence, and connection, at times entirely unrelated to actual talent. Many of my friends are brilliant writers creating masterpieces in the much-maligned genre of erotica. They contain brilliant fantasies just waiting to be acted out in bedrooms across the world. Their work deserves attention by media and masturbators alike.

Let the curmudgeonly kinksters continue to gripe and society gasp in indignation—because good women and men will continue to search for better sex, mind stroking, and erotic liberation one way or another.

MIDORI left her early life in Japan to join the sex-positive movement in San Francisco in the early 1990s and began lecturing passionately on alternative sexuality, women's issues, and identity through art. Midori is currently a full-time writer and educator on sexuality and intimacy.

As an artist, Midori understands the importance of identity and personal exploration as part of the foundations of society. She's a dedicated artist exploring the fringes of desire, nature of memory, and identity through art installations, performances, sculpture, and art activism. Exhibiting and performing internationally, she has also presented as artist in resident at Das Arts (Netherlands) and Tanzquartier Wien (Austria). Find her online at www.fhp-inc.com, www.ranshin.com, and Twitter/Facebook: PlanetMidori.

Fifty
Shades of
BDSM

RACHEL KRAMER BUSSEL

Kink and Condescension
Fifty Shades of BDSM Backlash

O HEAR SOME CRITICS TELL IT, *Fifty Shades of Grey* is bad for bondage, BDSM—and women. The bestselling erotic trilogy is being held up to a standard we don't ask of most fiction: to single-handedly portray a whole subculture, kink, accurately and in a good light. Instead, it's being excoriated both for causing the downfall of feminism and for making a poor case for BDSM.

First, let me be clear that I am not endorsing the trilogy as the second coming of erotica. There are plenty of erotic books and stories where both parties are actively interested in BDSM, proud of being kinky, and ready to take their desire to the next level. And there's plenty to criticize about the writing found within.

I'm also not arguing that James presents BDSM in a positive way. Did I find the story line, in which the sole reason Christian Grey is kinky and has never had vanilla sex is because his crack whore mother died when he was four, he was beaten by her boy-friend, and then was seduced by a family friend when he was fifteen, over the top? Of course. Who wouldn't? And the books are far more about Christian's penchant for dominance in and out of the bedroom than Ana's budding interest in submission.

However, the books are fiction, and should be critiqued as such, not as social commentary. On the kinky social networking site Fetlife, user bumblebee wrote in a thread in the Submissive Women group, "I wish they wouldn't portray BDSM as some sick twisted thing broken people do—but can grow out of with enough love and support! We don't need that kind of publicity." It's this last sentence that is at the heart of my critique. Fiction writers, and artists generally, would have very little to work with if all we were trying to do was create good PR for marginal-ized groups. Furthermore, the idea that BDSM needs "public-ity" in order to attract newcomers, like it's running a popularity campaign, is ridiculous.

I understand the impulse—if *Fifty Shades* is a reader's first introduction to BDSM, and they find it not to their liking, they may never read another book about the subject or think it would ever be of interest to them. But while fiction can be a catalyst for social change, and can indeed incite discussion about social issues, that's not its primary job, and to claim that it requires us to assume that readers are so gullible and naïve they will take anything an author writes at face value. It assumes that readers will get so lost in the story, they won't be able to differentiate it from real life.

When I attended an E. L. James luncheon, I didn't find women so swept away by Christian Grey that they were trying to turn their husbands into his real-life counterparts. Most of them sim-ply found the books a form of sexy, escapist fantasy. They were more than able to differentiate between the extremes of James' universe and their own bedrooms.

In romance, as in any story, there needs to be a conflict, and the central conflict between Ana and Christian is, in fact, that she wants a traditional, loving, monogamous, vanilla relation-ship—albeit with hints of spanking and BDSM play—and he has never considered this type of relationship before. James is heavy-handed with pretty much every aspect of her plot, but her job is not to convince the public that BDSM and love can go hand in hand. Imagine if it were—surely she would then be crit-icized for painting too rosy an image of kink, sans any thorns!

Another way media critics have condescended to readers is to assume that those who are interested in bondage, fictional or otherwise, are simply deluded. They, too, assume that simply because James wrote a story featuring a female submissive and male Dominant, that's all there is to BDSM, rather than room to play with both gender and power in creative, intelligent ways. When Gina Barreca writes that "maybe 'bondage' is just a sexy word for 'degradation,'"[6] she not only insults everyone who's ever shown an interest in bondage, but anyone who's read or considered reading *Fifty Shades*. She not only makes it sound like Ana simply offers up her wrists to be cuffed upon her first glance at Christian, she also assumes that the women flocking to read the series are being dictated and dominated by James, as if she has some agenda intent on grooming them all to become kinky docile subs.

Barreca also writes, "Just when we thought our daughters' futures would be defined, stronger positions in the worlds of the culture, the workplace, the family, and politics, it turns a lot of women are soaking up this message, 'You want me to make choices? OK, then! I am choosing to be submissive to a man who has a playroom of pain and who wants to decide what I eat, where I go and purchases my electronic devices.'" Not only does she misread the plot, in which Ana grapples heavily with Christian's interest in BDSM, trying to puzzle out what makes him tick, how his previous relationships have played out, and

---

6 "Women Falling for Fifty Shades of Degradation," Gina Barreca, the *Hartford Courant*, May 3, 2012.

whether she is that kind of girl, she misreads the basic tenet of BDSM: consent, and desire along with it. Women are not simply "soaking up" this message, but analyzing it, debating it, discussing it, with their friends, family members, and lovers. Many are reading a book of this genre for the first time and discussing it with their peers. Because it's now reached critical mass in terms of popularity, it means there are going to be countless friends and strangers with whom to discuss both the plot points and larger issues. This makes it even more ridiculous to claim that there is a single, simplistic takeaway from the books.

Barreca is not the only one making arguments like this. In the *Sydney Morning Herald*, Pamela Stephenson Connolly argues not only that "Christian Grey is a sexual predator with a dungeon,"[7] but also that, "All the work that has been done to establish that BDSM is not a pathological symptom, but one of a wide range of normative human erotic interests, is in danger of being undermined by the success of *Fifty Shades*." The only way that could be true is if we devalue readers to such a degree that we assume they will take everything they read as gospel.

Sex educator Tristan Taormino, editor of *The Ultimate Guide to Kink*, lamented to the CBC[8] that, "The inherent mistake in the book is Anastasia's question really early on, which is, 'Why is he this way?' I think it really flies in the face of everything I know about sexuality." I agree with her that your average kinky person is not coming from a similar position and that Ana's approach is not necessarily the key to a lifetime of happiness, since their fundamental goals, at least at the start, appear different. But again, if this is a mistake, it's a mistake in terms of plotting; if in the end Ana is still trying to de-kink Christian, it would mean that the end result, where they live happily ever after, married with children, wouldn't make sense. But to say

---

7 http://www.smh.com.au/opinion/fifty-shades-of-grey-giving-bondage-a-bad-name-20120709-21rm3.html.

8 http://www.cbc.ca/news/arts/story/2012/07/10/f-50-shades-of-grey-bdsm.html.

that this is somehow "bad" for BDSM as a whole gives much too much credence to James' power as an author, even an author of a 20-million-plus bestseller.

On the other hand, there are some places we'd expect to see these kinds of words. Christian blogger Dannah Gresh at Pure Freedom[9] wrote about why she's not reading the trilogy, causing an uproar among some of her readers. Among her reasons, aside from it inciting lust in its readers, is, again, kink (in the comments she rails against the use of the acronym BDSM for sanitizing what she sees as simply "pain and humiliation"). Gresh writes, "It seems to me that in our emasculating culture there is a hunger so great for strong men that women will stoop to bondage, dominance, sadism, and masochism for just a taste. Do yourself a favor, don't!" Once again, it's assumed that *Fifty Shades* and James, without trying, are imparting some instantaneous form of wish fulfillment in hungry, horny readers, who will instantly be so overcome with desire for a Christian Grey–like character they will try to turn their vanilla partners into sadists.

But the more disturbing examples employ a fundamental misreading of the nature of fantasy and reading. They assume that women are so easily gullible, far more so than Anastasia Steele, willing to be blindfolded down the path to complete sexual submission simply because the heroine of a novel was. They assume that the simple fact that readers are enjoying a story featuring an extremely kinky alpha male hero dominating a virginal heroine means that these caricature characters are exactly who we all, deep down, want to be.

Fifty Shades of Grey is not an instruction manual, though it has spawned several sex advice guides, with names like *Fifty Shades of Pleasure: A Bedside Companion* and *50 Ways to Play: BDSM for Nice People*. Many have hyped (I suspect overhyped) the degree to which *Fifty Shades* has invaded our bedrooms,

---

9 http://www.purefreedom.org/blog/?p=320.

with the *New York Post* touting a run on rope at city hardware stores,[10] imbuing this work of fiction with nearly superhuman powers.

I believe that fiction is vital to us, both for entertainment and to tell us certain truths that extend beyond the bluntness of nonfiction. As Lisa Cron writes in *Wired for Story*, "Stories allow us to simulate intense experiences without actually having to live through them." Readers can and are living vicariously through Ana, but that doesn't mean they're checking their brains at the door, and if it did, it wouldn't be E. L. James' fault. Cron gives insight on her blog[11] into why *Fifty Shades of Grey* has been such a success: "There's something that prose gives us that nothing else does—not real life, not movies, not plays. Prose provides direct access to the most alluring and otherwise inaccessible realm imaginable: someone else's mind."

We can appreciate, or even talk back to, Ana's mindset and journey, without trying to hail her as an ambassador to BDSM. Neither she nor any hero or heroine could live up to that vaunted role. However, when we look down on readers by assuming they are taking their erotic fiction so seriously that they are even more entranced by the spell of Christian Grey than Anastasia Steele, we have a problem.

Reading is an active task, and while I doubt people are studying Fifty Shades with a highlighter, we need to separate our critiques of the plot and writing with our critiques of BDSM. E. L. James didn't invent kink, and it'd be tough to argue that she's espousing it as a lifestyle, considering Ana's ongoing quest to tame the kinky beast that lurks in Christian. You don't need to be a fan of the series to recognize that it's not about being a cheerleader or detractor of BDSM, but of telling a story, where BDSM is a vehicle to carry the plot. *Fifty Shades of Grey* has clearly set

---

10 http://www.nypost.com/p/news/local/ny_gals_learning_the_ropes_at_fifty_sVWWKeksj9WKUto2lTg1KK.

11 http://www.wiredforstory.com/fifty-shades-of-story-vs-%e2%80%9cwell-written%e2%80%9d/.

the publishing industry on its head, but let's give it credit—or discredit—in concordance with its role as fiction, not as some grand manifesto being obeyed without question.

RACHEL KRAMER BUSSEL (rachelkramerbussel.com) is a New York–based author, editor, and blogger. She has edited over forty anthologies, including *Spanked, Bottoms Up, Fast Girls, Orgasmic,* and *Dirty Girls,* and is the Best Bondage Erotica and Best Sex Writing series editor. She edits the weekly sex diaries for *New York* magazine's blog Daily Intel, and has written for *Bust, The Daily Beast, The Frisky, Inked,* the *New York Observer, Penthouse,* Salon, *Time Out New York,* xoJane, and other publications. She blogs at Lusty Lady (http://lustylady.blogspot.com) and Cupcakes Take the Cake (http://cupcakestakethecake .blogspot.com).

SASSAFRAS LOWREY

A Queer Leather Reluctant Support of *Fifty Shades*

S A CRUSTY PUNK KID just barely eighteen, I walked down SW Broadway St. in Portland, Oregon, past the now erotically famous Heithman Hotel, bruises forming on the beaten, warm flesh of my shoulders and ass and a leather cuff tight around my wrist. Everyone I knew were other homeless and precariously housed queer kids. Living lives filled with leather, we were having play parties in punk house basements and collaring each other in the shadows. We didn't know anything about international title contests and barely had seen a book that talked about kink.

It never would have occurred to me that a little over a decade later a book with explicit BDSM themes would top the *New York Times* bestseller list and outsell the famed Harry Potter that was just becoming a phenomenon as I found leather. I'll admit that I've been a little snarky about *Fifty Shades of Grey* and its success. I may have even been quoted that writing this critique/

exploration of the book was "more painful than the six strokes that Ana Steele took by the end of the book."

A key issue that continually arose for me while reading *Fifty Shades* was Ana Steele's construction as a character who is the ultimate reluctant submissive. To make her attractive and relatable for straight mainstream women, it seems as though she can't appear "too freaky" or somehow too eager for the sensation-based experiences she's having with Christian Grey. The result: a character who I imagine is somewhat safe for sexually repressed readers to identify with. Because ultimately she isn't responsible for the experiences she's having, she's able to maintain her "good girl" identify while getting fucked or tied up with Mr. Grey's tie. But she is also a character who lacks sexual autonomy, which, given the profound reach of these books, makes me nervous.

Ana is presented as weak, naïve, and ultimately susceptible to being led into the darkness of Christian's "fifty shades" instead of a willing explorer eager to push herself toward new experiences. As a leather person and as an author, I found it disappointing that in this moment of representation, which had the potential to reach so many people and give them the opportunity to perhaps gain a better understanding of our culture/community, readers are shown a duped submissive who is essentially manipulated and feels abused by the situations she consents to being part of.

Similar to my concerns and critiques of Ana as the reluctant, manipulated submissive are my frustrations with the construction of Christian Grey as a childhood abuse survivor. As a survivor myself and someone who speaks and writes regularly about the intersections of kink and childhood abuse, I believe that it's extremely important to bring abuse out of the shadows, and I'm eager for it to emerge as a publicly discussed topic. However, what we witness in the pages of *Fifty Shades* is not a representation of abuse survivors who take their bodies/experiences/sexuality back and make empowered decisions. Instead, abuse survivorship is conflated with kink. Specifically, Ana routinely presents as fact her perspective that Christian is the way he is (read: kinky) because of a difficult, troubled childhood and the sexual abuse he experienced as a teenager. This tired argument is levied at many of us in the leather community on a daily basis, and the idea of it being perpetuated in such a public way is disappointing. All through *Fifty Shades*, we get glimpses into Christian's troubled past—his biological mother the "crack whore," how he "knew hunger," and then the "darkness" (read: kink) that began to surround him as a teenager. Especially because he is positioned next to Ana, who is practically the epitome of wholesomeness, Christian's relationship to kink is essentially presented to mainstream readers in a way that furthers larger cultural stereotypes that only "damaged" individuals have kinky desires.

Of particular interest to me, and one of the more complicated plotlines within the book, is the relationship between Christian and Mrs. Robinson and the debate within the text between Christian and Ana about the ramification of their relationship. Over the course of the book, we learn that as a teenager he was collared by Mrs. Robinson, who initially exposed him to BDSM. From his perspective, it was healthy, consensual, and set him on a positive track in life that kept him from following the dysfunctional path of his biological mother. I found especially compelling the fleeting moments where we learn about Christian's collared submissive past, which were the most nuanced moments of the book. In particular, when describing his own journey into kink, Christian discusses how Mrs. Robinson had loved him in the only way that was "acceptable" to him at the time, and how their dynamic had saved him from following in the dysfunctional path of his biological family. This was the first moment of *Fifty Shades* that I could personally really identify with.

I came to leather very early, barely eighteen, homeless, and trying to make sense of the abuse and abandonment I'd experienced. It was through leather that, for the first time, I learned to really allow someone to get close to me. It was how I could allow myself to be loved and how I was able to find myself.

I was disappointed that Ana only reacts with anger toward Christian's submissive past and Mrs. Robinson. It seems to be her mission to convince Christian that he was abused as a teenager and that Mrs. Robinson is a dangerous pedophile. Conversely, Christian's abusive and specifically stalker behavior toward Ana receives little comment and gets somewhat looped into their dynamic despite any real consent. I fear that this has the very real possibility of leaving kink novice readers with the impression that kink and abuse truly are one and the same.

One of the queerest moments—and simultaneously one of the more troubling aspects of the text for me—is Christian's aversion to touch, thus presenting what in the queer community might be referred to as stone: a sexual way of being that doesn't involve being physically touched. In queer trans and leather dyke communities, this is not uncommon, and it is respected as simply another way of relating to our bodies. However, within *Fifty Shades of Grey*, Christian's boundaries are treated like an obscure damage, a result of his childhood abuse. Ana continually sees his boundaries around touch during sexual activity as abnormal and unacceptable, despite how happy and satisfied he is with his embodied reality of sex/play and his ability to clearly articulate those boundaries to a partner. Regardless of his clear articulations, the virginal "good girl" repeatedly strikes deals to "normalize" Christian. She strives to convince him that he should want to be touched, even if the sensation is traumatic and unpleasant for him. At the end of the first book, Ana even goes so far as to convince herself that if she takes the "as bad as it gets" six-stroke beating, he will let her touch him, and so she actively pushes against his hard boundaries. We're swept into Ana's crisis and left with no room to question her intensely manipulative actions.

Every day while riding the New York City subway, I look around and see at least one woman reading *Fifty Shades of Grey*. While I may not find the books the best-written or most engaging texts, I experience a powerful moment as a pervert, and a former sex educator, to take a peak over someone's shoulder and see "safeword," "contract," and "negotiate" jump off the page. Friends in the community who work at sex and leather shops report an increase of women coming in after reading the book and feeling comfortable discussing kink-oriented fantasies for the first time. I used to work at a leather shop down the street from the Heithman Hotel and remember vividly the struggle many women experienced stepping through our doors, let alone talking about even the tamest of fantasies they'd had. If a book can help them consider the possibilities of what is erotically available to them, then who am I to criticize?

But as someone who lives a life in leather that extends far beyond my bedroom or any "Red Room of Pain," I struggle with the worry that perhaps the women I see reading these books are being indoctrinated into thinking that perhaps it's okay to be a little sexually adventurous so long as you resist a little bit, aren't too turned on or too excited—so long as you don't take it too far. Basically, so long as you don't create a life that looks like mine or the lives of those in my community, because then you'd be "fifty shades of fucked up."

While I might personally feel disconnected from *Fifty Shades of Grey*, and while I don't feel it offers a reasonably accurate representation of any aspect of the leather community, I would be lying if I said the book was without merit. As backwards as it sounds, the book's greatest strength is its popularity, and the possibilities that popularity suggests. We, as leather folk, are poised at a cultural turning point. The outcome may be unclear but what is clear is that, at this particular moment, we have an unprecedented opportunity. Millions of people are being exposed to BDSM, providing a gateway toward a moment of education.

In trying to draw my thoughts together for this piece, I went where I always turn: to my leather community, to the people and the culture that have built me up and saved me. A friend reminded me that this is not a new fight, that both the fear of my culture and the misrepresentation of my community are very real, but that this has happened before and that, if we are strong, we will succeed. It happened in the online community when the internet became widely available and panic ensued over a perceived flood of wannabes. But BDSM became less shadowy and with more recognizable shades of darkness then. Perhaps, for this new generation, *Fifty Shades of Grey* is our new internet, even more insidious in that it comes with a prescriptive story line.

The book certainly isn't an accurate portrayal of our community, but at the same time, it isn't really meant to be. As a reluctant and skeptical tentative supporter of the novel I hope that *Fifty Shades of Grey* will serve as a gateway to our world. I must believe folks who are truly called to the lifestyle, who are called to live a life in leather, will find us—perhaps, thanks to Christian and Ana, a little sooner than we all expected.

SASSAFRAS LOWREY is an international award-winning queer author and artist who came into a gutter punk leather community a decade ago. Ze is the editor of the two-time American Library Association–honored and Lambda Literary Award finalist *Kicked Out* anthology. Sassafras' first novel, *Roving Pack,* will be released in the fall of 2012, an excerpt of which earned hir an Honorable Mention in the Astraea Lesbian Writers Fund for Fiction, and ze is currently editing *Leather Ever After,* a BDSM fairy tale retelling. Ze tours colleges and community organizations across the country, facilitating workshops that support LGBTQ and leather people telling their stories. Sassafras lives in Brooklyn, New York, with hir Daddy, two dogs of vastly different sizes, and two bossy kitties. You can learn more about Sassafras and hir work at www.sassafraslowrey.com.

SARAH S. G. FRANTZ

The History of BDSM
Fiction and Romance

EPICTIONS OF BDSM activities are carved into the walls of Egyptian pyramids, painted onto Greek urns, tiled into Roman mosaics, and illuminated in medieval manuscripts. It is no surprise, therefore, that BDSM fiction has a history almost as long as the history of the novel.

The term "BDSM" itself is a very recent one, established in the early 1990s. It is a combination acronym of a variety of connected sexual practices: B/D stands for Bondage/Discipline, D/S for Domination/Submission, and S/M for Sadism/Masochism. Bondage can include any sexual restraint, from the most vanilla of sex play with scarves and blindfolds all the way to elaborate rope bondage, rope suspension, and the Japanese erotic rope art, Shibari. Discipline ranges from the practice of "punishing" naughty submissives during encounters that often include role-play, to specific fetishes like over the knee (OTK) spanking and caning. Domination, submission, sadism, and masochism are all both sexual practices and sexual identities. Domination and submission refer to power exchanges in which one partner is submissive to another, doing what they are ordered, usually (but not always) in sexual situations. Sadists are sexually aroused by inflicting pain on their partners, while masochists enjoy having pain inflicted on them.

Despite these activities' apparent universality, the details surrounding them—how they are done, what society thinks of them, and what the people who do them think of themselves—all depend on the culture and the time in which they are performed. A sexual proclivity that is taken for granted in one culture might be completely alien to another culture, with different relationship expectations and sexual mores and even different technology. This means, of course, that the representations of these activities (stories, pictures, film, etc.) change over time and across cultures. These representations also build on each other, using conventions previously established by other representations. This affects not only how BDSM has been portrayed in novels over the last 250 years, but also how romance novels are structured and, most tellingly for a consideration of *Fifty Shades of Grey*, how BDSM and romance come together.

The early novel has a diverse ancestry, but it solidified into the form we recognize today in the early eighteenth century: specifically, in the 1720s, with Daniel Defoe's character studies, Penelope Aubin's adventure stories, and Eliza Haywood's racy, explicit exposés; and in the 1740s, with Samuel Richardson's extended character studies, Henry Fielding's domestic adventure stories, and the demure stories of a reformed Eliza Haywood. Right in the middle of this flourishing of the British novel, John Cleland published the first pornographic novel in English, *Memoirs of a Woman of Pleasure* (1748), much more famously known as *Fanny Hill*.

During the course of her sexual adventures, Fanny, a young prostitute, is introduced to a Mr. Barville, who was "under the tyranny of a cruel taste: that of an ardent desire, not only of

being unmercifully whipped himself, but of whipping others."
On a "sudden caprice, a gust of fancy for trying a new experiment," Fanny agrees to (paid) relations with Mr. Barville and
they engage in mutual flagellation: Mr. Barville achieves satisfaction as Fanny whips him, but Fanny is only moved to sexual arousal after Mr. Barville finishes whipping her. She is not,
"however, at any time re-enticed to renew with him, or resort
again to the violent expedient of lashing nature into more haste
than good speed." That is, Fanny was game once but is uninter-
ested in pursuing more after that first experience.

Mr. Barville, in modern parlance, is more masochist than
sadist, but has enough switchy tendencies that he partakes in
both sides of the activities. But of course, no one had that vo-
cabulary in the eighteenth century. A few things to note about
this short interlude: First, Mr. Barville is depicted as relying on
the BDSM activity for sexual arousal and satisfaction. It's not
just something he enjoys doing; rather, it's necessary for him.
Second, he insists on doing it in an ethical manner, stressing the
mutual consent of both parties. Finally, the activity is remarkable enough to be unusual for Fanny, but not disgusting to her,
as when she later sees two men engage in anal sex.

In 1791, just more than forty years after *Fanny Hill*, the no-
torious French aristocrat Marquis de Sade published *Justine;
or, The Misfortunes of Virtue*. The story reverses the typical
eighteenth-century narrative of virtue rewarded because the
more virtuous Justine is, the more misfortune—rape, impris-
onment, sexual torture—she suffers. The novel makes explicit
the fact that if she bent just a few of her strict morals, she
would suffer fewer horrific attacks. In 1797, de Sade published
a sequel: *Juliette; or, Vice Amply Rewarded*, the story of Justine's
sister. Unlike her virtuous and miserable sister, Juliette is utterly debauched sexually, completely amoral, and lives a happy, successful life. Contrary to the nonconsensual flagellation
incident in *Fanny Hill*, de Sade's narratives revel in the nonconsensual sexual torture and murder of innocents, especially

early adolescent girls and boys. Because of his published writings, de Sade was imprisoned by Napoleon for the last thirteen years of his life, and after his death his family burned many of his unpublished manuscripts.

In 1869, almost eighty years after de Sade's novels were published, Leopold von Sacher-Masoch published his infamous novella *Venus in Furs*, a fictional representation of Sacher-Masoch's relationship with his mistress Fanny Pistor. In the novel, as in real life, after the hero convinces his mistress to dominate him cruelly, they go on a trip together to Florence, during which the hero enacts the role of manservant and is abused by his mistress, even as she disdains him. While the relationship is consensual, male submission is seen as a weakness and the heroine eventually finds another man to whom she wants to submit. The novel makes clear this ending returns the genders to their expected, "normal" societal roles. This return at the end of the novel to "normalcy," to the way things are "meant" to be, becomes an enduring structure in BDSM fiction and romance (and is prominent in *Fifty Shades of Grey* itself).

A generation later, in 1886, psychologist Richard Krafft-Ebing published his *Psychopathia Sexualis*, in which the terms "sadism" and "masochism" were used for the first time in a scientific context. Krafft-Ebing appropriated these terms, obviously derived from the names of the most famous authors of each practice, from the code used in newspaper advertisements by people looking for like-minded partners—a nineteenth-century version of Craigslist. *Psychopathia Sexualis* was a notable addition to the explosive growth of psychology and psychoanalysis at the end of the century that attempted to examine and explain the vagaries of human sexuality. No matter how medicalized these terms have become, however, it is important to remember that they derived first and foremost from literary representations, from writers who had the courage to share their fantasies—no matter how disturbing—with the rest of the world, shaping all future representations of those fantasies. Then as now, literature functions as an outlet and a framing mechanism for sexual desire.

Despite—although some argue because of—the sexual repression of the Victorian era, there was a veritable flood of erotic novels about BDSM activities in the second half of the nineteenth century. Besides *Venus in Furs*, one of the most famous was *The Whippingham Papers*, a series of poems, plays, and stories about flagellation, published anonymously in 1887. Many of these stories were set in English schools, in which corporal punishment was practiced. In fact, caning, birching, and spanking were so associated with British schoolboys and their later adult sexual practices that they became known as the English Vice. As the preface to *The Whippingham Papers* states, "The propensity which the English most cherish is undoubtedly flagellation...this vice has certainly struck deeper root in England than elsewhere." Algernon Swinburne's anonymously written contribution to the *Papers*, a ninety-four stanza poem, "Reginald's Flogging," gives us a taste of this culture:

> "And how do you like it, Fane?" he says, "does it sting?
>   does it sting you, Fane?"
> Oh, fain was Reggie to rub his bottom,
> To rub it with his shirt;
> As he laid the rod on Reginald's bottom,
>
> "Does it hurt, my boy, does it hurt?" he says,
> "Eh, Reggie, my boy, does it hurt?"
> The first six cuts on Reggie's bottom
> He hardly winced at all;
> But at every cut on Reggie's bottom
>
> You could see the salt tears fall, my boys, the thick tears
>   gather and fall.
> But wae's my heart for Reggie's bottom,
> When the seventh and eighth cuts fell,
> The red blood ran from Reggie's bottom,

For Reggie was flogged right well, my boys, for his bottom
   was flogged right well.
The next three cuts on Reggie's bottom,
They made it very sore,
But at the twelfth it was bloody and wealed,
And he could not choose but roar, poor boy, he could not
   choose but roar.

However, for almost a hundred years after the publication of
Venus in Furs, most of the flood of stories and poems and plays
were only available for reading audiences who knew *to* look for
them and who knew where and how to find them. It wasn't
until 1954 that another BDSM story became famous enough
to become a part of the public consciousness: Pauline Réage's
Story of O. Réage was the pseudonym of Frenchwoman Anne
Desclos, who wrote her sadomasochistic fantasies in an attempt
to keep the sexual interest of respected French literary critic
and publisher Jean Paulhan twenty years into their affair. He
encouraged her to publish the novel and wrote a preface. In
1955, *Story of O* won the prestigious French literary prize the
Prix des Deux Magots, given to provocative works outside the
mainstream. The controversy this created and the speculation
over the novel's true authorship kept it at the center of public
attention both inside and outside France: for a while, it was the
most widely read French novel in the world.

   The novel tells the tale of a beautiful Parisian fashion photog-
rapher who is taken by her lover to Roissy, an estate run for the
benefit of an exclusive club of men. There she willingly submits
to beatings, abuse, humiliation, and oral, vaginal, and anal sex
with any of the men who inhabit or visit the chateau. By the end
of the book, after being passed from her lover René to his English mentor Stephen, and then on to a number of Stephen's associates, O is utterly debased—naked, pierced, branded, masked,
and treated purely as an object by those around her—but is
transcendently happy, although not unambiguously so.

In 200 years of novels that explore BDSM topics, conventions emerged, and were adapted and built upon. As with *Fanny Hill*, O consents to everything that happens to her. As with *Venus in Furs*, the story tells of relationships. Desclos' innovation is deep character development, to the extent that the novel is more *bildungsroman* than love story, depicting O's emotional journey and exploring the erotic process by which O finds fulfillment and happiness—even ecstasy—in her voluntary submission. In comparison, *Fanny Hill's* tale, in typical early eighteenth-century fashion, is one of individual erotic scenes strung together without much connection between them and with little development of the character experiencing them. Neither de Sade's Justine nor her sister Juliette learns anything during the course of her story: they are merely the object lessons in their creator's twisted morality tales. The couple in *Venus in Furs* are not happy in their desires. In comparison, although it is unclear at the end of the book whether O is passed to yet another master or whether she dies, over the course of the story she grows and changes and finds a form of contentment, her own happy ending within herself. None of these books, however, are romance stories.

After *O's* success in the 1950s, the 1960s and 1970s offered four separate narratives of BDSM relationships that impacted the public imagination in very different ways. First, in 1966, John Norman published *Tarnsman of Gor*, the first of a twenty-seven volume series of science-fiction/fantasy stories about the planet Gor, on which is practiced a deeply hierarchical sexual Master/slave dynamic between men and women. These novels gained a cult following, resulting in BDSM practitioners still today who call themselves Goreans and try to follow the precepts set out in the novels.

Second, beginning in 1972, Avon Books started publishing blockbuster historical romance novels (often called "bodice rippers"). The first of these books, published and marketed in innovative ways, was Kathleen Woodiwiss' *The Flame and the*

Flower; the second, in 1974, was Rosemary Rogers' *Sweet Savage Love*. The blockbuster historicals grew from this start and became so popular that in the late 1970s, they accounted for a quarter of all books printed (just as the Fifty Shades trilogy accounted for 20 percent of all books sold in the second quarter of 2012). The blockbuster historicals were not explicitly BDSM-focused, but they certainly exploited many of the same conventions that make the Fifty Shades trilogy so popular: the virginal heroine; the older, domineering alpha male hero; the heroine's sudden sexual awakening, matched with the hero's sexual obsession; a focus on sexual violence; and finally the complete reformation of the hero for the sake of his love for the heroine.

Third, 1978 saw the publication of *Nine and a Half Weeks*, Elizabeth McNeill's memoir of her D/s affair with a stranger, in which she finds herself as debased by and as dependent on her lover as O does. However, rather than finding any transcendence in the relationship, McNeill's character is deeply unhappy and, after the eponymous nine and a half weeks, finds a way to escape. The novel, of course, was made more famous by the well-done film of the same name from 1986 with Kim Basinger and Mickey Rourke that became a cult classic.

Finally, starting in 1979 and finishing in 1980, the iconic gay Leather magazine *Drummer* serialized John Preston's *Mr. Benson*, a fascinating mirror image of McNeill's story. In it, young Jamie meets the eponymous Mr. Benson in a random bar, and the story relates their adventures as they establish and explore their D/s relationship. Unlike the characters of *Nine and a Half Weeks*, Jamie and Mr. Benson accept, explore, and enjoy their BDSM desires, use it to build a relationship together, and through it achieve their happily-ever-after ending. As a result, this story of two deeply kinky gay men finding themselves and each other in their BDSM play is the first BDSM romance as we understand the genre conventions today.

In *A Natural History of the Romance Novel*, literary critic Pamela Regis defines eight essential narrative elements of a romance:

1. Problem in society or with the protagonists that the romance narrative will help solve
2. Meeting between protagonists
3. Attraction between protagonists
4. Barrier preventing protagonists from finding their happy ending immediately
5. Point of Ritual Death or the Dark Moment, at which it looks like all hope of a happy ending is lost
6. Recognition as to what can overcome the Barrier, solve the problem, and keep the protagonists together
7. Declaration of love between the protagonists
8. Commitment between the protagonists to stay together, usually a marriage, sometimes a betrothal, sometimes just a verbal agreement

Almost every romance novel will have each of these elements. They might not play out on the page in front of the reader, they might be more or less important to the specific narrative, they might happen in a different order—but to be considered as such, every romance must have all of the elements. And a romance that is specifically a *BDSM* romance must explore Regis' elements particularly through, by, and with one or more of the kinky sexual practices encompassed in the combination BDSM acronym. Rather than using a kinky activity merely as spice in a sex scene, as a standard erotic romance might, in a BDSM romance the kinky activity must be integral to the characters' individual emotional trajectories *and* to the successful relationship they build together. This is what Preston's *Mr. Benson* provided for the first time: the story of a BDSM relationship in which the lovers achieve a happy ending together *because* of their kinky explorations with each other. With *Mr. Benson*, BDSM *fiction*—a category that includes all fiction that uses BDSM activities and identities as integral to the narrative—added a subgenre of BDSM *romance* fiction. Of course, it can also be said that *romance* fiction added the subgenre of *BDSM* romance, even if it took a while for the genre to notice the addition, considering the separation of gay Leather publishing from mainstream mass-market romance publishing.

In 1983, the year *Mr. Benson* was published as a stand-alone novel, Anne Rice, writing as Anne Rampling, published *Exit to Eden*, a heterosexual BDSM romance. The novel explores a female Dominant/male submissive dynamic, an unusual pairing in fiction. Unlike *Venus in Furs*, there is a happy ending, a fulfillment that can perhaps be traced to the influence of the women's movement. Also in 1983, but as A.N. Roquelaure, Rice published *The Claiming of Sleeping Beauty*, the first of a trilogy of BDSM fantasies based on fairy-tale conventions. Her goal with the Sleeping Beauty books was to strip them of everything except the pure exploration of sex. Using the fairy-tale format, she could ignore character development and motivation and believable plot to focus instead on sexual fantasies that would appeal specifically to women. While the trilogy has a nominal happy ending—in that Sleeping Beauty, after many sensual tortures and much sexual training, marries a prince—the happy ending is rather beside the point. The fairy-tale nature of the books and the lack of both character development and a clear hero mean that the books, although influential in BDSM fiction, can't truly be considered BDSM romance.

In the 1990s, the focus on positive portrayals of female sexual fantasy heralded by Rice's books became a veritable flood of erotic literature for women. Pure erotica, without a romance narrative line, flourished, particularly at new publishing houses like Black Lace, which opened in the UK in 1993. Erotic romance also exploded as a genre, both through new publishers like Red Sage, which opened in the US in 1995 with the publication of its first Secrets anthology, and through established houses releasing full-length novels of erotic romance. Authors like Susan Johnson and Robin Schone, for instance, hit the New York Times bestseller lists with their erotic historical romance (Schone's first book begins with the heroine thrown back through time and into a different body during a masturbatory orgasm). Publishing company Kensington released highly successful erotic romance anthologies starting in 1999.

As erotica and erotic romance flourished, BDSM-focused fiction also carved out a niche for itself. In 1993, Laura Antoniou published The Marketplace, the first of a series of novels about a secret worldwide society of BDSM practitioners who train and sell consenting sexual slaves. The first novel follows four slaves through their slave training, examining their desires and needs to be sexual slaves and their experiences as they succeed—or fail—in their training. In 1995, future romance author Pam Rosenthal, using the pseudonym Molly Weatherfield, published Carrie's Story. Rosenthal claims to have wanted to write a novel with "creative sex laced with intellect, voice, and irony." The story very much reads like a cross between Story of O, McNeill's Nine and a Half Weeks, and Rice's Sleeping Beauty: a woman in New York City narrates—with a typical New Yorker's sarcasm—how she finds herself in a BDSM relationship in which she explores submission and pony play. She consents, she very much enjoys herself, but she's very conflicted about the activities her lover helps her to explore, especially as they seem to conflict with her own feminist feelings. Neither Antoniou's nor Weatherfield's books are romance according to Regis' essential elements, but they both explore relationships, develop fully rounded characters, are deeply erotic, and expand the boundaries of BDSM fiction.

Erotic romance author Emma Holly has the distinction of being the first to combine the subgenres of erotic romance and BDSM fiction. In 1999, she published two BDSM romances with Black Lace: Velvet Glove follows a male Dominant/female submissive couple, while *The Top of Her Game* follows a female Dominant and her male lover (but not submissive). While both books explore the BDSM desires of the characters, together and apart, at the end of both novels, but especially *The Top of Her Game*, the couples have "normalized" their relationships, eschewing their BDSM identities and most of their kinky activities. While not necessarily "cured" of the "need" for BDSM activities, the characters retreat from seeing BDSM as part of their individual identities and as essential to their romantic relationships and will admit only to perhaps using it to add flavor to their future sexual interactions. This structure hints at the much more focused rejection of BDSM "perversion" that we find in the Fifty Shades trilogy, in which Christian is cured of his need for alternate sexual expression by his partner's healing love and happily-ever-after commitment.

Although BDSM literature and erotic romance existed in parallel universes during the 1990s and came together momentarily in Emma Holly's novels, they didn't truly marry until the innovation of digital publishing at the start of the new millennium. Ellora's Cave was the first and most successful of the digital presses of the early 2000s dedicated to publishing erotic romance. Started in November 2000 by Tina Marie Engler because she was unable to sell her sexually explicit erotic romances to traditional print publishers, Ellora's Cave—with its digital-only business model, stable of authors with few other places to publish, and readers with few other places to buy what Ellora's Cave sold—quickly became a multimillion-dollar-a-year company, establishing a business model that's still growing today—a model that E. L. James took advantage of when she first published *Fifty Shades of Grey* with a small digital and print-on-demand publisher. Digital publishing expanded the erotic romance genre—usually set historically—into contemporary, paranormal, and futuristic settings. It also greatly expanded the market because of easy accessibility to an online audience who were no longer restricted by dependence on bricks-and-mortar stores' willingness to stock potentially controversial books.

In 2002, Ellora's Cave published their first novel by Joey W. Hill, probably the most well-known author—some would even say the founder—of BDSM romance. Hill was one of the first, and is certainly one of the most successful, erotic romance authors to use BDSM to construct both the identities of her main characters and the trajectory of their romance narratives. In Hill's novels, the BDSM play is not simply consensual, but practiced by characters who are individually BDSM-identified, to the extent that the barrier to the happy ending is often precisely that the characters need to recognize and accept how deeply rooted their BDSM identities are in their identities as a whole. That is, unlike Holly's characters and unlike Christian and Ana in the Fifty Shades trilogy, Hill's protagonists cannot achieve their happy ending without integrating it with their continued BDSM identification. Hill's most famous and critically acclaimed book is *Natural Law* (2004), the story of female Dominant Violet and her submissive lover Mac Nighthorse, who not only solve the mystery of a serial killer who is stalking male submissives, but also grow individually and together through their BDSM play with each other.

In the decade since the beginnings of digital publishing, erotic BDSM romances—and the digital houses that publish them—have become an essential part of the romance publishing landscape. As such, while E. L. James' *Fifty Shades of Grey* might be unique in capturing the imagination of so many people, it is by no means unique to the world of fiction. The trilogy takes its inspiration not only from the characters and—to a lesser extent—plot of Stephenie Meyer's Twilight series, but also from centuries of literary exploration of BDSM practices, identities, and relationships. Rather than being unique, it uses the well-worn and much-loved conventions of romance fiction, BDSM fiction, and BDSM romance.

The barrier to the full expression of love between Christian and Ana is Christian's apparent identification as a Dominant and sadist and his stated need for BDSM sexual activity. But rather than growing individually and together through their BDSM sexual exploration, Christian is saved from his "perversions" by the love of pure, virginal Ana, who helps him realize that he doesn't actually require BDSM activities to be fulfilled. Much as the happy ending of romance has been rewritten countless times, so, too, has this exploration of BDSM. However, the journey is the thing, not the ending, and it is a journey that the many millions of readers of the Fifty Shades trilogy have taken and enjoyed.

SARAH S. G. FRANTZ is Associate Professor of English at Fayetteville State University in North Carolina, and President of the International Association for the Study of Popular Romance. She has published academic articles on Jane Austen, J. R. Ward, Suzanne Brockmann, Joey W. Hill, popular romance fiction, and BDSM romance. She has coedited (with Katharina Rennhak) *Women Constructing Men: Female Novelists and Their Male Characters, 1750-2000* and (with Eric Murphy Selinger) *New Perspectives on Popular Romance Fiction: Critical Essays* (McFarland, 2012). She is also a freelance romance fiction editor and BDSM manuscript consultant at Alphabet Editing.

SHERRI DONOVAN

The Legal Bonding
of Anastasia and Christian

CLOSE FRIEND—actually one of my divorce clients—asked me what I thought of the contracts presented in the Fifty Shades trilogy, and it made me imagine how I would have counseled Ana and/or Christian if either had sought my legal advice. I had just returned from a national lawyer convention where every female attorney was talking about these books, yet no one had talked about the contracts.

I had a field day.

I looked at the ins and outs, legally speaking, of the relationship between Anastasia and Christian. I tried to imagine the rules and contractual provisions that would best enhance their pleasure as well as serve and protect the submissive Anastasia and Dominant Christian.

Anastasia and Christian are sexual partners who dabble in bondage, paddles, whips, and commands. If they hope to have their deepest desires met while utilizing the process of legal bonding and fair negotiation, they clearly need a unique agreement: a special prenuptial, or nonnuptial (if marriage was not foreseeable), agreement with terms that recognize and embrace their roleplaying. This would be similar to a domestic partnership document, however it would focus less on housekeeping and more on tying the knot through ropes and chains. Ana and Christian would need a contract that permits them to engage in a sexual BDSM rendezvous in the Red Room of Pain without getting sued and with each adult maintaining safety. I would have told the submissive Anastasia in particular that she needed a paper and/or digital file that expressed her wishes and rights equally to the Dominant, Christian.

But first we have to explore the philosophical and legal question is: Can two people consent to physical aggression towards each other? The criminal code and family law protect a partner from violence against the other if it is against one's will and is intended to cause harm.

What if the painful acts are intended to give pleasure and are desired by both parties? Does it matter if the beatings are solely inflicted by Christian against Anastasia? Should the submissive, Anastasia, be permitted in the contract to switch roles if she wants to become the Dominant, compelling the Dominant Christian to play the role of a sex slave? Can pain and pleasure exist at the same time, and if so, is there a limit? How many lashes or strikes are physically permitted so as not to cause harm, injury, or death?

These are the kind of questions and issues a lawyer would raise.

But let's return to the book itself, and look at the legal agreements found there.

Nondisclosure Agreement (NDA)

The first step in the process of legal bonding between Christian and Anastasia in *Fifty Shades of Grey* is the Nondisclosure Agreement (NDA). A nondisclosure agreement is a contract to keep certain items or a subject confidential. It is a document to keep a secret. NDAs are valid under certain circumstances, but the one that Anastasia signed would be subject to challenge.

A good lawyer would question whether Anastasia was of sound mind to sign a legal document when she was filled with desire and yearning. She barely read it and did not have representation or the advice of counsel. It was fully drafted by Christian's lawyer and given to her in a nonneutral setting, in a nonbusinesslike manner. Anastasia was at Christian's house on a date; sexual heat was in the air. I do not know if you could go as far as suggesting this was entrapment, but it was certainly enticement. It is hard to think clearly and soberly when endorphins are kicking in, not to mention the distraction and awe of being in the company of a wealthy, glamorous man with Christian's lifestyle—the helicopter ride and the luxurious abode.

Anastasia was literally swept off her feet into a different world; she was under the influence of seduction.

Did Anastasia and Christian have equal bargaining power? Their difference in age and experience suggests a lack of the preparedness and astuteness needed for Anastasia to sign a document legally binding her to Christian.

Until she met Christian, Anastasia was a virgin, in not only sexual but also legal and business matters. The NDA was Christian's idea, as he had carried out relationships with seventeen others before Anastasia. The process of legal bonding requires mutual consent, and that consent must be given of one's free will, without duress or coercion. It also requires mutual benefit and consideration. In other words, you give to get. If the NDA bound both lovers to silence, it could be argued that both benefited, if both desired confidentiality. However, in this case, it appears that Christian had more of an interest in and concern for secrecy, to protect his reputation in business and thus his wealth. Anastasia may not have realized her own interest in confidentiality to protect her reputation and future career. But there is no mention of Christian's obligation to ensure confidentiality in the NDA. Admittedly, he states that in return for Anastasia's submitting to his NDA and the "rules," she will get a "huge" benefit. He did live up to his promise that first night and gave it to her good.

If I had been Anastasia's lawyer, at the very least I would have added a clause to the NDA with an exception for:

a) a couple of personal confidantes, like Kate
b) doctors
c) mental health professionals
d) financial advisors
e) lawyers

I also would have suggested that the NDA include a clause that neither party could speak with the press and that each could obtain a gag order from a court if need be for any potential slips of the tongue.

The Contract and Suggested Amendments

Christian, in all fairness, gives Anastasia time to think about the rules independently, away from his presence. He sincerely wants her to make a thoughtful and informed decision. He recognizes that these provisions are asking a lot of Anastasia and wants her to be sure that she is ready and consents for the adventures ahead. He hands her the contract and tells her to research it. He also encourages her to add her own rules and limits.

The full contract grants both parties confidentiality (thus correcting the NDA) and safety, and includes protection from sexual disease. However, the contract is very strict in its requirement that the submissive offer the Dominant pleasure at his request, without hesitation or question. It sets out that decisions concerning everything from schedules to hygiene to the type of sex play are to be made solely by the Dominant, and the submissive must negotiate for her preferences. It also provides for punishment and discipline for violations as the Dominant determines. These punishments may include flogging, spanking, whipping, corporal punishment, restraints, and handcuffs.

Christian's hard limits give some important protections from physical harm as a result of that punishment; in particular, there is to be no blood and there may be no acts that can cause permanent marks. The contract emphasizes the submissive's health and safety more than once, noting that all instruments used must be hygienic. (A sense of some ethics is also displayed in Christian's hard limits, in his prohibition against the inclusion of children and animals. But the submissive must determine if she is comfortable with not looking at or touching Christian without permission.)

I like the specificity and the lists of the type of sex, toys, bondage, and restraints that can be used. But I would argue that the Dominant should not be able to do anything not listed, and a clause should be added specifying that. The types of punishments to be utilized should be itemized. I'd also suggest adding an opportunity for both to consent to items and acts not specified in the contract.

I like the submissive safety code words: yellow—close to her limit; and red—actions cease. Anastasia can decide herself whether she cannot tolerate any more. The code words give her significant control of the situation.

As an additional safety measure, Anastasia should be able to determine by herself if she needs to go to the doctor, and clause #15.8 should be amended so that she can get medical attention at any time she sees fit. The way it is currently drafted, the wording is vague and overly broad. And it is not necessarily in Christian's interest to send her to the doctor and disclose what he is doing.

Christian's rules and the hard limits he would like as part of the contract include many vague and broad terms, like obeying any instruction and agreeing to any sexual act except those on Anastasia's list of hard limits. The contract needs more specificity in these areas, as well as on exactly what beauty treatments

Anastasia, as submissive, will undergo. Perhaps Anastasia could have made her own list of what she would not do treatment-wise as well sexually. (It should be noted, however, that contracts for sexual favors are void as a matter of public policy. They are not legally binding or valid in America.)

The rules provided by Christian require Anastasia to be monogamous to him. This requirement should be mutual, something Christian would likely not object to, because he likes and wants monogamy.

In this sort of agreement, there should be escape clauses and a sunset clause. If either party wants to stop at any point for whatever reason, the curtain should rise. And indeed, there is a sunset clause included. The three-month contract automatically expires without a signed renewal. The renewal provides the opportunity for further negotiation and modification. There are also several escape clauses: one providing that all that occurs must be consensual; another that if there is a breach of the contract, it is void; and a third stating that if the Dominant violates the safety clause, the submissive can leave without notice. In addition, the Dominant can stop the contract at any time; clause #13 states that the submissive cannot, unless the Dominant gives permission. I would argue, however, that according to the contract, she can. Clause #3 says that all actions will be consensual. Thus, if the submissive, Anastasia, does not consent to an act, she is not obligated. It just needs to be stated more clearly, so there is no misinterpretation.

Anastasia's Initial Reaction and Subsequent Negotiation

Anastasia is bright and becomes a good negotiator for herself. She first negotiates for when she will wear the clothes Christian purchases for her and how often she wants to exercise with the personal trainer Christian will provide. Anastasia also solicits and receives Christian's verbal permission (which should have been put in writing) for an exception to the NDA—to disclose some issues in the contract with her best friend, Kate.

Once Anastasia returns home, she reviews the contract more closely in her bedroom. Her immediate concerns are that the contract is too short and Christian will be on to the next girl very quickly. She is extremely worried about a lack of commitment on his part.

She also thinks that it imposes too much on her time by committing her to be with Christian every weekend. She wants a weekend a month to herself. She shudders at the flogging and whipping, thinking that she could tolerate the spanking and the hand restraints but is not comfortable with the request not to look into his eyes and not to touch him unless requested to do so. Part of her is excited about the whole arrangement, however; her inner goddess jumps up and down at the thought. Anastasia enjoys Christian; he turns her on like electricity and she likes his playfulness.

Anastasia does research about the contract on the computer that Christian has given her, which he has the password to, meaning he could check her browser history. He even tells her how to start the research—nearly as unfair an advantage as the bribery via expensive gifts, first edition books, the laptop that was not on the market yet, a new car, and oysters and wine.

Christian and Ana had agreed she would be able to think about the contract away from his presence. However, Christian distracts Anastasia's independent thinking when he comes over unexpectedly and they have sex. Christian gives her a taste of what is to come if she signs the contract when he ties her hands above her head and teases her, covering her eyes with her shirt and using ice, bringing her close to orgasm but not completely, using the technique as punishment.

Doing so before Anastasia is about to sign the contract puts her under his influence, a sexual drug of endorphins that affects the brain and prevents her from approaching the discussion from a rational, sober, and neutral place. Christian even resumes their discussions of the contract immediately after sex. He only does so, however, to encourage Anastasia to share her issues and questions and to negotiate with him. It is not a take-it-or-leave-it contract. This makes it more of a document based on mutual consent and input by both parties. Anastasia asks about being collared by Christian and states that she does not want to do it.

Once Christian is gone, Anastasia puts together a more formal response to the contract in writing, but it is not compiled with much contemplation or after any discussion with a lawyer or mental health professional. The response is written almost immediately after sex, and with Anastasia upset at feeling like a sex receptacle, in addition to being concerned about Christian not being able to give her the commitment or affection she desires.

In her response, Anastasia makes it clear to Christian that she feels the contract is for his benefit. She also asks about his drug use, in order to protect her safety. She notes that she likes that she can terminate the contract at any time if Christian violates it.

Anastasia requests a shorter term of one month instead of three months, and suggests three weekends a month instead of four. To her credit, she asks for specificity concerning how Christian can use her body sexually or otherwise. She also recognizes that to obey in all things and accept discipline without hesitation is very broad, and notes that she wishes to discuss this further.

She is concerned about sadism, and expresses a lack of desire to be whipped, flogged, or subjected to corporal punishment. She also does not want to be restricted when it comes to masturbation. She questions why she cannot touch him and look into his eyes. The food list is also a deal breaker. (Many women might differ on this, liking the idea of having a healthy food list and a nutritionist and making the deal breaker some of the violent actions.) The clothes and exercise issues had been negotiated previously, without a hitch.

Anastasia rejects or questions only a couple of the soft limits, like fisting, genital clamps, and suspension. I was surprised she did not reject or add more limits. I was also surprised to read that Christian thought she quibbled with too many points.

Christian and Anastasia later meet in person to negotiate before finalizing the contract. They both verbally agree it is legally unenforceable—that it exists only to set parameters for their relationship and expectations, but that the agreement will help stop any lawsuits and make Anastasia less subject to legal maneuvers from Christian.

Christian responds to Anastasia's written points one by one. He agrees to state that the contract is for the benefit of both of them, not just him. He discloses that he does not do drugs and is clean of all sexual diseases. He agrees that she can walk away anytime but then coldly points out that, if that occurs, it will be the end of their relationship and contact with each other.

Christian does not compromise on Anastasia obeying him. She shares her concerns with him about getting hurt emotionally and physically, but eventually gives in to obeying Christian. Both agree that there will be no suspensions. Christian counteroffers Anastasia's request for days off away from him by giving her one day out of one weekend per month, in exchange for her spending a midweek night with him that week. She accepts.

Christian pushes for his terms on the three-month contract length and on discipline. Christian gives in about ordering Anastasia on the eating issue. He does not give in about not allowing her to look at or touch him, or masturbate without his permission.

He does agree verbally to go slow. Anastasia points out Christian's leverage points, using sex and seduction to get what he wants. When Christian is in front of her it is more difficult for her to refuse him, and many of the times that Anastasia is required to make decisions, there is wine involved. She also recognizes her lack of experience compared to his, and leaves without consenting to the contract and without giving in to her desire to have sex with him.

Sealing the Deal

Christian has by this point made it clear that the Dominant/submissive roleplay is the only way he knows (or wants) to be in a relationship. It is a complete question mark at this point which way Anastasia will go, given her preference for affection and emotion.

But at her graduation, Anastasia consents to the contractual offer.

When Anastasia expresses to Christian that she wants more from him, the "hearts and flowers" of a relationship, and Christian asks her to try the relationship he has suggested, she softly responds, "okay." That little quiet, verbal murmur seals the beginning of their Dominant/submissive contract and entry into the Red Room of Pain. She then confirms and accepts the contract in writing by scribbling on the wrapping paper of the first-edition Thomas Hardy books gifted to her by Christian. But although Anastasia has accepted the conditions, she never actually signs the contract.

The legal bonding process continues after their agreement on the Dominant/submissive roles, however. At their next meeting, they review the soft and hard limits—what will and will not take place. Christian agrees to no fisting and agrees to go slow with anal sex and not to pursue it further if Anastasia does not like it the first time. Many items that Anastasia does not understand, she goes along with, like butt plugs, beads, and eggs. She glosses over most of the bondage terms, except the spreader bar. After Christian defines it, she consents to including it in the contract. Anastasia still has issues with gagging, and Christian takes a note of this but does not delete it. Again, a discussion of the contract is occurring with alcohol; perhaps if she had been sober, Anastasia would have pressed him to remove gagging entirely.

Next, they review items that can cause pain. Genital clamps are deleted and caning gets taken off the list. Christian verbally agrees to go slow and then only later increase the intensity.

Anastasia appears to be in shock, and she remains concerned about punishment and violence.

Christian does offer "more" after Anastasia's request and agrees to try one night a week together outside of their D/s contractual relationship. Christian is agreeing to go outside of his comfort zone a little, but this is a verbal promise, not a provision in the agreement. In return, Anastasia must accept Christian's graduation gift of a new car.

Finally, they seal the contract not by signing it, but with a verbal consent, passionate kisses, and thrusting. The legal bonding of Anastasia and Christian is sexually consummated!

The Final Contract

The crux of Christian and Anastasia's final agreement is as follows: Christian needs permission to punish Anastasia from Anastasia herself. However, she may still be punished if she breaks the rules, as she has agreed to be obedient to Christian.

Despite this agreement, Anastasia remains still as uncomfortable with punishment as Christian is with being touched, and states that she accepts punishment only for his benefit because he needs that in a relationship. Anastasia wants to be with Christian and she does not want to lose him. She does not hate the contractual relationship, but she does not like the discipline and the pain and she would prefer the contract without it. Anastasia is very worried about being hurt, physically as much as emotionally. Their contract does not protect her from this.

Near the end of the book, Anastasia revisits and raises issues in the contract. Christian makes it clear that he wants them to continue to follow the rules all of the time and to follow the spirit of the contract when they are in the "playroom." And at Anastasia's request, Christian breaks the rules to punish her, hitting her with a belt on her ass, very hard, six times in a row, and further, spanking her repeatedly, eighteen times.

In both instances, Anastasia ends up in tears, sore, and injured. And so in the end, whatever their final arrangement, the two must include in their relationship a clause, whether written or verbal, that there will be no punishment. It is clearly too much for Anastasia to bear and does not make her happy. Unwanted punishment violates the very purpose of the contract: for *both* parties not only to be protected, but also have their most fundamental needs and desires met.

SHERRI DONOVAN has over twenty-five years of experience in divorce and family law and has operated her own law firm, Sherri Donovan & Associates, P.C., since 1988. Ms. Donovan is a certified mediator, parenting coordinator, professor of family law, published author, and neutral evaluator for New York City courts for matrimonial cases.

Ms. Donovan is the author of *Hit Him Where it Hurts: The Take-No-Prisoners Guide to Divorce, Alimony, Child Support, and More*, and has recently published an article on special needs children and divorce in the *Huffington Post*. Ms. Donovan is a seasoned public speaker and lectures extensively for a variety of organizations that include the United Nations, New York County Lawyers Association, and New York City Bar Association. Ms. Donovan has spoken on many public forums, including television appearances on CBS, NBC, and MSNBC, and radio appearances on WWRL Radio Program, *The Joey Reynolds Show*, and over fifty syndicated shows across the country. Ms. Donovan has many professional affiliations, including but not limited to: member of the United States Supreme Court Bar; professor at the Gordon F. Derner Institute of Advanced Psychological Studies, Adelphi University; divorce clinic specialist for the National Organization for Women (NOW), New York City, since 1990; and legal counsel for New York City's Small Business Congress.

DEBRA HYDE

Wanted: Fifty Shades of Sexual Wholeness

OT LONG AGO, a dominant man near and dear to me complained that *Fifty Shades of Grey* was far too pious for far too many chapters. "I mean, no sex for a hundred pages?" Call him a typically impatient male if you must, but I don't wholly disagree with him. While the slow burn of erotic romance can be a delicious torment, keeping readers squirming while waiting for that yearning desire to flare into the fires of consummation, *Fifty Shades*' flame took so long to ignite, I wondered if its pilot light had gone out.

And while we waited, we weren't teased and tormented with a convincing escalation of slowly unfolding attraction. Instead, E. L. James wooed us not with what I had hoped would be Christian Grey's dominant nobility and Anastasia Steele's smart innocence, but a showy parade of conspicuous wealth. She marched out the spacious private office, private helicopter travel, luxury cars, and the elegant, extravagant private residence to entice us into the world of BDSM in a Daddy Warbucks kind of way (complete with Ana's wide-eyed clueless innocence standing in for Annie's bug-eyed optimism).

I had hoped for a more thoughtful, and well-paced, examination of a woman's sexual self-discovery, of the mutual responsibility both Dominant and submissive share, and, ultimately, the promise of a future together where erotic intimacy and exploration would remain paramount. (What can I say? I love a happy ending. Especially one that promises orgasms for all.)

But a book can't be all things to all people. And since James' trilogy was predicated on certain Twilight structural elements—the story arc of falling in love, marrying, and starting a family; the male protagonist's troubled, brooding, moody nature—its plot and characters could deviate only so far.

Still, I can't help but wonder what the books might've looked like had the Twilight influence been less overarching. For one thing, we'd have more fascinating, less exasperating protagonists.

In some ways, Ana is a competent submissive. She's receptive, able to soak up her erotic experiences with Christian and incorporate them into her identity with an ease I bet many of us long for in real life. Ana is conscientious, reasonably transparent, and honest, and that's a pretty good starting point for a woman exploring submissiveness (and sex) for the first time. She doesn't top from below and manipulate Christian into giving her only what *she* wants sexually. Instead, she tries what he wants, then advocates for herself. She agitates to have her needs met only after the pitfalls of Christian's limitations reveal that her emerging needs will go unmet.

Nor is she characteristically a smart-ass masochist (SAM), a "bottom" who goads a top into punishing her. A SAM routinely creates drama *within a scene* to secure *specific* forms of pain play a *specific* way. When Ana engages in tugs of war with Christian, it's within the context of the overall relationship and not during a scene. And that's a notable distinction when we're talking about BDSM. BDSM relationships have no special immunity to the vagaries of life, and because they live and die the same as other relationships, smart couples (and more extended polyamorous configurations as well) handle problems as a matter of their relationships, not their play.

That's not to say that Ana's infallibly is well constructed. Initially, she's an untidy character and we have to suffer through an unrealistic level of clueless Ana before we get to the smarter and discerning Ana. I had far more difficulty with her blatant ignorance than I did her virginity. My children and their friends are roughly Ana's age and, frankly, I know who among them are virgins and who aren't. A number of them aren't sexually active and don't plan to be until someone meets their rather particular standards. But at the same time, they aren't ignorant. You don't get through college or into young adulthood these days without learning that BDSM exists. You may not be an aficionado, you may not even dabble, but you know its basic tenets and practices. Heck, BDSM FAQs were available online back when we paid for internet by the hour twenty years ago.

While Ana earns some admiration from me, I have bigger, ongoing problems with Christian Grey. Clearly, E. L. James borrowed his moody, temperamental brooding from Twilight's Edward Cullen, and then built a scaffolding of BDSM around him in an effort to make him even more morbidly fascinating. Unfortunately, damage and dominance don't mix well. "Fifty shades of fucked up" isn't a bragging right. It's a red flag, and any knowledgeable submissive would think twice before taking up with a damaged Dominant. (Of course, Ana isn't knowledgeable, so . . .)

I'm not a big fan of Christian's knowledge base, either. An experienced Dominant would know not to use silk neckties. Fabric was the first thing I was taught to abandon when exploring bondage; back then, it was silk scarves, but silk neckties pose the same problem. If a submissive thrashes about, the fabric tightens up. Ignore it and you run the risk of having your circulation cut off, maybe even suffer nerve compression. That's how leather handcuffs became *de rigueur*. Madonna's kinky prancing and posing, no matter how hot and convincing her performance, had nothing to do with it.

(Disclaimer: One can tie neckties or silk scarves in ways that minimize unwanted stress and injury, but it's not exactly beginner's fare. Plus, Christian isn't exactly a bondage technologist.)

So what would the mutual responsibilities of a Dominant and submissive look like? First, the Dominant really needs to have his shit together. If he has childhood abuse issues, he better have the metaphoric baggage unpacked and put away so neatly that his dresser drawers look like those of a compulsive neatnik. Self-control and self-discipline better be his best assets. He should be perceptive, and capable of reading his submissive's state of being whether it's during an erotic scene or when she wakes up on the wrong side of the bed. He should encourage post-scene postmortem discussions where both parties review what worked and what fell short, a skill-building approach too many people overlook. A postmortem helps both parties understand one another more fully in the early months of a relationship, builds a practice of shared communication, and, done right, makes for some damn fine pillow talk. But overall? A sound Dominant needs to be really good at being in a relationship. He can't afford to be "fifty shades of fucked up."

Which means if she comes to you as a virgin, for Pete's sake, don't treat her virginity like an inconvenience, Bub. And you damn well better know that the odds of an inexperienced submissive falling in love with her first Dominant are extraordinarily high.

A responsible Christian would likely point Ana to a master's degree worth of required reading. (Okay, maybe a certificate's worth.) Ana, conscientious lass that she is, would delve into it and educate herself. Yes, Christian would orchestrate and lead her through a battery of incredible and tangible experiences, but he would also want a well-versed submissive, one who did not exist by his word alone.

Mind you, I don't expect Christian to be a perfect Dominant incapable of error. Neither do I expect him to be a knight in shining armor, there to give Ana a perfectly princessly existence. I simply want Christian to be less messed-up. I want him to be a whole human being and reasonably well adjusted.

More of the BDSM artifice surrounds Christian than Ana and, although Ana quickly realizes she has a complicated Dominant on her hands, she doesn't sacrifice too much of her autonomy in loving him. If anything, her autonomy grows over the course of the trilogy. But I often found myself wishing she'd had a few trustworthy go-to submissive friends. Few people engage in BDSM in a friendless vacuum and I too often imagined how James might've employed a submissive women's discussion group to provide occasional didactic reality checks.

I was, however, impressed by Ana's self-awareness at the end of *Fifty Shades of Grey*, after she urges Christian to use the belt on her. Yes, the aftermath's a maelstrom of emotional confusion, but she astutely realizes how entrenched their individual limits are, how those limits prevent them from truly bridging one another's deep-seated needs, and, seeing no way out of the impasse, chooses to leave.

Looking back over my reading experience, Ana clearly became an acquired taste for me. She's not a highly perceptive person at the start of *Fifty Shades*, but she does learn quickly from concrete experience. Experience becomes her avenue to insight, and immediate hindsight is her GPS. She finds a way to navigate life, no matter how messy the route. She gains life skills and a stronger sense of self as she goes. In fact, Ana redeems herself well enough that I almost forgave her initial ignorance.

Perhaps I've forgotten the tenuous nature of first love's discovery, how difficult it is to chart a course when you've never tested love's waters before. We learn as we go in our first relationships, building our skills and competencies. Complicate a first relationship with Dominance and submission and the learning curve becomes all the more profound, the journey more arduous. Even if you come into BDSM with sexual and relationship experience, you'll still face a learning curve.

Perhaps it's easy to forget those early lessons once we've integrated our experiences and transformed them into personal competencies and proficiencies. It's easy to castigate the beginner when we forget our own long-ago neophyte struggles.

While I came close to forgiving Ana her ignorance, I remained hard on Christian Grey's shortcomings. Christian remains locked in a pathology that's too nineteenth-century sex-negative for far too long into the trilogy. His sexual tastes strike me as a Krafft-Ebing paresthesia, a misdirected sexual desire. Combine this poorly constructed BDSM scaffold with an already brooding character and Christian becomes far too restricted in his ability to maneuver as a character—too unrealistic, as well. How can someone as brilliant and successful as Christian be so self-unaware? How can he be completely blind to the fact that he's stuck, repeatedly acting out his broken BDSM scenario? That's just too big a blind spot to ignore.

Thank God the good Dr. Flynn hands us a deus ex machina near the end of *Fifty Shades Darker*. When Ana seeks his opinion of Christian's psychological makeup, the doctor explains that Christian had used BDSM as a coping and compensation avenue, somewhat successfully, too, until he met Ana. With Ana, according to Dr. Flynn, he "found himself in a situation where his methods of coping are no longer effective. Very simply, you've forced him to confront some of his demons and rethink." At this point, James moves the trilogy beyond its shades of fucked up—convincingly, too, despite the artificial ploy.

Much to my dismay, however, Ana and Christian turn away from BDSM as Christian resolves his inner turmoil. I was keenly disappointed that James adopted a "he's fixed now and doesn't need this deviant stuff anymore" direction for her trilogy. Certainly people's sexual tastes can change over time and their erotic repertoire can grow or diminish through the years. And I'm inherently enough of an erotic romantic that I can't help but hope that sexually fulfilled and self-aware people find their happy ending in continued sexually rewarding experiences, whatever those experiences may be.

But I've also seen what happens when people turn away from their deep desire for BDSM because they can't resist a competing, as-deeply-ingrained anguish that they're wrong to want this and they stuff their need for BDSM away. They suppress and sublimate, sometimes succeeding for long periods of time, only to have the erotic need burst like a dam stressed by too many days of torrential rainfall. Often, they go on the down low, hunting down BDSM encounters outside of their marriages. Christian is, in my view, very much at risk for this behavior—and I want better for him and Ana.

So let me imagine them celebrating their silver wedding anniversary as I'd like to see it. Christian's hair is graying at the temples. The lines of his youthful intensity have etched themselves in his face, giving him a distinct gravitas. Ana remains beautiful and breathtaking but youth no longer defines her looks. Grace and wisdom do. Coming into her own over the course of the trilogy has served her well beyond its pages.

They're sharing a private candlelight dinner, Christian in a three-piece suit, Ana stark naked. Elegant silver handcuffs encircle her wrists. A length of silver chain connects them but allows enough leeway that she can feed herself. We're treated to a sweet nostalgia as they harken back to nascent times and charmingly address one another as Miss Steele and Mr. Grey like the British *Avengers* television characters from the 1960s.

Somewhere in their marriage, Ana and Christian rediscovered their kinky tastes and integrated it into their lives, where it serves as a healthy means to a passionate end. Yet they employ it for more than sexual pleasure; they use it to express their deep love and appreciation for each other and all they've shared through the years. They *honor* each other with it.

And when Christian takes Ana to bed later that night, he'll bring out that necktie, now ratty and threadbare. This time, he'll know the proper way to tie together Ana's wrists—he'll apply a bit of Japanese rope bondage technique and wrap the tie a couple of times between her wrists.

Finally, orgasms for everyone. Through good times and bad, for better or worse, until death do them part. Yes, I love a happy ending. Especially if, in this case, it brings Christian and Ana fifty shades of sexual wholeness.

DEBRA HYDE has four erotic novels and dozens of erotic short stories to her publishing credits. Her lesbian BDSM novel, *Story of L*, won the 2011 Lambda Literary Award for lesbian erotica. A modern retelling of the classic *Story of O*, it updates the original tale to reflect the contemporary lesbian leather world and the women in it. *Romantic Times Book Reviews* magazine named it and her heterosexual novel, *Blind Seduction*, to its "Fifty Hot Reads Beyond *Fifty Shades of Grey*," calling *Blind Seduction* "a story about what happens after the BDSM seduction." When not writing, Debra cocurates the monthly New York City reading series Between the Covers, bringing erotic storytelling to curious and avid audience-goers alike.

A Requested Evaluation of the Mastery of Christian Grey

Or, A Week Spent Observing
Fifty Different Shades of Grey

I RUN THE WORLD'S oldest BDSM training chateau, La Domaine Esemar. Masters, Mistresses, and slaves from around the globe come here for training and evaluation. This week, I did my first evaluation of the mastery of a fictional character: the coldly fascinating, impressively erotic Mr. Christian Grey. I divided the book into a week of reading, exploring his character as if each day were one day of a weeklong visit by a young Master.

Day One: My initial assessment is that Mister Grey, based on his early interactions with Anastasia, appears to be arrogant. Arrogance always strikes me as an indicator of insecurity. It is a trait that has little to do with dominance, and in fact is often antithetical to that purpose. However, as day one's reading progresses, I begin to see a man who enters my world of BDSM with reasonable modesty.

As I look more closely at his character, I realize that he uses his eyes to manipulate others: I surmise that if he were to meet another Master he would—slightly and almost imperceptibly—lower the level of his own gaze. I suspect that, if Christian Grey were to actually come to La Domaine for training and evaluation, his first words to me would be spoken with a soft voice, one well controlled, and I would encounter in him a great desire to find warmth that can be both given and taken simultaneously. I am reasonably certain I would find, in his character, a great desire to reveal his own courage and need. I sense he would want his very private soul mercilessly examined. Although this would not be enough to indicate his level of either mastery or self-understanding, I consider it to be a positive sign.

At the end of day one, I find Mr. Grey hard to fully conceptualize. Christian appears to have polished his reticence as one would polish a fine gemstone. He clearly is plagued by a great inability to reveal himself. Of course, I wonder why the author has done this, particularly in regard to what that implies about Mr. Grey's ability to be as open and honest as a great Master needs to be. After all the comments on his "powers" I had heard from real women who had read the book, this certainly was not the level of self-mastery I had expected to find. I also wonder what that will mean regarding everything that will follow as I read through all fifty shades.

At La Domaine, we believe a Master should reveal himself as completely as he reveals his slave's self. I will have to pay attention to this process of revelation as the book progresses and see if this first impression is warranted. And I find myself thinking that, if this character were real and was actually visiting Esemar, I would undoubtedly have the great pleasure of opening Christian Grey.

Day Two: On day two of reading, I start to see that Christian possesses a powerful magnetism, one that would allow him, with relative ease, to put any driven slave firmly in his control. Mr. Grey clearly has the makings of the Master he wishes to become. My only serious reservations about the potential of his mastery, after my first reading of his Red Room of Pain "dungeon abilities," are based on his lack of warmth and his continued avoidance of revealing himself, not only to his slave, but to himself.

Christian Grey is a character that cannot let go; the result is that he has a psychological perimeter that contains far too much. On my second day of reading, it is becoming clear that he needs to learn how to fully accept and explore his drives, his fears, his need to give, and his desire to trust and be trusted.

At La Domaine, we teach that it is not about how much you can take; it is about how much you can give. It is evident that Mr. Grey understands this when the value exchange is directed from slave to Master. However, it is not at all evident that he grasps the emotional implications regarding his own mastery: as Master, he must also give of himself.

I observe an inherent sense of inequality between Master and slave, in the way Christian conducts his relationships. This is an inequality entwined with the character's understanding of giving and taking in our sexuality. Will this be a consistent current in Christian's dominance, or by the book's ending, will he have opened up and be giving, if not freely, then with the passion and compulsion found in greater self-acceptance?

Day Three: Christian certainly knows how to submit. Even before we learn that Christian had been trained for several years, it was evident to me that he had submissive experience—and a great deal of experience at that. Clearly, his former Mistress had him well trained. If the depth of his submissive abilities is any indication—and of course it is—then Mr. Grey has a remarkable potential depth still to be discovered in his powers of dominance. I hope we'll see that depth before the book's end.

Today I observed how personally fulfilling his early training was. Clearly it introduced him to the richly rewarding path he is now walking. It also seems that somehow, hopefully yet to be revealed, the submission he learned, the submission he has mastered, is a large part of what is driving him to become the incredible Master Grey I, as a reader, envision. Day three's reading has led me to the conclusion, perhaps premature, that Christian has not been able to fully accept this submissive part of himself, or at least nowhere near as thoroughly as the vastness implied in his previous submission. Clearly he has been deeply moved and shaped by the depths of that experience, yet it does not appear to strongly impact his dominance. I wonder if his character is past that intensely submissive period in his development or if submission still holds a place of desire and honor for him. I hope he is not past the former; maintaining his own submission would certainly serve his needs well in addressing the latter. The question that is becoming apparent as I read further is: Will Grey show any substantial level of respect for his own passions, both past and present? For without the successful inclusion of his past, his present relationship will not be as fulfilling and rewarding as it could be.

By the end of the day's reading, I feel that, unquestionably, Christian Grey needs to proudly accept and value what his previous Mistress accomplished with him and allow this to be a cherished area of his growth. Yet I feel some other ethereal element that I cannot yet comprehend, which is preventing this. Perhaps Christian holds a belief that he should feel disdain for what he did when he was young? If so, he surely will need to embrace his past.

That seems to be a consistent challenge within Mr. Grey's character: the ability to embrace. Specifically, he needs to learn to embrace his sexual dominance as a successful metaphor for his wants and needs. Perhaps then Mr. Gray will be able to allow Ana, and others, to touch him.

Day Four: Today's reading has me wondering about the boundaries Grey has established between his Ana and his heart, and the boundaries he has established around himself that contain him and keep him from accepting and enlarging his capacity to love.

Christian is gradually coming to understand that he is in love with Ana. It is clear that he has never loved any of his slaves before. He has merely possessed them. The voice of his character has the hollowness of a man who thinks he may be so alone because he is undeserving or, perhaps even worse, incapable of love. It could be that he believes both to be true. In any case, it is evident that he is madly in love with his new slave, as well as extremely overwhelmed and confused by this love. I wonder: Does this confusion belie his mastery? Does it, like some outside force, control his ability to master others, or does it show that his mastery is simply nonexistent?

I am starting to see that, in some as yet unclear way, the intensity of his love is currently interfering with his ability to be "Master." Will his virgin slave continue to unwittingly amplify the already observed conflict between his arrogance and his potential as a Master, or will Christian submit to these new currents that are flowing within him now, not melt at her every fear and whim, and actually see this relationship through with a commitment to who he is and what he feels is right for his life?

Part of this will depend on how firmly he trusts his own dominance, his own development, his own sexuality. If he stays within his arrogance (if he fails to extend his love of her into his love of himself—and others—in a more day-to-day way), then I fear he will not find the trust in, and commitment to, his own belief system that would allow his love with his Ana to remain a power-filled BDSM love. As I read further, I begin to think this may well depend on whether or not he gains a firm understanding that *there is nothing wrong with his sexuality*, that he has a healthy sexuality and that his desire to share this with his Ana is a positive one. That should allow his mask of arrogance to be removed and replaced with the stunning confidence he shows in so many other areas of his life. However, I fear high-altitude winds here.

Day Five: Today's reading finally clarified the issue for me. Ana feels that Christian's sexuality is not healthy. She mocks him through that, and he allows this disrespect. He feels that he is "fucked up" and that she "tolerates" him because she loves him. Yet, whether or not they both recognize it, her character is extremely aroused by his Dominant sexual persona. This reveals that BDSM sexuality must also reside deeply within her. Every time they approach this together, she comes as much as he does, often far more. As I explore this problem in his mastery, I can see that for his character to become fulfilled, he will have to face the inevitable, and absurd, line of thought that people who are into our sexuality are there because they have been abused as children. After seeing literally thousands of individuals and hundreds of couples here at La Domaine in the past two decades, I am convinced that the assumption that childhood abuse correlates with BDSM sexuality is a false premise. In this specific fictional case, it is obviously false as well, as Ana, the innocent, gets as wet as Christian gets hard. Their sexual prowess together is based on their compatibility and resonance. All readers need to see that his shades and hers are very similar, even though one has an "abused" background and the other does not. As much as Christian needs to recognize this, I feel that Ana needs to see it even more, or else socially induced misconceptions, and Grey's fear that "she might be right," will inevitably undermine the compatibility and resonance between them, just as it does with the couples we see here at La Domaine.

As I read further, I find that I have taken a great liking to Christian. I like his technical skills, such as flying, and I like how he delegates authority to his workers (although the lack of thanking them indicates a further lack of mastery), as well as his techniques in the Red Room. He does confuse generosity for giving, but through Ana, he is gradually learning to give. However, the more that Ana shows her growing care for Mr. Grey, the more Christian's veils and shadows appear. It is almost as if any approval of his dominance, coming from his chosen slave, leads to a lack of mastery, or at least an avoidance of it. I wonder how this will affect his growth with Ana as the story continues.

As the book starts to draw toward its end, I find myself wondering how Christian reacts toward mastery in others, and specifically, how that would affect his growth if he were here at La Domaine. I can easily see how he grew with his former Mistress, the book's only indication of his ability to accept mastery in others. I sense that as I continue reading, I will soon know what lies behind his continually veiled countenance and what is lacking in his mastery. The answer is here somewhere; I feel like I can almost see it; I just need to clarify, for myself, what the problem is. I sense it has to do with something that this stunningly handsome, rich, and powerful man is lacking. Two more days of reading and contemplating and I hope I shall be able to fathom his many shaded depths.

Day Six: I once again note how Grey's use of arrogance interferes with his mastery. It is a simple observation; he does not thank Ana for anything. At La Domaine, we have a precept: thank you is always appropriate. I wonder how often Grey thanks those who work for him. I have yet to find any of that in the book. He has so many contradictions. He has shown the ability to give so much, but he really must learn to accept more.

Today's Christian—the Grey of day six—once again has his hair tussled, his shirt open, and his pants hanging on his hips in that delicious manner that every Mistress, Master, and slave here would love. I know I would not even have to tell my slaves to be as seductive as possible with him throughout the day. Their eyes would all glaze over with possibilities. But I suspect that the young Master would go through the day hardly noticing.

At La Domaine, we teach our Masters and Mistresses and slaves to use all their senses. When a slave is told to offer, even from several feet away, a La Domaine Dominant can scent a slave becoming aroused. I would have no need to point this change in scent out. That is something a trained Master should be able to observe and utilize. On day two of my reading I could tell that one of the better components of Mr. Grey's dominance is his use of his senses. He is a keen observer. Yet he still misses many signals. By day six, I have come to feel that Christian does this unknowingly, only as a natural occurrence, creating an emotionally unsafe place for both Dominant and submissive. La Domaine training would serve him well.

When Christian has his slave neatly tied, I can see that is for her pleasure, as well as, in some way, for his own sense of security. It also is one more indication of the extent of his implied technical skills, skills he shows throughout the book. Interesting: the more his slave becomes aroused, the more Grey's eyes glow and, conversely, the more distant he becomes. He delivers a tremendous whipping and brings Ana to a devastating orgasm, and then, only momentarily, the reader sees the distance turn to warmth. He goes to her and lightly caresses her face. The way he touches her skin is very moving. It occurs to me that, except for his love for spanking and bringing slaves to orgasm, he seldom seems to touch. He releases the slave and sends her to take a shower. Oh, dear Christian, allow yourself to receive some warmth.

The book is drawing to a close, and although he has definitely made a connection with me, it seems he has not done the same with any other member of the Fifty Shades family—a family that includes his own blood family, Ana's, and virtually everyone else who is drawn to him in the story. Perhaps his heart will not let him. One would think he would be entering people, other than Ana, much more deeply and far more sincerely.

Day Seven: The book is done, and now it is time for the Final Evaluation of Mr. Christian Grey's Mastery, by Master R.

Mr. Grey has excellent technical skills, but he has too great a reliance on them. He has superb abilities when it comes to arousing slaves, and understands and truly appreciates his sexual gifts, yet he has far too many many ways to avoid being touched to allow his mastery to attain fulfillment. No contact on his chest and the constantly worn shirt—metaphorically covering his heart—are just two examples. The extremely powerful way he uses his eyes, both in observation and in the practice of avoidance, troubles me. That he uses his eyes for both purposes is a contradiction in dominance, and I have become certain that it is caused by his fear that he is irregular and damaged. This indicates, for all his accomplishments in business and sexuality, a lack of true confidence and self-acceptance. Christian's mastery would be greatly improved by self-acceptance. I fully enjoyed and approve of how Mr. Grey uses his senses to feed his intellect; however, Christian must learn to channel the information he receives from those senses into positive emotion as well as into that appealing intellect.

If Christian Grey were a reality, and were here at La Domaine seeking counsel, I would end our week together by offering him the following thoughts and summation, based on our brief, albeit literary time together:

Mr. Grey, you consistently appear tense, as if you have accepted a challenge or are facing an internal devil. Yet I am drawn to several aspects of your person and reflections of your personality. Your clothing is impeccable. I love the fine line of your lips and I wonder if I am immediately drawn to that fine line because of its tension, because your lips imply a greatly repressed sensuality, or simply because you are portrayed as so intensely beautiful. Ana feels your hair looks like it needs to be tussled;

by the end of my first day reading, I felt your entire demeanor needed to be tussled.

As the philosopher Santayana said so well: "Love is a physical drive with an ideal intent." BDSM is nothing more (or less) than your type of loving. I suspect you are a wonderful man, with terrific potential as a Master. As you were revealed to me, I came to understand through Ana's voice that, as Mr. Grey, your physical drive is superb, yet Christian has a great deal to learn about ideal intent. You need to learn to first reveal, next cherish, and then confidently share your love. In this process you will become the master of your own potential. I am certain, if you learn to open your heart, you can learn to love who you are, and that will make you a great master. In short, Mr. Christian Grey, you need to master love.

But then, don't we all?

Our week together is done. My involvement with fiction draws to an end as I metaphorically show this young Master to the door. If this were a reality, I would allow myself the pleasure of a farewell touch to his sculpted face, and I know I would fully enjoy the excitement that small connection would generate.

A final thought, from a real Master to a fictional visitor: Good-bye, Master Grey—I hope we meet again.

MASTER R was a professional submissive in NYC in 1969. He began exploring his dominance in 1978. In 1993, R created La Domaine Esemar, now the world's most respected BDSM training chateau, where he has been deeply involved in the training of hundreds of Masters, Mistresses, and slaves. His writings have appeared in kink magazines from around the world, including *Secret* (Belgium), *Marquis* (Germany), and *Skin Two* (Great Britain). His autobiography, *Master: The Unauthorized Autobiography of Master R*, is a well-received and compelling life story, which explores not only the gradual emergence of his Mastery but his work as an accomplished musician, singer/songwriter, free thinker, and political activist. In addition, as Robb Goldstein—The Troubadour—he had a twenty year career exploring the relationship between American fine art and American folk culture, a pursuit which led to his speaking at over one hundred and fifty museums and universities across the US between 1985 and 2005. R's proudest moment was winning a major Free Speech/First Amendment decision in 1978, "Goldstein vs. Nantucket," a decision that extended Free Speech protection to all the street artists in the United States. Although Master R has recently retired, he still, whenever his expertease is needed, maintains an active role at the extraordinary La Domaine, as Master EmeRitus.

The Collar of Blue Stones

*I*T'S ALL MY FAULT. I'm not like Ana, an innocent accidentally falling in love with a dominant man. No, not me. I knew exactly who I was messing with the moment that I met him. Oh, I might have uttered "holy cow" a few times. But if there was any blush in my cheeks, it was there because he put the color just where he wanted it. I didn't flee my sadist, as Ana fled hers in *Fifty Shades of Grey*. Instead, every day for three months now, I've put on a beautiful necklace made of blue crystals and stones. Not a day goes by without someone noticing it and telling me how lovely it is. Every time they do, my fingers wander up to the blue crystals and I smile. They think it's simply jewelry, but for me it's my beautiful secret. When they compliment it, I feel like they are telling me that my surrender is beautiful. That my commitment is beautiful. Of course they don't know that it is my "day collar," placed there by the Blue Flame, the man who tops me.

Blue Flame has a lot in common with Christian Grey. No, he is not a mega-millionaire, but he understands what he wants from a woman. These words that Christian utters to Ana so beautifully could easily have been spoken by my Blue Flame to me: "I have rules, and I want you to comply with them. They are for your benefit and for my pleasure. If you follow these rules to my satisfaction, I shall reward you. If you don't, I shall punish you, and you will learn."

My friends don't know that every morning when I put my necklace on, it reminds me of my submission to him—this man who lives across the country and is not mine except for this agreement that we have. They don't know that every night when I take it off before I go to sleep, my mind flashes to bits of memory of my visits with him: Sitting at a sushi bar with his ropes tied into a harness under my dress. His arm around me, gently tugging on them through my clothing. My body yielding to the push-pull of the ropes. Sitting in a coffee shop in San Francisco, taking off his black heavy boots and rubbing his feet as he reads the paper and sips his coffee. The pleasure that I feel in my body when I please him. Me, on my belly, tied to a four-poster bed, completely open to him as he places a vibrator underneath me and canes me while I am having dozens of orgasms. The necklace is my constant reminder, the trigger of sense memories that feed me between the long stretches of separation, that stitch our visits together. The memories can hit like a smooth wooden paddle. They can land soft and smooth with a gentle caress or strike so hard that I lose all of my breath. Because, for me, being with the Blue Flame is all of those things.

Domination and submission, power and surrender, mean different things for different people. For some it's about having a chance to trust someone else to take control. For others it's the pure physical sensation—spanking, flogging, licking, restraints—that bends the mind, the antithesis of thinking in straight hard lines.

Being held in just the way you need to be by someone stronger than you are in that moment, being told what to do in the safe context of a mutually agreed upon power exchange, is pretty damn intoxicating. That is what Christian was trying to offer

Ana. But she had too much resistance to truly understand the gift that he was offering. For her, it was an aberration—something that seemed broken and disturbed. For me, it is nothing less than perfection.

No one would guess that I am a submissive woman, that I take pleasure in serving. After all, in most of my life I am the one giving the orders or, at the very least, taking charge. Perhaps that is why surrender calls to me. It is the path not taken, or perhaps it is the path that, as an American woman, I was taught was beneath me. Something to be avoided at all costs. Yet I would risk a lot to have this.

There is a transformation that comes over me in surrender. A softening of the hard intellect and practicality that is my usual way of being in the world. I love my yielding woman. I find her bewitching. My collar leads me to her.

My mind wanders to my last visit with him. We are in my hotel room and it's our last day together before we go back into our real lives. It will be many months before we're together again. We are not supposed to be sexually intimate today, that was the plan—to make going home easier. We are in my hotel room. I offer him a glass of wine. I don't want to transition. I am hungry for him. The heaviness of months without physical contact with him looms over me like a bad cold. I nestle into his body and implore him with my eyes. I take off the blue collar of stones. He reaches for our play collar. It's made of leather with one blue crystal dangling. This is a good sign.

Blue Flame asks me to kneel. He likes to start with me on my knees. I am asked to kiss my collar. He beckons me to lift my hair. I can feel his strong hands. They are the hands of a man that does things, and they feel steady as he places the leather around my neck. There is ritual to mark this time of my submission. He always pulls the collar very tight at first before he settles it into a comfortable snugness. This always startles me, almost as unexpected as me finding myself on my knees. Yet I hunger for this, as much as my hunger embarrasses me.

I feel so self-conscious every time I participate in this ritual. Imagine, me kneeling. Kissing his hands in gratitude for whatever they will offer me in these moments. My eagerness to do this even though I almost have to force myself to my knees is unyielding. The freedom I feel in this physical expression of giving myself to this man so wantonly, the pleasure of my submission, rushes my body like a river overflowing a dam. And at the same time, I know that this scene would make some feminist somewhere completely crazy. Women getting spanked and men loving to do it? It's scary for a lot of people. Miss Steele is not alone in her fear. It's not politically correct, but it's my desire. And that's where decades of feminism should have brought us—to every woman being able to speak and have her own true desire. And I was claiming mine.

For all the pockets of sexual freedom in which people can and do have their desires met, there are vast expanses where people live blunted lives because this deep, dark stuff must be relegated to porn or fiction or TV or freak shows. Why is that? Is it because we conflate BDSM with abuse? Unfortunately, it is even linked there in *Fifty Shades of Grey*—and that is where the book fell short for me. We are once again hiding desire and sexual instinct behind a veil. The story that somehow Christian became a dominant man because of abuse is so unfortunate in that it perpetuates the myth that BDSM is a psychological disorder.

But that is not my experience with men who dominate women and the women who enjoy surrendering to them. BDSM and abuse are not the same, and we can't intellectualize sexual desire away. Public discussion by "sensible" people inevitably harkens back to what a woman will put up with for "love" (especially if the guy is loaded and handsome with a buried broken heart just yearning to be held). I'm so sick of hearing that women do "this" to please their man, that they submit for love. They may. We do lots of things for love. But I think we hide behind "love" so we don't have to take responsibility for our desire, which may have nothing at all to do with gushy emotion and everything to do with raw sexual pleasure. That is Ana's story. It's not mine.

How about the fact that lots of women want to feel dominated because it feels good. Period. And I was now on my knees and loving it even if I was debating my right to be on my knees in that very moment with my unseen critics. In this place, my pleasure comes from serving this man.

We find our way to the bed. Perhaps I will get what I want after all. He is smiling, lying back on the pillows, sipping his wine. He beckons to me. I make my way to his arms and he holds me. I feel his kisses on the top of my head, his hands playing with my hair. Oh God it feels so good! My body is on fire in an instant. I begin to kiss his body through his clothing. Soon, they are more than kisses; I am trying to get to his flesh. I want him to want me. I use my teeth and gently bite through his clothes. I feel his body relax, and he puts the glass of wine down. I have his full attention as I pleasure his body. I can feel his hard-on pressing against his blue jeans. I somehow try to give him a blowjob through his clothes.

"Please," I ask softly. He knows what I am asking for. I am asking him to get undressed. He shakes his head no. I whine and moan softly. "Oh God...please?" He laughs at me.

"May I get naked, Sir?" I ask. He nods yes.

I pull off my clothing and rub my body against the coarse Levi's, locked down with a leather belt and silver buckle. He pulls me to sit astride him, as if I was making love to him. He looks at me with eyes that love and mock me. He loves my struggle to have him.

I know he wants me. I can feel his desire rock hard beneath me. His eyes never leave mine. And soon mine are full of tears.

"Please. Please. Please," I beg. He shakes his head no. "Don't you want me?" I weep.

"Yes, of course I want you. I want you just like this," he says.

I collapse for a while on his chest, sobbing. I hate him. I love him. Why is he doing this to me? I cannot believe that I just begged for a man to make love to me. It was incredibly humiliating and he was enjoying the show. I wanted to claw his face. Instead I allowed him to hold me, as I moaned, and kissed his body everywhere and tried to find release like a cat rubbing up against a tree. My pussy is burning, hot and wet. How could he not want me? How could he possibly leave me like this, I ask myself again and again.

Blue Flame's hands are mostly steady. He holds me as I tremble and he just asks for the same simple thing. He asks me to yield to him. To know that I am desired. His requests for me are to simply melt into that. Easier said than done. I can still feel the candle of my surrender fight against the flame with words and endless debate and pleading. Submission does not come easy for feminists with big lives and even bigger mouths.

His joy in my suffering is the only pleasure that I can find. And it is in the end the pleasure that I seek. He is a sadist, after all. But another wave of resistance bubbles up, even as I gently touch the pleasure. I want to pound his chest. I tell myself to stop. To yield. To surrender. I am the submissive, and he is the Dominant. He gets to call the shots. But I am used to the shots being called mostly around things that give me pleasure. Bend over? Sure! Where?

Canes always frighten me, but I am developing a taste for them because Blue Flame enjoys playing with them. I want his pleasure to be my pleasure. But can I find pleasure in my own sexual hunger? Can I surrender so deeply that I can find joy in my own pain if it pleases him? Can I allow myself to care about him like that? Apparently so.

Blue Flame has found ways to torture me that I never considered. It is humiliating to beg. To literally weep at his feet. In this moment, on the bed in this hotel room, he is asking me to yield everything to "his way" on the deepest of levels. He wants me to go home hungry.

The physical pain of wanting, and knowing that I will be wanting for a long time. The cruelty of that. The pain of not understanding the why of it. The knowledge that I am not supposed to be busy in my head with the why of it. That is not my business. That is not my concern. On the deepest of levels, I am simply to find my pleasure in the sadistic grin on his face while he enjoys my struggle and the same tears that I am shocked and humiliated by. My place is in the acceptance of it.

Was I really crying? Was I really pleading for him? It is unreal to me, now, away from him. I can remember his hands holding me, telling me that it was okay to cry. His desire was clear and stated again and again in so many ways. It is for me to find my pleasure in his pleasure. Sometimes that does include many orgasms for me without him taking a single one. Not this time.

This time his pleasure is so painful to me that even the memory of it rips my heart out. But in my memory his hands are right there to catch my heart and kiss it. He looks at me with his beautiful blue eyes and places my heart right back inside my chest. I can hear him right now, "Breathe, Pamela...breathe." I smile into our shared giggle of breathing into the hard stuff.

I receive praise with my burning, angry sexual desire. I receive praise with my spirit crumbling. He loves me with gentleness after he asks me to calm my sexual energy and put away my arousal, after a good long time of allowing me to raise it fruitlessly, sitting astride and naked on his dressed body as he smiles into my crying eyes and I buck like a wild mustang caught by ropes.

Reluctantly, I dress as he watches me. I kiss the fur on his chest with one more moment of hopeful expectation. But he takes off my play collar and replaces it with the necklace of stones. I want to kick him. And despite all of that I want to go deeper. I can't wait for next time. On some deep level I know that I am a moth that can't wait to fly into the flame again and again.

I remember feeling powerful in my body, as I knew that I met the challenges of the day. I felt submissive pride, and more...I felt a pleasure that was way more interesting to me than the orgasms that I was leaving behind. His pleasure was mine.

We go for a coffee.

We hold hands as we walk through shops. I buy dark purple flowers for him. They remind me of what my sex must look like, all filled with blood with no place to go. I give them to him. Let them sit on his table. A reminder of my desire left unfulfilled on our last day. Dark and beautiful. The pain of my surrender is beautiful in the petals.

It is morning, two or three days after my trip. I reach for the blue stones. My pretty little necklace that someone will admire today. My fingers touch the stones, and my hips open gently into the softest of surrenders that will guide me through my day. I think of Anastasia fleeing, and how I stay. Well, she is a girl who doesn't really understand her desires yet and shouts no as she flees from herself and her lover. I am a woman, and I whisper, "Yes, please, Sir. Thank you, Sir," as I learn to stay.

A pioneer in fertility advocacy, **PAMELA MADSEN** is the Founder and first Executive Director of The American Fertility Association. She is a fearless advocate for women's health and integrated sexuality who leverages her raw honesty and well-informed wit to help strip the stigma from infertility, female desire, and body image.

Pamela is a veteran speaker, educator, and renowned blogger for *Psychology Today*, *The Fertility Advocate*, and *Care2*. She is the author of *Shameless: How I Ditched the Diet, Got Naked, Found True Pleasure…and Somehow Got Home in Time to Cook Dinner* (Rodale, January 2011).

Pamela has appeared on *60 Minutes*, *Oprah*, *CNN*, *AARP Primetime Radio*, *The Dr. Laura Berman Show*, *The Jane Pratt Show*, and *Playboy Radio*.

To learn more about Pamela's Shameless Community, coaching, retreats, blogs, and her book, please visit www.beingshameless.com.

DR. KATHERINE RAMSLAND

Being Stretched
The Risks and Riches
of a "Limit-Experience"

*I*N *THE LITTLE PRINCE*, Antoine de Saint-Exupery writes about a pilot who is stranded in the desert with a defunct plane. A little man comes along who claims to be the prince of a different planet. As the pilot tinkers with the plane, the prince describes his journey. Time passes. The pilot grows increasingly afraid he might die out there. The prince dismisses his concern. He says that they need only go into the desert and find a well. The pilot thinks the prince is nuts. It's better to remain with the plane, he thinks. If he just keeps working on it, he will make it fly. But the prince has faith in the unknown. They must go, he insists. Only when the pilot realizes that his best efforts are futile does he reluctantly agree.

They trudge across the desert for some time, but find no well. The pilot's initial doubts grow into panic: *They should never have left the plane!* But just when he is certain they have made a fatal miscalculation, the prince discovers the well. It's all about risk and trust. Playing it safe was a dead end.

Anastasia Steele and Christian Grey both love this story. They appreciate the line, "There is a poetry of sailing as old as the world," and they probably noticed the book's central theme, that "anything that's essential is invisible to the eyes." Grey knows this from experience, whereas Ana's appreciation is literary. Thus, Grey is more willing to engage in "edgework," i.e., explore an arena that could strip him of control and thereby transform him. He recognizes that the alchemy of desire and uncertainty can tap a hidden well of vitality within him.

Ana, on the other hand, does not grasp this. She ventures beyond the plane, but never quite leaves it. This explains one aspect of the appeal of *Fifty Shades of Grey*. It explores the forbidden without risk. It's dark but safe.

However, the suggestion from Grey of greater gain from greater surrender offers the daring reader a jump-start, even as it affirms female power.

Edgework

Women of all ages are drawn to the Beauty and the Beast archetype found in the Fifty Shades trilogy, wherein the strength of a man's love is measured by his willingness to restrain his aggression. It's the ultimate female fantasy. Grey tells Ana that it's his "nature" to be controlling, but for her, he would fight the urge.

Grey's appeal is more than this, however. Grey has wealth, beauty, an impressive appendage, and a "Master of the Universe" aura. He's an alpha male, so when he defers to Ana, he serves her "inner goddess." Yet there is more to this picture than just the full attention of a devoted lover. Grey also asks something of Ana that forces her to ponder desires she has never before explored. He hopes she will consider stretching herself, literally, into his world.

As a virgin, Ana offers a clean slate on which to write an erotic agenda. She has no preconceived ideas about what will happen in a Dominant/submissive relationship, so a "Dom" can more easily mold her as a "sub." She tries a few bondage and discipline experiences, but ultimately she elects to stay safe. She does wonder why she can't "take a little pain for my man," but her "hard limits" prevent her from grasping what she's turning down. She doesn't trust enough to look for the invisible well.

Ana's point of view offers female readers a fantasy of empowerment and sensuality, but it's Grey who reveals a world in which pleasure beyond what we had imagined is possible. The Dom is the doorway through which we must step, and trust is the key that unlocks it. We must be willing to engage in a relationship that could involve things we fear. Thus, we face the "limit-experience."

A limit-experience, as the postmodern philosopher Michel Foucault expressed it, touches untamed energy that pushes our minds and bodies toward what feels like a breaking point. It's scary but can also be exhilarating. Its purpose is to erase boundaries between the conscious and subconscious, as a lifelong preparation for self-annihilation.

Well, this doesn't sound like much fun, and we can understand Ana's reticence about submitting. However, Grey attests to the power such experiences bring. He knows there's a life-giving well because he's drunk from it. "I found myself," says Grey in *Fifty Shades Freed*, "and found the strength to take charge of my life."

To achieve a limit-experience, we must push into unknown and seemingly dangerous terrain. We have to break with what's familiar and get free of self-imposed restrictions. The possibility exists for an ecstatic euphoria unlike anything we've ever known, but there's risk. The limit-experience gets us as close as possible to the extreme erotic intensity of life's negation without a total wipeout. It's the obliteration of a psychological orgasm.

The result of edgework is enhanced sensuality and greater self-determination. Foucault thought that S&M practices offered the best avenue for a limit-experience because the surrender to powerlessness forces personal redefinition.

Exquisite Agony

BDSM holds that the physical body has a secret wisdom that can be tapped only when pushed against its physical and emotional limits. Whatever makes one feel utterly, erotically alive is enabled within a safe framework. This might mean being tied up and blindfolded during sex, or being spanked or whipped, or being cemented into a tub (as one Dom told me about a sub). The goal is to transcend the sub's ego boundaries, to guide her into something larger. When her identity is reduced to the suffering body, it can provide such intense immediate pleasure that she feels effaced.

The Dom's role is pivotal. Doms must discern how the sub can reach this goal. In fact, superior Doms will have experienced the role of sub (as Grey did) and so can grasp the intricacies of the sub's fantasy. Because this experience involves exposing secrets, the relationship also acquires deeper intimacy. With the Dom's validation, the sub can throw off self-conscious restraint and pull out all the stops. She can simply feel—and *stretch*.

The most extreme form of BDSM is sadomasochism, which involves consensual violence...to a point. A person might wish to be burned, whipped, have a loaded pistol placed in his mouth, or be trussed so tight he can't move. The Dom inflicts pain and humiliation to help the sub reach emotional catharsis. This reportedly feels like a radical transformation into a sense of openness and full existence. However, not all BDSM participants will take it this far.

The Psychological Frame

So how does edgework actually work?

Both participants understand that mutual consent makes it happen, and they must choreograph the scenario together before they can fully play it out. However, once things are in motion, the memory of consent and design must recede.

The intense roleplaying produces an altered state of consciousness in which the sub feels forced. Under the auspices of having "no choice," she gains erotic benefits from the illusion of total surrender to the Dom's will. If she trusts that there is no risk of serious harm, she can agree to be dominated in unpredictable ways. This allows the anxious edginess of anticipation to produce the most intense stimulation. As Grey states in *Fifty Shades Darker*, "It's all about anticipation."

The idea of being pushed into something that one both fears and craves sparks a fierce tension that draws body and mind together in heightened arousal. Applying restrictions to the body in the form of bondage or discipline draws out its capacity for physical sensation. It's an absolute surrender to the full impact of the flesh. As the sub endures and emerges intact, he or she becomes stronger, wiser, and more self-aware.

This synergy of resistance and momentum can be highly exciting. Subs who yield as if they have no real choice are more pliable. With the Dom's guidance, they can break through and experience more.

What a Dom Says

I've interviewed several Doms and "Lady Ro" agreed to describe her work. "I have used branding, piercing, tattoos, and scarification," she said, "because these practices bring one to new heights of sensual and chemical awareness. It's all about direct manipulation of physicality and about how the brain responds to things like sensory deprivation."

Her preference is to leave subs unbound. "I don't like to tie them up, because then I have to serve them. I like willing subjects who want to stay there. If someone is submitting to me, then it's their willingness to stay that's a turn-on. I don't use safewords [phrases that would stop a ritual because it's gone further than the sub can bear]. I demand complete trust. I don't want to mess someone up and make them miserable. To me, it's more about sensuality. If they don't like it, what's the point?"

Their fantasies become her launching pad. "I try to get into their fantasy and make it my own. I don't just cater to their fantasy, I twist it. I try to find something that fascinates me about it."

Both partners in these arrangements have strengths and weaknesses, and both variously exploit and complement the other. To make the dance work, Lady Ro explains, they need each other. Thus, before anything begins, they must be explicit about the terms: what each desires and what each needs to feel satisfied and safe. If they operate in total trust they can achieve a delicate but edgy equality. The experience can be mystical when shrouded in a playful self-deception that allows each participant to fully engage in its erotic choreography.

Fifty Shades of Edgework

Grey goes over the BDSM rules because he wants Ana to understand her limits before trying to push past them. He reassures her every step of the way. When he is poised to take her virginity in *Fifty Shades of Grey*, he tells her, "You expand, too." He's saying much more than just a biological fact. He's telling her that he can move her into a new awareness, if only she trusts.

The narrative moves through a series of "firsts" for them both, and while Grey embraces the unknown (with more reason to fear it), Ana takes baby steps. She calls Grey's playroom the "Red Room of Pain" and compares it to the Spanish Inquisition. Thus, despite the pleasure Grey gives her, she sees only the negative. This is her safety mechanism, her form of a safeword.

Ana views this arena as Grey's world, not hers. A plain metaphor captures it: As she steps into the playroom for the first time in *Fifty Shades of Grey*, she notices a chest of drawers. She wonders what the drawers hold. She can't see what's inside and wonders, "Do I really want to know?"

Her reaction shows the caution of a generally fearful person (as does her distancing mechanism of sarcasm and defiance).

She is the pilot who stays with the plane. Despite Grey's constant assurance that he will not hurt her, she sees only the rules, not the door they open. She describes an impulse to run screaming from the room and talks about her constant trepidation. She believes this adventure is the "edge of a precipice" from which she must jump rather than a potential launching pad into greater power and perception. To her, edgework is too scary.

In her limited manner, Ana sees just two things: Grey is "dangerous" and he's wounded. She keeps telling herself that she's willing to enter his disturbing world so she can save him and show him what it means to love.

Ana is at the center of a narcissistic fantasy that she controls. She overthinks, which allows her to rationalize her surrender to BDSM as "saving" Mr. Grey. She doesn't make it to the limit-experience because she always finds a reason to pull back. Even when she's secretly disappointed that Grey does not want to install a playroom in their new home, she fails to fully own her desires. (She could have asked to have the room installed herself.) She prefers the safety of the self she knows (the plane) to the one she could become (the well).

Understandably, Ana's reticence confuses Grey. She seems to enjoy everything he does, yet she keeps him at a distance. He reveals things to her, despite his fear of being rejected, but she fails to move into this intimacy with him. Her safe harbor is not love, as she tells herself. It's her "thinking zone." She does not want to free-fall very far, not psychologically or emotionally.

Anything That's Essential Is Invisible

Women often hear that they are either "too this" or "not enough that." In other words, they aren't "just right." However, Ana frequently hears from Grey the words that women crave: she's perfect. She also receives the attention of a man who has carefully studied female sexual response. This removes the burden of having to explain what feels good and allows her, as the recipient, to just surrender. She also gets to feel powerful by bringing a wealthy, creative, and controlling man to his knees. She is Beauty to his Beast. However, if she were to dissolve this dichotomy in BDSM, she could experience him more fully and still be "just right."

By the end of the third book in the trilogy, Ana still hasn't entered this zone, although she's gone further in. She has the self-empowering fantasy of Beauty and the Beast, but she fails to transcend it. She's still stuck inside herself, which buffers her from the richest possible intimacy with Grey. To return to the love they share for *The Little Prince*, she *could* have so much more—she could fly *without* the plane.

Readers, however, have the benefit of not just soaking in Ana's fantasy but also of doing more with it. From Grey, they've learned about BDSM and the rewards of trust, so they can decide for themselves if they want to stay with their plane or go with the prince (Grey) to look for a well.

Note to Ana: Please reread *The Little Prince* with Grey so you can catch up to him. There *is* a poetry of sailing. Go for it.

DR. KATHERINE RAMSLAND has done journalistic searches for the limit-experience inside the vampire and BDSM subculture. The bestselling author of forty-two nonfiction books, two novels, and over one thousand articles, she teaches psychology at DeSales University in Pennsylvania and writes a blog, Shadow Boxing, for *Psychology Today*.

Whose Shades of Grey?

ERHAPS I SHOULD be embarrassed that, as a sex educator, erotic writer, BDSM enthusiast, professional Dominatrix, and lifestyle S/switch, I had absolutely no desire to read *Fifty Shades of Grey*. But I am not embarrassed. I could have gone my entire life without reading it and been perfectly happy. In fact, with my reading focused on biography or sex education and research these days, I haven't picked up a piece of fiction in ages. I was never one to read Harlequin romance novels anyway. My tastes in erotic literature were always decidedly more sophisticated. In fact, the one time I attempted to read a cheesy romance novel with Fabio on the cover, I was bored to tears and gave up. By contrast, classic erotica stimulated my thinking and allowed me to identify with the characters and experience physical satiation. I spent most of my teens exploring my sexuality through the works of Anaïs Nin, Henry Miller, Laura Antoniou, Anne Rice, and Pauline Réage. Later I discovered self-help material on sex and BDSM in the sexuality section of my local bookstore. Believe me, cheesy romances couldn't hold a candle to these authors and books.

While my curiosity toward *Fifty Shades of Grey* was limited, each time I read or heard a sex industry professional or BDSM practitioner reference the book, there was little that encouraged me to read it. I finally downloaded the book on a flight from Australia to the States and tried to approach the book with an open mind. I tried not to brace for the worst.

I regret to say that this book was perhaps the most daunting literary undertaking of my life. Not because of the poor, middle school style of writing. Not because of its poor example of a BDSM relationship that will mislead "vanilla" people about what kinky people and their relationships are like. I found *Fifty Shades* daunting because of heroine Anastasia Steele. Perhaps in my spoiled, black feminist bravado I failed to find Steele's weak-minded, overeager desire to please both her roommate and Christian Grey endearing. And her indecisiveness toward committing to Grey's desire for a relationship directly contradicts her undeniable interest in Grey and the tears she sheds over him along the way. Ana "tops from the bottom," and at the very worst she's nothing more than a tease.

Yes, I know women with poor self-esteem and limited life experience can be easily impressed by wealth, beauty, and charisma, and Anastasia Steele seems to be one of those women. But she also lives as a paradox, both impressed and appalled by it. She allows her wealthy best friend to dress her in her clothes, but refuses Christian Grey's desire to purchase some of the same for her because it would make her his "whore" or "mistress." She allows her best friend to manipulate her into actions that ultimately benefit only the roommate (e.g., interviewing Grey), but refuses any direction from Grey that might advance her personal and professional life. She is strong enough to tell Christian that his gifts of a new laptop and car are "on loan," but not strong enough to determine whether her gift of submission might be on loan as well.

Ana's failure to identify Christian's behavior as potentially dangerous (tracing her phone calls, acquiring both her home address and her mother's address) concerns me as well. It reads as a poor example for young women readers by normalizing stalking behaviors.

Christian Grey's stalker tendencies aside, I found Steele's constant babbling about his looks and her astonishment over his interest in her tiresome. She cannot seem to grasp hold of her self-worth long enough to determine why someone like Grey would desire her. Steele is painfully shy, uncoordinated, often unprepared, and lacks direction in her life. She is weak, suggestible, and her innermost thoughts read like a young teenager, not like a young woman graduating from college.

Worse, she is completely disconnected from her sexuality and desire almost to the point of being asexual. Her lack of sexual partners and sexual experience certainly doesn't qualify her as a partner for Grey; while Grey invites Steele down the rabbit hole without much guidance, I found Steele's willingness to explore questionable, given her lack of expertise with sex overall.

But what bothered me most was Steele's attempt to change Grey, to "bring him into the light" and out of the "darkness" of his sexual proclivities. It bothers me that Grey's sexual interests are brushed off as the result of both a difficult childhood and sexual abuse at the hands of a trusted family friend. By following this route, author E. L. James creates a platform for Ana to treat Christian's advances as a deviance. Ana never has the chance to use Christian's proclivities as a vehicle for welcomed mutual exploration. Given Ana's overall lack of experience and eagerness to please her new partner, I wonder why James made Steele a sexual prude when it comes to BDSM. If she was going to be so disagreeable about BDSM in general, why didn't she maintain that stance during all of Grey's queries?

I have met women who were willing to do whatever a man asked to make him happy, but when it comes to BDSM, you either get it or you don't. I found it quite unbelievable that Steele would dream and fantasize about Christian tying her up and flogging her—to the point of nocturnal emission—but then wince at the idea in her waking hours. In demonizing Christian's sexual desire, James makes him into a sexual predator and Anastasia Steele into his victim and a woman only trying to love an otherwise unlovable man.

I wish the book had taken a more open-minded approach toward BDSM and alternative sexual lifestyles. It paints its dominant practitioners as sexual deviants who prey on the weak and make victims of their submissives. Grey's childhood and his introduction to BDSM do nothing more than to offend the many people who choose BDSM as a lifestyle and are not the product of victimization. For me, it was like hearing people say all gay people were molested instead of being born that way.

The author misses quite a few other points with me as well. I could no more believe Anastasia had never, as a twenty-one-year-old, masturbated in her life than I believed she'd graduate college without a personal email address. I found it disgusting that Grey would introduce the idea of BDSM with Steele in the form of a limited-term contractual relationship. As he went through his checklist of potential activities, I waited patiently to read Ana asking him to show her the types of instrumentation mentioned on the list or take her to play parties to watch them being used on others. I hoped he would introduce her to people in the BDSM community (and not women he had previously had sexual relationships with) so she could ask questions about the lifestyle. Christian's inability to explain his penchant for BDSM was ridiculous—most people involved in a BDSM lifestyle can pinpoint why they have an inclination toward such play. They are usually insightful, articulate people.

I was disappointed that Grey never explains the differences between a submissive, a slave, and a bottom to Steele, and never gives her the opportunity to explore her sensual desire on her own terms.

What's more, Grey's lack of guidance in Ana's research frustrated me. She needed to discover whether she'd prefer maintaining play in the bedroom or extend it to all aspects of her life (as he initially requested). I cringed when Christian told Ana to start with Wikipedia when the website's not consistently reliable in its material. Especially when countless reliable sources do exist for the BDSM beginner.

Had James given careful thought and consideration into her book, she might have produced something truly helpful to curiosity seekers wanting to explore their Dominant and submissive fantasies. As it is, her book is a dangerous piece of fodder that has more potential to do harm than good. One can only hope that the film adaptation consults with people with real-world BDSM experience and sex-positive educators and discovers better ways to portray BDSM people and practices. Because one can then hope we'll see a movie in which a young woman doesn't sign away her life and become a sex slave to a wealthy man without the necessary life experience and careful negotiation.

SINNAMON LOVE is an adult film star, fetish model, professional Dominatrix, writer, radio personality, and single mom of three teenagers living in Brooklyn, New York. Since 1993, Love has appeared in over 250 hard-core movies and numerous men's magazines, and has made countless appearances on *Playboy TV* and *Playboy Radio*. In 2010, Sinnamon went on a yearlong tour with the Punany Poets (of HBO's *Real Sex* fame), a sex-positive erotic poetry and sex education theater show. She is a frequent guest on *Shade 45* on SiriusXM radio.

Love is currently a staff writer and relationship columnist for TheWellVersed.com. She was inducted into the

Urban X Awards' Hall of Fame in 2010, followed by induction into the AVN Hall of Fame in 2011. She is an outspoken Autism/Asperger parent advocate and has recently taken on improving sex education in inner-city schools.

Love can be heard on DTFRadio.com every Thursday night from midnight to 2:00 A.M. on her radio show, *Sex Love & Hip Hop*. *Sex Love & Hip Hop* is a relationship advice show featuring good music, well-known and underground hip hop artists, sex educators, adult stars, and everyday people discussing real topics for the urban demographic.

CHRISMARKS AND LIA LETO

A BDSM Couple's View

AS TWO PEOPLE who have individually and as a couple been involved with BDSM and D/s for many years, we find it encouraging that the Fifty Shades trilogy has become such a cultural phenomenon. E. L. James' books seem to have created an expanding space wherein the general public can participate in an evolving conversation about creative sexual dynamics.

Ironically, we met on a popular "vanilla" dating website. We each hinted in our profiles about our dark predilections, which were often overlooked by our prospective matches. Our initial emails revealed that we each desired a partner who sought a relationship involving Dominance and submission. In contrast to the trilogy's main characters, we brought to our relationship over twenty years of BDSM experiences between us.

Once we met it became evident that we shared incredible chemistry, and we soon fell in love. Three months later, I offered Lia my collar and we signed a contract acknowledging our devotion and commitment to our respective roles. For us, our relationship is an unfolding journey that nurtures our vanilla lives and allows us to explore our deepest passions and darkest desires.

About Chris: College educated and a professional in the marketing field for many years, I was aware of my interests in certain BDSM practices from a young age. Thinking that my interests were strange, I suppressed my desires for activities like spanking for most of my life, only trying out a little here and there. About fifteen years ago I became curious about flogging and bought my first flogger. Flogging is something that many readers of the trilogy have reacted to with horror, some even suggesting that it is abuse. I use leather suede floggers similar to the ones described in *Fifty Shades of Grey* to elicit a wide range of pleasurable sensations. I began attending classes in the BDSM community and learned how to use various toys and tools with care and skill. I now lead workshops to share what I have gleaned along the way with others seeking to explore this aspect of their natures.

About Lia: An overeducated alpha in the vanilla world, I identify as a bisexual Switch, meaning that I am as comfortable as a Dominant as I am as a submissive. Aware of this duality early in my life, I was as happy dominating others as I was fantasizing about being Wendy Darling, tied to Captain Hook's mizzenmast, at the mercy of the pirates. For most of my adult life, I have been dominant in my personal relationships. Ten years ago, I realized that in order to create balance in my life I needed to explore the depths of my submissive self, so I began the search for my ideal, worthy Dominant. In Chris, I have found a partner of remarkable honesty and power. I am honored to be his submissive. We are creating our journey as a couple in love by exploring a power-sharing relationship and sharing what we learn with others.

Our intentions and experience stand in sharp contrast to the characters in Fifty Shades. The BDSM scenes in the trilogy are fairly brief and do not reflect the forethought and preparation that we and many others in the community practice. We thought it would be useful to elaborate on how one of our scenes comes together and share our individual perspectives as Dominant and submissive as we prepare for and play out a scene. Chris will discuss how he envisions and plans a scene, stages it, and moves through it. Lia will discuss how she prepares her body and mind for the physical and psychological rigors she experiences during a scene.

Contemplation and Preparation

Chris: Lia and I share a wonderful vanilla sex life although I often physically dominate her by grabbing her hair and being more controlling in our lovemaking. We have a very dynamic range of sexy and loving behaviors that we bring to our intimate moments.

However, there are times when I plan for a more elaborate BDSM scene. These times are extra special, and I dedicate more time and energy to thinking about what elements of BDSM I will bring to our next encounter. I may purchase something special to make that happen. One day Lia commented about chains making fun sounds, so a few weeks later I purchased some metal chains, some locks, and cuffs, which I use to secure her to a St. Andrew's cross. As we previously negotiated our respective limits for play, Lia no longer has a say in what will happen to her. I have the control to make the scene follow my plan, and in this way I reinforce our Dominant and submissive roles.

Lia: From the moment I know that Chris and I will be having a scene together, a myriad of feelings and thoughts begin to swirl in me. On the practical side, there are certain rituals I practice in order to be fully prepared for whatever Chris may want to do with me. I ask him how he would like me to dress and then choose my attire carefully. For some scenes he insists that I am naked, which arouses me and sets my nerves on edge.

Sometimes he suggests a color scheme for my lingerie. Often he gives me permission to surprise him, which I love to do.

I consider the preparation of my body a crucial way to express my devotion and love for Chris. An hour or so before our scene, I undertake my ritual cleansing, shaving, and oiling. It is then, in the intimacy of the shower, that I feel all my senses rising in anticipation of what is to come. I take care to not let my hands linger on my tender parts, for they are for Chris' pleasure, and I know that they will undoubtedly receive intense attention during our scene. I dress with deliberateness. My pulse quickens ever so slightly as I put on my makeup and signature scent. Before I present myself to Chris, I check myself carefully in the mirror from all angles. Throughout my preparation I smile expectantly, wondering how Chris will test my limits and what new sensations I'll be experiencing at his hands.

Our Scene

Chris: One of our favorite scenes begins with my tying or chaining Lia to a St. Andrew's cross in preparation for a flogging. It may begin with her wearing some clothing, but frequently I will tell her to strip. Sometimes I will undress her. I use the former strategy to build tension and uncertainty, which of course also builds Lia's excitement. If my goal is to increase our romantic connection, I will undress Lia myself while gazing at her and caressing her body.

Once Lia is secured facing the cross, I check to see that she is relatively comfortable and, most of all, safe, making sure she does not have any restrictions that could end the scene prematurely. It will be my intention to hurt her but not to harm her. When I am feeling more romantic, I may begin with some kisses to her shoulders, whispering tender words, or sensuously caressing and teasing her. If I have begun the scene in a more brutish manner, I may be rough with Lia but will give her one or two loving touches to reassure her that I am caring for her.

I begin Lia's flogging by draping my matched set of floggers over her shoulders and letting the tips rest on her breasts. I watch as she leans her face into the leather to inhale their sweet, musky scent. I drag the floggers slowly toward me and trail them down her back. I caress her body softly several times with each flogger. This warm introduction often brings goose bumps to Lia's skin and even the occasional shudder. The sensuous dance of leather on skin begins. Starting slowly, I bring the floggers down on her body. I am focused on two things: where I land each blow and how she reacts to the impact. I watch to see if she flinches or tenses, stretches into the sensations or shies away from them. I can vary the blows, the timing between them, and the locations, changing the quality of the impacts by increasing the intensity, the rhythm, and the duration with which the floggers land on her skin. I render sharp stings by grazing Lia's body with just the tips of the flogger. Laying on more length of the leather results in heavy thud impacts. My ritual of flogging follows a pattern that is fairly traditional, with milder blows leading to heavier ones followed by a pause during which I reconnect with my lover before I begin again. With each pause I will do something soft and tender; I might trickle a feather-touch of my fingers from the nape of her neck down her spine, or offer an encouraging word or a kiss. In that moment I gauge Lia's breathing and ascertain how well she is experiencing the scene thus far. Each series of impacts brings forth a biochemical response in Lia's body, especially endorphins, which are her body's natural painkillers. By playing with the timing of each series of blows, I am able to effectively give Lia a natural high, which not only feels good to her but also makes it possible for her to accept more severe sensations with increasing pleasure. After twenty to forty minutes I will often switch to using either my long single tail whip or two of my Dragon's Tongue whips. I begin as gently as the whips allow. The sensations are sharp and sting Lia even when I am stroking her softly.

Watching Lia is a pleasure; she is my lovely goddess. I thrill to see her body respond to my floggers and whips. And then there are her sounds. Her whimpers make me smile as they remind me of the sounds she makes when we make love. Our dance, the dance of the Dominant and submissive, continues for an hour or more. I have never timed one of our scenes, as I am so focused on throwing my floggers and whips on Lia, on how she looks and reacts, and the wonderful sounds she makes. I lose all sense of time; I am deep in a state of flow; my intention and attention on Lia is palpable, my energy is loving and challenging and deeply committed to bringing her all manner of sensation and pleasure. In our scene, I am the conductor of the orchestra, the leading man, and the choreographer of a spontaneous ballet that builds to a glorious crescendo for us both.

Lia: The beginning of a scene sets the tone for our activities to come, and all my senses are on high alert. Chris will usually speak softly but firmly to me as he secures my body to a cross, table, or other equipment. With my arms and legs in ropes or chains, I realize that escape is futile and begin my dreamy descent into "subspace," a state of mental and physical being wherein my mind and body experience waves of release by way of a vast spectrum of hard and soft sensations.

Chris usually starts our scenes by flogging me. The gentle brushes of the long, leather strips against my back and shoulders at first feel like a soothing massage. I relax and sway to the rhythm of his strokes. He frequently stops to caress me, to kiss my face and my neck, and I feel his love in this attention. He continues the flogging, combining both hard and gentle impact on my back, buttocks, and legs, and I sense the heat rising in my skin. My muscles pulse with energy and I find myself craving equally the heavy thudding of Chris' floggers and the pillow softness of his kisses. When he steps away from me, I miss his breath on my back and gird myself in anticipation of the next round of blows.

Suddenly I writhe at the first crack of a sweet new pain as he uses one of his whips. And then another. Back and forth the blows rain, and I writhe uncontrollably beneath two whips. The pain slices and flares reliably, then dissipates, echoing throughout my body. From excruciation to relaxation, tides of intensity wash over me again and again. I can hear my blood pounding as it courses through my veins. My cries and whimpers erupt in counterpoint to the cracks of the whips and I am an instrument in the symphony of sounds around me.

Throughout it all, I feel Chris' laser-sharp focus on me. Once he has turned me around to face him, I suffer his lashing on my breasts, belly, and thighs. My eyes are riveted on him and I marvel at his artistry, in awe of the swirling arcs he creates with his whips. I want to please him; to outlast the pain of the stings, to make him proud of me. The intensity of the lashes rises and falls with my breath. Seconds could be minutes or hours, as I've lost all sense of time and place. When finally my legs quiver beneath me and my knees give way, Chris comes to me and embraces me. He kisses my face and my neck. He is smiling at me as he quickly frees me from my bonds and wraps me in his strong arms.

Aftercare

Our post-scene process of reconnecting is very important to us. In the afterglow of our shared delight, we admire the resulting marks on Lia's skin, both of us pleased that the crimson evidence of our play will remain on her for several days. Reveling in a natural high that will last for hours, we snuggle and share our feelings about the scene and our love for each other.

Our Hopes

We are grateful for the opportunity to contribute to the national conversation sparked by the trilogy. The current mainstreaming of BDSM sexuality encourages us that the general public's curiosity will lead to greater acceptance of alternative styles of loving. While Fifty Shades is arguably not great literature or even great BDSM, it does feature several aspects of BDSM that are important: consent, negotiation, and BDSM as components of a caring and loving relationship.

We feel blessed to have found in each other a partner that honors and nurtures all the aspects of our lives: the professional, the mundane, and the intimate. We hope that those who enjoyed reading Fifty Shades are equally blessed and inspired to find fun and creative ways to live and love.

CHRISMARKS is a self-described Sensual Sadist. He teaches BDSM workshops for his private educational group, Black N Blue U., as well as for other regional organizations and national BDSM conventions on various topics including: BDSM ethics, limits, and safety; massage techniques; spanking; flogging; short whips; and his newest workshop, "Kissing for Maximum Erotic Effect." ChrisMarks is pursuing a path to a master's degree in counseling, is an ordained Non-Dominational Minister, and his interests include the intersection of BDSM with psychology, spirituality, and disability issues. He runs Black N Blue Trading and is a designer and manufacturer of whips and floggers. He also has over twenty years experience as a trained massage therapist. In his free time ChrisMarks serves on the Board of Directors of the Community-Academic Consortium for Research on Alternative Sexuality (www.CARASresearch.org).

LIA LETO has been an active participant in BDSM sexuality for over twenty years. She is submissive to her partner although dominant in the rest of her life where she is a college professor, a novelist, and the founder of a non-profit serving survivors of sexual and domestic violence. Lia earned a master's in ethics and world religions and a Juris Doctorate. She has worked as a judicial law clerk, as first assistant to a district attorney bureau chief, and as a researcher for leading ethics and legal scholars. For over two decades she has taught group and private fitness classes in strength, flexibility, and self-defense at top health clubs, universities, and corporations nationally. Lia enjoys copresenting workshops regionally with her partner. She is also an experienced bodyworker—a fact her Dominant, ChrisMarks, really loves.

SUSAN WRIGHT

Fifty Shades
of Sexual Freedom

IFTY SHADES OF GREY combines three of my favorite things: it's a romance novel with kinky sex that caught the attention of the media. I've been tracking the media coverage of alternative sexuality since 1997, when I started the National Coalition for Sexual Freedom, working to de-stigmatize BDSM and helping people who have been hurt by the negative stereotypes associated with kinky sex.

Suddenly now everyone is talking about BDSM because of *Fifty Shades of Grey*. Reviewers typically describe the book like this: "Ana is a young woman who signs a contract with the wealthy Grey, who controls everything from when she exercises to what she eats." But that's not true—Ana never signs the contract. It's simply introduced as the first step of the extended dance they do with each other.

Much of the tension in the book is created by the characters' desire for each other without a desire for the kind of relationship the other wants. Grey wants a formalized relationship where each person maintains a certain role in their power exchange, while Ana wants a "hearts and flowers" romantic relationship. They set hard limits for themselves while also compromising and doing certain things to fulfill each other's needs. That's what makes it so hot. A couple talking to each other about their deepest desires? Who doesn't want more of that?

That's why so many women are responding so enthusiastically. There *is* a way to get the amazing sex you want, and it actually involves talking about it. One of the easiest ways to get that conversation going is to show your sex partner a book and say, "Hey, check out this scene." That way you don't have to say, "I'd like to try bondage and a blindfold tonight, dear." Instead you can indicate interest in the activity through the characters, and that way if your partner dismisses the idea, it's not you personally they're rejecting.

We've been led to believe for too long that great sex happens magically. That there's no need to tell your partner what you really want because, if you're really meant to be together, somehow they'll already know.

But in *Fifty Shades*, instead of the spontaneous, rock-your-world sex that you get from typical romance novels, Ana and Christian email, text, and talk about what kind of sex they want. Neither expects the other to be a mind reader. *Fifty Shades Darker* begins with Christian asking Ana why she didn't use her safeword if she didn't like the intense spanking he was giving her. He points out that he can't trust her if she won't communicate with him. That's why they talk after each scene to make sure they both understand how the other felt about what happened.

These characters explore their feelings and desires with each other in a way that is very typical of real kinky people. When you're playing sex games, you have to lay out the rules and set the boundaries together in order to be on the same playing field. Playing with power and intense sensations, as you do in BDSM, requires trust, communication, and honesty, and that creates true intimacy. From there, you can go anywhere together.

Unfortunately talking about sex makes many people uncomfortable. We aren't taught how to talk about sex, so when anyone tries to speak up publicly, they usually get shushed. Consider the fact that *Fifty Shades of Grey* was banned from libraries in several counties in America. Other romance novels—notably the paranormal romances written by Laurel K. Hamilton and J.R. Ward—include graphic kinky sex. So why was *Fifty Shades* treated differently?

The content of *Fifty Shades* didn't get it banned; its reputation got it banned. *Fifty Shades* has gotten the mainstream media trumpeting about BDSM in an unprecedented way, so social conservatives have made their own statement by refusing to acknowledge the book despite the big demand for it. Libraries should encourage more reading—yet when it comes to sex, politics triumphs over good sense once again.

A few people, like Dr. Drew Pinsky, question this sudden public interest in Domination and submission, and fear where it will lead. They claim BDSM is "violence" (which it's not) and people must be protected from it—even though everyone in America is free to skydive, rock climb, and play football, all of which cause far more physical harm than BDSM.

The people who don't get BDSM want to know *why* we do it. They figure it must come from some kind of cultural imprinting of the patriarchy or be a rebellion against the pressures of work and family or even some kind of emotional or mental health issue. There are fears that women, in particular submissive women, who enjoy BDSM are suffering from self-hate or insecurity, or are victims of abuse.

In actuality, some people are just hardwired for more intensity with their sex, whether that intensity is emotional, mental, or physical. We take the symbols that exist around us and use them to heighten our erotic response. And coincidentally, by working with your partner to get to these more intense places, you build an incredible trust and acceptance that goes beyond the mere physical.

Some people will never want to surrender themselves sexually, and some people will never want to dominate another person sexually, but a significant number of people do enjoy BDSM. We shouldn't be shamed or told our choices aren't contributing to the enlightenment of humanity. Sex is a powerful drive and ignoring or subverting it throws everything else out of whack. It's hard to be a powerful person when you're busy denying who you are.

So why is kinky sex still taboo? The persecution is so pervasive that I conducted two surveys in cooperation with the National Coalition for Sexual Freedom (www.ncsfreedom.org) to find out exactly how widespread it was. We had 1,000 respondents in 1998 and 3,000 in 2008 and found that one in three kinky people have been attacked or discriminated against because of their sexuality. Some people lose their jobs because of their sexual behavior in their private lives; others lose custody of their kids. Some people are shunned by their family and friends because they're having kinky sex with consenting adults. Others have been shamed by their doctors and their therapists.

Even law enforcement officials have discriminated against BDSM practitioners, prompting 90 percent of the respondents who reported they had been the victim of persecution to *not* report the crime for fear of additional persecution. As one survey respondent said, "I was sexually assaulted and because I was engaged in SM, my claim was not taken seriously and I was blamed for the incident. In the SM community, 'no' still means 'no.' People do not understand that."

Kinky people are caught in a catch-22: sex sells, so we are saturated with sexual images in the media, yet our roots in the Puritan culture lead to sexual repression. We have a tendency to judge other people to determine if they're doing right or wrong according to our own personal choices. Some religious political extremists have a self-righteous belief that theirs is the only true way to live. Those people work very hard to stop BDSM educational and social groups, to shut down events and prevent other adults from accessing one of the few places where you can safely explore your sexuality.

And yes, this kind of discrimination is also proof that we are living in a patriarchal society, one that is accustomed to controlling sexuality, usually women's sexuality, most recently demonstrated in the fight around reproductive health rights. Men are allowed more sexual freedom—unless you're a gay or bisexual man, in which case you're fair game for any kind of abuse.

But when it comes right down to it, as long as your sexual behavior involves consenting adults, how you express your sexuality is nobody else's business. We need to grow up and be responsible about our own sexual choices, and this national discussion is a good step. Anything that gets people talking about sex—not just sensationalizing it or making fun of it—is a good thing for Americans. We can see from the reaction to *Fifty Shades of Grey* that people are eager to explore their sexuality.

This may be BDSM's Stonewall, our breakthrough to the mainstream and greater understanding. Who would have thought it would take Twilight fanfiction to get us here?

SUSAN WRIGHT has published over thirty novels and nonfiction books on art and popular culture. Susan is the spokesperson for the National Coalition for Sexual Freedom, which she founded in 1997, and has published articles and presented workshops at professional organizations and universities on discrimination against kinky people, BDSM versus abuse, and media influence on the persecution of alternative sexuality.

Fifty
Shades of
Writing

RYAN FIELD

The Delicate Balance

*T*HERE'S AN INTERESTING STORY behind how I discovered *Fifty Shades of Grey*. It wasn't at a pool party, like the one I attended a few weeks ago where *Fifty Shades* was the topic of conversation among half the guests during dinner. It wasn't at the supermarket, where I ran into someone who was reading *Fifty Shades* and asked me if I'd read it because he knows I write erotic fiction. And it wasn't at a graduation, where some of the guests were whispering and giggling about this new steamy book on all the bestseller lists.

I actually found *Fifty Shades* while perusing the internet about two or three months before it went mainstream. There's this one book review blog I frequent often, because I usually find that the negative book reviews they publish are almost always books I know I'm going to love. It never fails. On that particular night, there was an extremely scathing book review for *Fifty Shades* written by a serious BDSM reader and I knew immediately I had to buy and read it. Practically every single negative comment in that review was something I knew would keep me reading. So I went to Amazon, downloaded it to my e-reader, and found myself drawn into the story line the moment I started reading. This happened back in February 2012. At the time there were a handful of Amazon reviews for *Fifty Shades*. Last time I checked there were now over 8,000.

As a published author of gay erotic romance and erotica, I'm not as familiar with the BDSM subgenre as I am with others. Although I'd written truncated stories with light BDSM scenes that I'd worked into less complicated plots over the years, I'd never actually written a full-length novel where the love, emotion, and erotica revolved around a BDSM theme or "lifestyle." It was *Fifty Shades* that inspired me to do this. And not because it was a huge bestseller; I read *Fifty Shades* and posted about it on my website months before it went mainstream. *Fifty Shades* inspired me because BDSM was a topic that I'd kept at a distance for too long, partly because I didn't feel comfortable writing about it and partly because I wasn't certain I could do it justice.

When I finally decided to try, in a full-length BDSM novel titled *Jonah Sweet of Delancey Street*, I set a few personal goals—including avoiding the same mistakes BDSM readers thought *Fifty Shades* had made. Those who are avid writers and readers in the BDSM genre take it very seriously. From what I read in various reviews about *Fifty Shades*, many in the BDSM community seemed to think essential elements of the "lifestyle" were not included in the book. Ironically, I also think this is why so many in the mainstream who knew nothing about BDSM loved the book and made it a huge success. They were all curious about BDSM, in the same way I was when I first heard about it, but didn't know enough about the "lifestyle" to see any flaws.

By listening to readers and other writers who have very strong opinions about BDSM erotica and erotic romance, I learned more about the important elements they felt *Fifty Shades of Grey* lacked. While I don't believe there are too many mistakes one can make in writing BDSM fiction, because it's hard to find a set definition of BDSM anywhere, I do believe there are a few key elements that are essential to BDSM fiction, which readers come to expect. And yet I still couldn't understand why the serious BDSM readers were so upset about *Fifty Shades*. As an amateur, I didn't see any problems with the book, and from reviews I've read and comments I've heard, neither do most other amateurs.

I needed more information for my novel, and I needed to dig deeper to find out why there were so many differing opinions about what was required in a BDSM novel and what this all meant to *Fifty Shades*. So I asked questions both of people who were and weren't serious BDSM readers. Almost every single avid reader of BDSM I spoke to during my research mentioned one element I found fascinating: the delicate balance between what happens during erotic BDSM scenes and what happens during non-erotic scenes.

It's not the only element BDSM readers look for, not by any means. Serious BDSM readers tend to be extremely articulate and they know what they want. But this one element was important to all of them, with respect to character development and how the BDSM moved the story forward. In erotic romance where there is BDSM and love is the focus, some even said they believe this element moves the *love* in the story forward. And it adds to the trust and respect that are both necessary to all BDSM stories, long or short.

I knew I had to be careful with my own story; it worried me for a while, to the point where I almost didn't tackle the project. What had inspired me so innocently with *Fifty Shades* might also hurt me with my own book. I might not be equipped to write BDSM material convincingly, and I knew my audience would lean more toward serious BDSM readers than the average mainstream reader who knew nothing about BDSM (though I wasn't opposed to attracting mainstream readers who weren't experts on BDSM in the same way *Fifty Shades* attracted so many readers). I knew I had to balance the important erotic BDSM aspects with the equally important psychological and emotional elements in non-erotic scenes. As significant as the distinctly defined roles of the submissive and Dominant are to all BDSM books in erotic scenes, it was just as significant for characters in BDSM books to find an emotional balance in non-erotic scenes if the love or the relationship was going to endure.

Another factor that seemed to be important to serious BDSM readers was that the characters had to be open and willing to try the "lifestyle." In other words, the character has to want to do it from the very beginning and not be forced or coerced into doing it. I found that most serious BDSM readers didn't think this happened in *Fifty Shades*. In fact, I heard from more than one reader that the *only* issue they had with *Fifty Shades* was the fact that Anastasia was not interested in BDSM and Christian was. As a novice reading the book, this aspect of *Fifty Shades* was not a problem for me. I'll even admit openly that I found it compelling and intriguing. I was reading *Fifty Shades* for escapism and entertainment. And I could understand why it would *not* be a problem for all the mainstream readers who were captured by the story line. In the same respect, the more research I did, the more I could understand how it would frustrate serious BDSM readers.

In a general sense, I learned that most BDSM readers aren't fond of weak, lackluster sub characters in non-erotic scenes. Like most readers in any genre, they hate dumb characters altogether. And many considered Anastasia to be both dumb and weak. They don't mind gentle, sensitive characters. And they don't mind quirky fundamental flaws. But weakness and being a submissive in a BDSM novel do *not* go hand in hand. More than that, being Dominant doesn't necessarily mean a character is stronger in an emotional sense in non-erotic scenes than a submissive character. I've heard some say they prefer it when the Dom has certain vulnerabilities in non-erotic scenes.

This is where I learned that the complicated balancing act between what happens during erotic D/s scenes and non-erotic scenes begins. The Dom character can be emotionally vulnerable, with more than one hidden insecurity, and carrying a great deal of baggage. The mask of dominance and the desire to inflict pain he or she possesses, and the need to control everyone and every single situation, could be nothing more than a façade to keep the world from knowing the harsh truth—that the character has deep insecurities. But he or she can't be too aggressive in non-erotic scenes. And he or she definitely cannot be a sexist or misogynist. On the other hand, if the sub character comes off as weak and pathetic in non-erotic scenes it can be just as obnoxious as having the Dom be too aggressive.

This balance-of-power aspect in BDSM books can be deceiving for readers and writers who aren't familiar with BDSM erotica. It was for me in the beginning. New readers often have the preconceived notion that the Dom character will be controlling in all aspects of the relationship and that the sub will always be nothing more than a doormat who carries with him or her psychological issues from the past that have made him or her a sub. Those readers familiar with BDSM find this mindset condescending at best and insulting at worst. Some would even go on to say that those into the "lifestyle" in real life don't have any baggage; they just like BDSM. Period.

No one could argue the point that in a D/s situation during a BDSM scene the sub releases all power to the Dom, allowing the Dom full control. If the sub is inexperienced, it's the Dom's job to use good judgment and keep things from getting out of hand. The stronger the Dom is, and the more the sub trusts the Dom, the more intense the scene will be. By relinquishing all power to the Dom the sub finally experiences the emotional intensity that can't be found anywhere else. But all that should end as soon as they both get off.

The separation between what happens to the characters during the D/s scenes and what happens while they are functioning in non-D/s scenes becomes a crucial element in the plot and in the depth of the characters' relationship. In my book I decided to make the Dom an aggressive, controlling individual who came close to being a narcissistic sociopath. He didn't cross the line, but he always seemed to be on the verge. The reason he didn't cross the line is because the sub in my book wouldn't let him. My sub wouldn't be controlled outside the sex scenes.

The sub in my book was the gentle, sensitive type who tended to trust people more than he should have. He also had a secret yearning for the "lifestyle" and didn't have to be talked into doing BDSM. It would have been simple to make him a doormat in all aspects of his life. But that's not how it works with most subs in real life. I gave my sub an inner strength that some might even say meant he had a stronger personality than the Dom. He also had a way of taking control of the relationship without trying too hard when they weren't involved in the BDSM scenes. And when faced with situations that didn't involve the erotic BDSM aspects of their relationship, my sub made it clear from the beginning that my Dom would not control him in every aspect of the relationship. I ultimately found this brought the story to another level, even though it wasn't exactly what I read in *Fifty Shades*.

What did all my research with BDSM mean for *Fifty Shades*? The basics I loved most in *Fifty Shades*, and what millions of other readers seemed to love, too, weren't elements that worked well with people who are serious readers of BDSM. It took me a while to figure that out and to fully comprehend why they didn't work. But I think it's vitally important to understand that this is not in any way a bad thing. Writers in any subgenre are always trying to attract a new audience that isn't familiar with that subgenre. No one can say that *Fifty Shades* didn't break that proverbial glass ceiling for BDSM writers by introducing BDSM into the mainstream. It's opened doors for other BDSM writers that have been nailed shut for years. It shows that writing BDSM fiction covers a great deal of territory and sometimes books focus on one element over others. And I would venture to guess that if *Fifty Shades* had followed more of the guidelines that serious BDSM readers and writers follow, it might not have become as popular in the mainstream as it is now.

RYAN FIELD is a gay fiction writer who has worked in many areas of publishing for the past twenty years. He's the author of the bestselling Virgin Billionaire series and the short gender-bending story "Down the Basement," which was included in the Lambda Award–winning anthology *Best Gay Erotica 2009*. You can check out his website at www.ryan-field.blogspot.com.

Was It Good for You?

O, WAS IT?

There's not much point discussing whether *Fifty Shades of Grey*, which has sold 40 million copies and climbing, is a good book. Reviewers and critics have been merciless in their assessment, deriding the story as implausible, the characters as one-dimensional, and the style as laughable. At the age of twenty-one, the beautiful heroine, Anastasia Steele, has never dated, has never even been attracted to anyone, has never felt the faintest frisson of sexuality—until she meets billionaire Christian Grey, described as "heart-stoppingly beautiful," a man who likes to take control. The first time she's in bed with him, she comes three times. Ana is young and pliant, up to a point; Christian is psychologically wounded, which has left him with a need to control women and a fondness for inflicting pain. He does not like to be touched, she does not want to be beaten—and they are in love. Will he let her stroke him? Will she let him beat her? These are the book's great questions. Ana proclaims, "I know it will take an eternity to expunge the feel of his arms around me and his wonderful fragrance from my brain."

Sentences like this haven't slowed sales one click. Some claim that the Fifty Shades phenomenon is partly explained by the growing popularity of electronic reading devices. Without a cover to reveal what we are reading on our Kindles or Nooks, we are free to pursue sexually explicit books in virtual anonymity. But the new electronic secrecy could lead us to read classic (and classy) erotica, books like *Fanny Hill, Story of O,* and *The Image.* Instead, we are sinking deep (or sinking shallow) into the Fifty Shades trilogy. Why is that?

For one thing, in erotic fiction, as in all genres, there is a need for contemporary material. Fiction helps tell us how people live; contemporary fiction tells us how we live now, which is why, despite the great writers of the past, we always need new authors. Today's writers chronicle our society, our anxieties, our joys. *Story of O* is still a highly charged book, but it was written before AIDS, and condoms were not a part of the picture. They're certainly part of the scene today, and part of Fifty Shades. Condoms are probably mentioned fifty times in the first book alone! The book's very zeitgeist is contemporary, with an unabashed worship of wealth. Christian's Red Room of Pain is notable for its luxury as well as its bondage devices. Readers of the Fifty Shades trilogy are titillated by scenes of dominance and submission and fabulous wealth. They read on to learn just how much the lovers will submit to each other. Then they recommend the book to their friends.

Why is that? Not for the plot, not for the characters, not for the style: women read *Fifty Shades of Grey* for that timeless erotic situation—the man urging the woman to go further; the woman slowly submitting—in a contemporary setting. And people also read it for the sex scenes. So, it is valid to ask (indeed, absurd *not* to ask): How good are those sex scenes?

A good sex scene contains enough erotic detail and pacing and originality to get us excited, which is sufficient for pornography but not for fiction. Beyond being arousing, the sex scenes in mainstream novels and short stories must offer more.

Here it must be acknowledged that the line between pornography and mainstream fiction is sometimes difficult to draw. Women often need story and setting and emotion to get excited, so those elements are featured in pornographic novels for women, making them more like non-erotic fiction. And non-erotic fiction for women is often sexually explicit, because many serious women writers are bold about sex.

How do we even judge sex scenes in fiction? Novelist and critic Elizabeth Benedict offers some guidelines. Her lively, well-informed book, *The Joy of Writing Sex,* published in 2002, examines the question of what makes a good sex scene, and Benedict offers instructive criteria.

Let us use these to evaluate a single representative erotic encounter in E. L. James' *Fifty Shades of Grey.*

First, the scene. At three pages, it's shorter than most of the sex scenes in the book, but just as explicit. It occurs about halfway through the book (starting on page 273 in my paperback edition). Grey is in Anastasia's apartment. They are alone; her roommate, Kate, is conveniently away. On the threat of being punished, Grey warns Ana not to roll her eyes at him, but she rolls her eyes saucily anyway. "Come here," he says. "I told you what I'd do. I'm a man of my word. I'm going to spank you, and then I'm going to fuck you very quick and very hard. Looks like we'll need that condom after all." He makes a grab, "tipping me across his lap... very slowly he pulls down my sweatpants. Oh, how demeaning is this? Demeaning and scary and hot." Grey proceeds to give her a spanking, alternating his blows with fondling and caressing. "My body is singing, singing from his merciless assault." Then he takes her from behind, slamming against her sore backside. After they come, he breathes, "Oh, baby. Welcome to my world."

According to Elizabeth Benedict, a good sex scene:

1) is not always about good sex but is always an example of good writing;
2) should always connect to the larger concerns of the work;
3) is driven by the needs, impulses, and histories of the characters;
4) depends upon the relationship the characters have with each other.

So how does this scene rate?

1) E. L. James is not a graceful writer nor a keen observer nor an original thinker. The scene includes the lines: "My insides practically contort with potent, needy, liquid, desire" and, "The feeling is beyond exquisite, raw, and debasing and mind-blowing." Although these pages are not always clumsy, no one would claim they were "an example of good writing."
2) The book is about control. Christian Grey is looking for a good submissive. In allowing him to spank her, Anastasia finds unexpected "radiance" when she gives him the control he craves. The scene not only connects with "the larger concerns of the work," it embodies them.
3) For weeks Christian has been exploring Anastasia's sexuality and urging her into greater and greater submission. His deprived early childhood and his adolescent introduction to sex by an older "Mrs. Robinson" have shaped his psyche, and he has a great drive to dominate women. His need to spank Ana comes from a deep place, as does her excitement at being spanked. The scene is certainly driven by the characters.
4) Sex can make lovers grow closer, and in this scene it does. Grey has been begging Ana to sign a contract making their relationship explicit, but she keeps postponing it. By letting him spank her, she is showing her love for him, just as he shows his for her by the gift of an Audi. Spanking

Ana, and knowing she enjoys it, Grey exultantly cries, "Welcome to my world." The scene utterly depends upon "the relationship the characters have with each other."

So in three out of four of Benedict's criteria, the sex scene discussed here succeeds. It feels essential to the growing closeness of these two rather improbable characters and leads us to the next stage of Ana's submission. Perhaps the secret to the success of *Fifty Shades of Grey* is simple. Whatever else E. L. James does or doesn't do, she knows how to write a good sex scene.

Anyway, it was good for me.

CATHERINE HILLER is the author of five novels, most recently *Cybill in Between* (Ravenous Romance) and *The Adventures of Sid Sawyer* (Armadillo Central). She has also written a book of erotic short stories, *Skin* (Carroll & Graf), which was praised by John Updike. She has a PhD in English from Brown.

The Story Is in the Sex

O N THE SURFACE, *Fifty Shades of Grey* is about the struggle between Ana's desire for emotional intimacy ("more") with Christian, and his desire for the security and distant that he gets from dominating his partners. Ana sees Christian's need for control as being the opposite of her desire for love. He is "in the dark"; she wants to bring him "into the light." To Ana, "dark" means sad, angry, controlling, emotionally distant, while "light" represents love, happiness, and interdependency. But Ana is in for a big surprise: Christian isn't the only one with a dark side. Ana, who is so innocent at the beginning of the story that she has never even masturbated, is completely unaware of her sexual self. She insists that she isn't submissive and doesn't enjoy sexual bondage or pain, but her thoughts and reactions during sex tell us a different story. The battle between "light" and "dark" takes place within Ana herself as she is forced to confront and finally embrace the "dark, carnal place" within her own psyche.

Although Ana and Christian spend a lot of time talking about sex, including contracts, hard and soft limits, and "debasement," they don't get physical until chapter 8. Because Ana is a virgin who has never had an orgasm, this is her introduction to sexual pleasure of any kind. In spite of Christian's claim that he doesn't "make love" but "fucks hard," he takes things pretty slow with Ana. Sure, it's hot, but compared to what they've discussed so far, it's pretty tame. Christian even follows the stepwise progression that we all know from the baseball metaphor. They've already kissed, in the elevator, so he started out with a single. He fondles her breasts (second base), stimulates her clitoris (third base), and they have intercourse (score for Christian!). Hell, the first time they do it is in the missionary position, which is about as "vanilla" as one can get. The second time he takes her from behind, which is a little more adventurous but hardly the kink he threatened (promised?) earlier. He then surprises them both by sleeping with her, something he has never done with any of his previous partners.

Ana clearly enjoys sex with Christian (who wouldn't?) but has trouble letting go and giving herself over to what she feels. She tries to keep her breathing "under control," but the sensations Christian provokes are "disordered, chaotic." Her thoughts continue on a similar path through the early scenes (chapters 8 through 12). Her words give the impression that she is not acting but reacting, not experiencing but observing something happening outside herself. Everything is described in the third person, like someone else is in control: "my breasts press into his hands" (instead of "*I* press my breasts into his hands"), "my body resonates," "my body writhes."

The next day Christian ups the ante sexually, introducing Ana to light bondage with the infamous gray silk tie. When he brings her to orgasm while her hands are bound, she is not only out of control physically, but emotionally and mentally as well, losing "all sense of self" and "all cogent thought." Christian restrains Ana again after she sends him an email saying, "Okay,

I've seen enough." This time he not only binds her hands but also loops the tie through her bedpost so she can't even touch him. Here, Ana seems to be losing the struggle for control for her own body: "I fight my body as it tries to arch in response," "My hips flex automatically," "my body bucks beneath his expert fingers," "I'm helpless, lost in an erotic torment."

What Ana *Really* Wants

For the first third of the book, Ana is relatively passive in the sexual scenes. Not because she's supposed to be submissive (she's not very good at that), but because she's just too inexperienced to know what she wants. In fact, she's so sexually clueless that she can't even recognize that the sensations and emotions she feels during sex are reflections of *her own* sexual needs, not just reactions provoked by Christian's expertise. But this starts to change in chapter 14. While Ana's not yet fully aware of what she wants, her subconscious starts to make its desires known— like a taste for "kinky fuckery" like bondage and submission, in spite of what she claims.

How do we know this is Ana's desire and not just something she's willing to do to please Christian? She *dreams* about it. In her dream, Christian brings her to orgasm with a riding crop while she is completely restrained. Although Christian is the actor here, it's Ana's fantasy. Or maybe her subconscious has really come out to play. In her sleep, Ana can't hide from her desires, she can't distance herself from what she wants—and what she wants to do is *submit*, to be at Christian's mercy while he pleasures her with the kinds of toys she has seen in his playroom. After being introduced to sex by a master, Ana's sexual self is emerging—and it is *kinky!*

If the earlier scenes revealed Ana's desire for submission, the spanking scene (chapter 16) starts exploring the sexual possibilities of pain and punishment. She is ambivalent at first and the feeling of being out of control returns. She's clearly confused by her reactions, describing the spanking as "demeaning and scary and hot." Again, she distances herself: he "makes" her feel this way and she's unwilling to take responsibility for what she feels: "my traitorous body explodes in an intense, body-shattering orgasm."

Ana embraces the pain-pleasure of spanking when she and Christian play with the Ben Wa balls. In that scene, Christian pushes her to *ask* him for the spanking, demanding that she recognize that she wants it as well. She acknowledges her feelings when she says, "I'm lost in a quagmire of sensation" and admits that the pain is not only "manageable," but "yes, pleasurable."

Ana starts to embrace her own desires, which in turn helps Christian become the partner she needs. When she submits to him sexually, Christian is able to relax his need for total control outside the bedroom and emotional intimacy develops between them. Ironically, as Ana gives over control to Christian in bed, she *stops* describing her feelings and reactions as being out of control or overwhelming.

Ana has come a long way from the inexperienced girl who fell to her knees in Christian's office. When they have sex on Christian's desk (chapter 21), *Ana* is the aggressor. She is no longer the naïve girl who believed that love was only "hearts and flowers": "This is not making love, this is fucking—and I love it." She can acknowledge her own feelings and desire—not just love but *lust*: "It's so raw, so carnal, making me so wanton. I revel in his possession, his lust slaking mine."

Ana Embraces the Dark

The two sex scenes that take place in the hotel in Georgia show how far Ana has come. First, Christian decorates the bathroom with candles—an example of the "more" that Ana wanted (and that Christian insisted he didn't do). Christian is still in charge, of course, and tells her what to do ("Put your hair up," "Lift your arms"). This time, Ana doesn't hesitate or second-guess her own actions—she just does it. Because she is becoming more comfortable with herself sexually, she is able to "ignore [her] natural inclination to cover [herself up]."

Christian caresses Ana while holding her hands so that she is really touching herself. Since Ana has never masturbated, this is a first—learning to give *herself* pleasure. Her thoughts make it seem like he is in control: "I am a marionette and he is the master puppeteer," but she's the one doing the touching. Her pleasure is truly in her own hands.

Christian takes Ana from behind, standing up. He is physically in control but Ana has learned that there is a difference between submission and passivity: "I grip on to the sink, panting, forcing myself back on him." Afterward, Ana acknowledges the depths of her own desire when she wonders if she will ever get enough of him.

The scene in the hotel bathtub (chapter 23) is a major turning point. Physically, Christian is in charge: "He clasps his hands on either side of my head and kisses me. Deeply. Possessing my mouth. Angling my head...controlling me." Her response? "I'm kissing him back and saying I want you, too, the only way I know how." He is in control and she knows it. She accepts that possession is "what he likes... [and] what he's so good at." At first, he holds her hands but later when she asks he lets go and pleads with her not to touch him. This is *huge*. Previously, Christian held Ana's hands not because he liked restraining her (okay, not *only* for that reason), but because he has a phobia about being touched in certain places. Now, however, he can let go because he trusts her to respect his boundaries. She is no longer "out of control" during their sexual encounters—she has acknowledged her needs and can rein herself in enough to respect his needs as well. As before, there is no language about losing herself or being overwhelmed. She understands and welcomes what is happening: "I am starting to recognize this delicious tightening... quickening."

How does Christian respond to these changes in Ana? When they're back at his apartment (chapter 25) it's *his* control that "unravels," and when he comes, he groans "incoherently." Because Ana is meeting him in the giving and taking of pleasure Christian can let go and allow himself to lose control. She has also come to see the pleasure of BDSM, describing the feel of his thrusts as "punishing" and "heavenly" in the same sentence.

The climax of Ana and Christian's sexual arcs come in the final sex scene, which takes place in the playroom, which Ana refers to now as the "Red Room of...Pain...or Pleasure." Kneeling by the door, she is "excited, aroused, wet." She no longer thinks his desires are something evil, to be changed: "This is so...I want to think *wrong*, but somehow it's not. It's right for Christian." (And evidently for her, too, since she's turned on and he's not even there yet!) She gives herself over to Christian completely, recognizing that submission brings both of them pleasure. She is tied spread-eagle to the bed, totally vulnerable as in her dream/fantasy, blindfolded, unable to even hear his movements.

Sex and Love in Shades of Grey

In the beginning of the novel, Ana equated Christian's desires and need of control as being "in the dark" and pledged to save him by bringing him into the "light." Now she has discovered that darkness *within herself* and learned to embrace it. Her desire while she is waiting is "dark and tantalizing." When he begins to flog her, she is "dragged in to a dark, dark part of [her] psyche," and realizes that she's "entered a very dark, carnal place."

Ana has come a long way from viewing the world in black and white. By opening her mind and body to new sexual experiences, she has come to see that love and pleasure come in many shades of grey.

JOY DANIELS writes erotic romance because she likes to expose her characters completely—strengths, flaws, and scars. Before turning her attention to love and lust, Joy studied oceanography and spent her days trying to save the world one fish at a time. She writes and grows veggies in the Washington, D.C., area with her scientist husband and two curious kids. Since moving south of the Mason-Dixon line, Joy has developed passions for NASCAR and country music and both feature prominently in her stories. She is currently working on a Nashville novel, and her debut novella, *Revving Her Up*, will be released by Samhain in January 2013. She can be found online at www.authorjoydaniels.com and @authorjdaniels.

STACEY AGDERN

Sexually Positive

S A BOOKSELLER, I see the rise and fall in popularity of many books; today's hottest bestseller is often the book that gathers dust on the shelves two months later. I've learned all too well that the impact of a title on the reading public can never really be judged in advance. But what strikes me most is when a book forces a change in people's reading habits. These are the kinds of books that alter people's perceptions of what they can and will read. *Fifty Shades of Grey* is one of these books.

Really? What? Yep. Absolutely. I have seen multiple examples of customers who swear all they'll read are books by authors like Franzen, Wolfe, Safran Foer, Lahiri, and Kingsolver become completely obsessed with authors who have names like Day, Hart, and Burton. All it takes is *Fifty Shades of Grey*.

But why? Why this book? First, because *Fifty Shades of Grey* is so popular, most people will shove their genre-based prejudices aside in order to stay current. As anybody knows, the ability to join a conversation on a topic of current interest is crucial to fit into society. Water coolers, trains, coffee shops—in each of these places people are talking about "that book." As a result, everybody is reading it.

But there's something more than being at the center of a trend that makes *Fifty Shades of Grey* the kind of book that changes people's reading habits. What is the intangible factor that makes this book sparkle—that makes it stay with a reader and forces them to reevaluate the way they look at reading? The sex, of course.

It's not just that there is sex in the book; if that were the case, there would be an entirely different conversation going on in contemporary society. No, the fact is that, in *Fifty Shades of Grey*, E. L. James has created an atmosphere where sex is seen as a good thing, a source of enjoyment. In short? It's sexually positive. As a result, it reintroduces into contemporary society the idea that it is okay to read a book where characters obtain enjoyment, and—gasp!—pleasure from mutually beneficial sex.

What makes a book sexually positive?

Two different elements: The first is the reaction of the book's characters to the sex that takes place during the course of the story. The second is the way the sex itself is written.

First, and foremost, Ana Steele is not painted as a slut or a whore by any of the characters that the reader is supposed to respect after she has begun to have sex with Christian Grey. In fact, instead of being ostracized, she is encouraged both by family and friends to continue her relationship with Grey. Her mother and her best friend in particular are both his champions. They may chime in with advice to be careful if it seems he is going too far, but it is quite clear to the reader that they are on Grey's side.

Nor does Ana's professional life suffer as a result of her engagement with Grey. She is shown studying for finals, working a part-time job, graduating from college, searching for postcollege employment, and working in her new full-time job. None of these things has anything to do with Grey, despite how much he wishes to involve himself.

Second, there is the writing in the sex scenes themselves. The writers who are usually nominated for and win *The Literary Review's* Bad Sex in Fiction Prize are the kind of writers who make sex seem boring, routine. Winners of this award include illustrious names like Norman Mailer and Tom Wolfe; nominees also include Jonathan Franzen, not to mention John Updike, who received the organization's Lifetime Achievement Award. In short, most critically acclaimed literary writers seem to believe that it is all right to write about sex as if it is the sort of thing that only those who have lost their mind would engage in.

E. L. James, on the other hand, writes her sex scenes with an eye toward demonstrating that the characters get enjoyment out of the act. Even when there is pain involved, Grey is shown to be adamant that "Miss Steele" finds pleasure. And as the sex happens from Ana Steele's first-person perspective, the reader is absolutely certain that Ana has in fact done so.

These two elements, when combined, demonstrate James' interest in creating a story where sex is seen as positive and pleasurable. It is also these two elements that draw readers from *Fifty Shades of Grey* to authors like Sylvia Day, Megan Hart, and Jaci Burton.

From *Fifty Shades*, readers often turn towards Sylvia Day's *Bared to You*. Although the heroine of *Bared to You*, Eva, is employed by the corporation owned by the hero, Gideon Cross, there are no negative consequences to her professional life once she enters into a relationship with him. Her boss, who becomes her friend, jokes with her and counsels her, but by no means does he encourage her to stay away from Gideon. There are also no personal consequences; none of the people in Eva's personal life that the reader is supposed to identify with and respect believe that a relationship with Gideon is a bad thing. And Sylvia Day's depiction of the sex between Eva and Gideon is electric; she is able to demonstrate to the reader, through Eva's first-person point of view, how much pleasure both characters derive from the scorching sex they have.

But *Bared to You* adds an extra element to the basic sexually positive atmosphere that *Fifty Shades of Grey* brings to the table. Eva is much more experienced than Ana Steele in both life and sex. As a result, the sexual relationship she enters into with the enigmatic Gideon Cross is more of a give-and-take on multiple levels. Eva is not afraid to challenge Cross and his dominance, and in return Cross is smart enough not to push her.

Switch by Megan Hart is another book that readers reach for after they finish *Fifty Shades of Grey*. It's a completely different kind of story, but still sexually positive. This is the story of Paige, a young woman who is searching for...something in her life. There are no professional consequences for this young woman as she goes on her journey of personal and sexual exploration. There are also no personal consequences directly related to Paige's sexual exploration. She is neither ostracized nor judged for her interest in sex. And Megan Hart's writing is beautiful, painting Paige's sexual fantasies with gorgeous language that demonstrates this woman is really finding the pleasure she needs.

The element that *Switch* adds to the basic sex-positive story is the emergence of a Dominant female character. The "something" Paige searches for, and finds, is the ability to channel her need for control into all aspects of her life. It is an internal struggle she goes through until she learns how much being in control pleases her. And, of course, pleases the person she has sex with—namely her ex-husband, with whom she has had a tumultuous relationship.

Finally, we have Jaci Burton's *Taking a Shot*. It is the story of a young woman and her relationship with the last person on earth she would expect to have a relationship with. Jenna, the book's heroine, gets no flak from her family and friends about her relationship with Ty, the book's hero. She is neither ostracized nor insulted at work, nor by anybody the reader is supposed to respect. The way Jaci Burton crafts the story is simply amazing: emotional when it needs to be and hot enough to melt ice when it should be. It is very obvious that both characters are enjoying the sex they have together.

There are two elements that *Taking a Shot* adds to this sexually positive dynamic. First, the hero and the heroine are both dominant, they are equals, and they find themselves meeting in the middle more often than not, to their mutual benefit. In fact, unlike the other three books mentioned, this story is told from *both* Jenna and Ty's perspectives, taking full advantage of the third-person point of view.

But the second element this novel adds is more important than the first. Despite the scorching sex, *Taking a Shot* is about more than just lust or dominance. It is about the *relationship* between two people and the intangible aspects that make the best relationships work. It is more than just sexually positive: it is relationship positive.

Books that treat sex in a positive manner are not revolutionary. Unfortunately, due to contemporary prejudice against pleasure reading, most people have a tendency to dismiss these kinds of books as irrelevant. However, thanks to being introduced to the sex-positive atmosphere of *Fifty Shades of Grey*, readers have been discovering a wide and varied genre full of amazing characters, wonderful stories, and hot sex written by authors who are capable of burning up a page. It is too early to tell whether this is the kind of paradigm shift that will last long after people have forgotten *Fifty Shades of Grey*, but it is a shift worth watching nonetheless.

STACEY AGDERN is the award-winning romance specialist at Posman Books, an independent bookstore located in New York's Grand Central Terminal. She has written reviews and commentary for publications such as *Heroes*

and Heartbreakers, Romantic Times Magazine, Romance at Random, and *Romance Novel News*. She has given presentations on the effective use of booksellers at regional and national conferences. She is a regular correspondent for Barbara Vey's "Beyond Her Book" column at *Publishers Weekly*'s online site and shows her geeky side as a member of the BlackStone Podcast. You can find her on Twitter at @nystacey.

My Inner Goddess

I WANT TO FUCK HIM.

Baldly put. Far too blunt for the average person, much less a young college student such as *Fifty Shades of Grey's* Anastasia Steele.

Ana is a week away from her final exams when we first meet her—and when she first meets gorgeous billionaire Christian Grey. She is overwhelmed by everything she encounters at his office, from the battalion of blondes who greet her, to the view, to how Christian strokes his index finger against his lower lip.

It's clear, from the way Christian responds to her, that something is happening, and Ana has no clue what it is. Neither do we, but both of us are dying to find out.

As their relationship begins, Ana needs to find a way to express what she is feeling when she is near Christian—needs a personification of the newly sprung emotions and desires he summons in her.

And thus her inner goddess is born.

It's not as though Ana doesn't have inner thoughts before beginning a relationship with Christian, but her thoughts are not personified by any kind of deity—they're more along the lines of "Wow" and "Holy crap." Much more immature and insecure. But as soon as Christian engages Ana in sexual discourse she needs a better spokesperson, hence the development of her goddess.

The inner goddess is not a new concept born of *Fifty Shades of Grey*—there are an endless number of shops and websites with the name selling goods designed to make you feel more satisfactorily womanly. "Inner goddess," in that context, evokes images of patchouli, beaded curtains, and women-only bonding sessions.

But those goddesses are not Ana's goddess.

Ana's goddess harkens back to a far earlier concept, albeit one that is derided as much as the patchouli people—Sigmund Freud's concept of id, as part of his larger explanation of the unconscious, comprised of the id and the superego. The id is the part of us that is all about pleasure, sexual and otherwise. The id is the bad boy of our psyche—pushing us to satisfy basic urges, needs, and desires.

Which, in Freud's terms, is a Bad Thing.

In *Fifty Shades*, however, it's a very, very good thing. Ana's goddess "sways in a gentle victorious samba," even though Ana herself is, as we know from the first scene with Christian, awkwardly clumsy. Ana's inner goddess doesn't wear tie-dye or Birkenstocks; this bitch is decked out in sequins and stilettos, doing her Olympic pole vaults and cheerleader leaps with equal aplomb.

Plus, Ana's goddess isn't only about the pleasure principle; she wants Ana to take charge. To be dominant, even if Christian is the Dom.

So she sulks, and pouts, and attempts to be brave as Ana faces the redoubtable Christian.

Ana's inner goddess is everything that Ana wishes she could be, even though she's never realized she had the wish in the first place. She is the inner voice that heroes and heroines of romantic fiction listen to when they are in doubt about their own desires—when they doubt those desires' validity and rightness.

That Ana's inner goddess espouses positive, helpful action is what makes her a romantic fiction id—as contradictory as that might sound. In literary fiction, the inner voice often encourages self-destructive behavior: "Have another drink," one might say, or "Go ahead and sleep with your husband's brother." Not self-affirming at all, but again voicing secret desires. In romantic fiction, however, the id helps vault the protagonist into positive action—usually falling in love—where the hero and heroine are too foreshortened by their own insecurities, issues, or whatever to allow themselves to take the action on their own. They need support to accomplish their ultimate happiness.

There are numerous examples of heroines, in particular, who can only reach their Happily Ever After if they finally listen to the voices inside their heads, and not in a *Three Faces of Eve* or *Sybil* kind of way. In *Jane Eyre*, Jane escapes from Thornfield Hall and ends up with the Rivers family, two sisters and a brother who are perfect in every way. Too perfect. Jane knows she cannot accept second best by marrying St. John Rivers, no matter how foxy he is; she doesn't love him, her soul yearns for Edward Rochester. And so, when she hears his voice inside her head calling for her, she doesn't question it. She takes off, returning to Thornfield Hall where she finds she can at last be his equal partner (that he is now blinded and crippled says something about author Charlotte Brontë's own sense of self-worth, but that's a subject for another essay).

These voices are a way for the writer to reveal the heroine's innermost desires, but they aren't the only way writers have for doing this. In many early romantic novels, the letter or the diary of the heroine is used to allow the woman's feelings and thoughts to emerge unscathed from the unconscious. Many literary critics and scholars have noted the diary device in writers of early nineteenth-century literature, from Elizabeth Gaskell to Wilkie

Collins to Charlotte Brontë's own sister Anne. In Anne's *The Tenant of Wildfell Hall*, for example, the book unfolds through a series of letters written from Gilbert Markham's viewpoint, and then segues into a diary written by Helen Graham. Helen's diary entries not only describe the events, but also Helen's feelings about them, in a poignant, passionate way. Helen's "diary" is her only outlet to express how she feels about the deterioration of her marriage, since she won't allow herself to voice her opinion about what is happening because she feels as though she owes her husband that much respect. But even in the context of her own diary, Helen won't put words to her own deepest desire. She edges close to what she wishes would happen, but doesn't state it in so many words.

Of course the best example of diary entry as manifestation of inner voice is in Helen Fielding's *Bridget Jones's Diary*. If Bridget had not expressed so much of herself within those pages, *Fifty Shades*—and other books where women get to be sexual, and insecure, and clumsy, and somehow entice an incredibly attractive man into their romantic midst—would never have happened.

Bridget's diary entries are more a superego/id hybrid, because Bridget herself has so many opposing wishes and desires within herself. She does want things, but she is equally adamant about what she does not want, which Ana's inner goddess isn't. For example, Bridget says, "I will not fall for any of the following: alcoholics, workaholics, commitment phobics, people with girlfriends or wives, misogynists, megalomaniacs, chauvinists, emotional fuckwits or freeloaders, perverts." If Ana's inner goddess had suggested that to Ana, that would have ruled Christian Grey out entirely, since his personality fits at least four of those categories. Bridget recognizes her own temptation, though, following that proclamation up with, "And especially will not fantasize about a particular person who embodies all these things." Neither Ana nor her inner goddess are that conscious—literally—of how Ana's manifestation of id is acting on her desires.

Let's return for a moment to Freud, and how he saw the role of the unconscious in guiding a person's actions. Not to be so presumptuous as to dismiss him as entirely wrong, but Sigmund, you gotta lighten up a little—satisfying "basic urges, needs, and desires" is not a bad thing. Especially when it comes to women, who—to cast a huge, stereotypical blanket over an entire gender—tend to do for others rather than for themselves. "Basic urges, needs, and desires," when satisfied in a positive way, means great sex (or great chocolate, but again, another essay).

It wasn't until authors of romantic fiction recognized that women's "basic urges, needs, and desires" weren't being met that readers got to meet inner voices like Ana's inner goddess. Ana's inner goddess knows what Ana really wants, and tells her in no uncertain terms.

And what does Ana want? Well, she wants to fuck Christian Grey. Many, many times. And harnessing, so to speak, her inner goddess in the service of those wants means that Ana doesn't have to feel ashamed—or much ashamed, at least—of her desires.

Is it cowardly for Ana to appoint an inner goddess as the mistress of her desires and not speak for herself? Perhaps, but it also makes the book far more compelling. Ana can't, but her inner goddess gets to dance the salsa, do pirouettes, merengue, sit in the lotus position, jump up and down (both with and without pom-poms), glow, pant, roar, plead, and fall prostrate after Christian has satisfied her.

Who wouldn't be better with a little more inner goddess waving pom-poms in her brain? Not the inner goddess who would whisper that it's okay to have the dessert, you deserve it—that's more like your Aunt Betty, who's stuck in the house with the cats and the Diet Coke—but the inner goddess who would encourage you to explore what it is you really want. Want to get in a helicopter with a control freak billionaire? Sure! How about inserting silver balls up in your lady business because it sounds like it'd be fun to do? Hell, yeah! Or biting your lip, even though you know it makes that same control freak billionaire crazy? Heck, you want him crazy. Crazy for you, and therefore for your inner goddess, who is your real you.

Where Freud was perhaps too reductive in his conception of the human psyche is in applying moral judgment on what the id, the ego, and the superego do for the conscious human mind. There are nuances here—fifty shades of nuance, to get cute about it—and castigating Ana's inner goddess as merely being a conduit for satisfying Ana's needs and desires is simplistic and lazy. Not that one would call Freud either simplistic or lazy; anybody who could be that many shades of fucked up himself is not simple. But his theories don't take into account the inability of people—such as a certain Ana Steele—to articulate, on their own, what they really want.

Ana's inner goddess might be annoying at times—she certainly makes her voice heard on far more occasions than some readers might like—but it's her inner goddess who can articulate what Ana wants to do.

And when Ana gets to do what she wants, the results are very pleasurable. For Ana. For Christian. And for the reader.

MEGAN FRAMPTON writes historical romance under her own name and romantic women's fiction as Megan Caldwell. She is the Community Manager for the Heroes and Heartbreakers website (www.heroesandheartbreakers .com), lives in Brooklyn, New York, with her husband and son, and usually wears black. She can be found at www .meganframpton.com or at @meganf.

Intermission

LAURA ANTONIOU

Fifty Shades of Holy Crap!

"AT LAST!" the longtime BDSM erotica author cried upon reading the news. "Finally, I see what people really want in their smut! Apparently I have been doing it all wrong. No matter. I will correct twenty years of my career by writing exactly what the public wants." Her maniacal laughter echoed through her apartment as she furiously typed...)

Book One: Fifty Shades of Sellout

"Double Crap!" Tiffany extrapolated, as she realized her perfectly perky 37D breasts had gained another D overnight. "Now what will I wear to meet and interview Mr. Momzer Macher, the new President and CEO and CFO and C-something-O of the Ridiculously Huge Seattle Startup Company?"

Sighing with frustration, the gorgeous blonde who didn't actually know how naturally attractive she was, gazed at her mirror image and fingered the honey-gold waves of her naturally wavy hair. "Darn my much more interesting and pretty roommate for getting sick and leaving me to make these hard decisions! I know! I will wear that daring leather bustier that my gay BFF talked me into buying at that strange street fair he took me to in San Francisco! Gee, I wonder if he worked things out with that hunk he met that day. He said he was into leather, but when I asked him where to find a good purse, he just laughed."

She blinked her cerulean eyes at the memory and then went to get her fetching outfit. It was tight in all the right places and really emphasized her 37-24-36 shape, and the leather felt so stiff and hot and sexy against her alabaster skin! And how it molded to her perfect 110 pounds! *How will I ever get through the night without fainting?* she wondered as she strapped her tiny, delicate alabaster feet into her four-inch heels, deciding not to take the *really* high ones. *Good thing I already threw up.*

At the party, everyone was in their fanciest clothes and the music was awesome and loud and there was dancing and great foods like chicken fingers and the little hot dogs in teeny buns and sushi and tapas and stuff. Tiffany, having never seen such wealth, such style, or such alcohol, despite being about to graduate from college, chose a cherry popsicle that had a fancy imported liquor in it, and was on her third when suddenly she saw . . . HIM.

Like. OMG. There he was, so freaking hot. In his leather pants from Dolce & Gabbana and his black silk shirt and really expensive black tie and black jacket and black diamond stick pin through the really expensive black tie and his ink-black hair and jet-black eyes and his big feet in big black boots. Oh, he was *so* into black!

"You're Tiffany," He murmured as he leaned in toward her, gracefully looking at her plunging cleavage and her heaving alabaster breasts.

He was so tall! Even with her lithe 5'7" frame enhanced by those four-inch heels, He was at least a foot taller! And His piercing black eyes pierced her to her very soul.

"I...I..." Tiffany stammered, letting her booze popsicle drip, drip, drip down her hand to splat, splat, splat on the floor. She bit her full, ruby-red lips in luscious lasciviousness.

"I'm disgustingly rich and dominant," He sneered dominantly. "You will be Mine!"

"Oh, wow," Tiffany seized. "Um. Wow. Okay. Sure. What does that mean, exactly?"

"I have a checklist," He said triumphantly while texting a URL to her. "Go to My webpage and fill it out, and tell Me whether you like, dislike, or are neutral about the three hundred activities and fetishes listed there, and whether you've done them before and with whom, and what you thought about it, and then rate them on a scale of one to ten on whether you'd like to do it now, tomorrow, next week, or after the Mayan Apocalypse."

"Um," Tiffany coughed out, a delicate flush gathering on her porcelain features, her beautiful, full lips, her high, sculpted cheekbones, her delicately feathered eyebrows, and her oh-so-cute upturned nose. "But I'm sure I haven't done anything on your list at all! Despite being an adult in 2012, having been through college in a very trendy urban area, I am still completely virginal and know nothing *at all* about kinky sex! I am beautiful, although I don't actually believe that." At this painful honesty, she blushed, stumbled, chewed her lip, and wiggled her ears in panic.

His anthracite eyes brightened under His heavy, midnight brows and He gazed at her with an acquisitional hunger, like a Guy who hasn't had anything to eat in days. And yet she could see some painful memory, some dark—dare she think *black?*—secret lurking behind those onyx eyes.

"Then you're *really* going to be Mine!" He thundered. "Because I Alone can teach you the gift of submission, give rise to your slave heart, grant to you the loving dominance of My Masterful Aggression, all tempered, of course, with rationality and with all due care and attention given to risk-aware negotiation. I will teach you to serve Me with your submissive soul, your passive power, your girly gushiness, train you to come at the snap of My Fingers and find true freedom in your complete subjugation to My Will. Yes...you will even learn...bad grammar."

"Triple crap!" Tiffany declaimed. "All that? But...how is that possible? It all sounds crazy! And yet...when I look into your charcoal eyes under that irrepressible lock of ebony hair, as I run my searching, trembling fingers across the steel buttons on your sable silk shirt, all I can think of is...Jesus Christ, I am so horny I could die. I think. But I don't really know, because of the virgin thing? It's a pity I was never exposed to sex education in school. Or owned a computer. Or knew how to work that Google thing."

Mr. Momzer Macher took her pale, shaking hand and led her gentle, undulating form away from the party into his private boardroom, where the table could be set up like a bed, and tumbled her back onto it.

"I will teach you, little one," He said with intrepid confidence in himself. "And you will be my prized little party girl, slave possession for all time. Just like the last seventeen subbies I had."

"Oh, quadruple crap!" she extremed, as He tore away her leather bustier with one hand and fell on her like a ravening wolf. A ravening *black* wolf.

Book Two: Fifty Shades of WTF?

Tiffany accepted the large package delivered by the uniformed messenger and added it to the pile inside the door. Already, she had a computer from the future, hand designed by Steve Jobs with more memory than any Apple computer available, boxes of flowers, trays from the Fruit of the Month Club, and mysterious objects from the Dildo of the Month Club, a complete, mint set of *Sheena, Queen of the Jungle* comic books (she had been a comic book major in school), and even more mysteriously, a BlackBerry instead of an iPhone, also from the future. Having just discovered the existence of email, Tiffany was learning all about the exciting new world of "cyber things."

"Jesus Christ, Tiffany," said her prettier, much more interesting roommate, Plotitia Device. "Is this guy trying to buy you, or what?"

Just then, Oprah popped through the door and squealed, "And you get a CAR!" at Tiffany, tossing her a set of keys. "From Momzer Macher. Bye now!"

"Oh, holy crap," Tiffany sighed. "I just don't know what to do! I should probably return all this stuff, except I kind of need a car and I never owned a computer and the fruit is good for me, although He insists I eat the whole box whenever we're together. I hate that almost as much as the way He keeps threatening to beat the shit out of me in His Purple Room of Punishment. Which I hate almost as much as the way He tracks me through this thing He tagged me with." She tugged at the radio transceiver stapled to her ear. "And I hate that almost as much as the way He threatens any man I ever talk to and pretty much goes ballistic if I make any plans that don't include Him."

"Call me crazy," said Plotitia, "but he sounds kinda messed up. Maybe you should back off and go slower with this stuff."

"If only there was a way for me to understand His Desire to do such awful things!" Tiffany sniffled. She remembered how, a few days after their tremulous meeting, she had turned from restocking the expired toothpaste from China on the shelves of the Super 99 Cent Depot where she worked, and there He was. Momzer Macher, all tall and wide shouldered and narrow hipped, with His pants hanging off His narrow hips (He forgot to wear a belt that day) and all His black clothing and His inky boots and midnight hair and soulful dark eyes hiding some mysterious, anguished past. He looked down at her and sneered dominantly, "Do you have plastic cable ties? And bungee cords? And hemp rope? And cotton rope? And burlap sacks? And two-by-fours? And clothespins? And gimp hoods?

And the trademarked Rabbit Pearl Vibrator, as seen on *Sex and the City*? Oh, and extra batteries?"

"Aisle three," she stammered, wondering 1) what on earth He wanted to do with all those things, and 2) why a gazillionaire was doing His own shopping at the Super 99 Cent Depot. Then she stumbled, bit her lip, fluttered her eyelashes, and wrinkled her nose.

"When you do those things," He said to her, leaning forward so she could smell the scent of Him, all clean, like He'd recently bathed, using soap, "I wanna do bad things with you."

"Oh, crapola deluxe," she whimpered. Yet, little did she know then, in the Super 99 Cent Depot, just what "bad things" meant. Because later on, after she accepted His invitation to coffee, after she allowed Him to rescue her from getting drunk and making out with a guy, after she met His mom (but not really His mom, but she didn't know that yet), He then showed her that darn contract and took her to His Purple Room of Punishment. Which was His fancy name for a fuck room with a revolving, round bed, mirrored ceiling with disco ball, and stacks and stacks of cheap-ass bondage materials, plus a well-thumbed copy of *The Frugal Dom's Guide to Kink on The Cheap*.

He had told her she needed to make the decision whether to become His Total, Complete, 24/7, Lifestyle, Gorean, Old Guarde, Euro, Submissive, Slavegirl. And then He started sending her all these presents.

"But I don't understand what it all means!" she cried, chewing her lip and wiggling her toes and swallowing hanks of her tawny, wavy hair. "How on earth could I ever learn anything about this stuff in Seattle?"

Just then, the mail came, with an invitation to a Doms and Subs and Friends Together Munch, a flyer for the upcoming Living & Loving in Leather conference, and a catalog from the Pacific Northwest Dykes Who Make Whips. She tossed them all on top of her MacBook Pro from the Future, and shook her head sadly, bursting into tears, as she usually did when thinking of

Momzer Macher. "There's just no way I could ever understand Him!" she wailed.

"Then you shouldn't see him again," pronounced Plotitia, who, despite actually having done some journalism, also didn't know how to research things.

"Okay," said Tiffany, stumbling over her gifts. "I'll just return all this stuff, now!"

Suddenly, her phone rang.

"Come on out with me, baby," purred the deep, dark voice of Momzer Macher.

"I was just talking about you!" Tiffany squeaked.

"I know, I bugged your apartment. Come with me at once, let me take you flying and show you a world of wealth beyond your deepest, most submissive dreams! Then we can go for pancakes. I'll get you the Rooty Tooty Fresh 'N Fruity, if you're a good girl."

Deep in her heart, Tiffany knew she should say no. After all, this guy was fifty shades of crazy, what with His super-secret dark past that He wouldn't talk about and His kinky sex fantasies and how He wouldn't let her touch Him except when He was fucking her or holding her or she was sucking His cock or they were kissing and the mysterious fact that He could make her orgasm by doing pretty much anything, even though she had never even jerked off before, and His muttering, frequently, that He wanted to beat the shit out of her and that creepy thing He said about her looking like His mom, like, oh, eww, and that annoying way He kept stalking and spying on her and scaring off all her friends and trying to keep her from visiting home and that fucking annoying way He said "laters" instead of "goodbye" like a normal person, but…but…

Pancakes.

"Okay!" she said cheerfully, and she dashed out the door and ran right into him, as He was right there, totally kneeling so He could look through the keyhole. And He swept her off in His black helicopter and they flew around and had pancakes and went back to His place where finally, like after 800 pages, He actually hit her in a way she was pretty sure she didn't like AT ALL. After, she argued with Him and assured him, repeatedly, that it was totally okay with her and she knew her safeword, dammit, and then totally forgot to use it.

"I didn't actually like any of this kinky shit, ever!" she screamed at Him, finally. And He was very upset and she was upset and they both cried and said dumb things and broke up forever, which is really not true, because if they did, there wouldn't be a...

Book Three: Fifty Shades of Happily Ever After

"Let's get married," Momzer Macher said to Tiffany one day.

"Okay," said Tiffany with all the unconditional love she had in her deep heart. Inside, her inner fairy princess was doing a *pas de deux*, with a little bit of tango and a smattering of an esoteric Brazilian martial art that sort of looked like dancing except that you could totally maim someone if they didn't duck in time.

How she loved Momzer Macher, dressed for their tropical vacation in His usual black leather pants, hanging off His narrow, sexy hips (*I have to remember to buy him a belt*, Tiffany thought) and a black shirt and black tie and black boots and black bikini underwear. *How sad that I didn't understand His complicated past!* she thought, gazing into His deep, dark eyes, harboring the saddest past anyone ever had.

If she hadn't been threatened by her boss, who had a grudge against Momzer Macher, if she hadn't been stalked by several of His seventeen former slaves, if she hadn't learned the true secret why He liked to play His sick little disgusting S&M games, if He hadn't had to rescue her, repeatedly, from everyone who wanted to hurt Him by hurting her, why, she could have been working for a living, without a computer from the future, a new car, a new house, and a contract of all sorts of weird rules she never had any intention of signing, but He always forgot to actually ever have her sign.

Oh, and she wouldn't be pregnant.

But that wasn't her fault at all! Because Momzer Macher had told her He didn't like using birth control, so *she* had to, and then she had these shots all lined up, but forgot to go get them, what with the kidnappings and midnight helicopter flights and crazy former submissives and the way they kept fighting and making up and having great sex with simultaneous orgasms.

Simultaneous orgasms made a girl somewhat forgetful!

Maybe I should tell Him about the pregnancy, she thought. She consulted her inner fairy princess, but that twat was too busy spinning around in a dervish to Bhangra with some Watusi-inspired sidesteps. So, she looked into Momzer Macher's deep, dark, pained eyes and said, "Could we get married soon? Because I am sort of knocked up."

"What? Bad girl! Bad slave! What the fuck! I hate you!" Momzer Macher leapt up, shaking with fury. "How dare you!" And then He ran off, screaming, leaving her there to burst into tears.

"Oh, crap to the tenth power!" she wailed. "Holy, goddamn, motherfucking crap!" How stupid and clumsy and unattractive she was, to not have realized that the fear she constantly had about telling Him bad news was actually a sign that telling Him bad news meant He'd act like a complete dick and run off to seek comfort with one of His many ex-lovers or abusers. If only she had trusted friends to advise her and comfort her! But He had chased them all away with His jealous, controlling rages, which were all really just proof that He really loved her.

Meanwhile, Momzer Macher totally ran off and got drunk with one of His bad influences and acted like a dick. Then He sighed and came back and said to Tiffany, who had cried a whole lot, "Okay, let's get married anyway."

"And you won't make me do any of that kinky shit?" Tiffany asked, having gotten a little wiser in the past 600 pages.

"No. I mean, yes, but only when you want it. Or, when I really need it, unless it upsets you. Or the baby. Whatever. It's just that I have realized, Tiffany, you are the perfect woman for me. You look like my crack-whore mommy, and your submission is entirely fictional, yet you love me so much you collapse into complete hysterics at the mere thought of my leaving you. Somehow, that just says you are the most amazing natural subbie. Let me buy you more stuff. And then maybe a little spanking?"

"Hm," said Tiffany, one hand cradling her pregnant belly. "Nah. But maybe some more action with the Ben Wa balls. After we get married. I bet our baby will like that a lot." Her inner fairy princess made a *ca-ching!* sound and nodded in satisfaction while doing the hustle.

"I can't wait to taste breast milk again!" enthused Momzer Macher, now more or less completely submissive to His formerly virginal, sexually ignorant bride. And that was not creepy *at all*.

LAURA ANTONIOU has been writing erotica for over twenty years. Best known for her Marketplace series of BDSM novels, she has also edited and appeared in many anthologies. Her most recent finished novel is *The Killer Wore Leather*, a comedy murder mystery set within the Leather/BDSM world. Her website is www.lantoniou.com.

Fifty
Shades of
Fanfiction

CECILIA TAN

Fifty Shades of Stories

THE SUCCESS OF *FIFTY SHADES OF GREY* may seem sudden, but like many "overnight sensations" the apparent suddenness is the result of two forces: one, the cultural blindness that makes books like this invisible until they reach a tipping point into mass consciousness, and two, the many sociological and commercial forces that have been continuously at work in the background in the years previous. I want to examine one of those forces, the still-burgeoning but long-established world of fanfiction, or "fanfic" for short.

Most folks know the story by now. *Fifty Shades* began life as a piece of Twilight fanfic, but an "alternate universe" version in which Edward isn't a vampire, but merely a mysterious rich man, and Bella isn't a high school student, but in college. What most people may not know is just how incredibly common it is for preexisting characters and/or universes to be used as a vehicle for intense erotic fantasizing onto the page (or screen) by women all over the world. Fanfiction.net, an online archive, has 25,000 Twilight-based stories alone, and if the site allowed explicitly sexual stories, there would be even more. The Archive of Our Own (AO3), a fanfic archive begun in 2008, has over 400,000 fics archived, with more being added every day. In December 2010 the site drew almost 250,000 unique visitors. As of June 2012, that monthly number had grown to 1.5 million. That is, simply put, a lot of stories and a lot of readers. And that's only at one of hundreds of websites where fanfic can be found.

. . • . •

While not all fanfic is romantic or erotic, a huge portion of it is: about 20 percent of what's on AO3 is marked "explicit" and another 20 percent or so is marked "mature." Three of the tags most frequently applied to stories at AO3 are "romance," "relationship(s)," and "sexual content." Which means thousands of writers and millions of readers are participating in an online culture that produces huge volumes of sexy stories. And the vast majority of both those writers and readers are women.

This hotbed of female-driven expressions of lust and love is not new. It predates the internet. Fanfic's modern roots are in the 1960s and the growth of *Star Trek* fandom, whose write-in campaigns famously kept the TV series on the air. Camille Bacon-Smith published one of the defining works on the subject of *Star Trek* fan writers and the fanfiction community twenty years ago: *Enterprising Women*, a 1992 University of Pennsylvania Press book. In it, she calls the world of fanfiction "a conceptual space where women can come together and create...outside the restrictive boundaries that men have placed on women's public behavior." She also names the writing of fanfic "a subversive act, undertaken by housewives and librarians...under the very noses of husbands and bosses who would not approve and children who should not be exposed to such blatant acts of civil disobedience." And women banding together to read and write love stories about pop culture icons *was* a highly subversive act.

Which was more subversive in its time: the fact that fan writers used copyrighted characters as the vehicles for their fantasies, or that they wrote and shared such vivid fantasies about sex and romance in the first place?

Today, a new generation has grown up from that same community and has proliferated wildly in the hothouse of anonymity that is the internet. Is reading and writing sexual stories and romance still seen as civil disobedience? Is it still something to hide from the genteel sensibilities of the menfolk? I would say yes, at least in some quarters, judging by the number of fans who feel the need to use pseudonyms. But many others are much more empowered. And the breakthrough of *Fifty Shades of Grey* presents an opportunity not only for fanfic writers and readers to come out of the closet, but also for female readers of erotica and erotic romance to, as well.

Romance has long been the biggest selling segment of all published fiction, and yet for all the decades that it has topped the moneymaking genres list, it is still thought of by some readers to be a "guilty pleasure" and a source of shame instead of a source of pride. Shouldn't something "everyone" is doing be a cultural norm? Perhaps one of the best things about the runaway success of *Fifty Shades of Grey* and its pervasiveness is that it blows open the closet door, at least in terms of itself. I saw no fewer than three women reading the book while waiting to board an airplane recently, and none of them were making any attempt to hide it. And who knows how many others, in that same airport terminal, were reading it on their Kindle or smartphone invisibly? And how many beyond them read it in its original fanfic form?

There is no longer a compelling reason to hide writing or reading fanfiction, and there are fewer and fewer compelling reasons to hide enjoyment of erotic books. Fear of being judged by others for what we read remains the main one, but fewer women suffer that fear now than in the past. And some readers are empowered enough and uninhibited enough to feel entitled to their fantasies. They want their erotica and they want it now. They will be the tastemakers who define what flourishes in the "post–*Fifty Shades*" marketplace.

Since fanfic is not bound by the strictures of commerce, creativity flourishes in infinite diversity. No fan writer is being steered by an editor toward what stories "sell" best to bookstores. Instead, the fan writer answers only to the audience itself. Erotic fanfic topics encompass not only BDSM, but "kinks" as varied as bubble baths, healing sex, male pregnancy, frenemies, comfort sex, bromance, and much more. Which will be the next hot trend? Fan writers will know before book publishers do. Fan writers receive instantaneous feedback on whether their stories succeed in moving the audience or not. Since feedback from readers, in the form of comments, is the only "payment" or validation a fanfic author receives, comments are highly prized. A fan writer knows immediately whether a story accomplished what was intended. Did the readers cry, sigh with ecstasy, or reach for their vibrators?

By all accounts, the fanfic originally known as "Master of the Universe" (MotU) had many English-speaking women the world over reaching for their vibrators and eagerly awaiting the next chapter. It is not alone in this regard, as there are many thousands of stories like it. (AO3 shows over 3,000 current stories tagged with "BDSM.") Also not unique to MotU is the fact that it was eventually collected as original fiction with the "serial numbers filed off" and published by a small press specializing in such "filed off" fiction. Did you know there are numerous small presses doing exactly that? Writers Coffee House Press, the house that originally published *Fifty Shades*, is but one. Omnific is another. (And more are certain to spring up in the wake of success.) Even before the runaway success of *Fifty Shades of Grey*, these publishers recognized two key things. One, that the readers of fanfic have their erotica-loving analogs in the non-fandom world: women who may not be clued in to fandom but who share the same desire for sexy stories. And two, that there are many fanfic stories just waiting to be cherry-picked where, although an established story, character, or universe served as the initial inspiration, the fan writer ended up quite far from the original.

So it was with "Master of the Universe," which used Edward and Bella as a kind of virtual Ken and Barbie, merely familiar vehicles for the writer's fantasies. Some might complain that *Fifty Shades of Grey* is not the best-written piece of literature. Some might feel it isn't deserving of the attention it receives when there are literally thousands and thousands of erotic fanfics out there that could be considered more original and better written. But the fact remains: this fanfic was incredibly popular among online readers. Whatever one might argue about E. L. James, the popularity of the original fanfic proved that her writing touched a nerve. It moved readers. That's the ultimate test, and in the seething underground of female lust that is the fanfic world, where thousands of other choices are freely available for just a mouse click, MotU passed that test. In its "filed off," professionally published form, it continues to do so.

CECILIA TAN is "simply one of the most important writers, editors, and innovators in contemporary American erotic literature," according to Susie Bright. Tan is the author of many books, including the groundbreaking erotic short story collections *Black Feathers* (HarperCollins), *White Flames* (Running Press), and *Edge Plays* (Circlet Press), and the erotica romances *Mind Games*, *The Prince's Boy*, *The Hot Streak*, and the Magic University series. She discovered how much fun it is to write fanfic in recent years and is a supporter of the Organization for Transformative Works (OTW).

Editing Fifty

IN 2009, a good friend I'd met through the Twilight fandom introduced me to the story "Master of the Universe." According to her, the lead male character—Fifty—was everything I'd been looking for in a good fanfiction Dom. He was mysterious, calculating, demanding, jaded, and best of all, panty-dropping hot.

"Master of the Universe" or, as we now know it, *Fifty Shades of Grey*, held me captive from the first chapter. I was drawn to Ana's unbelievable innocence, and I found Christian's ability to take command of Ana in the bedroom and otherwise a huge turn-on. While I'd read several BDSM Twi-fanfictions by the time I came across *Fifty Shades*, something about the way E. L. James wrote her characters made their story unique compared to the others.

It didn't take long for *Fifty Shades of Grey* to garner a following in the Twi-fandom. People could read it on FanFiction.Net as well as at the Twilighted community. I followed the story via FanFiction.Net. By the time I really got into the story, James must have had over 2,000 reviews from fans. I'd never read a fanfiction novel that had received so many comments in so little time. People were passionate about the direction the story took from update to update. Fans would get irritated at Christian for being too demanding of sweet little Ana or angry at Ana for not being more understanding of Christian's needs as a Dom.

I visited the Twilighted threads a few times during the months I was reading the fanfic. Twilighted is where James built her original fan base—the Bunker Babes. The Bunker Babes are a group of *Fifty Shades* fans that supported and backed James no matter what direction she took the story. They promoted *Fifty Shades* all over Twitter and the fanfiction communities. They were her sounding board and cheer squad, and were a force to be reckoned with.

I loved reading the story because James took a nonconformist approach to intertwining the BDSM and vanilla aspects that kept the BDSM elements from being too in-your-face. The sexual tension between the two characters made me so hot and bothered that it was sometimes difficult to contain myself, and I wasn't the only one. Thousands of women all over the world were reading about the "Red Room of Pain," using the phrase "Laters, baby," and begging for more between James' updates.

Prior to reading Twi-fanfiction, I'd had very little experience with erotic romance. As a matter of fact, in college I'd fallen in love with, and studied, Victorian literature, captivated by works such as *Villette, Frankenstein, Dracula, Heart of Darkness,* and *Jane Eyre.* Victorian literature is nowhere near erotic in nature, instead focusing on virtue and goodness. *Fifty Shades of Grey* changed everything I knew about literature and myself—it increased my curiosity, not only in erotic romance as a genre, but also in BDSM as a lifestyle.

In early 2010, I was asked to help in the development of an e-publishing house for the Australian-based company The Writer's Coffee Shop. The Writer's Coffee Shop began online as a site for worldwide discussions centered around books, authors, blogs, and more, and eventually evolved into TWCS Library, where people could post original works as well as fanfiction. I worked alongside the original founders of TWCS' site to build a publishing house that catered to the needs of aspiring authors. I became a managing and acquisition editor and worked with erotic romance manuscripts more often than not.

As an editor of erotic romance, I feel that the genre opens the doors of the imagination into worlds most readers have never traveled. An erotic romance manuscript should capture the excitement and naughtiness of a first love—the one you lost your "V card" to. It needs to combine sensuality and kink in ways that make the loneliest person *feel*. It should be romance, adventure, love, loss, suspense, and unbridled desire all rolled up into one story. James' *Fifty Shades* did just that and in a manner that didn't scare off first-time readers of the erotic romance genre.

From the launch of TWCS Publishing House, we knew we wanted to acquire and publish the story that had set the Twilight fanfiction community afire, and we were thrilled when E. L. James chose to publish the series with us. Due to my background in editing and writing erotic romance with the publishing house, as well as my experience in the lifestyle, I was the only choice for editor of *Fifty Shades of Grey*. Many would have been nervous taking on such a task, but I was excited. I knew from the moment we signed James that this would be the chance of a lifetime.

I was given a little over a month to edit and finalize the manuscript with James. Reading through it for the first time after the rewrites was a surreal experience. The structure and characters were the same as the original story that first caught my attention in 2009, but the changes in details made it feel like a first read. James had managed to take her Twilight-inspired story and turn it into a manuscript that was truly *hers*.

It didn't take long for word of the rewrite and potential release to spread worldwide. James had a huge following of readers prior to publishing *Fifty Shades of Grey*, and this helped in initial sales. It also made the task of editing the book and keeping it true to James' intent very important. We knew James and her readers would not take kindly to an editor coming in and red-penning *her* story, and I was advised by TWCS to handle James and *Fifty Shades* with kid gloves. At times it was difficult for me to hold back my natural desire to make changes I thought were necessary; after all, I have been lovingly dubbed "Comma Bitch" by those I've edited. Looking back, I'm glad that I refrained from making drastic changes to the story and allowed the characters to speak for themselves, but agreeing to handle the manuscript and James delicately went against everything I stood for as an editor—and if I could do it over, I'd go with my gut instinct rather than sugarcoat the process for those involved.

When I edit, I like to send "bundles" of edited chapters to the authors I'm working with—bundles being four or five chapters at a time. James would get a bundle and sort through it. Once she was done, we'd have a Skype session and go over the changes I'd made, suggested, or questions I had. Sometimes we agreed, sometimes we didn't. In the end, she always had the final say-so. This was her baby—months upon months of her hard work. It was very important for her to be able to guide the process.

We went through the manuscript twice together in this manner before our final Skype session. The last edits we went over together were those we got back from the publishing house pre-reader. We spent an entire Saturday, seven or eight hours, grinding through the manuscript. As a team, we agreed on some of the changes that were suggested while axing the ones we didn't find relevant or necessary. It was a lengthy process, and by the time we were done, we both let out a huge sigh of relief.

Working with E. L. James was not as daunting a task as one might think. She was no more particular about her work than any other author I've worked with. As a matter of fact, James' quick wit, tenacity, humor, and the simplicity in her writing are all traits that contributed to the enjoyment and challenges of editing *Fifty Shades*. Our final thoughts, on that last day of edits, were about the potential backlash from some in the literary community due to the nature of the story and its original life in fanfiction form. It's a chance we all knew we were taking—a chance I am so thankful James had the balls to take. The genre of erotic romance has been forever changed, as has the world of e-publishing.

I like to think that I had a *little* something to do with it.

TISH BEATY was part of the team that developed The Writer's Coffee Shop Publishing House, where she worked closely with E. L. James and edited the *New York Times* bestselling novel *Fifty Shades of Grey*. She has a bachelor's in psychology and minor in English literature. Tish has been writing since childhood and dabbles in erotic romance. She currently resides in southwest Missouri with her two energetic boys and husband, and can be found online at www.tishbeaty.com.

MALA BHATTACHARJEE

Throwing Shade

How *Fifty Shades of Grey*
Broke Fandom's Rules

/S, BDSM, S&M... there are a lot of letters that come to mind when discussing the sexy doings of erotic fiction. Two that you may not know about? The capital "F" Fandom and the lowercase "f" fandom. Capital "F" Fandom is the all-encompassing term for the entire culture of primarily internet-based fan communities who participate in individual lowercase "f" fandoms. E. L. James was a celebrated member of Twilight fandom, whose success with *Fifty Shades of Grey* would eventually turn the floodlights on Fandom as a whole.

Fandom, you see, is like Fight Club. The first rule of Fandom is that you don't talk about Fandom. It's a subculture, like any other, that operates largely under the radar of mainstream society. Sure, you may use Facebook, you might have a Tumblr or a Twitter account, but engaging in discussion and creation of fanworks with others is a whole different level of interaction. There's a secret handshake, a subtle head nod, a sense of being a part of something that spans time zones and countries and languages. It requires a certain amount of mutual respect (and often some mutual disdain as well) and trust. It's a trust that no one is going to laugh at you for liking *My Little Pony*. It's a trust that someone else understands what it's like to watch BBC's *Sherlock* and think Benedict Cumberbatch is the hottest thing since sliced bread. It's a trust that you can write whatever you want and someone, somewhere, will find it wonderful.

When E. L. James altered her wildly popular Edward and Bella alternate universe fanfic "Master of the Universe" and published it with a new title and new character names, she broke one of Fandom's oldest social contracts: Thou shalt not profit from thy fanfiction. A "rule" instituted long ago, primarily for legal purposes—studios and publishing houses were far more "cease and desist"–happy than they are now; it would've been a given that Stephenie Meyer's people would take on *Fifty Shades of Grey*—it also serves the purpose of keeping fanworks *for the fans.* "Going pro" with your fic means going public—and involving people outside the fan community. Once you involve a showrunner, actors, an author, or the media, it's like someone standing over your shoulder as you organize your stamp collection—or your sex toy collection. You're being judged for your geekery, for your "mommy porn" (heaven forbid!), and your autographed season two cast shot of *La Femme Nikita*. It changes the fannish experience.

Why is that such a big deal? Because the fannish experience, for many, is a deeply personal one. For a lot of women, it's a way to explore their creativity and their sexuality without facing scorn and censure. There's a long-standing joke about the internet known as Rule No. 34: if it exists, there's porn about it. There is nothing under the sun that hasn't been written about and posted in fanfiction forums, on journaling sites like LiveJournal.com, or on large-scale fiction archives like FanFiction.

Net. A lot of the so-called "porn" is written by women and consumed by women.

Similar to the published romance and erotic fiction industry, fanfiction is a haven for self-expression, for exploration of
kinks and tropes that you can't necessarily talk about with your
friends over a glass of wine. You don't have to be ashamed if you
like forced seduction or May/December romance or ménage—
you'll find a group or an archive or an anonymous meme that's
into the same thing. Because of the relative anonymity of internet handles and commenting systems and the ability to present
yourself however you see fit, it is all done in a way that makes
the writers *and* the readers feel safe. And there's no money being traded in the process. It's done for pure enjoyment, for the
satisfaction of sharing a story and perhaps receiving a few comments in return.

Sometimes, fans receive even more. The CW's *Supernatural*
acknowledged vocal portions of their fanbase in meta commentary–laced episodes featuring Becky the fangirl. The team
behind MTV's *Teen Wolf* was entreated to involve characters
in a same-sex relationship. And while many authors, like Anne
Rice, Diana Gabaldon, and George R.R. Martin are vocally anti-
fanfiction, still others—E. L. James' inspiration, Stephenie Meyer,
among them—are openly supportive of fanworks. Fandom advocate and bestselling author Naomi Novik (the Temeraire series) even continues to *write* fanfiction.

At the core, fanfiction and participation in Fandom is about a
shared passion for the source material. So when E. L. James put
a price tag on something that was previously free, it changed
the very *intent* of her stories. "Master of the Universe," something written for fellow Twilight fans, turned into something
that needed—no, *demanded*—a wider audience. One that was
willing to pay for what previously had been shared with a select
community of readers. It doesn't matter if you wrote under a
name like Snowqueens Icedragon (James' alias) or SamDean-
Fan42: when you shed that persona and outgrow the audience

who supported you when you wore it, a certain amount of hurt feelings ensue. It's as though positive comments aren't enough—as though tangible profit has become a bigger draw than the give-and-take of your favorite fandom. And that, to some, is yet another broken rule of the fannish Fight Club. (It should probably be noted that I've broken several just by writing this.)

Mainstream media, in their lurid, almost viciously gleeful coverage of the Fifty Shades phenomenon, have tarred legions of female readers with a torrid brush. They've called out the women who hunch over their Kindles on the subway, laughed at the library hold lists that number in the hundreds, and offered a general sense of bewilderment at the idea that women might find something with adult content enjoyable to read. But for decades, even before the advent of the internet, Fandom was welcoming such women with open arms: bring us your tired, your poor, your kinky masses. Creating this constantly shifting and expanding home for the sexually curious is not a professional, paid endeavor but a philosophical one. Consequently, *Fifty Shades of Grey*'s success, and the ensuing media circus, has a lot of people who have lived in the virtual neighborhood for years shaking their canes and muttering, "Get off my lawn," at those who come in wielding cameras and waving microphones.

After all, women were successfully indulging in their fantasies online, and off, long before Christian Grey handed Ana Steele a contract and started monitoring what she ate. This isn't *new*. Spanking, beating, toys...I can guarantee that everybody from Harry Potter to Buffy Summers to the members of 'NSync have been chained up and flogged into next Tuesday because someone thought it might be hot...and because it was perfectly acceptable within the confines of Fandom to do so. Fanworks have never been "mommy porn." Fandom is not a skit on *Saturday Night Live* or a set of buzzwords in every newspaper's competition to boost their sales—and it's certainly not over 20 million copies sold and counting.

Fandom is like Fight Club. The first rule is that you don't talk about it. But, rules and regulations be damned, *Fifty Shades of Grey* certainly started one hell of a conversation about women, reading, and sex.

Longtime pop culture writer **MALA BHATTACHARJEE** is the former news editor of *Soap Opera Weekly* and current features editor at *RT Book Reviews* magazine. She also writes interracial and multicultural romance under the name Suleikha Snyder. Mala lives in New York, where she constantly refurbishes her soapbox and occasionally shares the results at her blog, www.badnecklace.com.

ANNE JAMISON

When Fifty Was Fic

"IT'S NOT JANE AUSTEN."

My mother's blanket critique of all books, excepting the six of which it isn't true, applied with equal disapproval to Samuel Beckett and, I would imagine, to *Fifty Shades of Grey,* although my particular mommy is not likely to make it through the first page of *that book.* (As in, Mom, I'm in the *Wall Street Journal.* —how exciting, what for? Amateur BDSM erotica, what else? —is this about *that book* again?) My mother would apply her phrase equally to *Twilight,* which she's also unlikely to read, although Stephenie Meyer claims a "classical inspiration" for each of the saga's books and identifies the first volume with *Pride and Prejudice.* Presumably, Meyer has in mind the basic structure of "Boy meets girl. Boy hates girl. They are destined to be together," and less, say, elements of style.

I often teach Jane Austen. I also taught "Master of the Universe" (or MotU), the fanfiction version of *Fifty Shades of Grey* (names changed to protect the copyrighted), which was loosely based on *Twilight,* which was loosely based on Austen. I confess, however, that I teach Austen in courses labeled "literature" and taught Snowqueens Icedragon, now better known as E. L. James, in a course labeled "popular culture." While Jane Austen would qualify as pop culture (now with more zombies!), Fifty Shades is unlikely to be designated as literature in the critical hive mind anytime soon. E. L. James would probably agree. She may have name-checked *Tess,* but she knows it's not what she's writing.

"It ain't Kansas."

A phrase from a popular 1980s T-shirt, featuring "New York" with a picture of a gun. I sometimes fanfic it in my mind: "Twilight. It ain't Austen," with a picture of hands holding an apple (the original New York reference retained in a big apple, because that's how fic evolves, a series of echoes). Or now, "Fifty Shades. It ain't Twilight," with the Twilight hands bound together by understated (grey) handcuffs, no sign of New York or its echoing apple. The original referent long gone, only the basic structure remains.

Retelling known and loved stories is nothing new. Jane Austen's ne'er-do-wells Mr. Wickham and Willoughby are recognizable reiterations of "The Rake," a stock character in Restoration drama. Does that make it fic? What is the difference between revisiting or revising myth and the writing we refer to as fanfiction? Does the distinction rest on how closely the revised vision resembles its source, or on whether the source is in the public domain, not copyrightable? Or does it simply come down to a label and finances: if you can earn money from it, it's no longer fanfiction—a commercial distinction that makes no claims about literary value (whatever that is)? Is a text simply fanfiction when it is labeled as such, this label, in turn, proclaiming amateur status?

I taught Twilight fanfiction in a course that examined genre in both the traditional and popular sense of the word. In the more traditional literary critical sense, *genre* means simply a kind or category. If certain formal, stylistic, or thematic elements are common to a group of stories, these stories constitute a genre. In contemporary and popular usage, however, "genre" fiction refers only to certain genres, which are also understood as distinct from "literary" fiction, and as a term it is often used pejoratively. The course was dedicated to "genre" in this sense, as well: the Western, science fiction, detective fiction, and ... Twific. We looked at all-human (no sparkly vampires), alternate universe, novel-length, Edward/Bella fanfiction as a stand-in for the romance genre, but also in order to pose questions about genre in both senses. Was this body of work simply another variation on an established category? Did it behave enough like a genre to be one in its own right? Or was it something else entirely?

During the class, though, we kept returning to the same broader question: What makes fanfiction different from *any fiction?* I asked a group of contemporary novelists, all participants at a 2010 Comic-Con panel on retelling myth, what besides copyright separated the work they did from fanfiction. One jumped in faster than the others with an acerbic single-word answer: "quality"—and this wasn't a *New Yorker* panel. This was *Comic-Con.*

Such attitudes, even in geek culture, are remarkably entrenched. If genre fiction is something like literature's ugly cousin (from literature's point of view), and romance is sci-fi, fantasy, and detective fiction's annoying *girl* cousin, a tagalong picked last for the team, then fanfiction has long been the ugly cousin's stepfamily's misshapen mixed-breed dog, the one everyone is too ashamed to let out in public but unable to quite put down or even neuter.

One goal of my course was to examine the assumptions that underlie our understandings of categories like "literary," "genre," and, particularly in the case of fanfiction, "originality." Students soon identified one of the primary assumptions people have about a "literary" or "original" work as its autonomy. It's the kind of myth that the literary economy is so reliant on, it does not matter how frequently or systematically each top-selling work of fiction gives it the lie (pitches read like this: "It's *Emma* meets *Terminator*!" And not: "You've never read anything like this before"). It's one of those myths we simply know is true: work is more valuable if it originates with its author and afterwards can stand on its own, and less valuable if it is derived or in any way requires propping. A copyright holder owns the rights to derivative works. They cannot stand on their own: it's illegal.

When we read fanfiction, though, this question of a work standing on its own is not at issue. Although an individual fic may be *able* to stand on its own (be read without knowledge or consideration of its source), it *doesn't*. Fanfiction invites readers, collectively and collaboratively, to *join in*. Clicking on a fanfiction link is like joining a perpetual online writing and reading party, a party that celebrates, consumes, and jubilantly re-creates a loved (or at least a known) work. Fanfiction identifies a particular taste and promises satisfaction—a particular kind of satisfaction, with warnings for plot twists that may seem to deviate. (A typical warning from a summary: "Edward starts out with Tanya, but don't worry! This fic is Bella/Edward all the way!")

When E. L. James/Snowqueens Icedragon wrote for this system, what did she get out of it? How is what she did different from sitting down to write a novel, alone in a room? If Fifty Shades started as fic—and it did more than start that way, the text is all but identical—is it still fic after selling (at current count) over 20 million copies? How does the way the narrative was produced, self-consciously derivative and interactive, affect the end result or how we judge it?

Like a Dickens novel, *Fifty Shades of Grey* (and the whole Fifty Shades trilogy) retains traces of its serial origins—a looser, more sprawling structure, but also more cliffhangers. Certainly, in the case of Fifty Shades, more climaxes. Can these serial rhythms and even the book's perceived flaws help explain its popularity? In many respects, Fifty Shades is the antithesis of more than a century of narrative and stylistic orthodoxy: say only what you must to get your point across, to get your character from A to B, and not more. Less is more. These are values that have been associated with literary fiction and commercial storytelling alike, as it happens, and these qualities are often what we mean by "good" writing. Fanfiction, on the other hand, and Fifty Shades in its wake, is founded on the principle that more is more. We are not done yet, fanfiction says; more would be better. Why not? Women like multiples.

Other traces of its fanfic origins mark Fifty Shades—again, at the level of construction. Fan writing, as fan writers who also write "original" (traditionally authored?) novels are quick to explain, allows a number of shortcuts. Usually, new fiction doesn't come complete with a cast list, but fanfiction based on television and movie franchises does. So, fic tends to catalogue certain perfunctory details of appearance that cue known quantities (Bella: bites lip, stumbles, soft brown hair, smells of fruit, can't imagine why Greek gods look at her, etc. Edward: sex hair. And other impossible perfections). In much the same way, character names foreshadow plot trajectories: in Twilight fanfiction, you know that no matter how nice that fellow James may seem to be, he's up to no good. James will betray you; Edward will rescue you. The Jacob character may appeal to Bella and cause a jealous scene, but if the fic has an Edward/Bella label, the reader can rest assured Jacob will not prevail (Jacob fans have their own subgenre).

E. L. James/Snowqueens Icedragon took all these shortcuts. Her descriptions of Christian/Edward and Ana/Bella closely conform to fandom standards, with only the slightest cosmetic changes to the published version. When she took her story from its fanfiction context and published it, though, it turned out that a lot of that "missing" characterization and attention to setting that even high school–level creative writing instruction stresses was superfluous for millions of people. James' readers simply didn't need a fully detailed world or finely wrought characters. The Twilight template was working fine for them even without reference to the original. Less is more, in some cases, after all.

I confess, I don't really read that way. I would argue—somewhat quixotically—that E. L. James' Fifty Shades was more valuable from a literary perspective when it did *not* stand on its own, even though the fanfiction and the "original" published novel are all but identical. I'm not arguing that Fifty Shades somehow *can't* stand on its own (20 million+ readers say otherwise), but rather that the same work was more literary (read: more complex, discursive, critical, stylistically motivated) when it didn't. "Master of the Universe" was more engaging intellectually as part of a complex system of interwoven, mutually commenting fictions and character studies than it could ever be on its own.

As Twilight fanfiction grew more widespread and its community more diverse and sophisticated, it drifted farther and farther from its Twilight source, often revising or reversing it very pointedly. Bella's not graceless, she's a ballerina, or a gymnast—but still, undeniably, this poise is understood in relation to that initial annoying stumbling, a reversal of a known quantity we're reminded of every time we read her name. Those revised fanfiction stories end up functioning as commentary: reversing grating characteristics or, alternately, imagining what circumstances could have led to the *Twilight* characters' troubling passive (Bella) or controlling (Edward) behavior. Fanfiction Edward, for example, often grew up emotionally stunted after watching his mother die in some horrible way—whether culminating years of abuse or neglect, as in "Master of the Universe," or violently curtailing an idyllic Oedipal bubble. Would this be enough damage, each successive fic asked, to explain Edward's withholding, controlling tendencies? What trauma could lead Bella to her perpetual state of passive acceptance, her lack of self-insight, of basic self-worth? This was a fandom game my students loved to watch: What exclusively human trauma would make the behavior of Twilight's main characters seem psychologically earned? A different take on these traits could be found in BDSM Twific: Bella's a sub; this isn't psychological trauma, this is sexuality, and Bella can be self-aware about it, assertive and proactive about her desire to be controlled in the bedroom, without having these desires take over her whole personality and life.

Fifty Shades, then, grew not out of one source—Stephenie Meyer's Twilight Saga—but out of a system of mutually derivative and transformative texts. In fact, another reason for teaching "Master of the Universe" was that it *was* so multiply derivative: The "Office" genre. "Mogul" Edward. The BDSM fic. The more-assertive Bella (submissive Bellas were *always* depicted as more assertive than Meyer's original characterization). The dial-a-childhoodtrauma game. "Master of the Universe" read like a pastiche of all these established moves.

This isn't cheating. Drawing obviously and explicitly from other fics is standard practice in fan writing communities. Watching it happen is like watching genres develop at warp speed. Someone writes a popular faniction—take "The Office" by Tby789. Edward is a corporate type—a CFO—and Bella is his assistant. They hate each other. They have sex. A LOT. They are destined to be together. (The *Pride and Prejudice* template— now with more sex! Etc.) This fiction takes off, inspires countless variations on a theme.

When I first became interested in Twilight fanfiction in 2009, "The Office" was one of *the* stories people were talking about, and it had just been taken down from the web by its author. At that time, it had over 2 million hits on FanFiction.Net. The fandom assumed the author was trying to publish it (she wasn't), and this was already causing anger and rancor. Although the original "Office" story was "gone" (officially, but old fanfictions, even "Master of the Universe," are never really more than an archived PDF away), its mark was everywhere. By the time I finally got a copy of the story, I had seen it recycled, recast, retold so many times, I felt like I was rereading it.

"The Submissive" was the well-known BDSM romance that rose in popularity before MotU was first posted. Edward is an emotionally damaged, wildly successful, piano-playing corporate executive Dom; Bella is a librarian and a willing, eager, but inexperienced sub. They have secrets: the secrets are feelings. Can a Domward love Subbella and continue to pursue the lifestyle they both want? Can BDSM, a relationship based on trust and honesty, fail to hurt in the decidedly wrong way when partners hide their true feelings and motivations? Can Bella help heal damaged Domward to love? And, crucially, can she overcome his anxiety about her diet for long enough to seduce him by brushing against him while cooking? Of course it all sounds familiar. It's *fanfiction*.

When *I* started reading MotU, I immediately recognized elements of Stephenie Meyer's Edward-point-of-view *Midnight Sun* fragment (posted on her website) *and* of the parody "Midnight Desire" by Twilightzoner, in which Edward's shocking monster is nothing more than a healthy teenage boy's libido—which nonetheless soon takes on a life of its own as a character, cheering complete with pom-poms when it seems that Edward might finally get laid. MotU had reversed the dynamics so that Bella, rather than Edward, was arguing with her inner monster, or her "inner goddess," a more adventurous (if strangely detachable) sex drive than she could acknowledge as fully a part of her. When seen as a gender reversal of teen Edward's lack of sexual self-awareness, Bella's naiveté takes on a different tone. In their fanfiction context, the "inner goddess" dialogues worked well as a parody of two distinct, known quantities, the kind of inside joke with which fanfiction rewards dedicated "inside" readers.

It wasn't just plot points, settings, or scenes from other fanfiction that Snowqueens Icedragon built on. It was also strategy. By many accounts, for example, "The Office" was one of the stories to really spur Twific's departure from "canon" characterizations and story lines. Angstgoddess' "Wide Awake" (Snowqueens Icedragon claims to have spent sixty pounds sterling downloading it to her phone in Spain) was another—likely still the most universally admired story in the fandom. There, both characters have suffered childhood traumas, and will go to any measures to avoid sleep and its nightmares, a reimagining of canon-Edward's vampiric sleeplessness. In "The Office," however, the narrative was driven by the (all human, nonsparkling, sexually voracious and adventurous) characters' sex lives. Sex wasn't an embellishment or endgame; it *was* the story. On the other hand, there *was* still a story; it wasn't what fandom calls "PWP" ("Porn without Plot" or "Plot? What Plot?"). Before "The Office," Twilight fan writing had often explored the Twilight characters' sex lives, following the well-established "missing scenes" or "continuation" fanfiction tradition. After "The Office" (and a few other stories that were subsequently published by the fandom-derived Omnific publishing venture), canon and vampire stories experienced a drop-off in popularity. Twilight itself soon contributed little more than a paradigm for some of the most popular fanfictions, offering a basic plot trajectory and characterizations along with a ready-made cast to be manipulated onto porn images, transformed into electronic banners and icons, or montaged onto videos. These evolutions in Twilight fanfiction paved the way for both MotU and its reframing as "original," by which, here, I mean copyrightable.

It was quickly clear to my students that most of the fanfiction we read was at least as "original" as much published work, and very often more so. Yes, certain characterizations and outcomes were given, but their paths could be extremely varied, more full of surprises than traditional novelistic structure allows. Nonetheless, most of the fan writers we talked with assumed that their work, however different from its source, could not stand on its own. It appeared, after all, on a Twilight fanfiction board, usually with a disclaimer and a firm statement of its amateur, nonprofit status. It was not original by definition.

Many of these writers also understood the work's nonautonomy as key to another way writing fanfiction differs from the "original" model of a writer alone with a blank page (or screen). Jane Austen read aloud to her family in the evenings, of course; the Brontës shared with each other. But an audience of friends, family, even editors, is not quite the same as an anonymous target audience of thousands of active, and interactive, readers.

In fanfiction, this interaction can get quite elaborate. On some sites—including Twilighted, one fanfiction archive where MotU was hosted—authors hold court after publishing a chapter, engaging and chatting with fans, taking suggestions, sharing jokes, and, in the case of Snowqueens Icedragon, virtual Oyster Bay Chardonnay. I was taken with her sometimes funny and desperate pleas about narrative pacing: *How do I move time forward?* On other social media platforms, fan authors answer questions—sometimes as their characters. Also, many stories have editors (betas)—Twilighted had its own team of (volunteer) editors, and authors given permission to post there were required to use them, although big stories that drove traffic to the site (MotU was one) could choose to ignore their suggestions.

Even with a good critique group, no novelist gets a cheering squad quite like this while the work is in progress. And it's not just cheers or even jeers: it's illustrations, contests where fans can campaign and vote for stories, promotional videos, posts on review and recommendation sites—all in exchange for stories given freely. Most fan writers will tell you that this kind of interaction is what fanfiction is about. Writing a novel, on the other hand, is largely a lonely business.

Then, too, it's not just the writing that's collective, it's the reading. My students and I read ten different Bellas, ten different Edwards, all the same and all different, encountering ten different iterations of the same problems and issues—distinctive, but not quite distinct. It was a big narrative conversation. The authors talked to us—they were happy to! And then the *names*. How much does it change things that these related characters all have the same names and undergo such similar trajectories? No matter how many times you read *Pride and Prejudice,* Darcy's still Darcy, and very different from Mr. Knightley in *Emma*. It would be weird to talk about "that Darcy" from "the one where Elizabeth's father was sickly." It would be strange to think of

Mr. Woodhouse as a revision of the caustic Mr. Bennet. Names mattered more than we thought, going in. For the most part, E. L. James just changed the names to create Fifty Shades, and it does, indeed, make for a very different reading experience.

In terms of our initial course questions, students found that Twific operated as genre in the broad sense: a category or kind of romance narrative, an obsessive love story that evolves across a literalized power gradient. At times, however, it seemed Twifics were at once too similar (the names, the plot structure) and too disparate (so many different settings! So many different traumas!) to function as genre in exactly the way genre fiction traditionally has, although reading so many fics in close succession felt closer to reading extensively in a single genre than any other reading experience we could think of. More broadly, though, my students also felt that fanfiction puts a kind of microscope to the way fiction works—genre fiction certainly, but not only genre fiction. Our studies served as a reminder that novels and characters are always in conversation with one another. Read in its context, among systems of stories, fanfiction "lays bare the device," as Russian formalists aspired to do to literature, revealing narrative and character as a cobbled-together patchworks of preceding traits, stories, and styles. Our notions of originality and autonomy in fact are relatively recent, tied to the ability to profit from our writerly labor, which is tied, in turn, to the rise of mass literacy and the technology of print. Fanfiction muddies the system by offering labor and its products freely given—but to a mass audience. Fanfiction is fiction with its seams showing, its threads becoming "original" only when authors successfully lay claim to them, as E. L. James has, in print.

ANNE JAMISON is associate professor of English at the University of Utah, where she teaches and writes about literature and culture from the eighteenth century to the present. She holds a PhD in comparative literature from Princeton and is the author of *Poetics en passant* (Palgrave, 2009), the forthcoming *Kafka's Other Prague,* and a blog on teaching Twilight fanfiction that has been cited in publications from the *Wall Street Journal* to *Entertainment Weekly*'s PopWatch. Go figure. Anne's forthcoming book on fanfiction (www.smartpopbooks.com/fanfiction) will be published in late 2013.

Fifty
Shades of
Pop Culture

MARC SHAPIRO

Fifty Shades Is Where You Find It

KAY. Let's get the obvious out of the way. E. L. James is indeed all that.

She's literature's White Knight. Her Excalibur is called Fifty Shades. Her books, *Fifty Shades of Grey*, *Fifty Shades Darker*, and *Fifty Shades Freed* get people hot and bothered. The exploits of Christian and Anastasia are all in our faces. Those enticing book covers are everywhere we look.

And on just about everything.

Because *Fifty Shades of Grey* is pop culture personified. You don't fight it as much as you ride it out until the next big thing comes along. In literature, we've seen it before: J.K. Rowling, Stephenie Meyer. They've had their day and, while far from dead and buried, they've gone the way of *what have you done for me lately?*

Now it's E. L. James' turn.

And as expected, there's a lot to go around, because Fifty Shades and E. L. James are like blood in the water for people who live and die by the next big thing. The interest is not so much about the relative merits of Fifty Shades' odyssey as it is about what that odyssey means. And the pundits are having a field day with the notion of the books as a lightning rod for the new erotica and the middle-aged woman who's gotta have it. You can almost hear the heavy breathing coming from the enterprising journalist who coined the phrase "mommy porn."

Not too far behind is the breathless examination of the dollars and cents of it all and what E. L. James means to an industry that has, admittedly, seen better days. The skinny is that the formerly bastard stepchild known as fanfiction has suddenly taken on an air of respectability, and the marginal world of e-book erotica is the new minor leagues for the major league publishers beating the bushes for a proven track record to bring up to the bigs.

But on a deeper, personal, and ultimately more important level—women of all ages are talking openly about sex. Many are blushing but they are definitely talking.

However, what is being studiously avoided in the rush to canonize E. L. James is that Fifty Shades has become a cash cow. You can find the brand just about anywhere and in any form. Take the books for example.

If you're an erotic reader of a certain age, you're well aware of what were known in the trade as "fuck books" whose heyday ran from the '50s to the '70s. Simple line drawing covers, crude and rude titles, pages upon pages of hard-core and extremely raw sex buttressed by a simpleton story. Traveling salesman knocks on the door. Woman lets him in, they have rough sex for what seems like an eternity. It was the *War and Peace* of its day for the genre. You could find them in most book and magazine shops on both the good and bad sides of town. The key to this kingdom was that you had to be twenty-one to go into the section with the "dirty books."

But society has put lipstick on the Fifty Shades brand and that respectability has translated into point of purchase targeting where these mommies live. Walk into any supermarket or warehouse store whose name is ten letters or less and you won't have to look far for a stack of Fifty Shades, rising phallic out of the floor on aisle four, a mere spitting distance from the creamed corn. Go in for steak and come out with the sizzle. It's all too spot on and perfect.

Booksellers who, in the old days, would walk on the other side of the street to avoid acknowledging the form are now courting erotica as if it were the second coming. Those coveted front-of-the-store tables and end-of-the-aisle endcaps, primarily reserved for the latest offerings by "branded" bestselling authors or the hot "serious literature," are now stacked to overflowing with the Fifty Shades trilogy. And who's to blame booksellers for changing their tune? There are light bills to pay and doors to keep open at a time when, sadly, brick-and-mortar bookstores are dropping like flies. In the immortal words of the bard, "Money talks."

Librarians have raised the expected stink and a few have made token attempts at banning the books outright. But patron demand soon had them falling in line.

So much for the source material. Here come the moneybags that are inevitably late for the dance. Movie rights? No biggie there. You knew that was coming. Hell, there's already a soundtrack of Christian Grey's favorite tunes to spice up the aural centers. Notice I said aural and not...well, you get the picture. Been to a mall department store lately? It's like a journey into Christian Grey's Red Room of Pain. The lingerie, Christian Grey–style boxers, T-shirts with pithy come-hither slogans, caps, journals...don't forget the pink furry handcuffs. They're all emblazoned with a variation on the Fifty Shades logo.

And this is just the authorized stuff that lawyers signed off on, where major money was exchanged.

Further down the evolutionary trail of cashing in is the fringe market. Unofficial Fifty Shades books (lifestyle guides that will spend 50,000 words telling you what you already know) and graphic novels, knock-off erotic novels reconfigured to reflect the Fifty Shades lifestyle. Adult shops catering to the hardware of kinky sex are noticing an increase in the sales of whips, handcuffs, and restraints. Some enterprising erotic outlets are reporting big attendance at hastily formed couples therapy/sex workshops.

You get the picture. Who knew that a pop culture phenomenon, chopped and channeled for mass consumption, could be so laughable? But this is what happens when one writer sits down and comes up with the most brilliant idea on the planet. At least for the moment.

Because the ball is now in E. L. James' court. Continue to write the books that are making millions of women sing and you're locked in for the hall of fame. Rest on your laurels and pocketbook? You, too, could be a trivia question of the future.

Mercenary? More likely just good business. Cynical? Sure. *Fifty Shades of Grey* is not only literature but an immensely important cog in the pop culture cycle. But there is an upside to all this mass marketing. People are once again reading in a very big way.

Thank you, E. L. James. You're the stuff Pulitzers are made of.

MARC SHAPIRO is the author of thirty-six celebrity bios and entertainment books. His young adult biography *J. K. Rowling: The Wizard Behind Harry Potter* was a *New York Times* bestseller. His biography *Justin Bieber: The Fever* was a bestseller in Canada. His most recent biography on singer Adele is currently available, and he has just completed writing *The Secret Life of E. L. James, An Unauthorized Biography*. He is a published short story writer, poet, and comic book writer. He does this for a living. Don't tell the authorities.

How I Lost Christian Grey at Auction

’M AN EDITOR. Actually, I'm a romance editor, and because of that very few of my friends ask me about the books I work on. But ever since *Fifty Shades of Grey* started gaining traction, every person I know has asked me about E. L. James' series of erotic novels. They want to know what I think—are they well written? Are they really that scandalous? Am I somehow embarrassed because they actually made it out of the shadowy world of fanfiction and into the mainstream hands of women everywhere? Are they trash?

From my editorial and publishing standpoint, my position on *Fifty Shades* is simple: we read it in-house, we bid on it, we lost, and we wish we'd won—won the auction, that is.

What is the "untold" publishing backstory of *Fifty Shades*? Well, it all began fairly simply, with the submission itself (which is, of course, far different than the "submission" in the books). We first heard about the project from scouts—those somewhat mysterious people who are tasked with finding projects to develop for the movies. We often get leads from scouts, but this time they were all abuzz about this work that had originated in fanfiction and was now selling—yes, actually selling!—for the impressive price of $9.99. It had a movie deal before it had a US book deal. Within a week the first book had hit the e-book *New York Times* bestseller list, and that's when things really began to get interesting. What did this book have that others did not?

Because I was busy, I had a few trusted colleagues read it in-house first. Their reports didn't reveal anything that would normally lead us to believe that this would be a publishing sensation; they said that this was the same sort of story that Harlequin had been publishing for years. Yes, this book had more sex, but what's surprising is it didn't really have *that* much more sex than some of the steamier historical romances published back in the 1980s.

One report said, "Could see why story is resonating with so many readers. You have strong, stoically handsome billionaire hero. He's emotionally damaged, sexually charged and yet is tamed and redeemed by a young, innocent, and virginal woman. Despite the BDSM and Room of Pain stuff (also loved the contract Christian had her sign detailing how many days she should work out), it's actually a classic romance, sweet in a way. Heroine helps him work through his tortured past/childhood, heroine gets all-consuming love and unlimited money. Storytelling is good."

For those of us who have read a lot of romance through the years as well as a fair amount of erotica, none of these elements are particularly unusual. Which is precisely what the readers who have come to *Fifty Shades of Grey* often don't know. These aren't romance readers who are flocking to this book. In fact, most of these readers would probably be horrified to be told that what they are reading is, at its heart, a romance novel.

Yet we were intrigued that it was selling for $9.99 as an e-book. And the price for the trade edition was higher than most hardcovers. So we made an aggressive bid, but it was not aggressive enough. We didn't know how high was up when it came to *Fifty Shades*, which brings me to why—why is everyone reading this book?

Perhaps it's one of the first big stories of the digital reading age—because while it's doing well in print, it's also doing well as an e–book, maybe because no one sees a cover when you're reading on a device. The appeal could also be the characters, because in addition to the sex, readers seem fascinated by Christian Grey and Anastasia Steele. As of this writing, the search for the actor to play Christian Grey is getting as hysterical as the long-ago search for Scarlett O'Hara. Plus there is that connection to Twilight.

Yet maybe it is the sex. Could it be that the women of America are finally ready to embrace the dark side of their sexuality? Therapists have told me that patients are talking about this book endlessly in their sessions. Or perhaps it is that the hero of *Fifty Shades* is sexier, more attentive, provides better, and treats his partner more as a physical being than the guy sitting in the living room watching ESPN?

Fifty Shades is, at its heart, a fantasy: I'm pretty sure most women know that some man of incredible fortune is not going to sweep her off her feet. I keep thinking of the *Washington Post* essay "Reflections on Jake Ryan of the John Hughes Film 'Sixteen Candles'" and its reminder that "Jake Ryan . . . is never coming to get you," because, let's face it, neither is Christian Grey. But maybe the bottom line is that *Fifty Shades* is *fun*, at a time when we could all use some fun. Some distraction.

One thing I believe: *Fifty Shades* is a phenomenon, unlikely to happen the same way again...and, as an editor, I still wish we'd won that auction. Oh, and if you liked it, ask me what other books you might like. I'd be happy to welcome you to the world of romance novels.

EDITOR X has been an executive editor of romance fiction at a major publishing house for a very long time and has many *New York Times* bestsellers to her credit.

ANGELA EDWARDS

Making Fifty Shades into Cinema

HE FILM COMMUNITY'S PURSUIT of the rights to the Fifty Shades trilogy was unlike anything I've ever seen. It's always the case that when a few studios or producers want something, everyone else is bound to want it, too. No one wants to be left out. However, even under these circumstances the competition was fierce, with every studio going for it, regardless of whether the material suited the tastes of the creative team or not. There was a frenzy. It rivaled the competition for *The Da Vinci Code*, if it didn't surpass it. Often a studio—or more likely a producer—will option a book that suddenly and unexpectedly becomes huge. Harry Potter is the most often cited example. But in this case, people knew what was at stake and everyone pulled out all the stops to get it.

There are all kinds of rumors as to why the eventual winner, Universal Studios, succeeded, but in many of these cases it's simply who the author responds to and how a particular studio's vision for the film is conveyed. People wanting to option rights to a book are expected to have a "take": ideas as to how something should be adapted. A creative conversation that fully engages the author and expands on his or her story in intelligent and unexpected ways is also effective. These encounters can inspire, flatter, and reassure the author and agent. I'm sure it's a tough decision to make when so many powerful people are falling at your feet. It's a nice problem to have, but that doesn't make it any easier to know whom to go with. Everyone going for this book would have had smart things to say about it.

In the case of some properties, there's the risk an option may not lead to a film being made, simply because the process of adaptation requires deep development and a lot of resources. In many cases, people lose interest or a book's cultural domination fades. Sometimes the reason is as simple as sales having slowed down by the time the right script emerges. But there is no doubt, now that the trilogy is breaking all sales records, that in this case the film will be made. The studio will have paid far too much for it to let it go quiet, and there's the waiting, built-in audience of Fifty Shades' readership ready to flock to the cinema to see it. People who don't normally even read books, or at best read one book a year, are reading this. The main challenge here is not in getting the film made, but in making a film that will not disappoint millions and millions of readers. This is a really tall order. If one replicates the book too closely—I believe this was a criticism of at least one or two of the Harry Potter films—a boredom factor can creep in. Stray too far and people get angry. This book succeeds in people's minds, their fantasies. Making it flexible and layered enough to work on these levels for a wide enough audience will be the main hurdle.

In my informal polling as to why so many women (and they mostly are women) like or even love these books, I seem to get different answers. But there is, ultimately, a unifying theme. What they are drawn to is simply the *romance* of it. This is not what one expects from a novel that features an unequal power relationship and unconventional sex of the kind where even a reader who is paying close attention may have a hard time imagining what's going on. I certainly couldn't work it out all the time. The appeal lies in the fact that most of us reading these books are projecting our own wishes, our own romantic notions, onto the romance between Ana and Christian.

In addition, there is one fantasy there that I feel sure a lot of women share: the fact that Ana is able to change her man, to get him to love her in exactly the way she wants to be loved. That's very powerful. How can a film adaptation live up to all that? Bringing Ana and Christian to life, with all their longing, all their passion...all the sex.

Everyone is wondering how the sex scenes will be filmed. This won't be an X-rated film, so how does that work? I don't think this is as difficult as some people think. Because there's so much paraphernalia involved in BDSM sex, it's easy to suggest what is about to happen without actually showing it. And its effects—wincing from pain or pleasure—are far easier to convey than rapturous orgasmic reactions, which can border on parody. We can all count on one hand cinematic sex scenes we think have worked. Many people mention the one from *Out of Sight*, starring Jennifer Lopez and George Clooney, as being particularly memorable. Part of the appeal of that, of course, lies in the chemistry between the two characters the actors are playing. But, part of it, if I recall correctly, was in the waiting for them finally to get together. Equally importantly, a lot of it was suggested, which is almost always the most effective way to film these moments. No one is looking for porn here, even if the ubiquity of the Fifty Shades books has made some soft porn writing suddenly acceptable.

No one really knows why some sex scenes work, but we all know when we see something perfunctory. Often the sex is so boring we're disappointed that the filmmakers felt they even had to show anything. There was a recent, wonderful quote from the actress Maggie Gyllenhaal, who described a conventional film sex scene (I'm paraphrasing here) as a woman wearing Victoria's Secret underwear and arching her back.

With Fifty Shades, it seems, conversely, that certain hurdles can be overcome by the sheer fact it will be out of the ordinary. The Red Room of Pain in Christian's apartment will say more than a hundred of the soft-core sex scenes we are used to. Here there's also the heightened aspect of it all—Ana's longing to have Christian in the way she dreams, his own frustration. They are both experiencing something powerful, but in different ways. The sex means different things to each of them.

The minute the actors are cast, things can begin to unravel. Every woman has her own idea of who Christian is, and the book's readership spans adults of all ages. I've heard of mothers and daughters sharing this book. A twenty-three-year-old's idea of Christian is going to be different from a fifty-three-year-old's. Christian can't have bland model good looks or he will risk losing the other qualities that draw Ana and the reader. And Ana—how pretty is she? So pretty that she seems too remote, that all the insecurities she suffers in the novel could ring hollow on-screen? Any actors will simply have to take up the gauntlet and run with it, not looking back too much or else the net of expectations will entangle them.

The book offers as many gifts as it does challenges to a film-maker. Glamour is a significant aspect of these stories. Christian has it all; Ana has nothing. He gives her everything, and even if she feels a bit strange taking anything, she adjusts quickly. I don't know how many women really do fantasize about being swept off their feet in this madly unrealistic way, but it seems pleasing on the page. This is the easiest part to film; movies are the perfect medium for showing this over-the-top wealth. It will be great fun to see Christian's apartment, his cars, and so on. (I've heard it said that E. L. James admires the Pierce Brosnan/Renee Russo remake of *The Thomas Crown Affair*; the overriding image in that film is of great wealth: beautiful people, beautiful houses, beautiful clothes, etc. The glamour shouldn't be a problem for the filmmaker of Fifty Shades, as it seems the easiest part to get right.

The hard part is maintaining the overall fantasy. No one should try and make this what it isn't by overintellectualizing it. There's nothing feminist about this; it's pure escapism. Even the sex is escapist. Nor is the story making any observations about romance in our times. Everyone's just captivated by it, pure and simple.

Anyone looking to adapt a novel to film is grateful for the "hard ground of narrative," as the great master of adaptation, the late Anthony Minghella, put it. Any future adapter of the Fifty Shades trilogy has more than enough action to contend with. A lot happens in this relationship, and the books are action-packed on every level. So it bodes well in that sense. No one has to go looking for things to happen, for visual interpretations; it's all there.

There are a lot of smart people working on this film, though— as we know—that doesn't guarantee success. A lot of smart people have worked on a lot of adaptations that have not lived up to how their source material lives in the imagination. A film adaptation has to both be true to itself and complement the book. It has to allow its audience to stop comparing the minute the first frames appear; it has to take their minds off the book while taking them back to it in a way that embellishes what they might have seen in their minds' eyes. That allows just enough room for the audience to still be able to project their personal wishes and desires onto the story, to get involved. The nice surprise would be if it manages to allow us to have a swooningly romantic time, a chance to escape into glamour, impossible love, youth—and amazing sex, whatever form it takes.

ANGELA EDWARDS is the pseudonym of a London-based film executive involved in trying to secure the option to the Fifty Shades trilogy.

ANDREW SHAFFER

Fifty Shades
of Grace Metalious

S HORTLY AFTER *FIFTY SHADES OF GREY* topped best-seller lists, the *New York Times'* Maureen Dowd could hardly contain her disbelief that a woman like E. L. James was the author of such dirty books. "The plump, happily married forty-something mother and former television producer seems like a normal lady," she wrote. Dowd's condescending tone was typical of the media coverage surrounding *Fifty Shades*, as if James was the first "plump mother" to ever write a dirty book. In actuality, James was following in the footsteps of Grace Metalious, who faced similar critical derision over fifty years earlier for a dirty little book called *Peyton Place*.

"It's an odd book to come from the typewriter of a plump, thirty-two-year-old mother of three children, but Mrs. Metalious is no ordinary housewife," her editor wrote. Metalious was lower middle class, wore blue jeans and flannel shirts, and lived in a tiny house with no running water. Howard Goodkind, who worked as

339

a publicist for *Peyton Place*, later recalled, "All over the United States there were women with children saying they could write, but Grace Metalious had gone ahead and done it."

Prior to Metalious, bestselling women writers such as Edith Wharton, Dorothy Parker, and Edna St. Vincent Millay were typically upper middle class and lived at the heart of the publishing world, New York City. Most importantly, these women were childless. It was regularly assumed that if a mother was writing, she wasn't spending enough time raising her kids. "You live in a town, and there are patterns," Metalious said of Gilmanton, the conservative New Hampshire small town where her family lived. "The minute you deviate from the pattern, you're a freak. I wrote a book, and that makes me a freak."

Her husband, George, was a school principal—a sweet, honest man by all accounts, but what was his wife doing writing a *book*? When, prior to the publication date, Metalious' publicist let it slip that not only was *Peyton Place* a great book, but it was also "a very dirty book," a scandal erupted.

Without even reading a line of *Peyton Place*, the people of Gilmanton were swift in their judgment. "Word has got around that it's a shocking book. People suddenly decided that George is not the type to teach their sweet innocent children," Metalious told a reporter. "I feel pretty sure of one thing," Metalious was quoted as saying by the Associated Press on the eve of her book's publication. "It'll probably cost my husband his job."

When the *Boston Traveler* ran an AP story on August 29, 1956, under the headline, "TEACHER FIRED FOR WIFE'S BOOK: Gossipy, Spicy Story Costs Him His Job," the public took notice. The truth, however, was less sensational: George's contract as school principal in Gilmanton was set to expire at the end of the school semester, and the school board had no intention of renewing it. Still, George backed up his wife's story, saying, "They told me it was because of my wife. They don't like her book." The three-person school board, however, denied that their decision had anything to do with *Peyton Place* (which none of them had read at the time the story ran). "His wife's book had absolutely nothing to do with it. It was a personal matter," William Dunn, chairman of the Gilmanton school board, said.

Metalious denied that Gilmanton was the basis for Peyton Place. "It's a composite picture of life in a small New Hampshire town, but it's not Gilmanton. As a matter of fact, the book was three-fourths written before I moved here," she said. "To a tourist these towns look as peaceful as a postcard picture, but if you go beneath that picture, it's like turning over a rock with your foot—all kinds of strange things crawl out. Everybody who lives in town knows what's going on—there are no secrets—but they don't want outsiders to know." *Peyton Place* threatened to kick over the stone on Gilmanton and every other picture-perfect New England town.

By the time the book was finally published on September 24, 1956, the entire country was curious to get a glimpse inside the book that had cost the author's schoolteacher husband his job. "Whatever the merits of the Metalious case [George's dismissal], the novel lives up very fully to its advance billing," an enthusiastic *New York Times* review read (headline: "Small Town Peep Show"). At a time when the average debut novel sold about 2,000 copies over the course of its shelf life, *Peyton Place* sold 60,000 copies in hardcover in just ten days. It hit the *New York Times* bestseller list, where it stayed for an astonishing fifty-nine weeks.

Peyton Place was banned in several cities and in Canada. "Letters to the editor debated the book's merits; libraries worried whether to purchase it," Emily Toth wrote in her biography of Grace Metalious, *Inside Peyton Place.* In Beverly, Massachusetts, a sign at the public library read, "THIS LIBRARY DOES NOT CARRY 'PEYTON PLACE.' IF YOU WANT IT, GO TO SALEM."

"Novelist Metalious suggests that sex is never long out of the town's mind; anyway, it seldom is out of hers," *Time* magazine wrote in its review. "Her love scenes are as explicit as love scenes can get without the use of diagrams and tape recorder. The low animal moans produced by Peyton Place's mating females must be audible clear to White River Junction."

Metalious countered with, "Too much sex? How can you write a novel about normal men and women, let alone abnormal ones, with no sex in the plot? We all had a mother and father!" The millions of middle-aged, married women who read *Peyton Place* likely agreed, even if they hid the book from their children and husbands. (The kids got hold of it, regardless: "Everyone was passing that book around," novelist John Irving, who was fourteen when the book came out, recalled in an interview with the Associated Press on *Peyton Place's* fiftieth anniversary.)

The book was brimming with taboo topics for the 1950s, including casual sex, underage sex, pseudo-incest, adultery, and abortion. But just how *dirty* was the book? Not very, it turns out—at least not in an erotic sense, a la *Fifty Shades of Grey*. A sample passage: "He grunted like a rooting pig, and he breathed like a steam engine puffing its way across the wide Connecticut River, while from Nellie there was no sound at all... Lucas grunted harder and puffed louder, and the old spring on the double bed creaked alarmingly, faster and faster. At last, Lucas squealed like a calf in the hands of a butcher and it was over."

If it's difficult to imagine just how *Peyton Place* could have been considered the epitome of the "dirty book," one only has to look at the state of culture in the 1950s: Elvis Presley had only recently made his national television debut, in January 1956. In a world where the wiggling of hips was considered the height of obscenity, it's easy to see the moral majority getting their panties wet over lines such as, "You have the long, aristocratic legs and the exquisite breasts of a statue."

Thanks to the controversy, *Peyton Place* was the third best-selling hardcover novel of the year and eventually sold 300,000 copies in hardcover. Big-city critics praised the book—if it wasn't a work of art, it was at least art of a certain type—but small-town critics and self-proclaimed moral guardians ripped Metalious' book apart. In a front-page editorial that ran in 1957,

New Hampshire's *Union Leader* called the book "literary sewage," before adding, "This sad fascination [with sex] reveals a complete debasement of taste and a fascination with the filthy, rotten side of life that are the earmarks of the collapse of civilization."

"If I'm a lousy writer, then a hell of a lot of people have got lousy taste," Metalious said. When Dell released the mass-market paperback in 1957, it became the top-selling paperback of the year, with more than 3 million copies sold. Dell eventually sold over 10 million *Peyton Place* paperbacks, and it was estimated that one in twenty-nine Americans had read *Peyton Place*.

After Metalious sold the film rights for $125,000, movie talk heated up. "Somehow, the smoldering bestseller would be filmed. Each important casting decision got play in the newspapers," Metalious' biographer wrote. The route from page to screen was a rocky one. It was never clear that the men who produced, wrote, and directed *Peyton Place* ever understood their source material: screenwriter John Michael Hayes offended Metalious by asking her if the book was her autobiography. (She threw a drink in his face.) Still, the film debuted on December 13, 1957, and had long legs: despite being toned down for censors, *Peyton Place* was the second highest–grossing film of 1958.

Metalious, flush with cash from her advances and royalties, looked forward to a long and prosperous career. "From now on everything was going to be wonderful forever. Life was going to be all beer and skittles and nothing unpleasant was ever going to happen to me again," Metalious said. In 1958, she divorced her husband and married her business manager, a radio disc jockey, three days later. She'd never been happier, she told the press. New husband Martin "was the only man in my world who made me feel intensely female. A stallion type."

Even with her success, she stayed true to her lower middle-class roots: "I don't waste any time shopping when I'm in New York. These Fifth Avenue stores are strictly for jerks. I get all the clothes I need [locally]," she said. Despite being a celebrity, she made no effort to get her plump figure into shape. "I'm just fat and happy," she said. "I think diets are stupid."

Unfortunately, her comment about "beer and skittles" was a little too on-the-nose: she drowned herself in alcohol, which led to a quick end for her second marriage. She then reunited with George. "I'm taking her home to be a mother mainly," he told reporters. "Being a writer is just incidental." Privately, he told colleagues he wanted to "help get Grace sober."

The newly reunited couple bought a hotel on the shores of Paugus Bay in Laconia, New Hampshire. They named it, of course, "Peyton Place." Still, George was unable to help his wife. "All I have left is five hundred dollars, and I'm going to drink myself to death," she said. In fact, five hundred dollars was a bit of an overstatement: she owed the IRS hundreds of thousands of dollars in back taxes, and now, with the hotel purchase, was hopelessly in debt. The only way out was for her to write more, faster—which was complicated by her alcoholism.

Meanwhile, her hardcover and paperback publishers were hungry for more *Peyton Place*. A sequel, *Return to Peyton Place*, was released in 1960 to drum up interest in a second movie. When Metalious complained to reporters that Hollywood producers had coerced her into writing it against her wishes, her producer wrote, "I did not guide her hands across her golden typewriter." In fact, *no one* had guided her hands: Metalious had written what amounted to little more than a screenplay treatment, which was fleshed out by a ghostwriter into a full novel ("A foul and rotten trick," Metalious later said).

The second *Peyton Place* book still sold 5 million copies in paperback, about half of what the original had sold. Critics, however, were less kind to *Return*. One of her publishers suggested that Metalious write a "spring break in Peyton Place" book—even though Peyton Place, a town of less than 4,000 residents, had no college. "Couldn't you just put a college there?" her publisher asked. Metalious was dumbfounded by the request. Peyton Place may have been a fictional town, but it was real to her.

Metalious wrote two more novels, neither of which were associated with *Peyton Place*. They were met with diminishing returns—both commercially and critically. When her final book, *No Adam in Eden*, was published in 1963, *Newsweek* wrote, "Yes, fans, the sensational author of *Peyton Place* has run another one through her typewriter, just the way you like it. But you'd better hurry. The author's supply of talent is strictly limited." Their words would prove eerily prophetic.

On February 25, 1964, Metalious died suddenly of cirrhosis of the liver, the result of drinking a fifth of liquor a day for several years. She was just thirty-nine years old. In its obituary for her, the *New York Times* took a final shot at her. "It is debatable whether literary merit alone sold so many copies or made it one of the most talked-about novels in the United States," they said in a postmortem on *Peyton Place* and its author.

In the wake of her death, a prime-time television soap opera and nine ghostwritten sequels from Pocket Books followed (sample title: *Pleasures of Peyton Place*). The soap opera, in particular, sanitized Metalious' gritty fictional New England town, rendering it almost unrecognizable. Her family earned next to nothing from the continued exploitation of *Peyton Place*, in part due to the front-loaded contracts Metalious had signed and the money she still owed the IRS at the time of her death.

There were worse threats on the horizon, though: a year after Metalious passed away, the police chief of Manchester, New Hampshire, banned Terry Southern and Mason Hoffenberg's novel, *Candy*, calling it "the worst I've ever seen." Chief Francis P. McGranaghan added, "This book makes *Peyton Place* look like a Sunday school text." By the seventy-fifth anniversary of Grace Metalious' birth, in 1999, *Peyton Place* was out of print and mostly forgotten.

Today, things are looking up for Grace Metalious' legacy. *Petyon Place* is back in print. And while her name was long considered an embarrassment to her hometown of Gilmanton, New Hampshire (population: 3,060), Metalious' old estate has been turned into the Gilmanton Winery, billed without shame as the "Home of *Peyton Place*." A fitting tribute, indeed.

ANDREW SHAFFER is the author of *Fifty Shames of Earl Grey*, a parody of *Fifty Shades of Grey*. His writing has appeared in such diverse publications as *Mental Floss* and *Maxim*. An Iowa native, Shaffer lives in Lexington, Kentucky, a magical land of horses and bourbon.

LYSS STERN

Fifty Shades of Diva Frenzy!

WHEN E. L. JAMES did her first US book tour in May 2012, people were surprised that two of her stops were sold-out luncheons (at $85 per person, no less) at country clubs in Long Island and Westchester hosted by a group of suburban New York moms. I'm the woman behind *Fifty Shades of Diva Frenzy,* and the founder of DivaLysscious Moms, and www.divamoms.com (which I always describe as *Sex and the City* meets Mommy & Me). I knew E. L. James spoke for us and knew she *had* to speak to us.

I had read the first two books back in November and honestly could not put them down. I knew that *Fifty Shades Freed,* the third book in the trilogy, was going to be released in January, and I knew that the DivaMoms.com book club had to launch the book as we've done for so many other amazing authors. I decided to email E. L. James in London and explain to her what I did, how much I LOVED the first two books, and that I would be honored to throw her a DivaMoms book club launch party.

A few days later she responded, telling me that she was the mom of two boys and that she would be honored to have us launch *Fifty Shades Freed* to the DivaMoms. She also said she would be in New York City in three weeks!

My work was cut out for me. I knew I had to get this event done! And so using my DivaMagic, I brought the DivaMoms launch of *Fifty Shades Freed* to a beautiful penthouse apartment in Chelsea. We reached out to over 380,000 of the most influential moms in the area via our database and social media. Just by posting the event on our Facebook page, we had 900 RSVPs in hours. But the event space could only hold 200 moms. I was in a panic. But we made it happen and the apartment was filled wall to wall with moms—women from Long Island, Westchester, Connecticut, Pennsylvania, and New Jersey who drove in to be at this event.

I knew then and there that E. L. James was going to be the next J.K. Rowling and that her big book and movie deals were just moments away.

The Fifty Shades trilogy has been nothing short of a whirlwind; moms everywhere feel like they are on a fantastic, erotic ride and never want to get off. We watch women of all ages from all over the country screaming for more, all hopeful that the story of Ana and Christian is just beginning. What started as the subject of whispered gossip between ladies has turned into the "it" book of the year—and its success and popularity is on an *upward* spiral. It has evolved into an absolute worldwide sensation. *Fifty Shades of Grey* has, without a doubt, tied women together—no pun intended.

The fans of the series have been the engine. The success of these novels has proven the power and effectiveness of women's voices, of women's interest in fetish, of what *women* want to see in the world of literature and in the world of romance! We celebrate our collective, bright inner light that won't be dimmed. We celebrate motherhood and our evolution from the sandbox to the Red Room of Pain. We celebrate E. L. James for reconnecting women with an aspect of their sexuality—a flame—that they may have left unattended. We celebrate *Fifty Shades of Fabulyssness!*

Women everywhere are turning their shy, giggly whispers into full, loud, and powerful expression, making their sexuality something to be nurtured and accepted rather than hidden and saved for "appropriate" times. The books have inevitably gotten *some* kind of reaction from every woman who has read them; even the women I have spoken to who say they would not engage in such sexual behavior *cannot* put the books down. Women cannot help but discuss specific parts of the book with one another, turning their reserved, "Would *you* ever do that?" conversations into free, open, matter-of-fact discussions—and that's the way it *should* be. As I always say to everyone, even my mom, "Everyone is reading them, everyone *should* be reading them, and there is nothing *wrong* with reading them."

Time magazine nominated E. L. James as one of 2012's "100 Most Influential People in the World." This happily married mother followed her dreams and in doing so became one of the most talked-about authors—and women—of the year. *Fifty Shades of Grey, Fifty Shades Darker,* and *Fifty Shades Freed* went "viral," so to speak, putting ladies everywhere into a perpetual orgasmic coma! While breathlessly turning pages, we tuned out the world, escaped reality, and tapped into a typically forbidden world of sexual intensity. Women's conversations have been consumed by this modern-day love story; our voices have been loud and our voices have been *heard*—Random House and Universal Studios are hearing us loud and clear! People who call the novels "mommy porn" simply have not yet fallen under the spell of Christian Grey. But they will. I'm sure of that.

LYSS STERN is the founder and president of Divalysscious Moms (www.divamoms.com), the luxury lifestyle company that caters to New York's well-heeled and trendsetting moms. After eight years, Lyss' company database boasts 380,000 members. Lyss is also the coauthor of *If You Give a Mom a Martini: 100 Ways to Find 10 Blissful Minutes for Yourself* (Clarkson Potter), which was recently optioned to be made into a feature film, and is the cocreator of the new NickMom short-form series Storytime for Moms. Lyss lives in New York City with her husband, talent manager Brian Stern, and their two sons, Jackson and Oliver, and spends her summer in Atlantic Beach and Southampton with her family and puppy, Jedi.

Imagining a Black Fifty Shades

YANKING. SPANKING. Dominating. Submitting. Orgasms. Shaking. Pleasure. Strokes. Moans. Screams. Control. Release.

The sex scenes in *Fifty Shades of Grey* have penetrated the imaginations of women across the world, challenging them to explore their sexual curiosities.

Anastasia "Ana" Steele is every woman, kind of. She's strong, yet vulnerable. She's smart, yet still learning. She's independent, yet dependent. But she's also different from me. We're both young. We're both sexually adventurous. We're both stubborn in relationships. However, she's pale, brunette, and beautiful. I'm caramel brown, kinky-haired, and gorgeous. We both have our own sex appeal, but her image sells to a wider audience.

Beyond urban and black genres, multifaceted stories of black sexualities have barely penetrated the fiction publishing market. It's difficult to attract nonurban or nonblack readers to the most frequent narratives of black American sex lives for a variety of reasons, but it's primarily due to the cultural specificity of the stories that are currently available.

There are two recurring scenarios in black and urban erotica. However, these common plots have made books successful in their own right without the mainstream nod. First, there's the story of the classic urban vixen who physically resembles a contemporary hip-hop video girl. She's usually participating in male pleasure–centered sexual intercourse, halfway getting her needs met and having to pleasure herself. Meanwhile, she's constantly in danger due to her sexual relationship with a drama-ridden rapper or drug-dealing man.

On the flipside, there's the Christian-centered story line in which the black female protagonist deals with the guilt trips of the Black Church. If she's single, she's experiencing the too common reality of black women being ashamed of satisfying their sexual needs outside of marriage due to their Christian beliefs. If she's married, she's either going through a lack of sexual fulfillment due to a cheating male spouse or having an affair herself.

The cultural specificity of these frequent fiction narratives of black female sexualities makes it more difficult for these books to cross over and gain recognition outside of the black and urban book markets. Authors like Zane and Eric Jerome Dickey have experienced wider audiences and longevity in terms of their careers, but that's because they've stepped outside of those story lines. Yes, authors like Noire and Kimberla Lawson Roby, whose books have plots similar to the ones listed above, have experienced popularity as well, but their popularity has been more limited to the urban and black publishing markets.

In general, it's rare to read about the diversity of black female sexual pleasure in literary works and mainstream media. When conversations do occur or books are written and published, they usually end up as a slight remix of the story lines listed above, even in black and urban erotica. There are few stories of black participants in pleasure lifestyles such as kink and BDSM that get any mass literary traction or media attention. Thus, it's not unexpected that most Americans would expect and easily imagine the main characters in book like *Fifty Shades*—a book that includes BDSM—as white.

A black Ana would require the acknowledgment that black women are into more than just vanilla sex and plain-Jane desire. While the stories of black women's diverse sexualities are limited in mainstream media, some like handcuffs, bondage, a bit of spanking, dominating sex talk, and submitting to their partners. Others might prefer to stay in control in the bedroom, dictating the actions of their lovers and guiding their every move. Or they might prefer something entirely different. That's the beauty of being human.

On paper, many black women are Ana. They're college-educated, career-driven, self-sufficient, and independent. Thanks to Michelle Obama and other intelligent, ambitious black women shining in mainstream media, very few would blink twice at the idea of a black Ana in terms of academic profile and social class. It's the sexual nature of her character that would give many people pause, as black women aren't known for doing *those* types of things or exploring certain approaches to pleasure.

Additionally, what about the controlling, yet oh so sexy, Christian Grey? Would a reader believe a young (white) American billionaire is sexually attracted to a black woman? Or even more brain twisting, could a young American billionaire be black?

While there are plenty of white men and black women in interracial relationships, there aren't any young black male billionaires even in the age of President Barack Obama. The white Christian Grey has Facebook cofounder Mark Zuckerberg as a real-life billionaire reference. A black Christian would be a total product of the imagination, which could be problematic for mass book sales, particularly outside of the black and urban publishing markets.

Part of what sells books is the balance between imagination and believability. Could two black characters, one with a believable social class and the other rich beyond the imagination, engage in kinky sex and have it appeal to the world? Would a black Ana make white American and British women fawning over *Fifty Shades of Grey* feel the same inspiration to explore and express their desires? Would a black Mr. Grey still make the majority of female readers moist down there and ready to get on their knees in a play dungeon?

Arguably, the whiteness of *Fifty Shades of Grey* was necessary for mainstream success, as the imaginations of many readers aren't prepared to embrace a black version of the book. Not to mention, many white writers are petrified to bring characters to life that don't look anything like them, so it would've been daring for E. L. James to describe her characters as brown.

Truth be told, there is a double standard when it comes to the appeal of brown bodies having mind-blowing sex versus white ones. For a society that's supposed to be "postracial" or able to see past color, *Fifty Shades of Grey* is just another reminder that there's much work to be done in order for us to really see ourselves in each other.

Black couples yank, spank, dominate, submit, orgasm, shake, please, stroke, moan, scream, control, and release in bedrooms and play in dungeons as well. With a bit of extra curiosity, mainstream readers would find that sex is a universal experience and how we do it isn't limited by race but rather personal interest.

We need more sex stories of characters that look different than Ana and Grey. We need more sex narratives by black women, because there is power in the variety of black women's desires, and it's important that they tell their many sex stories, too. And we need more examples of high-achieving black men to put to rest the stereotype of a young American billionaire automatically being white. Achieving this diversity doesn't have to be an "Affirmative Action" style initiative, but rather something that stems from our creative values as diverse erotica fans and readers.

ARIELLE LOREN is the editor in chief of *Corset Magazine*, the go-to magazine for all things sexuality. Embracing human curiosity, honoring sensuality, and celebrating sex, the downloadable publication caters to an international community of sex-curious readers. Learn more at Corset-Magazine.com.

DR. LOGAN LEVKOFF

The Professional Poster Child

'M NO STRANGER to provocative topics. I've been an advocate for lots of "controversial" subjects before. To name a few: sexuality education, talking to kids about sex, condoms, vibrators.

Despite my training as a sex educator and sexologist, I didn't anticipate that we, as a culture, would make such a big deal over a fictional book trilogy, or that the love of such a series would incite an extensive public discourse about women, fantasies, sex, and—dare I say it—feminism. And I never thought that I would be a part of this firestorm of commentary, as the effective professional poster child for *Fifty Shades of Grey*.

This is not to say that I am a novice to the erotica genre. At my all-girls sleepaway camp in the late 1980s, I was charged with buying Judy Blume's *Forever...*, Nancy Friday's *My Secret Garden*, and *Penthouse Letters*. Sure, *Forever...* isn't really erotica, but it was all about a budding sexual relationship. For many of us who had never had any sexual experience before, the sentiments and descriptions were highly erotic. As for the other books, I remember reading them aloud with my girlfriends, and I remember the electrical charge surging through my body. I remember watching my girlfriends squirm on their beds. Clearly they, too, felt something; they felt pleasure. It was thrilling to know that my body was capable of producing those types of feelings without having to do anything physical. Though I didn't know it then, it was the moment when I discovered how powerful my body was. Most of us would give anything to get back to that time when those feelings were new and anything was possible.

Fast-forward to 2012. Early this year, my husband and a close friend told me about a book they had heard about (and, knowing my line of work, thought I'd be interested in). "Fifty something," my husband said.

"What's it about?" I asked.

"I don't know. Sex, I guess. I was told you would like it," he replied.

We were about to go on vacation and would be living on a boat with three other couples in the middle of the ocean; I needed some books to read anyway and downloaded what I soon learned was titled *Fifty Shades of Grey* onto my Kindle.

We got on the boat on a Tuesday around noon. By 2:00 P.M. I had begun the book. One of my friends on the trip, Amy, was reading *Fifty Shades Darker*. Within twenty minutes, clearly motivated by what we were reading, we grabbed our respective partners and headed down to our rooms. Our girlfriends had seen this interaction and in the middle of the Caribbean Sea, thanks to technology and cell service, downloaded their copies, too. Needless to say, there was a lot of swaying on the boat that week that had nothing to do with the waves. There was sex—lots and lots of sex.

Suffice it to say, I loved these books. I loved what they did for my libido. But also, almost as much (dare I actually say as much?), I loved what they did for my friendships and the conversations that my girlfriends and I had with one another. We talked, we laughed, and we shared untold stories from our lives.

It was like summer camp all over again—only this time as an adult in a marriage. And these conversations were right on par with all of my professional media messaging: sex is good, pleasure is important, communication is essential. I was officially a Fifty Shades fan.

When I got back to land, it turned out the whole country was reading the trilogy. Imagine how happy I was, then, when I was asked to appear on the *Today Show* to talk about the Fifty Shades phenomenon. I had been on the *Today Show* several times, but they had never put me in the 8:00 A.M. hour. Sex and other "fluffy" stuff get pushed to 9:00 or 10:00 A.M., when it's Kathie Lee Gifford and Hoda Kotb, and there are usually cocktails somewhere on the set. But not this time. This time I was booked for an 8:13 A.M. segment to talk about *Fifty Shades of Grey* with Dr. Drew Pinsky, celebrity psychiatrist, television host, and a longtime professional friend.

It was this segment that ended up inciting a wild and irrational discussion about female sexuality, fantasies, and erotica. The anchor, Savannah Guthrie, said the book was demeaning to women. Dr. Drew said that the book's concept disturbed him and that *Fifty Shades of Grey* was more than the swept-away fantasy; it was violence against women. (He also said that he had not read the book.) I said that Fifty Shades didn't disturb me at all; it was a romanticized version of a particular community and an absolutely consensual relationship. (And I'd read all three books. In forty-eight hours.) What could have been a conversation about how our culture's unhealthy portrayal of sex has fueled women's desire for sex on their own terms (and in their own voice) evolved into a debate about whether the Fifty Shades zeitgeist perpetuates violence against women.

Let me be clear: I have no tolerance for violence against women (or violence of any kind). However, the assumption that Fifty Shades perpetuates crimes against women trivializes real violence against women. *Fifty Shades of Grey* and other types of nonvanilla erotica have nothing to do with this. And that's what this is really about, right? Nonvanilla sex. Nonheterosexual-man-on-top sex. Consensual BDSM. And women who get off on having (or thinking about) lots of it.

We don't like to acknowledge that female sexuality doesn't always present itself in the package of the "good girl"; it forces us to reevaluate everything we've been taught about sex. It forces us to challenge preconceived notions of men and women. Because there's no such thing as the good girl. We can be good, bad, or anything in between. We can be aggressive, demanding, or we can want our partners to take charge and tell us exactly what to do. We are not the same sexual person every day. It depends upon our mood, the context of our relationship, and our partner. It may also depend upon how big our bed is, and whether or not we are at sea—but I digress.

Women can be aroused by things that may be politically incorrect—like falling for a bad boy and believing that you can change him, or wanting a wealthy man to take care of you, or wanting to take a pair of silver balls out for a test drive, or wanting to be submissive. However, we don't control how and if we turn on to something or someone. We may not desire to have fantasies about losing control, but many of us do. It doesn't make us bad women or bad people. It doesn't even say anything about our psyche or whether or not we want to "lose control" in our daily lives. We may not have even known that we could turn on to a particular scene or experience until reading about it. There's no underlying psychological issue here. This is not about feminism or the demise of the women's movement. But that is what it has become. Our fantasy lives, our personal lives, the things that are innately ours, have become pathologized, politicized, and publicly demonized. Our culture can't handle women who own (and embrace) their sexuality. It hasn't been too kind to women who want sex (or merely talk about it). We have a word for them: "sluts."

Consider the effects of this hideous judgment. The inability to be our authentic sexual selves greatly hinders our ability to have fulfilling sexual and emotional experiences. It's why we don't speak up. Why we don't demand pleasure. Or protection. Or why we don't carry condoms in our purses. Why we don't share our feelings and admit that those feelings are very strong. Or why we don't admit that we're only interested in having no-strings-sex. Or that we want to use a vibrator or watch a little pornography or experiment with BDSM. Or just read a book about it.

Which leads me back to the *Today Show*. Do you know what is really demeaning to women? Telling us who we are supposed to be and what we are supposed to turn on to.

Anyway, I said all of this that morning on television. Though maybe not so eloquently; it was only a four-minute segment. (But I actually used the phrase "kink community" on the 8:00 A.M. hour of the *Today Show*, which for me says "success"!) I received an avalanche of feedback to my response; tens of thousands of viewers have watched the video on my YouTube page. People have lots to say about Fifty Shades. For me, this goes back to the liberation and fun I felt when I first read those books, first experienced the uptick in my libido, and laughed hysterically with my girlfriends. That is what sex and sexual health should be about: pleasure, fun, and communication.

As it turns out, I am actually thankful to *Fifty Shades of Grey* for giving us material that has brought women's sexuality back into the public discourse. But I am convinced that we're missing the big picture. There is an aspect to the Fifty Shades phenomenon that no one has mentioned. It's what makes me proud to be associated with this trilogy. For me, when it comes to *Fifty Shades of Grey*, it's not about the sex, the relationship between Ana and Christian, or the real-life drama or controversy. The Fifty Shades phenomenon isn't about the content: it's about the readers. The success of *Fifty Shades of Grey* represents women at our best. Sure, the Real Housewives are entertaining, but we're not all gossipy and catty backstabbers. We're friends, we're sisters, we're mothers, we're partners, and we want to support each other. And if we find something that enhances our lives—even our sex lives—we share the information. That's what *Fifty Shades of Grey* is all about. Women talking to each other. Women talking to their partners. All with the goal of bettering our intimate lives, because as we all know, it's very easy to put that part of our lives on the back burner when we have so much going on.

So sure, *Fifty Shades* has some seriously good sex. Sex that many of us have never experienced or even dreamed about. But it's also about love and it's also about becoming that inner goddess inside all of us. Because we all have her. We all are her. But sometimes it takes a while to remember that she's there, waiting for us to find ourselves again. Because we need that. We need to remember that we are more than just someone's spouse or mother. We have names; we are sex goddesses. We are definitely not sluts.

I will be the poster child for that message any day.

DR. LOGAN LEVKOFF is a nationally recognized expert in the field of human sexuality. She encourages honest conversation about sex and the role that it plays in American culture. As a thought leader in sexuality and relationships, Logan frequently appears on television as a pundit and sexual health contributor. She is the host of *CafeMom's Mom Ed: In the Bedroom* and the author of *Third Base Ain't What it Used to Be* and *How to Get Your Wife to Have Sex with You*. Logan is an AASECT-certified sex educator and received her PhD in human sexuality, marriage, and family life education from New York University and an MS in human sexuality education and a BA in English from the University of Pennsylvania. She lives in New York City with her husband, son, and daughter.

MELISSA FEBOS

Raising the Shades

MEAN, MELLY," my mother's voice emitted from the phone, "it's really a *phenomenon*."

I heard her clinking pots in her kitchen.

"Have you read it?" I asked, turning onto my Brooklyn street.

"I've read all three!" she laughed, both delighted and embarrassed by the confession. "And, honey, you could have written these in your sleep. Not that you ever would."

"Nope," I agreed, suddenly wanting the conversation to be over.

Friends were startled that it took me so long to hear of *Fifty Shades of Grey*. Not me. I had spent the past two years talking about my own experiences with S&M—a part of my life that ended (in practice) six years ago. I am not drawn to similarly themed subject matter. As a drug addict who has been clean for nearly a decade, I am similarly bored and repelled by most stories about active addiction. I'm over it—that part of it, anyway. But facing *Fifty Shades* was, of course, inevitable.

As a twenty-one-year-old college student in Manhattan, I'd answered an ad in the *Village Voice* and spent the next four years performing all the practices described in *Fifty Shades* (and many, many more) upon men who paid $200 per hour to see me. For the first two years, I worked out of a Midtown "dungeon," which provided the space, equipment, and administrative work necessary to cater to the fantasies of these men. The last two years, I worked freelance, teetering on my stilettos to hotel rooms and lavish homes with my tote bag full of rope, dildos, clamps, and floggers.

And then I wrote a book about it. *Whip Smart* began, as my experience had, with an anthropological experiment, followed by my immersion in the commercial realm of S&M fantasy, and ended with the surprising and inevitable realization that my most profound motives were based on neither finances nor curiosity.

I had never intended to write a memoir about my years as a Domme, nor the twists that landed me on the bondage table instead of my clients, nor any kind of memoir for that matter. But I was a writer, and it turns out that I can only engage the big questions by writing my way into their answers.

At twenty-one, or twenty-two, or twenty-three, I could not reconcile my feminism, my self-conception as an intellectual, with my desire to relinquish power. And I *was* curious, adventurous, and drawn to experiences outside of social prescription. So I stuck with that story, and the flimsy idea that I was fundamentally different from my clients and the women I worked with. I was also a secret heroin addict, and so already a master of compartmentalization and denial.

The abridged conclusion is that I was, and am, fundamentally interested in power dynamics. The eroticization of this, for me, was an effort to divorce my submissive desires from my "real" life. I had no interest in submitting to the mores of our sexist culture, but still had been socialized by them—and repressed tendencies have a way of creeping out in fantasy, in sex.

Most of my clients were also committed to an outward life of empowerment: they were Wall Street types, cops, politicians, and child abuse survivors. Repression of impulse and trauma had worked well for them—my clients were successful by mainstream measures—but their desires could not be erased. They paid me to scratch their hidden itches, and also created a space for me to scratch mine.

The experience of those years, and of writing and publishing the book, taught me how to integrate my desires into my life. I got honest with myself, and then with anyone who cared to read my story. I learned to accept the seeming contradiction of my beliefs and my fantasies. They were not at odds; they were working out a balance between what was and what I wished. If our society's pressure to fit myself into a submissive, sexualized female ideal were not insidious, I might not be so convinced of my feminism. These parts of myself exist not at odds but in tandem. What a relief it was to figure this out.

But there is a curious dynamic between having learned a hard-won truth and observing that process in other people. As a recovered heroin addict, I have deep compassion and love for other addicts. Still, I often find myself more repelled by them than any other class of people. I think it is somewhat universal, the instinct to judge most harshly those people in whom you recognize some vulnerability of your own. That kind of recognition on a national scale is no different.

I avoided *Fifty Shades of Grey* for as long as I could. Every day for a month I fielded phone calls, emails, and requests for comment. I avoided most articles analyzing the phenomenon. I cut my own curiosity off at the knees, and resisted indulging in others' proclamations of the book's terrible writing. I wanted it to be bad. I wanted it to be good and feared it wasn't. I feared what feelings bubbled in me every time the book was mentioned.

And then I bought it. I read the first half of the first book in bed next to my sleeping girlfriend. The writing was indeed terrible. But I still masturbated three times, iPad in one hand, the other tucked under the waistband of my pajama bottoms. With zero shame. My own experience had given me that freedom.

I didn't finish the book. Not because I was disgusted with it or myself. Not because I didn't find it compelling, despite the poor writing. I was simply trying to revise my own novel and am easily influenced by the voice of whatever I'm reading. I need to stick to works in possession of craft and nuance to which I aspire.

I'm not interested in condemning the book. I think it's my obligation, as a writer, to inform myself of what people are re- sponding to. Especially women. My most important goal as a writer is to acknowledge truths that readers already know, how- ever inchoately. My greatest pleasure as a reader is not to digest completely foreign information, but to identify my own expe- rience articulated as I have not yet seen or thought it. Writers are mirrors more than guides. For me, honest self-appraisal has been the best guide.

I read the Twilight series, and I read most of *Fifty Shades of Grey*. These books have not found success based on tricks or mi- rage—or at least none that do not already operate in the psyches of their readers, or the cultures that raised them. They are not great works of art, but they are great mirrors. They name what we are afraid to name within ourselves.

I do, however, believe in the responsibility of writers to also show us what *can* be. My own experience has shown me that I can accept my submissive fantasies and remain an empowered, intellectual woman. I can still wear my stilettos and expect to be taken seriously. I need not be defined solely by my own eroti- cism, nor our culture's eroticization of my body, my femininity, and its invented ideal.

I think it's likely that *Fifty Shades* could have named the de- sire to submit to another's power without endorsing the more complex and dangerous fantasy that one must be a naïf to do so. Need Christian Grey have been a wealthy businessman? Need Anastasia have been a *virgin* incapable of naming her own vagina? One can submit one's body, to another human being, can submit to one's own desires, without submitting all their worldly knowledge. I know this for fact.

This equation is a dangerous one: that we must sacrifice our maturity to obtain our fantasies. That we must have all the power or none of it. The myth lifts a curtain with one hand and drops another with the other. Women have been negotiating this shitty deal for a long, long time. If there is an illusion here, it is that we must continue doing so.

But the book is just a story—millions froth at every corner of our culture. There is no inherent threat posed by this book, per se; its pages boast no invention. And in that sense *Fifty Shades of Grey* is the most accurate mirror we have. The book has not revealed our deep-seated belief that women's sexuality threatens our independence, or that we are incapable of containing multitudes. Our reaction to the book has revealed this belief. E. L. James' choices evidence this as well. The products of our culture are often simply its symptoms.

I am glad that *Fifty Shades* was published because we need to see our secrets named. Because we need to make public a conversation of how this can be done without promoting our disempowerment. Empowerment does not come in reading this book; it comes in seeing what we are, and what we are not. Accepting our fantasies comes at a price, but that price is not the forfeiting of our intellect, our wisdom, our politics, or our dignity. Rather, that price comes from bravely deciding that there is enough room for all of our selves. And there is.

MELISSA FEBOS is the author of *Whip Smart* (St. Martin's Press), a critically acclaimed memoir about her years as a professional Dominatrix that *Kirkus Review* said "expertly captures grace within depravity." Her work has appeared in *Glamour, Salon, Dissent, The Southeast Review,* the *New York Times, Bitch Magazine, BOMB,* and the *Chronicle of Higher Education Review,* among many others, and she has been profiled in venues ranging from the cover of the *New York Post* to NPR's *Fresh Air* to *Dr. Drew.* A 2010 and 2011 MacDowell Colony fellow, and 2012 Bread Loaf fellow, she teaches at Sarah Lawrence College, Purchase College, New York University, and privately, and holds an MFA from Sarah Lawrence. She lives in Brooklyn, and is currently at work on a novel.

APPENDIX

Fifty Shades of Reading

HERE ARE A WHOLE LOT OF BOOKS mentioned in these pages—some are smutty, some are literary, some are educational. We've distilled them into a big reference list for you, so you can put them on your favorite reading device and become an expert on smut.

We left out the mainstream classics—we figured you could find *Gone with the Wind* and *Pride and Prejudice* on your own (and if you haven't, you should!).

We also divided the list into fiction and nonfiction. The fiction list is almost a best-of guide to the erotica of the past decade, plus a few BDSM standards.

Erotica expert Susie Bright put her own list together on Amazon's Listmania (where you can find many of the same titles) in which she summed up what it is about these books that makes them so compelling:

> Every once in a blue hot moon, a novel comes along that
> captures women's erotic fantasies. The female heroine is

plucky, headstrong, a little naïve—but with a sexual appetite that's never been tapped. When she finds a lover who is confident (alright, masterful!) and persuasive enough to push her over the edge—wow, just send all your messages to voicemail and lock the door, because readers will not be torn from these pages.

We hope you'll find something here whose pages you won't be torn from, either.

Fiction

Bared to You: A Crossfire Novel, by Sylvia Day

Best Gay Erotica 2009, edited by Richard Labonte and James Lear

Black Feathers: Erotic Dreams, by Cecilia Tan

Blind Seduction, by Debra Hyde

Blue Boy, by Rakesh Satyal

Candy, by Terry Southern and Mason Hoffenberg

Carrie's Story, by Molly Weatherfield

Childe Harold's Pilgrimage, by Lord Byron

Edge Plays, by Cecilia Tan

Exit to Eden, by Anne Rampling (Anne Rice)

Fanny Hill: Memoirs of a Woman of Pleasure, by John Cleland

The Flame and the Flower, by Kathleen Woodiwiss

Forever . . ., by Judy Blume

Gabriel's Inferno, by Sylvain Renard

Gabriel's Rapture, by Sylvain Renard

The Image, by Jean de Berg

Jonah Sweet of Delancey Street, by Ryan Field

Juliette; or, Vice Amply Rewarded, by Marquis de Sade

Justine; or, The Misfortunes of Virtue, by Marquis de Sade

Lip Service, by M.J. Rose

Lolita, by Vladimir Nabokov

Madame Bovary, by Gustave Flaubert

Magic University series, by Cecilia Tan

The Marketplace series, by Laura Antoniou
Mind Games, by Cecilia Tan
Mr. Benson, by John Preston
Natural Law, by Joey W. Hill
Nine and a Half Weeks: A Memoir of a Love Affair, by Elizabeth
    McNeill
No Adam in Eden, by Grace Metalious
Peyton Place, by Grace Metalious
The Prince's Boy, by Cecilia Tan
Return to Peyton Place, by Grace Metalious
Roving Pack, by Sassafras Lowrey
Secrets anthology series, by Red Sage Publishing
Seducing the Myth, edited by Lucy Felthouse
The Sleeping Beauty Trilogy, by A. N. Roquelaure (Anne Rice)
Smut by the Sea, edited by Lucy Felthouse
Smut in the City, edited by Lucy Felthouse
Story of L, by Debra Hyde
Story of O, by Pauline Réage
Sweet Savage Love, by Rosemary Rogers
Switch, by Megan Hart
Taking a Shot, by Jaci Burton
Tarnsman of Gor, by John Norman
The Top of Her Game, by Emma Holly
The Vagina Monologues, by Eve Ensler
Velvet Glove, by Emma Holly
Venus in Furs, by Leopold von Sacher-Masoch
The Whippingham Papers, by Algernon Charles Swinburne
White Flames: Erotic Dreams, by Cecilia Tan
The Wolf and the Dove, by Kathleen Woodiwiss

Nonfiction

50 Ways to Play: BDSM for Nice People, by Don Macleod and
    Debra Macleod
*Enterprising Women: Television Fandom and the Creation of Pop-
    ular Myth*, by Camille Bacon-Smith

Fifty Shades of Pleasure: A Bedside Companion: Sex Secrets That Hurt So Good, by Marisa Bennett

Inside Peyton Place: The Life of Grace Metalious, by Emily Toth

The Joy of Writing Sex: A Guide for Fiction Writers, by Elizabeth Benedict

Letters to Penthouse, by Editors of *Penthouse*

Master: The Unauthorized Autobiography of Master R, by Master R

My Secret Garden, by Nancy Friday

Natural History of the Romance Novel, by Pamela Regis

New Perspectives on Popular Romance Fiction: Critical Essays, edited by Sarah S. G. Frantz and Eric Murphy Selinger

The Passion of Michel Foucault, by James Miller

Pleasure: A Woman's Guide to Getting the Sex You Want, Need and Deserve, by Hilda Hutcherson

Psychopathia Sexualis, by Richard Krafft-Ebing

The Ultimate Guide to Kink: BDSM, Role Play and the Erotic Edge, edited by Tristan Taormino

Wired for Story: The Writer's Guide to Using Brain Science to Hook Readers from the Very First Sentence, by Lisa Cron

Women Constructing Men: Female Novelists and Their Male Characters, 1750-2000, edited by Sarah S. G. Frantz and Katharina Rennhak

ABOUT THE EDITOR

LORI PERKINS is the publisher of Riverdale Avenue Books, a digital-first e-publisher. She was the cofounder and former editorial director of erotica e-publisher Ravenous Romance and has been a literary agent for 20 years. She is the author of *The Insider's Guide to Getting an Agent* (Writer's Digest Books) and has edited twenty erotica anthologies and more than one hundred erotic novels, as well as published erotica under a pseudonym.

Want More
Smart Pop?

www.smartpopbooks.com

›› Read a new free essay online everyday

›› Plus sign up for email updates, check out our upcoming titles, and more